The *Christmas* GUARDIANS

JANICE VOORHIES

THE CHRISTMAS GUARDIANS

Copyright © 2019 by Janice Voorhies.

ISBN: 1670560759

Second Edition: September 2020

10 9 8 7 6 5 4 3 2 1

Tuesday, November 26

10 PM

THE WIPER BLADES SWEPT BACK and forth, making a whooshing sound as they washed sheets of heavy rain onto the hood of the little Prius with every pass. Ramona squinted, leaning toward the windshield and slowing the car. "Rain?" she muttered. "What the heck is it doing raining in November?" She shivered—partly chill, partly irritation. "More like Seattle than Utah." The heater vents around her on both sides of the dashboard rattled with effort, battling the fog from her breath. Most of the storefronts surrounding her on Main Street were dark; the only landmarks visible this late were lonely security lights fading in and out of her vision as she passed. She shook off the moment of regret she always felt now when driving down Main Street. Douglas Valley was slowly dying, and no one seemed to care.

Condensation gradually reduced her field of vision through the windshield, so she lifted her foot off the gas pedal completely and, grabbing a tissue from the box on the floor, she swiped futilely at the glass with her right hand, using her left to keep the car centered inside its lane. Despite her efforts, the car drifted across the asphalt and veered toward the opposite curb. "What the..?", she groused as she jerked the wheel back to toward the center of the street and slammed on the brake. Exhaling a sigh of relief, she realized there wasn't another set of headlights anywhere around her. She appeared to be the only one dumb enough to be out on a night like this.

Easing her foot back onto the gas, now the car was barely creeping along. Usually, it was only 10 minutes from the Town Hall to her house. "Ski resorts must be cursing this weather. What's it doing raining at

Thanksgiving, anyway? Shoulda stayed home." But the town council met on Tuesday, and no matter what the weather, someone had to keep tabs on the mayor and her toadies.

Intent on her limited field of vision, Ramona almost missed the office lights still glowing behind the counter of Apodoca's Dry Cleaning. Probably just Ada tallying the receipts, she thought. That woman loved to talk, so she never managed to close the till by quitting time. Ada would rather hear about some smart-aleck kid who hucked a rock through Johansson Dental's plate glass window, or that after all these years, the old Hunsaker's property had finally sold. But Ramona sympathized with the need to escape the heat and humidity by chatting with customers. "Can't imagine doing other people's laundry for 40 years. Bad enough to have to deal with their kids," she mused aloud.

She edged to a stop at the traffic signal in front of the boarded-up building which used to house Christensen's, her favorite department store. Now she had to go clear to Springdale Mall to find a dress decent enough to be seen in at church. The signal sat stubbornly red while she waited--not a soul in sight to either the right or the left. Beating unceasingly down on the Prius, the rain had become a low, threatening growl. When the light finally turned green, she edged into the intersection. To her left the insubstantial ghost of a neon palm tree curved along the side of the Seaweed Bar and Grill, curling over the edge of the roof and materializing through the downpour. She snorted as she always did. A thousand miles from the ocean, and that bar boasted sea breezes and the smell of salt. "Gimme a break!" she muttered in disgust.

It was then that Ramona saw her. At least she thought it was a her. She was hunched over some scrap of paper, turning it this way and that, apparently trying to read in the faint light of the neon sign. The rain had drenched both the girl and the paper she held, but a flash of something shiny blinded Ramona for an instant as the girl twisted her hands to better catch the light. "Hey, kid, go home," she yelled. But, of course, the girl— her water-drenched long hair concealing her face and dripping onto the paper--couldn't hear her through the closed car window. "Kids! Why don't they ever have a clue?" she wondered for the thousandth time, shaking her head as she guided the car further down the empty street. A university president she'd heard speak years ago was right—no matter how much time and energy you invested in helping kids mature, there was always another freshman class next year. And you had to start all over again. It was the reason she had retired--the same problems year after year. Sometimes she felt like she'd never even made a ripple in the bucket. But there was no use worrying about what she couldn't change.

As the car glided past the glare of the Seaweed's sign, the girl in the dim light disappeared. Only the sound of the rain down the silent, mostly empty block kept Ramona company. Once she rounded the corner of 500 South, it was just a couple of blocks past the library and then right to her neighborhood. She pulled into her narrow driveway, stopping at the edge of the front porch. Letting the car idle, she lingered in the warmth, staring into the night while the rain poured off the gutter above her head and raced down the slope to the street.

Like every other house on the street, her porch ran the width of her house and shielded the front door and windows from the weather. Built in the early 1900s, the weathered brick home was the place where she'd been born. After they'd been married more than 20 years, she and Amos had bought the house from her mother and moved back in to take care of the elderly old woman. Her mother was frail even then. Eventually, both Ramona's mother and then Amos had passed away. Because she had forgotten to turn the porch light on when she left, there was no sign of life to welcome her. Her only company tonight were memories.

As she reached to turn off the key, the image of the girl standing alone in the pool of light edged into her consciousness and won out over the sight and sound of the rain on the windshield. "Don't waste your time," she scolded herself. The detached garage beckoned from the darkness behind the house. She sighed. Too many years as a teacher, she supposed, or maybe it was that she'd seen so many children without anyone to keep track of them. She pushed the button to restart the car, pulled the transmission into reverse, and backed out onto the street. "Waste. . ." she repeated, but she headed out anyway.

When the Seaweed Bar again appeared out of the rain a few minutes later, no girl was standing under the streetlight. The sidewalk was empty. "Stupid, stupid, stupid." She shook her head in exasperation, but that didn't deter her from swinging around the corner behind the bar, just in case. The alley snaked along the back of several blocks of the mostly abandoned shops, only Ada's on the block behind her and the Seaweed next to her casting shadows from back porch lights. Looking over her shoulder at the dry cleaner's rear entrance, she could barely make out the pile of neatly stacked cardboard boxes ready for recycling.

Her headlights cast amorphous shadows on the half dozen barely visible wooden doorways which lined the alley beyond the Seaweed, most latched with padlocks. It was cold, and her right knee was still bothering her, so even the gentle force of her foot on the brake caused it to ache. Then, out of the corner of her eye, she saw another flash. It had come from somewhere behind the stack of Budweiser cartons which tilted precariously against the wall next to several barrels. Empty beer kegs, perhaps?

Ramona rolled down her window and yelled, "Hey, anybody there?" No answer. She didn't want to get out of the car, but she knew if she didn't, she'd spend the rest of the night stewing about being "an old fool," so she jammed the car into park, grabbed the umbrella she kept under the seat, and leaning heavily on the door to favor her knee, she climbed out of the car, limping over to investigate.

It took a moment for her eyes to adjust to the deep shadows between the boxes. With her left foot, she shoved a couple of soggy and surprisingly heavy cardboard containers out of the way, wincing as her weight shifted to her right leg. Her nose wrinkled involuntarily when an empty bottle slid off the back of the stack, shattering and spraying the last few drops of what she thought must be whiskey on her already drenched shoes. Someone sucked in a startled breath at the noise. Ramona's eyes snapped in the direction of the sound. "Come out of there, right now," she commanded and with her umbrella poked another box out of the way.

The girl was there all right, a tiny shadow huddled under a couple of dripping sheets of cardboard stuck together and forming a tenuous shelter above the child's head. She'd drawn her knees up under her sweatshirt with her face buried in its folds. She couldn't be sleeping. The weather was too miserable for that.

"Hey, kid. What are you doing in there? It's freezing out here. Come on. I'll take you home." The girl lifted her head. She made no effort to move; she just stared at Ramona.

"Come on," Ramona ordered. Again, no reaction from the girl. "In case you hadn't noticed, I'm trying to be nice here. But it's cold, and I'm wet and tired, and patience isn't my forte. Now get up outta there and get in the car." Deliberately, Ramona turned her back on the girl and headed for the warmth of her vehicle. After a moment, a small smile seemed to flit across her face as she heard the girl behind her reach up, shove aside the top of her shelter, and follow. Give 'em a little direction, and most kids will do what's reasonable, she thought. Intentionally keeping her back to the girl so as not to spook her, Ramona pulled open the passenger side door and gestured for the girl to get in.

The child tried to wring some of the moisture from her water-soaked long hair before she lowered her body and slid into the passenger seat. Ramona reached behind her seat and pulled out the blanket she kept for emergencies, handing it wordlessly to the girl. "The police station's no place for kids," Ramona assured herself.

The girl said nothing, but she pulled the blanket tight around her, curling the soft edges up against her cheeks. Ramona studied the child. Now didn't seem like the time for an interrogation. "Seat belt?" was all she said.

Apparently, the girl didn't understand. Finally, Ramona reached across the seat, pulling at the girl's seatbelt until it latched in place. Then she did what she could to tuck the blanket back around the girl. The girl exhaled and huddled more deeply into the soft fleece. Ramona noted with approval that the girl relaxed a little because she leaned back against the seat and closed her eyes.

Fifteen minutes later Ramona eased the car again alongside her house, this time pulling clear to the end of her long driveway. She parked in the detached garage, circled around to the passenger door, and helped the girl climb out, bundling the blanket around her small shoulders. Watching the torrents still pouring off the roof of her garage, Ramona waited until there seemed a slight break, then shepherded the girl across the short expanse to the shelter of the back porch.

Once inside the house, Ramona pulled the blanket off the girl's shoulders and hung it on the drying rack next to the back door. She led the girl past the laundry area and through the kitchen, flipping on light switches as they went. As always, Ramona felt a familiar pang of loss that Amos wasn't there reading the newspaper in his favorite chair. She had relied on him to help her figure out what to do next when confronted with problems she hadn't the slightest idea how to solve. But his worn chair sat empty and silent.

Flipping the switch inside the front door, Ramona bustled the girl to the couch across from the fireplace. She touched the gas control, and the flames sprung to life. "Let me get you some hot chocolate, and then we'll deal with the wet clothes." When the girl was settled, and Ramona was satisfied the child didn't intend to bolt, she headed back to the kitchen through the open archway. She automatically shed her coat, slipped her gloves into her coat pocket, and hung the coat on the hook just inside the kitchen door.

Calling back to the girl, Ramona asked, "Do you want to phone your folks, so they won't worry?" Dipping an extra scoop of chocolate into the cup and setting the microwave for one minute, she rinsed the spoon and set it in the drainer as the microwave dinged. She put the hot cup on a matching saucer and wiped the rim of the cup to contain any possible drips. Casting a surreptitious glance over her shoulder into the big mirror above the fireplace in the other room, she could see the reflection of the girl sitting silently on the edge of the couch, her shoulders hunched together and her hands reaching toward the warmth of the fire. The child was staring straight ahead. With a twinge of anxiety, Ramona realized she had occasionally seen other girls with expressionless faces like that through the glass of the doors at the counselors' offices at school. Oh Lord, she thought, and she wondered for a moment if she'd done the right thing bringing the girl home. Maybe I should have taken her straight to a hospital, instead? It was too late now.

When Ramona offered the girl the warm cup, the girl curled her hands around it and breathed in the steam rising from it. "It's hot; be careful," Ramona instructed. The girl looked directly at her for the first time.

"Thank you," she said.

Ramona was so startled, she dropped onto the couch beside the girl. "Glad to see you can talk." Next to her, the girl sipped the chocolate carefully, her body relaxing slightly as the warm liquid eased her chill.

"What's your name? I need to get you home before your family starts to panic."

The girl turned to answer. For a moment her face reflected puzzlement, her eyes focused inward. Finally, she lowered the cup from her lips and turned slowly toward Ramona. "I don't know," she said. "I can't seem to remember."

11:30 PM

"It took you long enough," Ramona chided the plainclothes officer as she opened the door at his knock forty-five minutes later.

He ignored the jab. "Yes, ma'am. Dozen accidents tonight because of the blasted rain. That's why you get a detective instead of a patrolman. Young guys get sent out in the weather; I've got seniority."

"Hmmph!" Ramona eyed him up and down. There was something very familiar about him. "Don't I know you?" She demanded sharply.

The detective sighed. A look of resignation crossed his face. "Yes, ma'am. Third period, Senior English, 2005."

Ramona stared up at him. "I remember. Gifford, isn't it? When you were a junior, you and Andy Hauer got suspended for throwing water balloons off the roof at the graduation processional. First time I ever saw graduates' faces wearing school colors. Took a whole raft of teachers to scrub that green stain off those poor kids. How'd you cover that up when the department did a background check?"

"I was a kid, Mrs. Zollinger," Gifford said dryly. "I grew up."

Ramona snorted. "Once a trouble-maker, always a trouble-maker." She motioned him into the living room and gestured toward the couch. "Well, get over here and start doing something useful. I found this girl out back of the Seaweed. She says she can't remember who she is. You got any calls about a child who didn't come home?"

When the detective turned to her, the girl flinched and slide farther back into the couch. Tucking her head down, she stared at her hands.

From the corner of her eye, Ramona saw Gifford note the reaction. Deliberately, he took two slow steps toward the girl, stopping a couple of feet in front of her so as not to alarm her even more. "OK if I sit down on the couch?" he asked, lowering his voice as he shed his raincoat and reached over to hang it on the coat rack next to the couch. Ramona winced when she saw water drip off the coat onto her carpet.

"What's your dad's name? I could call him for you if you want?" Gifford moved to the far end of the couch, it's length a buffer between himself and the girl. From her stiffened posture, it was obvious that she was listening, but she refused to look at him.

Ramona pulled her rocking chair up next to the girl's end of the couch, reached over, and patted the soft form that was the girl's knee, now enveloped in a terry cloth robe Ramona had pulled out of the guest bedroom closet. After instructing the girl to shed her wet clothes, Ramona had put them in the washer and shown the girl how to operate the hand nozzle on the shower. Though the girl was warm now, her wary expression had returned; she retreated instinctively toward Ramona. It was obvious she didn't like the intruder.

Ramona was agreeably surprised to see Gifford take in the girl's reluctance to face him directly. "It's OK," she told the girl. "He's not going to hurt you. I won't let him make any trouble; I promise." Ramona turned to the detective. "She says she doesn't remember who she is."

"Mrs. Z," Gifford fell into the old pattern of addressing Ramona without even thinking about it, "let her answer the questions, please."

Unbidden tears welled up in the girl's eyes and spilled down her cheek. She swiped at them impatiently with the back of her hand. "I don't like cops," she said.

Gifford nodded. "Lots of people don't." He adjusted his position against the back cushion of the couch, crossing his long legs into a less threatening posture. "I'm not here to arrest you. I just want to get you home safely." His voice was pleasant and relaxed. He could see it wouldn't take much to panic the girl. "Do you remember your dad's name?"

"I don't have a dad," Her eyes opened wider, and for a moment surprise registered on her face. How did she know that when she couldn't remember her name? "I can't remember my name. Why can't I remember my name?"

Gifford's posture straightened imperceptibly though his voice remained slow and even. "It's OK. Don't worry. It'll come back when you've had something to eat and a little sleep. You're probably exhausted," Gifford soothed. "Do you remember why you were hiding behind the bar? Were you afraid of something or maybe someone?"

"I wasn't hiding. I was waiting."

"Waiting for what?"

The girl considered her answer before she spoke. "I think I was waiting for her." She gestured toward Ramona.

"Do you know Mrs. Z?" Gifford registered surprise.

"Why would you be waiting for me?" Ramona demanded.

The girl shied further away from Gifford and leaned toward Ramona, speaking only to her. "Because you came," she said.

"What does that mean?"

"I don't know," whispered the girl.

"Well?" Ramona demanded of the detective. "What are you going to do now!"

Gifford raised an eyebrow at the teacher's voice he'd known so well. Things didn't change much in Douglas Valley.

Pulling the girl even closer to her in a gentle hug, Ramona reassured her, "Don't worry, child. We'll figure it out. I'm just glad you're not all alone in the rain."

The girl's smile was tentative, but it was a smile. Ramona smiled back.

"If she can't remember her name or where she lives," Gifford interrupted, "I'll have to call the Department of Child and Family Services. They'll find a safe place for her until her folks contact us, or she can remember. Right now, I guess we better take her to the hospital and have her checked out just to be sure she doesn't have a concussion or something." Gifford was deliberately conciliatory.

"She's fine," Ramona answered tartly. "Had a shower, a little hot chocolate. Now she needs a good night's rest. She can stay here in the guest room; we'll worry about finding her family tomorrow. Last thing she needs is to be poked and prodded by a bunch of folks at the emergency room who are guzzling caffeine to make it through the graveyard shift."

"Mrs. Zollinger, you can't just highjack the rules," Gifford said without raising his voice. "The law about runaways is clear. You know that. We are required to contact the Department of Family Services. It's their job to help get this young woman home."

"The law doesn't have a clue what to do with a kid who's scared and tired and needs to go to bed. If your captain doesn't like me watching out for her, tell him to call me. Who is it by the way? Still that rowdy kid, Oscar Merced?" She shook her head in disgust and whispered under her breath, "Unbelievable."

"Here, girl. Time for bed." Putting a protective arm around the child, Ramona pulled her to her feet. Looking at Gifford over her shoulder, she added, "She's not going to disappear. I've got her clothes," as she hustled the girl down the hall and through the door of the bedroom across from hers. "There's a new toothbrush on the shelf next to the shower," she told the girl. "I'll deal with the detective."

The girl nodded in obvious relief and obediently moved toward the lighted bathroom doorway next to the bed.

"Now what, Detective?" Ramona crossed from the hall back to Gifford, her arms planted at her waist. "What's the protocol," sarcasm highlighted the word, "for dealing with a lost child?"

Gifford chose to ignore it. "We start looking at missing children reports, contact schools and hospitals for accident victims," Gifford checked the list off on his fingers, "talk to DCFS, and find a foster home for the girl."

Ramona's eyes took on a steely glint. "Then you better get started. The girl's safe here. I'll see to her." She turned her back on the detective and dismissed him, "You can let yourself out. Good night, Detective."

Chewing the side of his cheek to keep from snapping at her, Gifford realized not much had changed since high school. Well, he reasoned, the girl would have as much trouble trying to escape from Mrs. Zollinger as he'd had when trying to sluff her class, and at least he knew where he could find the girl. The thought cheered him up so much that he put on his coat and let himself out as directed. He slammed the door more firmly than necessary just to remind Mrs. Z he was still in charge.

Down the hall Ramona was hustling about, rummaging through the old chest of drawers in the guest room. "This is your bed," she told the girl. "I keep it made up in case of unexpected company. But to be honest, I never expected you." The girl sat down on the edge of the mattress watching Ramona. "There's a nightgown somewhere in here—used to belong to my daughter. It'll probably be too big, but better than nothing. Anything else you need is in the cabinet with the toothbrushes. I usually have breakfast about eight. I'll call you."

"Thank you for not making me go with the policeman," the girl apologized as she sat down on edge of the soft mattress. "I don't like policemen." She made no explanation.

Ramona nodded without comment and filed away that bit of information for later consideration. There were a lot of reasons kids might not like the police—none of them good.

After the girl had finished and switched out the bathroom light, Ramona pulled back the covers and waited while the girl nestled down under the butterfly quilt Ramona had spent one whole winter hand-stitching. She smiled as she remembered Amos teasing her about wasting so many hours on a blanket for a six-year-old's bed. "She's just going to jump on it during the day and kick it off at night. She'll never even look at one of those tiny little stitches."

Ramona had agreed and laughed, pointing out, "But I'll know." She forced her mind back to the present. "Try to sleep," she advised the child. Pulling the covers up and tucking them around the girl, Ramona promised her softly, "Tomorrow we'll find where you belong."

"Thank you," the girl's voice was weary with exhaustion.

Ramona was tired too, but she forced herself to head back down the hall and through the kitchen to the laundry area. Once a closed-in back porch, it was now an efficient, if tiny, laundry center. She moved the girl's clothes from the washer to the dryer and put the load of wet towels the girl had used after her shower into the washer. It had been a long day. She locked the front door, turned off all the lights but the porch lamp, and headed for bed. As she passed the guest bedroom on her way to bed, she was surprised to see a light still shining from under the door. Turning the doorknob as silently as possible, Ramona inched the door open barely enough to see into the room. The girl was on her knees next to the bed, her head bowed, her arms folded, and her soft voice whispering unintelligible words.

"Well, well," Ramona murmured. "Didn't expect that either." And she pulled the door closed quietly.

After her nighttime routine, Ramona sat down heavily on the edge of the bed she had shared with Amos for so many years. Her knee was throbbing and bending down by the side of the bed was out of the question tonight—as it was most nights now. She figured that if the Lord knew her sins, He probably knew her pains too and would understand. She folded her hands in her lap and whispered her own prayers. "Lord, bless Ellie, wherever she is and send her back to me, if it be Thy will." The prayer was more repetition than actual entreaty. She knew Ellie had been gone too long. She was never coming back. But it wasn't in her nature to give up, so she prayed the same words every night. And every day she woke up alone.

She forced her mind back to today's problems. "Oh... and watch out for this new child sleeping in the other room. Some mother is worried about her tonight. And thank you Lord for the blessings I know you are sending," she paused, reflecting a moment, then adding, "even if I'm not sure what they are."

After the "amen," she sat gathering the energy to force her muscles from the inertia they settled into whenever she stopped moving. Then she eased herself under the blankets and pulled her quilt up to her chin. Without Amos, she was never warm anymore.

For a long time, she lay with her eyes closed but her head racing. Sleep didn't come easily. The truth was, it was comforting to have someone else in the house. She'd never expected to live out the last years of her life alone. Stewing over it won't change things, she scolded. She tossed from side to side for a while, briefly rehashing the events at the town council meeting before she'd found the girl. Jesse Simpson was at it again, trying to turn Douglas Valley into some upscale tourist attraction. Idiot. Too cheap to replace the street signs with something big enough us baby boomers can actually read. Instead, let's use the money to plow under the downtown at a cost of millions of tax dollars. In her head, she mimicked Simpson's smug pronouncements at the council meeting. Aloud she said, "Must have to forgo common sense as a requirement for election." Living alone, she'd gotten used to talking to herself, and because she always agreed with herself, she never had to worry about dissenting opinions.

But it was thinking about the girl that finally kept her thoughts from relaxing into sleep. Ramona had known enough kids to suspect the girl was playing some sort of game. Probably a runaway who didn't want to be found. Maybe the child thought feigning amnesia was an easy solution to avoiding something ugly at home. She speculated about possible reasons a child would want to hide from her family, but nothing concrete seemed to fit. So young, it was almost impossible to imagine that the child was involved in any of the ravages that many kids in modern society had embraced like drug abuse or alcoholism. And she didn't seem to have the restless, unfocused anxiety that a lot of young people nowadays displayed. Once her hands stopped trembling from the cold, the girl seemed oddly unconcerned about her situation. On the other hand, it was clear she didn't seem to like the police, so maybe this wasn't the first time she'd run away? Or maybe it was abuse? The girl had an elfin face—those big, deep blue-- almost violet eyes, the long fair hair, the otherworldliness of expression. It was an appealing face, but Ramona knew only too well that appearance really didn't matter when it came to sexual abuse. Power was the issue. Anyone could be a victim. She shuddered involuntarily.

At last her eyes grew heavy as she curled under the covers and was almost blessedly asleep when the image of the flash of light that had attracted her to the girl in the first place crossed her mind. She rolled over to her stomach and stretched, hooking her toes over the end of the bed in her favorite position. She clenched her eyes shut, but her brain refused to stop replaying the picture of the girl under the streetlight. Finally, she threw back the covers, groaning a little as her feet settled on to the floor.

She put her slippers on and switched on lights back on one at a time as she headed to the laundry room. She pulled the girl's clothes from the dryer--now warm and fresh. Digging into worn jeans and finding nothing in either the front or the back pockets, she tried the pocket of the T-shirt and finally both the pockets of the stained hoodie. Crumpled up in the corner of the right fleece pocket, she pulled out a lump of used Kleenexes entangled with what felt like several smaller items, the whole mess not quite the size of her fist.

Sorting through the shredded tissue fragments, she extracted an empty key ring attached to a red plastic advertisement in the shape of a heart, a piece of chewed gum stuck to part of the bundle, a few pennies, and entwined in the remaining tissue was a very crumpled piece of paper, only 5 or 6 inches square. She separated it carefully from the fragments of tissue and smoothed it out on the top of the dryer.

There was some heft to the paper—not quite cardstock weight, but more substantial than a sheet torn out of a notebook. Holding it up to the light above her head, she saw tiny hairs of fiber revealed in its linen-like texture, a slightly rough surface her fingers sensed as she rubbed them across the surface. It reminded her of the "parchment" she and her sixth-grade friends had made to send secret messages to one another in elementary school—they'd always singed the edges carefully to imitate the scrolls they had imagined princesses routinely used. Though there was no evidence of burned edges, the borders were uneven as if the paper were intended to be used as a fancy 'thank you' note or some similar purpose.

Puzzlement crossed across her face as she laid the paper flat on the top of the dryer. It seemed to ease itself of wrinkles ahead of her hand. A double border of gold ink formed a frame for the writer's message, glittering even in the dim light. She scratched with her fingernail across one of the thick, gold lines and was startled when the ink stubbornly refused to come free of the paper. That explained the flashes. Must be from an expensive printer, she thought. Maybe why it smoothed out so easily—no holes or crease marks though, and it had been crammed into a damp, shapeless lump, then tumbled through a wash and dry cycle. Truth was, the paper looked as if it had never been touched by the rain or been smashed into the pocket of an oblivious kid. Ramona squinted at the paper and twisted it in every direction, faint flashes of light whipping back and forth across her face. But no wonder the girl had had trouble trying to read it. As far as she could tell, the page was entirely blank.

Wednesday, November 27

8 AM

THE NEXT MORNING RAMONA AWAKENED to a pounding in her head. She'd rolled over, and the motion shook her body enough to realize that the noise was not imagination. Someone was pounding on the front door. Opening one eye, she could see the pale, grey light streaming through the window and hear the rain still beating against the glass. Automatically, she glanced at the clock and spent a moment savoring the fact that the high school was already well into first period, and she was still in bed. The pounding from outside got louder and more insistent. She pushed off the covers and slid to the edge of the bed, protective of her lower back-- which didn't like any kind of jarring. She sat for a moment on the edge of the mattress, then raised herself to her feet. The rhythmic pounding on the door had now turned to a steady ringing of the doorbell. "Viola!" she yelled. "Cut it out. I'm coming." The clamor stopped abruptly.

Grabbing her robe, she headed into the hall and toward the door. She'd almost forgotten the girl, who was now poking her head out of the guest room. She looked like she was ready to bolt. "It's OK," she reassured the girl, touching her shoulder as she passed. "It's just my neighbor."

Muttering with irritation under her breath at the interruption, Ramona made her way across the living room, unchained the latch, and opened the deadbolt. "What the heck's so dang urgent," she barked as she yanked the door open and steel-gray light poured into the room.

"Did you give up working on anger management?" Viola asked sweetly. "Sounds like you need to devote a bit more effort on the problem."

"You'd try the patience of a saint," Ramona snapped. "Just because

15

you like to get up at the crack of dawn doesn't mean the rest of the world needs to."

Viola grinned. "Time for you to be up anyway."

"I swear," Ramona continued, ignoring her jab, "if you thought for two minutes about anything, your brain might die of shock."

Viola shrugged in satisfaction, pushed her way past Ramona and plopped herself on the sofa, her short legs not quite touching the floor. "So, what happened last night that you had to call the cops? Was it a stalker?" Viola's eyes glittered with curiosity.

"You were afraid to come over after 11 o'clock last night, but 8 AM didn't deter you?" Ramona said sarcastically. "I swear, Viola ...."

"You already mentioned that.

"No. It wasn't a stalker, for Pete's sake. You watch too many of those Dateline shows on TV. Come out here, girl," she called down the hall.

The waif-like child stepped into the hall, her too-large terry cloth robe again wrapped tightly around her body, its extra length trailing behind her. Her flaxen hair glowed strangely in the pale morning light from the big front window.

Ramona's sweeping gesture indicated the girl, whose eyes widened at the intruder. "This is why I called the police," Ramona said as she crossed the room and put a reassuring arm around the child's shoulders. "Girl, this is my neighbor, Viola Pridgeon."

Viola was speechless. Ramona noted the moment with a small relaxing of her schoolteacher stare. Triumph flickered, then disappeared.

"Good heavens. A child—a girl," she corrected herself. "What have you done. Did you kidnap a kid?" She stared at the girl who lowered her head and leaned it against Ramona's ample shoulder.

"Found her," Ramona said. "In a stack of boxes behind the Seaweed Bar and Grill. It was raining," she added unnecessarily. "Here, Child. Sit down. She won't bite," Ramona nodded in Viola's direction, "although sometimes it seems like her teeth are pretty sharp." Viola ignored her.

Across from Viola, the girl obediently settled into Amos's rocker by the window, while Ramona took the other end of the couch.

"It was cold last night. You must have been freezing." Viola's tone softened as she spoke to the girl. "You have a name, Child?" Viola shifted in her seat; her posture straightened automatically into its old, familiar pattern. A child needed help.

Ramona held up a hand to stop the questions. "Leave her alone; she doesn't remember."

"Doesn't remember what?"

"Quit scaring her. She's got enough worries without you demanding information she can't give." Dismissing Viola with a nod, she told the girl, "Don't mind her. She's genetically predisposed to being nosey." The shadow of a smile crossed the girl's face. The teacher in her took over; good vocabulary, she thought, and began an unconscious list of clues.

A shrill buzz from a phone interrupted further discussion. Ramona grabbed her cell now vibrating its way off the end table next to her. She listened, then replied with irritation. "Isn't it a little early, Detective?"

"The judge would like to meet your houseguest," Gifford's voice was pleasant as always, but a tone of command underlined his words.

"What for?"

"As soon as I turned in my report, DCFS was on the phone to my boss demanding to take charge. You may remember that Judge Callister's sister is the program head? He was not happy when she woke him at 2 AM to tell him how you circumvented the law."

Ramona had a suspicion that Gifford enjoyed passing on this information, but there was no change in the timbre of his voice.

"John Callister likes ordering people around. Comes from his years as a Scout Master; never got over it. So--what does the judge think I'm going to do to solve his legal dilemma?"

"He'd like to talk to the girl at 9 AM this morning. Courtroom Two. Look forward to seeing you, Mrs. Z." The phone clicked, and Ramona glared at the now-silent receiver.

She growled under her breath. "Well, girl," she said as the anticipation of a bit of sparring settled onto her face. "It looks like the circus is about to begin. I guess we better get breakfast on the table." Ramona had always relished a good fight.

8:30 AM

It was halfway through first period at Douglas Valley High. Carrie Jane Plunkett pushed back the thick, unruly red hair which had fallen across her line of sight and looked up warily from her computer. A sixth sense told her the room was too quiet. And the day before the Thanksgiving holiday? Admittedly, it was pleasant to have quiet occasionally, and she was always happy to assign something to her students that engaged them enough to force them to really focus. But this quiet was abnormal. So quiet she could actually hear the rain slamming into the roof of the building. She looked around. Tristen Holyoak, front row, was chewing on the end of her pencil and staring thoughtfully at the poem by Gerard Manley Hopkins on the desk in front of her. Tristen liked poetry. In the seat behind her, Ollie Haverfield did not. Ah, that explained the quiet. Ollie was asleep, his head resting on his right arm with his textbook as a pillow. Momentarily, she was tempted to leave him alone. For a change, he wasn't whispering about tonight's game to his teammate across the aisle or glancing surreptitiously at his phone under the desk.

Carrie Jane sighed. "Ollie, wake up. We're on page 387."

Ollie slumbered on.

"Tyler, nudge Ollie and mention that if he fails English, he won't be playing for the rest of the season."

Tyler looked alarmed. "Hey, Ollie!" He hissed as he leaned across the row and poked at his friend with an elbow. "Dunk-It says you have to wake up."

"Did the bell ring?" a startled Ollie asked. The rest of the class laughed.

From a seat in the back of the room, someone muttered, "Jerk."

"That's enough," Carrie ordered. She turned toward the sound. "Eduardo, if that was you, you'd better think again," she addressed the young man in the last row next to the door. He was a taciturn kid, stand-offish and sullen, but she found him compelling, nonetheless. Maybe it was the sharply sculptured bones in his handsome face or the dark hair that curled over slightly at his ears and framed the unusual blue-green of his eyes. This was not the first time his barely concealed anger had tainted the atmosphere in her class. Fortunately for him, the bell chose that moment to ring, and he ducked out the door, avoiding eye contact with any other student.

Carrie Jane sent a fleeting look after him and absently reminded the rest of the class filing out the door not to forget the rough draft that was due Monday. "No points if it doesn't come in on time," she said over the noise of kids gathering backpacks, boys jockeying each other for an early position out of the door, and girls checking their cells. Most ignored her. For them, when the bell rang, class was over, especially the period before lunch.

It wasn't the first time that Eduardo had made insulting remarks under his breath; some days the hostility radiating in waves off him was almost palpable. He ignored assignments, never brought a book to class, and spoke only if forced to. Were he any other Hispanic student, Carrie Jane might have thought that English as a second language was part of the problem, but Eduardo was both articulate and possessed of a quick, dry wit that could skewer any student brave enough to venture a branch of friendship. Automatically, she did a quick once-over of the empty rows in her classroom, picking up the odd pencil and a couple of pieces of trash that were the detritus of every period. Maybe it was time to talk to Eduardo's counselor, see if there was anything he could contribute to her understanding of the problem.

9 AM

The Douglas Valley Court House was an elegant old brick building from an era when residents were happy to have their tax dollars spent on beauty as well as utility. It was situated in the exact center of the original settlement, and its structure and landscape took up an entire city block. A small VIP parking lot sat at the main entrance to the building with considerably more parking located in the rear. Surrounded by graceful gardens and walking paths, the area was a popular gathering place for families strolling in the coolness of a summer evening. Winter turned the park into a fairyland of frosted pines, and the small pond on the north side of the building became a natural ice-skating rink which was a beehive of activity as soon as school was out every day.

Streets which bounded the courthouse were labeled Center and 100 North in the direction of Salt Lake City, while Main and 100 East bordered its opposite sides in the direction of the Colorado border close to a hundred miles away. Like soldiers in a dress parade, the streets spread out in straightforward, compass-point order. The city had been planned by pioneer farmers and ranchers who wanted to avoid what they called the 'cutesy circles and curlicues' that had been gaining popularity in the East almost 150 years ago. Just keep it simple, they'd decreed, and still today, even a stranger could find most addresses in Douglas Valley without a fancy GPS.

Viola was already in the car when Ramona and the girl, dressed in the same clothes from last night but now clean and dry, had come out after they finished loading the dishwasher and locking the front door.

Ramona blinked, and her eyes narrowed. "Viola, what the heck are you doing in my car? Get out of there right now."

"Nope. You are going to need me," said Viola complacently. "You alone with an authority figure is not a healthy combination. You'll end up in jail for contempt. Keeping your mouth shut is not your strong suit."

The girl sucked in her breath, her eyes darting back and forth between the two women. Ramona was leaning into the car, her eyes never leaving Viola's face. Viola locked eyes with her friend. Neither flinched.

Blinking in alarm, the girl stood frozen at the passenger door, uncertain what to do next. Then, unexpectedly, a slow smile of amusement at the standoff crossed her face.

Finally, Ramona jerked opened the door in defeat. "Oh, who the heck cares?" Under her breath, she added, "Stubborn as an old mule."

"It'll be OK. I promise," Viola reassured the girl behind her. She folded her arms and put her purse on the floor in front of her. Tilting her head in Ramona's direction, she added, "At least she won't let the judge throw you to the wolves."

"Viola!" Ramona opened her mouth, reconsidered, and bit back the swear word on her tongue. No use in proving her exasperating neighbor right again.

Pulling open the back door for the girl, Ramona gestured for her to climb in the car. A good night's sleep and breakfast had eased the girl's apprehension, or maybe she had momentarily forgotten her precarious situation. She slid herself onto the seat and pulled the door shut after her, a smile still playing at the corners of her mouth. Ramona jerked the driver's side door all the way open and slung her purse onto Viola's lap as she lowered herself gingerly into the car.

"If you won't get out, the least you can do is keep my stuff from spilling out all over the car." Obediently, Viola grabbed the purse and sat it next to her own on the floor. She unsuccessfully tried to avoid looking smug.

Ramona gritted her teeth. She could almost hear Viola congratulating herself on being a gracious winner.

Though it was still sprinkling, the trip to the courthouse took a more reasonable ten minutes instead of the almost 20 minutes it had taken for Ramona to get home the night before. Pulling into the courthouse front parking lot, the old woman glanced over her shoulder at the child behind her. "Girl, we can't keep calling you 'girl'. You need a name. Anything sound familiar? Lisa, Carol, Elizabeth? Georgene, LaRue, Susan?"

With a roar, the girl's anxiety returned. Her eyes swung wildly from Ramona to Viola and back. Her mouth moved, trying to articulate a response, but no sound came out.

Ramona saw the apprehension in the girl's eyes and backtracked. "Now don't get all upset. We'll help you remember. What about if we just call you "Annie" for the moment? It's right at the beginning of the alphabet, so it'll be easy to remember. Then when we find out your real name, we'll switch to it."

"Annie?" The girl tested the name on her tongue. Catching Viola's eye in the rear-view mirror, she saw the small woman nod at her.

"I guess that'd be OK." The desire to please overcame the girl's trepidation. After all, Ramona was right. It wasn't a bad name.

Ramona eased the car into a spot near the main entrance, ignoring the Reserved for Elected Officials sign. She shifted the car into park and groaned slightly as she lifted herself out of the front seat. "City oughta have some reserved signs for 'Old People'," Ramona announced. "We deserve to park here; we've been paying taxes longer than any of those city council members."

Opening the door for the girl, Ramona gave the girl's--Annie's, she reminded herself--shoulder a gentle squeeze. Back when she worked at the high school, teachers weren't supposed to ever touch a student—too much liability, but Ramona knew a touch could be powerfully reassuring, and it didn't hurt that her behavior used to annoy the heck out of her control-freak principal.

The little group made their way through the metal detector inside the front doors and stood for a moment at the information desk. Ramona felt rather than saw Viola glance at her sharply. "I'll sign the register," her neighbor said quietly.

Ramona nodded, concealing her relief. She'd spent too much time in the police department down the hall after she'd lost Elinor. Viola had been with her and Amos then too, handling whatever minute details she could to make their ordeal easier.

Leading the way to the stairs and the second floor, Ramona paused a moment to take a deep breath and brace for the climb. She didn't intend to let age change her behavior, but stairs required fortitude.

Halfway through the long hall of the second floor, they stopped in front of a set of polished cherry double doors bearing a small brass plaque that identified the room as Courtroom II. When Viola pulled one side of the door open for Ramona and the girl, it slid easily on well-oiled hinges, despite its obvious weight. Inside was a compact chamber containing a judge's bench, a desk for the court reporter, and two larger platforms for opposing counselors mounted about eight feet in front of the judge's bench. A rostrum with a microphone was centered between the platforms. Only three rows of padded stacking chairs were provided for spectators, six or seven on each side of a center aisle. The audience was separated from the official court proceedings by a railing which matched the cherry of the entry doors. But there was no audience today. Unconsciously, the three slowed their steps, and even then, each step echoed in the empty, imposing silence.

Ramona paused and looked around. Seemed like a lot of formality for a few questions from the judge. The three of them sat down in the first row of chairs and waited. After about 10 minutes, the door opened slightly, and a head popped in.

"You folks here to see Judge Callister?'

The three nodded in unison.

"The judge wants to see you in his chambers. Follow me." The messenger held the door for them, smiling cheerfully; he nodded to Ramona as she passed. "Morning, Mrs. Z. Nice to see you again."

Ramona smiled back. "Henry," she acknowledged. "Glad to see the court is in good hands."

"One of your admirers?" Viola smirked.

Judge Callister looked exactly like a TV judge—black robes, bushy grey hair, and sharp, observant eyes. His appearance was a useful tool; it gave him an air of authority which was a bonus when dealing with reluctant defendants.

As Ramona walked through the door, he sat up straighter and folded his hands on his desk. "Morning, Mrs. Zollinger," he greeted her. "Thanks for coming." Without preamble, he directed his opening volley at her. "Of course, we could have avoided this little meeting if you had bothered to notify the proper authorities of your problem in the first place." He paused and apparently thought better of what he was going to say since she was obviously ignoring him. "Never mind. You're here now. The court appreciates your willingness to cooperate in this issue."

Ramona looked at the tall windows behind him which in the summer revealed a stunning view of the gardens outside. Now the flower beds were covered with compost and most of the shrubbery was drenched with rain and bent over from the force of its delivery. "Nice office, John."

"May I remind you that this is a meeting of record. I am an officer of the court."

"Nice office, Judge John," Ramona emphasized.

Consciously controlling his irritation, Judge Callister invited them to take the chairs arranged in front of his desk. The girl seated herself between the two women.

Just at the edge of her range of vision, Ramona noticed Detective Gifford seated in the shadowed corner to her left and slightly behind her. "Detective, you're looking well this morning."

"Mrs. Z," Gifford acknowledged her. He settled back in his chair, a smile playing on the edges of his mouth at the confrontation unfolding in front of him.

The Judge cleared his throat and looked down, referring to something in his notes. "Now let me see if I understand what's happening here. Ramona, how'd you happen to come across this young woman?"

"Annie."

"Beg your pardon? I thought she couldn't remember her name?" The judge's eyebrows moved closer together in inquiry.

"We decided to call her 'Annie' until we figure out her real name, didn't we, Girl, er . . . Annie?" Ramona tipped her head in the girl's direction. The girl looked uncomfortable but nodded in agreement.

"I see, "said Judge Callister, his stern expression making it clear that he didn't see at all.

Detective Gifford leaned the chair back on two legs, so it was braced against the wall. He clasped his hands behind his head. The scrape of the chair distracted Ramona, and she frowned at him. "Sorry, Mrs. Z," he said agreeably. Sometimes, he thought with satisfaction, this job could be quite entertaining. The judge rapped on his gavel, and Ramona's head spun back around toward him. "Just tell me the facts, Ramona," he ordered.

In a voice she used to reserve for 9th graders, Ramona recited the events of the night before. The judge withheld comment; he had given up trying to manage Ramona's attitude years ago.

Viola, who had still not heard the whole story--listened intently. "You mean she was just sitting there in the pouring rain?" she burst out. "What on earth were you doing there, Annie?" She used the name smoothly, without hesitation.

"It's my job to ask the questions," the Judge interrupted. "Try to remember I'm in charge here."

Viola smiled at the judge, who couldn't resist smiling back. "Of course, Your Honor," she replied.

Ramona almost laughed out loud. As a caseworker, Viola's ability to project a convincing guise of innocent helplessness had come in useful when, for example, she was presented with an angry, abusive husband. If the fellow was fooled into letting down his guard, Viola managed to have him arrested and in a jail cell before he figured out what happened. Didn't look like Judge John was going to be any different.

Turning back to the girl, the judge asked "Annie?" There was a pause while he jotted down a note on the documents in front of him. "Exactly what were you doing there?"

The girl looked directly at him. "I was waiting, Your Honor."

"Waiting for what?"

"I don't know, Sir. I remember standing on the corner trying to figure out where to go." Revisiting the events of the night before, the dam of Annie's under-current of anxiety broke, and a rush of words poured from the girl. "Nothing around me looked familiar. I couldn't remember how I got there, or where I was going. I was really scared." Her lower lip quivered. "I tried to go into the bar for help, but some guy yelled at me and said I was too young to be in there." She stopped, her eyes darting from the Judge to Ramona for reassurance.

"It's OK, Annie," Ramona soothed, reaching over and covering the girl's hand with her own. Simultaneously, on the girl's opposite side, Viola did the same. "Just tell the Judge everything you can remember," Ramona urged.

The girl's eyes turned inward, and she began to shiver as her memory relived the night. "It was cold, and my clothes were wet—really, really wet. I guess maybe I started to cry." She stumbled at the admission but took a deep breath and went on. "Then an old man with white hair almost touching his shoulders came by." She replayed the scene in her mind. "He asked me what I was doing standing there in the rain. I told him I was lost." Her voice pleaded in confusion. "He didn't even offer to help me. He just opened a pocket in his jacket and handed me a little piece of paper. He told me I would need it, and then he turned around and walked away. Why would he do that?" She turned to Ramona. "He left me all alone. I didn't know what to do." Her voice trembled as she clutched more tightly at the older woman's hand. "I thought maybe the paper was the address of a shelter or something, but the light from the neon sign on the building wasn't bright enough to read it, and the rain was getting harder." Beseeching Ramona to understand, she went on. "I didn't know where I was, and I was frightened. I ran down the street, trying to catch him, but he disappeared around the corner." Her body deflated. "So, I found a place out of the rain and waited." She stopped abruptly, and a small whimper escaped her lips.

"For what?" The Judge prodded her.

Annie took a deep breath willing herself to get control of her emotions. She straightened in her chair, withdrawing her hands from both women's grasps and settling them quietly in her lap. She looked straight at the judge and addressed him in a remarkably level voice. "I thought maybe if I waited until morning when it was light, I could figure out what to do."

Ramona's eyes widened. "Why didn't you tell me that, Annie?"

"You didn't ask," the girl said simply.

"Now we're getting somewhere. What can you tell us about the 'old man'?" Callister encouraged her.

Leaning forward in his chair, Detective Gifford's weight caused the front legs to bump the floor, and the sound snapped the girl's attention in his direction. Recognizing the detective, her eyes widened, and instantly she angled her body away from him, the intensity of his focus causing her to sidle even closer to Ramona. Her voice wavered. "He was just some old man. His hair was white," she added again as if that was explanation enough. "And that's all he said. Something about reading that paper and knowing what to do." She fastened her eyes on Ramona. "He scared me. I needed to find a place to hide in case he came back." Closing her eyes to remember, she added, "That's when I realized I had walked into an alley. There was a light by one of the doors. I couldn't stop shaking, so I shoved aside some boxes, and I crawled under them."

"Did the white-haired man say anything else? Threaten you in any way?" Gifford probed.

The girl's face clouded over again. "No. I don't think so. He just talked to me." She turned to the Judge. "Why didn't he help me?" Her eyes clouded. "I was so cold. . ." There was a pause, and she rubbed her shoulders at the memory. "When I saw the headlights turn into the alley, I wanted to run. But I couldn't get up fast enough, and then Mrs. Zollinger told me to get in her car—so I did." She strained to tell her story with straightforward clarity, by the time she reached the part of climbing into Mrs. Zollinger's car, her composure had reached its limits, and huge tears threatened to spill down her cheeks.

Viola automatically dug around in her purse and handed the girl a Kleenex. "What kind of person leaves a child stranded in the rain?" Viola demanded, her eyes narrowing.

Judge Callister's face softened. "Can you remember anything before you found yourself alone in the rain? Do you live around here? Go to a local school? What about your parents? Siblings?"

"No, Sir." Her eyes went blank for a moment. "Nothing. I can't remember anything before what I just told you." She withdrew from her memory. "Maybe I dozed off or something. It felt like a long time later when Mrs. Zollinger wrapped a blanket around me and took me home."

Ramona rummaged around in her purse and pulled out the sheet with the gold borders she'd found in the girl's pocket. "Here, Judge. This is the sheet she was trying to read when I found her. Unless there's invisible writing on it somewhere, there's nothing there."

Before she could hand it across the desk to the judge, the girl grabbed it out of her hand. "That's it! That's the sheet he gave me." Hope flamed across her face, giving her a startlingly ethereal expression. It faded abruptly as her eyes searched one side of the paper, then the other, the gold border flashing tiny reflections against the walls as she flipped the paper back and forth. She looked at the judge, her expression now puzzled and a little angry. "There's nothing on it." Disappointment flattened in her voice.

She kept starring at the paper, willing something to appear. "Why did he give me this if he didn't want to help me? What kind of a person does that?" She laid the paper on the desk in front of the judge. "What's going to happen to me?" she whispered.

Suppressing a desire to reach across the desk and gather the child in his arms, the judge said gruffly, "There, there. I'm sure your family is looking for you as we speak."

Bestowing the judge a look of patronizing disdain, Ramona reached across the gap between their chairs and encircled the girl's shoulders with both arms. "Shhhh. Shhhh. It will be OK. We'll figure it out, I promise," she coaxed, willing the girl to believe her. The girl rested her head on Ramona's arms; tears damping the sleeve of Ramona's dress.

"Judge?" Detective Gifford's voice was low. "Could I keep the paper as evidence? Maybe we can figure out where it was sold."

"It's been through a cycle of the washer and dryer. Probably washed away any kind of evidence," Ramona apologized to Gifford. "It didn't occur to me the stuff in Annie's pocket might become evidence."

Exchanging a look of sympathy with Gifford's direction, the judge leaned forward and passed the paper o him. "Do what you can."

To the girl, he said, "I know someone must be frantic to find you. My sister is the program director at the Division of Child and Family Services. She'll watch out for you until we find your family."

Turning to Ramona, he added, "You know you can't keep her. Lily will find a foster family for her to stay with."

"No, no, please." The girl shuddered. "I won't go." She twisted to face Ramona. "Don't let him take me," she pleaded. "I won't be any trouble. I promise."

Sympathy colored Callister's voice. "I'm sorry, Annie." The name seemed to suit her. "State law says that only a licensed foster parent can shelter a child in jeopardy. Don't worry. My sister's very good at finding families who genuinely care about the children they take in."

Ramona's body stiffened as she bent forward. "John, this girl's not going anywhere. She's staying with me. Can't you see she's terrified? Every person and place she knows is lost to her. Now you want to rip her out of the only safe shelter she's found?"

"Ramona," the Judge warned, buttressed by years of practice in dealing with Ramona's outbursts when they were young.

"Ramona, nothing!" she snapped. "I've seen what happens to kids who've been shunted from one foster home to another. That's not happening to this child. Come on, Annie. We're leaving." She rose from her chair, threw her purse over her shoulder, and grabbed Annie's hand.

Gifford was out of his seat before she got to the door. "Mrs. Z," he said softly, his body blocking her way. "You're not going anywhere."

Ramona glared at him. "Don't try to bully me, Mark." His first name came unbidden to her lips. "You know it won't do any good."

"Sit down, Ramona!" Judge Callister ordered; his gaze unblinking. "No one questions how much you care about kids. That's not the issue."

Ramona tried to stare down Detective Gifford, but he simply stared back at her. After a moment or two, resigned, Ramona walked back to the chair, motioning for the girl to sit down again.

"People in this state have spent a lot of time trying to figure out what's best for kids in trouble, Ramona. You know that. As I remember, you helped draft a couple of those laws. Now just calm down. We'll find a good home for Annie."

"Well, I'm a licensed foster parent," Viola interrupted. The three adults turned to stare at her. "Part of my job. Have been for years," she said complacently. "Can she stay with me?"

The Judge considered that option. "What about that, Annie?" He was surprised at how easily the name rolled out of his mouth. "How would you feel about staying with . . .. Excuse me, I don't believe Ramona bothered to introduce us?"

"Pridgeon. Viola Pridgeon," Ramona inserted.

"Mrs. Pridgeon," the Judge finished his question. "How would you feel about that, Annie?"

"Ms." Viola corrected him and looked expectantly at Annie. "I've got room, and I'd be happy to have you for a few days. Maybe you could have a couple of sleepovers at Ramona's house," Viola's eyes twinkled. "She's right next door you know."

The tension in the girl's body eased. "Yes," she said gratefully. "I'd like that." Her eyes went blank again for a moment. Then almost as an after-thought, she said, "Yes. That's good."

"Glad you approve," the Judge said dryly. His next words were directed to Viola. "We'll check your certification, of course, Ms. Pridgeon, but if you're on the Department of Child and Family Services' list, then this meeting is over. I'll appoint you the CASA (Court Appointed Special Advocate). Viola nodded in understanding. "You'll need to go over to Lily's office and fill out the paperwork later this morning if that's all right?"

"Paperwork is no problem." Viola assented. "Government work is paperwork. Probably thousands of forms with my signature on them in the state system."

"Thanks, Viola," Ramona said, genuine appreciation added to her unspoken relief.

Her friend smiled back at her. "Yep."

The older women thanked the Judge, albeit grudgingly in Ramona's case, and pulled on coats and gloves. This time Annie took charge of Ramona's purse as she whispered a 'thank you' to Viola. Detective Gifford followed them.

"Mrs. Z. Could I have a word before you head out?" Gifford asked

Ramona looked up at him speculatively, not surprised by his request. She nodded. "Viola, will you take Annie out to the car? I'll be along in a minute."

Taking Annie's arm, Viola guided her toward the stairs as Ramona turned back to Gifford.

"What can I do for you, Detective?"

"Did the girl—Annie," he didn't like the idea of a pseudonym. He was a cop, after all. "Did she have anything else on her that might help us identify her—slogans on her clothes, jewelry, anything like that?"

Ramona thought for a moment, her mind going over Annie's clothes as she had put them in the washer the night before. "Nothing that I can remember. Nothing on her clothes at all—they looked pretty worn. Holes in the knees of the jeans—that sort of thing. She had some odds and ends in one of the hoodie pockets. That paper," she gestured to the sheet Gifford now held, "some pennies and a couple of old Kleenexes, a key ring . . ."

"A key on the ring?" Ramona caught the attention with which Gifford asked the question.

"Nope. Just the ring," she stopped for a moment, a memory tugging at her.

Gifford was silent while Ramona sorted out the images in her head. "It was attached to a red plastic heart—probably some kind of advertising gimmick. . ." she said, eyes clearing as she spoke. "It must have been pretty faded because I didn't notice any words—and words were my profession," she reminded him. "But if you want to look at it, why don't you follow me home?"

Noon

By the time Carrie Jane got downstairs, grabbed a tray, filled it with her standard salad, and managed to navigate her way through the cacophony of the cafeteria and the main hall jammed with students carrying slices of pizza and soft drinks, lunch in the Teacher's Lounge was already in high gear. She slipped into a chair next to Flor and loaded her salad and a carton of chocolate onto the table. The half dozen round tables in the faculty room were so crowded, there wasn't room for her tray.

Flor raised an eyebrow when she spotted the chocolate milk.

"What?" Carrie Jane demanded.

"That bad?" Flor prodded.

Carrie Jane grinned in acknowledgment. Chocolate milk was code for an especially difficult day. "It's just that Caballero kid keeps making it harder to find any reward for surviving 3rd period. Yours?" she changed the subject.

"Excellent." Flor tucked a dark tendril of hair behind her ear with a satisfied chuckle. "We're getting ready for our Winter Carnival. Today we divided into groups and created games we can play outside--or inside if it keeps raining. I think the kids are really getting into it. The only rules were that the teams had to use events or actions based on the book we're reading. Every group is required to have evidence of the game's relevance to the novel, or the whole class wouldn't endorse it. Who knew a tragedy could be so much fun?"

Carrie Jane laughed out loud. Flor was teaching A Separate Peace, but she wasn't much for viewing the world from the "half-empty" point of view. She had long ago decreed there was enough misery in the world—so she not only managed to tease reluctant readers into tackling a complex novel, she'd convinced them to delve into the relationships between the characters and, on top of that, think it was an adventure. "You are amazing," she sighed. "Wish I could make learning so entertaining!"

Flor swiped impatiently at an abundance of curls out which fell into her eyes as she leaned toward Carrie Jane, so she could be heard above the din around them. "Really? That's your story, Oh Teacher of the Year last year?" Flor raised an eyebrow. "At least your honors kids want to think. My sophomores? Not so much. I'm lucky if I manage to convince them that 'learning' isn't a horror sub-plot from Nightmare on Elm Street. So," she said, changing the subject, "what's on the docket for tonight? That guy who's been e-mailing you call?"

"Nope. Not a sound. I'm thinking about canceling my subscription to Heavenly Matches and try Single, Inc. Three months of membership fees and not a bite."

Across the table, Leon from social studies looked up. "Hey, I keep telling you. Come out to a couple of bars with me, and I guarantee you at least one date by the end of the night."

Carrie Jane grinned good-naturedly. "Thanks, but I prefer my dates not to hook up with me through an alcoholic fog." Leon was nothing if not persistent. At least three times a week he tried to get her to go out with him and his buddies.

"One advantage of alcohol is that nothing seems too bad once you've had a couple of beers," he pointed out.

"Even you?" Flor teased him.

Leon recoiled in mock horror. "Watch it. Next time you want someone to cover your last period, I may not be available." His grin belied the threat. "Take your trash?" He scooped up the two women's paper bowls and cups. "See you two at the rehearsal tonight?"

Flor looked to Carrie Jane for approval. "Sure. Seven?"

"I'll be there," Carrie Jane nodded.

The tardy bell had already rung, and the halls were almost devoid of all but the most recalcitrant students by the time Carrie Jane opened the door into the counselors' offices. The usual line of students sat in the foyer waiting for their brief appointments. "Hey, Miss Dunk-It," a couple of them greet her as she went by.

"That's Plunkett," she said automatically, but it was half-hearted. Once Ollie had started calling her "Dunk-It" at the beginning of the school year, the name had spread like lightning through the basketball team, the seniors, and then on to the lower classmen. It wasn't so bad, she consoled herself. It was a term of affection—she hoped.

Counselors were assigned students in alphabetical chunks, sometimes as many as 500 kids a year to one counselor, so Carrie Jane went out of her way not to make their lives more difficult by pestering them unnecessarily. But Eduardo stumped her. He clearly had a fine mind as far as she could tell; he just never bothered to use it. She agreed with the old TV commercials which touted the idea that a "mind was a terrible thing to waste." If she had any say in the matter, Eduardo wouldn't be wasting his.

Jed Elman looked up from his computer screen and over his shoulder at her when she knocked at his open door. "What's up, Carrie Jane? Haven't seen you since last faculty meeting. Been hiding?"

"Just essays. The stack on my desk was threatening to reproduce after the lights went out, so I've been hunkering down for a couple of hours after school every day."

Jed hit the SAVE button and swiveled in his chair to face her. "No good assignment goes unpunished."

"That's what your daughter thinks. She told me last week that I wouldn't have to work so hard if I would quit giving them essays to write. She has a point."

Jed grinned in appreciation. "Yep. Makes me a proud father, she does. How's her grade?"

"Guess? ... Oh, never mind. I bet you check it every day."

Jed smiled. "Every day," he agreed. "So?"

"Eduardo Caballero."

"Ah . . .." He turned back to his computer and typed in the name. Studying the screen, he said thoughtfully, "He's failing your class."

"He has the lowest score in all my classes," she corrected. "But it's more than that. He's starting to scare me—and you know I don't scare easily. He's not threatening, exactly. It's more like he's a time bomb, and the clock is ticking toward detonation." She thought a moment to be sure she expressed the problem accurately to Jed. "He's bright, probably considerably brighter than most of his classmates, but to get him to participate requires my entire quota of emotional energy for that period. It seems like he's angry all the time. Now he's started intentionally baiting other students. It's getting worse. I was hoping you knew something I didn't."

Jed leaned forward, putting his elbows on the desk and staring back at the screen filled with figures and reports. "Hmmm. Looks like Spanish is his first language, but he's not an ESL student. Is he having trouble understanding what happens in class?"

"Doesn't seem to. In fact, I'd say just the opposite. This morning he called Ollie Haverfield a jerk—under his breath, of course."

"I take it Haverfield didn't hear it?"

"Nope. Fortunately."

Jed grinned. "Good thing. You might have had to referee a brawl otherwise. But look at this." Pointing to the screen, Jed scrolled through Eduardo's records from junior high. "Straight A's clear through last year." Jed turned back to face her and rubbed his chin. "From what you say, it doesn't seem like he fits the Shadow Generation profile."

"The what?"

"The 'Shadow Generation'—that's what I call kids brought to the U. S. by their parents when they were children. Most of their parents only speak limited English, if any at all. The kids have no green cards, no visas, no citizenship prospects. They're in limbo." His voice lowered; his eyes stared past her as if he were chronicling one student after another on an endless list.

"Shadow Generation." She thought about it for a minute. "I have several students who probably fall into that category. Like the kid in fifth period whose family owns the panaderia on Main across from the old Christensen's. But I don't get the feeling that's Eduardo's family. I guess I need to talk to his parents and see."

Jed shifted his chair back to face the computer screen, reading intently. "Says here he was born in Douglas Valley. Registered in the school system with a U. S. birth certificate. If he's bilingual, it might help to know where his parents came from. Some cultures foster a 'macho' image. Makes families too proud to ask for help." He studied the screen. "He's a good-looking kid," Elman commented, staring at the yearbook photo at the top of the page.

"That's part of the problem. What teenage boy ignores the girls in class who are trying to flirt with him? Even CC Mangum can't get a rise out of him. She's not used to being ignored, believe me. It just doesn't make any sense."

Elman ran his fingers through his hair, or at least what was left of it. "I'll call Eduardo down." Sighing, he added, "See if I can get him to open up. Maybe there's something else going on. At this rate, he's certainly not going to graduate." He shrugged. "Sad. He's so close." He swore under his breath. "Damn it. Can't these kids see how self-defeating it is to quit this late in the game?" Shrugging his shoulders in defeat, he asked Carrie Jane, "OK if I schedule him during your class sometime next week?"

Carrie Jane considered her next step. "The sooner, the better," she said. "I'll try to get in touch with his parents. Maybe they can give me some ideas on how to help him."

4 PM

By late afternoon the sky had cleared a little, leaving patchy spots of sunlight interspersed with the dark underbellies of storm clouds; a stiff breeze mocked the temperature gauge on Gifford's unmarked car. He plucked the small red plastic heart attached to the keyring Ramona had found in Annie's pocket from the drawer in his desk and fingered its shabby form through the transparent plastic evidence bag into which he'd carefully loaded it earlier in the day. The printing on the molded heart had all but worn away. The only imprint he could read for sure was a faint L-i-n and what appeared to be an image of an old-fashioned quill pen in an inkpot. There was probably an address under the illustration at some point, but now there was only an empty patch of smooth plastic. Not much to go on. Even with his treasured Swiss watch magnifying glass--his sisters' gift to him when he'd earned his Eagle Scout award at 14--he couldn't make out any more details. Well, he'd turn it and the gold-edged paper over to the lab for a closer inspection.

In Douglas Valley, the "lab" meant Templeton Ruggers, the physics teacher at Douglas Valley High, who moonlighted for the Sheriff's office as the one and only lab technician. The Sheriff joked that Temp only worked for their office because it was an excuse to get to spend more time with the fancy equipment he had talked the school district into purchasing for his program. But he had proven to be a crackerjack scientist as long as that equipment could handle the project. Gifford checked his watch. Four o'clock. Temp was probably still at school if he hustled over there.

Pulling into the parking lot never failed to evoke in Gifford the awkward, exhilarating, emotional roller coaster of his high school years. In a small town most of the lives of his upper classmates were already known to him--at least by rumor if not fact--long before he registered as a freshman. He'd hung out with their younger brothers and sisters in elementary school, often tagging along with his friends behind the "big" kids, hoping for a little acknowledgment from the older crowd and maybe scoring a free Slurpee from one of them. The hallways and classrooms of the high school were as familiar as the isles of the local grocery store by the time he began his high school career. He'd already been smuggled onto the buses which took what seemed like the entire student body to every away football and basketball road game, watched movies in the gym on PTSA Night, wandered through the exhibits of the annual Science Fair, and knew the reputations of virtually every teacher in the building.

That was more than fifteen years ago. Though he'd lost track of many of the kids he'd graduated with, the police headquarters in Douglas Valley was almost a community center for residents—often former classmates-- streaming through its offices on both sides of the law. Gifford didn't lose a lot of sleep over high school friends he'd been forced to investigate or arrest. He figured that was the price of coming back home to work after college. He liked his town, he liked its people, and he liked his history with them. He wasn't a huge fan of the demographics published in big city dailies that declared humanity was on a downward trend. In Douglas Valley people tended to remember what Gifford agreed was important in life—useful work, friends, neighbors, family, and a home. Of course, he had to admit he hadn't done a great job on the "family" part, but at least he hadn't given up on the possibility.

An institution at Douglas Valley High, Mr. Rugger's physics classroom was down the science hall at the back of the building. The whole wing had been remodeled and upgraded a couple of years before; now the halls were flooded with natural light from skylights and reflected in bright, cheerful lockers painted in the school colors—green and white. It was a significant improvement from Gifford's days when the old brick walls were grimy from years of kids' fingerprints and the occasional sly graffiti commentary on high school life.

"Hey, Temp," Gifford announced his arrival so as not to startle Ruggers, who was staring at a list of specs and checking figures on a stack of student papers next to it.

Temp looked up, pleased to have a reason to stop trying to figure out how the heck a kid could come up with answers so far from the accurate results. "Giff? What brings you back to class?"

"Fortunately, not a make-up test." He laughed. Temp was an extraordinary teacher, but Gifford's physics homework had taken an average of two hours a night—not a great option for a student who, as a senior, was a starter on the varsity basketball team. On the other hand, college physics had been no problem after Temp's class.

Walking across the room, navigating lab tables and stools, Gifford pulled the two plastic zip-lock evidence bags out of his pocket, each with the date and place of collection he'd neatly printed on the front. "Need some info about this notepaper and the plastic tab in the other bag. The tab apparently was attached to a key at some time, but the key is gone and the writing on the tab is almost worn off."

Temp reached for the bags. His fingers gently explored the materials inside, careful not to contaminate the evidence. First, he examined the notepaper with the gold border. "Pretty fancy," he commented. "No writing?" He asked the obvious aloud, his eyes still studying the paper.

"Nope. Doesn't appear to ever have been written on, but Annie claims it was supposed to have instructions of some kind."

"Annie?"

Gifford explained about the girl with no memory, adding the details about where Ramona had found her. "I'm hoping you can help us figure out who she is or at least where she might have been before she showed up behind the Seaweed Bar. I need to know if there was ever anything written there, and anything else you can tell me about what kind of paper this is. Seems like it's pretty unusual quality for the flyer or whatever the girl thought it must be."

Temp reached down and opened a drawer in his desk, grabbing out a set of long tweezers and using them to lift out the gold-edged paper. Twisting it back and forth, the paper flashed a myriad of reflections which leaped around the walls in front of his eyes. "No writing at all. Weird," He said to more to himself than Gifford. "Just the paper?"

"We're hoping you can tell us what kind of paper this is and where it's likely to be sold." Gifford pointed to the other bag. "As for the advertising tab, can you put it under a microscope and identify what it might have been advertising?"

"I'll give it a try. I might have a chemical or two that could bring out the imprint of the letters. It'll take a couple of hours though. Is tomorrow soon enough?"

"Yeah. Thanks, Temp. Give me a call when you find something. I owe you a six-pack of Diet Coke."

Temp laughed. "Yep, and I intend to hold you to it." Temp's addiction to Diet Coke was legendary at the high school. Giff and his buddies had occasionally sluffed a class to take an extended lunch and bribed their way out of detention with a six-pack. Ironic, Gifford mused as he headed out the classroom door. Now his job included catching kids who'd sluffed too many classes and were declared truant by the court. Lost in the vagaries of life, Gifford closed Temp's door behind him and turned straight into a tall redhead, almost knocking her over. He grabbed for her arm as she stumbled, scattering the papers she carried all over the floor.

"Well," she said, "nice to meet you, too." She looked up at him and smiled. "I wasn't all that excited about grading them anyway!"

"Sorry, I wasn't paying attention." He squatted down pulling papers toward him from every direction. "How about if I hand you the papers as I pick 'em up, and you can put them back in whatever order I destroyed?" He grabbed as many sheets as he could reach, pushing what appeared to be English essays into a kind of precarious stack in front of him.

"I'm Mark Gifford. I graduated from here a long time ago. I take it you're a teacher, not a student?" He looked up and introduced himself to a set of warm brown eyes and a string of freckles strewn randomly across her nose. As he spoke, he shuffled the nearest group of papers on end and tapped them a couple of times on the linoleum floor, pushing them into a reasonably orderly pile.

"Teacher. English. And, yes, I know," she teased. "You hated English when you were here. Everybody hates English." She laughed down at him.

Giff glanced at her and saw from the corner of his eyes a rope of hair that hung almost foot down her back in an untamed braid. I'd have probably liked English a lot better if my freshman English teacher had had a riot of red hair and freckles, instead of the old maid battle-ax with three chins and no neck, he thought. But what he said was, "How'd you guess?" He finished scraping together the last few pages, stretching for a page that had slid between two rows of lockers. He rose from his knees, apologizing again as he handed them to her. "Some of these pages got mixed up pretty badly when I bumped into you. Maybe I could figure out which ones go together?"

"I'll handle it. That's why I make them put their last name at the top of every page." She laughed. "More than one good reason to use MLA format." She held out her free hand and shook his. "Carrie Jane Plunkett. I was just going to check with Temp about a student we share who is having some trouble. Is Mr. Ruggers still in there?"

"Yeah. He does a little work for the Sheriff's Department now and then. I enticed him to put off grading lab reports for a hurry-up project we need. He didn't seem too upset," Giff admitted.

"You're a cop? You don't look like a cop."

"What does a cop look like?"

"Balding, sharp nose, slightly overweight, and rumpled … definitely rumpled." She reeled off the list without even having to think about it.

Giff grinned. "Give me a few years, and that'll be me," he agreed. "It's nice to meet you, Carrie Jane Plunkett. Good luck with those essays."

She shoved her stack of papers under her arm and turned to open the door to the lab. He caught the scent of something fresh, citrusy perhaps, as she passed him.

When he headed back to the parking lot, he found himself humming the Douglas Valley High School fight song.

7 PM

There was a steady stream of cars turning into the parking lot when Ramona, Viola, and Annie climbed out of the Ramona's Prius and headed for the south entrance of the church. The night sky had cleared, and the stars arched over the valley--which always meant a drop in temperature. Douglas Valley residents took the coming cold snap in stride. "Bout time," they greeted one another. "Rain the end of November? It's just not right."

Ramona had the black music folders tucked under one arm. Viola carried a basket with fresh cookies, handing Annie one as they walked through the door.

Annie took a bite. A shy smile lit the corners of her mouth. "Good," she said.

"For Pete's sake, Viola. She's anxious enough. Doesn't need a sugar high on top of that."

"I haven't tasted 'em yet. Annie's my guinea pig," Viola retorted. "If she's gonna spending time with me, she'll have to get used to sugar."

"That's an understatement," Ramona glared at her. Sometimes it felt like all she did was glare at Viola. It strained the imagination to think they'd been friends for 30 years. Shaking off her irritation, she led the way down the long hall past the large room with two basketball standards and a carefully tended wooden floor.

The girl looked curiously through the double doors which were propped open. A dozen or so boys and a couple of men were sweating profusely as they cat-called each other, one team teasing the other by tossing the ball around the key and back.

"This is a church?" Annie asked. "What kind of church has a basketball court?"

"It's a Mormon church. That room's the cultural hall. There's even a stage at the back. They sponsor a lot of activities for kids. I used to have quite a few students who were Mormons. Mostly nice kids. Pretty devout for teenagers, but hard workers." Ramona explained.

Viola chimed in. "They let us use the chapel for our rehearsals—free. Some of 'em are even in the choir."

A murmur at the end of the hall grew louder as they approached another set of double doors. The chapel was already starting to fill with singers sorting themselves into soprano, alto, tenor, and bass. They filed into the pews, filling the benches with the low rumble of cheerful chatter and the rustle of musical scores being organized alongside little explosions of laughter. By the time the latecomers arrived, almost every seat would be taken. At the front of the room, three tiers of empty choir seats faced the pews on the main floor. This choir was way too large to be accommodated by the 30 or so seats behind the podium. Instead, on the first tier of seats closest to the congregational pews, an organist, a pianist, and a string quartet were arranging music on stands, the strings tuning their instruments with the help of the piano.

Annie moved herself closer to Ramona. "There are a lot of people here," she said, her eyes darting from one side of the room to the other. "A lot of people."

"A couple of hundred usually," Ramona agreed. "It's a community choir. All volunteers. We perform the *Messiah* every year during the week before Christmas. If this crowd makes you nervous, you could wait out in the hall while we practice. It gets pretty loud in here. Viola and I sing alto, so we sit in that section," she pointed to a row of pews on the north side of the room. "The sopranos are on our right and the tenor and basses sit behind the women." She turned to Viola and ordered, "Save us a seat. I'm going to find a chair for Annie in the hall." She took Annie by the arm and attempted to lead her back out the double doors, but the girl had stopped and was gazing intently at the string quartet now practicing a fragment of music which drifted above the increasing din of choir members greeting each other and climbing past one another to find their seats in the pews.

Ramona and Viola exchanged a glance. Annie seemed mesmerized by the music. "Does that sound familiar?" Ramona had leaned down and spoken directly into Annie's ear to be heard over the noise. Annie nodded wordlessly, never taking her eyes off the string players. Ramona looked at Viola, whose slight tilt of the head acknowledged an unspoken agreement. Where had this child been that she recognized Handel's We Like Sheep?

"Here, Annie," Viola said. "Why don't you just sit here between us?" She scooted to her left and patted a seat next to her. Annie sat down automatically; her eyes focused on the players at the front of the chapel.

There was a squawk from the microphone attached to the podium as the conductor, a large woman with sparse mouse-brown hair and a baton in her right hand, tapped the microphone to be sure it was working. "OK, folks, let's get started." The crowd silenced immediately. The conductor cued the pianist, and the warm-up exercises began.

More than an hour later, Annie had progressed from a keen interest in the musical practice to looking over Viola's shoulder at the music and humming along under her breath. "What's going on here?" Ramona mouthed to Viola over the girl's head. Viola shrugged her shoulders. No idea.

Before the quartet began the introduction to the next solo selection, the conductor asked Mildred Schick to come to the podium and stand next to the strings exactly as she would in the final performance. When Mildred didn't appear, the musicians started the intro again, but still no Mildred. "Where is she?" the conductor demanded, straining her neck to search the choir seats, then tapping her baton impatiently against her music stand. "Mildred, are you out there? Get up here immediately. Please," she ordered, adding the last word as an afterthought.

"She fell in the parking lot getting out of her car." someone from the soprano section called out. Thinks she sprained her ankle pretty badly. Went to the emergency room,"

The conductor acknowledged the information with a long-suffering sigh. "Really? Why can't you folks take these practices seriously?" Then warming to her subject, "People! People! Let me remind you that dedicated musicians can sing over pain. Please, no more of these ridiculous excuses from any of the rest of you. We only have five more rehearsals. I expect EVERY ONE of you to be here for every rehearsal. And ON TIME." She gave up. "All right. We'll just have to make do today." Studying her score, she decided, "Let's have the sopranos who know it do the solo and remember the rest of the choir comes after the solo beginning on page 237."

Turning to the string quartet, she gave them a measure to set the rhythm and then cued the introduction. She pointed at the soprano section, indicating the starting measure by a raise of the baton.

"I know that my Redeemer liveth," they began, the stirring words ragged but enthusiastic. Resigned, the conductor decided not to bother with worrying about the quality of the performance. Sometimes one's emotional energy had to be spared for the battles one could win. She pulled the women along with her as the piano and organ joined the strings.

Annie leaned forward and turned the page on Viola's copy of the music. Her finger found the words on the score, and she began to sing along. Viola looked at her in surprise. On her other side, Ramona shifted in her seat, turning the page on her own copy of the music. Viola slid her score slightly left, so it would be closer to Annie's line of vision. The girl's voice grew stronger, the pitch clear and accurate. "I know that my Redeemer liveth . . .." Her voice rose, joining those of the sopranos in the set of pews on the far side of her. A couple of altos turned to see where the sound was coming from. Annie, her eyes glued to the score in front of her, seemed carried aloft by the power of the music and, in response, lifted the volume of her voice. Now the sopranos nearest Annie, puzzled by the voice floating across from them, swiveled in their seats, some of their voices petering away. Gradually, one or two at a time, the entire section paused, dropping out to listen to the voice, until the only sounds in the room were the string quartet, piano, organ, and the crystalline notes from the throat of the young girl who seemed to have become part of the music.

Ramona was stunned. There was strength in that voice, and

something else, something Ramona hadn't recognized in a very long time. It was joy.

As the music reached its crescendo, Annie's whole body echoed the words, "and because He liveth, I too, I too shall live!" She held the final note for a long moment, then her body went limp. She looked up a Ramona, seeking approval. Annie didn't notice that Viola's face was drenched with tears.

The choir burst into spontaneous applause. A few members whistled. "Well," said the conductor at the microphone. For a change, she could find nothing to criticize. Looking straight at Annie, she said again, "Well! I'll need to see you after the practice, young lady."

For the first time since Ramona had found Annie under the cardboard boxes, she saw Annie's radiant smile.

When the practice was over, choir members crowded around Annie, congratulating her on her magnificent performance. The words Great job! Where did you get a voice like that? were repeated a dozen times. Annie looked shyly as each speaker addressed her but made sure her hand stayed attached to Ramona's arm.

"Ramona, where on earth did you find that girl?" Carrie Jane had waited patiently until the crowd began to disperse, then she slipped through the remaining shoulders blocking her way. Flor and Leon were not far behind.

"Didn't find her. She found me," Ramona answered shortly. "Douglas Valley High still standing since I retired?"

"Yes, but it isn't the same. No one telling us what to do in the English department, so we are all just floundering around trying to figure how to keep moving without you. Sure you don't want to come back?" Carrie Jane tempted her.

"I think 40 years is enough. Time to give you young teachers a shot at tenure."

Leon threw his arm around the older woman. "That's why I love you, Ramona." He grinned in amusement when the older woman bristled at his touch. "Just what we want is tenure and that high falutin' salary that comes with it. Maybe you can get the Town Council to squeeze out a little more property tax, so we don't starve to death."

"Hmph! I'm not even sure a couple of those town council folks can read, much less draft a property tax increase." Ramona was only half-joking.

"Well, we miss you--that's for sure. Nobody to harass the administration means they harass us more often!" Carrie frowned at Leon, and good-naturedly, he let go of Ramona. "Now who's your friend?" she said nodding toward Annie.

"Just somebody I found hanging around a bar," Ramona answered.

Leon shot Carrie Jane a glance. "See?" he mouthed.

"Well, you sure can sing, young lady," Flor said. "Where'd you learn the *Messiah*?"

"She's not sure," Ramona could feel Annie tremble and answered for her. "She just absorbed it when she was a kid." It must be the truth, where else could a kid learn that kind of music? she thought.

"I like it. A lot." Annie said shyly. "Would it be OK if I came back next time?"

"That'll be a requirement," interrupted Janeen Whitlock, the choir conductor who was barreling down on the small group now clustered at the back of the chapel. "A voice like that doesn't happen in a small town like this. I want you here bright and early next Saturday morning before practice, so I can work with you privately."

"Now wait a minute, Janeen," Viola stepped in front of her before she got to Annie, who was already backing away from the conductor. "I'm Annie's official guardian, so if you want to speak to her, you have to go through me." For a change, Viola was not smiling. "Annie's got a lot going on right now, so you'll have to wait your turn."

Janeen looked down at least six inches to the short woman in front of her. She'd tangled with Viola before. And lost. That woman was as stubborn as a cat refusing to share her bowl with the family dog. Janeen backed off.

"It's all right," Annie said. "I'd like to sing. If it's OK with you?" She looked not at Viola but at Ramona. Ramona answered thoughtfully. "That might be the cog that jolts your memory."

"Saturday morning, then. 8 AM." Janeen looked from Ramona to Viola. They nodded in agreement for a change.

Friday, November 29

1 PM

ANNIE WOKE WITH A START. Someone was knocking. It seemed like someone was always knocking on that door. Shadows had washed across the back of the living room across from the warm little nest she had built for herself on the sofa. She must have been napping longer then she thought. She pushed the hair out of her eyes and listened for a moment. She could hear Ramona and the vacuum somewhere down the hall. They'd had a quiet Thanksgiving, just the three of them, and today Ramona allowed her to have a slice of leftover pumpkin pie for lunch. She was pretty sure it was her favorite, though how she knew that was a mystery to her. She'd curled up on the sofa when she was finished and pulled a worn afghan over her; the combination of being warm and full must have made her drowsy. She blinked. The knocking had stopped. "Is someone there?" she called.

"It's me," said a high-pitched voice. "*Hace frío. Abre la puerta!*" it commanded.

Annie tossed the afghan into the corner of the sofa and unlatched the deadbolt. She clasped her arms against the chilly wind and took a minute to focus her eyes. She surveyed the porch and the front yard. It was empty. Then something tugged at the hem of her T-shirt, yanking her attention to the steps at the bottom of the door. Standing just beneath her line of sight was a little girl shivering with cold—her thin arms scrunched against her chest, and her lips tinted blue. Tears streamed down her face, joined by her dripping nose. But even with the effects of the frigid weather, she was startlingly beautiful. Her naturally curly black hair rimmed dark eyes with impossibly long lashes— She couldn't be more than three or four, Annie guessed. "Who are you? Are you a friend of Ramona?"

"*¿Quién eres?*" the child asked. "*Tengo frío.* I cold. Let me in!"

Annie was taken aback by the authority in the child's voice. She scanned the surrounding houses for the adult who surely must be watching out for the child, but the street was quiet, vacant. "What are you doing out there--it's freezing! Where's your mom?" Annie pulled the little girl inside and pushed the door shut against the determined wind. "Are you lost?" she asked. Leading the child to the couch, Annie pulled the afghan she had been using around the little girl.

"No lost. *Trabajo*—I work," was the impatient reply. The child's accent was compounded by her shudders. In total command of the situation, she secured the blanket around her shoulders and climbed awkwardly up onto the sofa.

Not sure what to do next, Annie knelt eye-to-eye with the child. "You are working? How old are you? Where's your mom?"

"You will help me. Si!" It was an assumption, not a request.

"Help you do what?" Trying to imagine what on earth the little girl was talking about, Annie repeated, "What kind of work?" She could have sworn the little girl rolled her eyes.

"Christmas is coming and papa says we don't have *dinero para los regalos.*" She lapsed between English and Spanish with practiced ease. "Do you have dinero?" The little girl asked innocently.

Money. The little girl wanted money. Something about her father needing money for presents. "*No, lo siento.*" The Spanish words slipped out of her mouth without thinking. Annie blinked. Spanish? Where did that come from? Understanding began to dawn. "This is your work? To get money?" It took some amount of control for Annie not to laugh out loud. Instead, she called for backup. "Ramona!" She heard the vacuum switch off abruptly, and Ramona's heavy footsteps hustle down the hall toward her.

"*¿Quién es, Ramona?*" the child repeated the name carefully, a slight lilt to her pronunciation.

"What? What's the matter?" Ramona demanded as she charged into the room. The little girl gave her a sunny smile. Ramona didn't surprise easily, but she stopped dead at that smile. "Who the hell is that?" The realization dawned that she'd sworn in front of a little kid. "Crap!" she uttered, relieved she'd managed to choose a less offensive word and avoid compounding her error.

It had only been three days, but Annie already ignored the language. "We have company," Annie explained needlessly. "I let her in—it's cold outside. I hope that was the right thing to do."

"No," Ramona said, her attention focused on the little girl. Then she backed up when she saw the look on Annie's face. "I mean, yes, you did the right thing. And no, you couldn't leave a little person out in the cold . . ." Ramona studied the child. Worn jeans, plaid flannel shirt at least one size too big, mismatched socks, bright orange tennis shoes, and a little purse which hung by a bit of yarn from her shoulder. Ramona shook her head in irritation. Probably from the other side of town. Let their kids run wild over there. Under her breath, she muttered, "Doesn't even have a proper coat."

Settling in the easy chair by the fireplace, Ramona beckoned the little girl off her perch on the couch. "What's your name, honey?"—wryly she had a moment of déjà vu as Annie's arrival flashed into her head. She hoped this wasn't going to become a habit. She wasn't sure she had enough hot chocolate on hand for that.

The little girl showed no signs of fear at all; she was still shivering as she climbed down, walked over, and leaned her little body against Ramona's knees, looking directly into her eyes. *"Me llamo Marisa. Tengo cuatro años."* She held up four fingers.

Ramona smothered a flash of admiration. Royalty couldn't have been more at ease in a stranger's house.

"Four, eh? Aren't you kind of young to be out by yourself, Marisa?" Ramona imitated the girl's pronunciation of her name.

Marisa took offense. "I am big. I babysit Alejandro when Mama cooks." She announced.

"Well, that explains it," Ramona chuckled. "Where do you live? Does your Mama know you are here?"

"Mama wash clothes. I come. I work," she stated with pride. "I have dinero." She pulled the purse down off her shoulder and unclasped it.

Ramona peered down inside. It was crammed with maybe two dozen coins of various denominations and one crumpled dollar bill. "I see. And what is the money for?"

"Regalos," the child said triumphantly.

"Presents," Annie translated.

Ramona raised an eyebrow. Bilingual? She added another clue to her list of Annie's accomplishments. Leaning forward, she rearranged the blanket around Marisa's shoulders and lifted the little girl onto her lap. "So? You have money for presents. Are you going shopping?"

"No. I give to my papa. He buy."

"Ah," Ramona understanding at last. "And you are helping him by amassing funds?"

Marisa twisted on Ramona's lap. "No! What is this 'fund'?'" she asked. "I get money!" Emphasizing her mission, she pulled a handful of change from her purse. "¡Ver!"

"And you want me to pay you?" Ramona shared a glance of amusement with Annie. "Very enterprising," she murmured.

The little girl eyed Ramona shrewdly. It was obvious she knew who made the business decisions. "You have dinero?" she asked.

"Si," Ramona answered. "But why should I give it to you? If you are working, you need to earn it."

This response was obviously not what the little girl expected. She considered the problem. She eyed Annie with speculation. "I watch the girl? She naughty?"

Ramona pretended to think about the offer. "No. Annie's a good girl." She rubbed her chin in exaggerated reflection. "Let's make a deal. I will pay you 50 cents to show me exactly where you live."

"It is far. I will need more money," Marisa bargained.

"I can see that's a problem," Ramona countered. "One dollar, then. That's my final offer."

Marisa proffered her hand to seal the deal. Ramona shook it solemnly. The child was irresistible.

Ramona spent several minutes digging around in the closet of the office across from Annie's room looking for a coat or jacket small enough to fit Marisa. Finding nothing appropriate, she scooped up the fleece blanket and wrapped up the child like swaddling a baby. Marisa giggled, rubbing the soft material against her skin. "I like this blanket for *bebés*!" she declared. "It is soft like *plumas*."

"Feathers," Annie translated at Ramona's questioning glance.

Frigid air assaulted them as Ramona carried the little girl out the back door, heading for the garage. She wondered how long the child had been knocking on doors asking for money.

The sky had lost any pretense of sunlight and angry clouds now piled up against the horizon. The freshening wind promised even colder temperatures. Annie helped Ramona seat belt Marisa into the back seat of the car, then climbed in next to the girl, pulling her own seatbelt tight.

Ramona backed out of the driveway and paused at the stop sign at the end of the block. She looked over her shoulder, asked Marisa, "Which way?"

Marisa studied the street and struggled to point, but her arms were tied up in the folds of the blanket. Her solution was to point with her lips toward her side window.

"Left," Annie interpreted.

In the end, the child earned her money. She knew exactly where she lived, although Ramona would not have defined five blocks as 'far'. It was part of a large group of duplexes built on land that had been an open field beyond Ramona's house when she was a girl. Now the high density, low-income homes appealed to Douglas Valley's newest residents, a sizeable portion of them Hispanic immigrants who, in Ramona's view, probably collected unemployment checks on a weekly basis. Ramona surveyed the community with distaste. She'd never liked this section of town. 'Rundown' was a flattering description. Yards were fenced with chain link that had rusted or sagged with age; many doorways were covered with the grime from years of dirty handprints—not to mention a serious lack of scrubbing. Torn curtains were visible in random windows, and several driveways held junk cars, some of which looked like they'd been sitting in the same spots for years. The streets were lined with battered mini-vans, older four-wheel-drive trucks, and kids' toys propped against carport openings.

Marisa lived in a duplex on the far side of the complex, her house the last one on the block. A fenced yard surrounded a lawn mostly dead from winter's weather, but unlike her neighbors, the shrubs were neatly trimmed. A couple of rusted bikes were parked to the side of the asphalt driveway. From the lower edge of the front window, Ramona spied two pairs of eyes studying her covertly through the slats of yellowed mini blinds.

"Mi casa," Marisa announced with satisfaction.

Great, thought Ramona. Well, at least she didn't have to call Detective Gifford about another lost child. He'd probably consider taking her to jail for serial kidnapping. "I'll get her out of the car; you knock,"

Ramona instructed. Annie helped heft Marisa into Ramona's arms, and the two of them made their way to a small front porch, Annie bracing the girl as Ramona heaved her up the steps. The door opened without Annie's intervention.

A dark-haired boy perhaps seven or eight years-old stood in the doorway. Silently, he pulled the door wide and gestured for them to come in. Marisa chattered something unintelligible at him, and he answered back. He was "scolding her about something?" Annie interpreted.

"*Mama!*" Marisa called. "*Mama! ¿Dónde está?*" Ramona set the child on the floor and untangled the blanket wrapped around her.

A slender, slight woman with the same dark curls as her daughter came from the direction of a waft of spicy smells and a faint cloud of steam, wiping her hands on a worn apron as she came.

"Marisa," she cried, scooping up the little girl, hugging her tightly. "Marisa, Marisa," she murmured. After assuring herself that the little girl was safe, she started a heated Spanish conversation between the two, which ended with Marisa taking the purse off her shoulder and showing her mother its contents. Her mother looked appalled. She glanced up at the woman and the girl standing awkwardly silent in the middle of the room.

"Did you get any of that?" Ramona whispered to Annie.

Annie shrugged. "I think Marisa's in trouble for not telling her mother where she was going."

Setting Marisa down, her mother turned to them. "I am so sorry," she said, her English clear and accurate but tinged with a pleasing, almost imperceptible rhythm. "Marisa says you brought her home when she was cold. Please, please sit down." She gestured to the single piece of furniture in the room—a worn couch placed under the picture window, a cheerful, multi-colored blanket neatly folded across its back. The boy who answered the door and what looked to be a younger brother were seated there watching the discussion between their mother and sister with some appreciation. At their mother's invitation, they obediently got up and moved to the floor across the room.

"I am afraid the child heard her papa and me last night talking about how we were going to afford gifts for her and her brothers," she said, glancing at her daughter with affection. "She does not understand that it is not so simple. My Little One just wanted to help." She shrugged her shoulders. She turned and addressed the boy who had opened the door for them in Spanish. He nodded miserably. "Jesús," she frowned at the older boy, "saw her leave while I was bathing Alejandro. He said nothing." Jesús shifted uncomfortably. "Your Papa will hear of this," she warned him.

Marisa shot her brother a look of triumph. Now she was not the only one who was in trouble.

"I am so sorry," her mother apologized again. "When I found she was gone, I thought maybe she had gone across the street to the house of my mother. But her *abuela* said, 'no'. I began to worry. I called her papa. He has been looking for her for more than an hour." She laid her hand on Marisa's shoulder and looked down at her with disapproval. "What were you thinking, going out in the cold and asking strangers for money? Your papa will be very upset when he finds you have done this."

Crestfallen, Marisa's gaze dropped to the floor, "*Mama, es Navidad,*" she whispered, her brash confidence deflated.

Annie rose from the couch, knelt next to her, and put her arms around the little girl, whispering something in her ear. The girl brightened and agreed.

"Well, Marisa. Here's the dollar we agreed upon." Ramona saw the little girl's mother wince. "Next time you decide to solicit charitable funds, let your mama know where you are going," She instructed the little girl. Ramona then offered her hand to the mother. "Nice to meet you—I'm sorry I didn't get your name?" she said as they shook hands.

"Luz. My name is Luz. Thank you again." She held the door open. The two visitors waved good-bye to the little girl and leaned into the southern wind as they returned to the car. Ramona looked up at the sky. High above them, clouds were rolling past, and there was the distinctive smell of rain in the air. "Rain," Ramona predicted in disgust. "Rain again."

"What did you say to Marisa just before we left?" Ramona asked as she and Annie clamored into the car.

"I told her I'd come visit her next week."

Ramona stopped and stared at her. "What? Why?"

"I like her," Annie said. "She reminds me of someone." She sighed. "I'm just not sure who."

Saturday, November 30

8 AM

"YOU KNOW, ANNIE, YOU DON'T have to do this. If you'd rather stay home and avoid the whole music thing, you certainly can. Janeen is pushy and demanding. She's a little much for someone who isn't used to her bullying," Ramona said, oblivious to the irony in her words. She turned off the ignition and studied the girl in the seat next to her out of the corner of her eye.

It felt odd to go to practice without Viola, but Viola had been adamant--she had cookies to bake and only a couple of weeks till Christmas! She could mix up and freeze a whole batch of snickerdoodles in that extra hour. It was too much time to give up. Ramona didn't bother to argue. Viola, during cookie season, was a force to be reckoned with. It was the one thing Viola did every year that was wildly out of character for the woman who believed that time spent in the service to her fellow beings was far more important than the "foo-foo" of domesticity, an attitude she'd developed during her many years of social work. Viola's cookie routine took precedence over everything else. Despite that underlying dismissal of all things domestic, every year she created ornate cookies with delicate filigree snowflakes, gingerbread characters, or Christmas trees complete with presents beneath them to what seemed like every person she'd ever met in the valley. For Ramona, it was an incomprehensible paradox.

Ramona agreed to take Annie early, and Viola promised to be along at 9 AM when the regular Saturday practice began. She shifted in her seat, glancing at Annie again. Truth be told, the attachment she'd already formed for the girl made her uneasy. Ramona was a realist. She knew that any day now, Detective Gifford would figure out where the girl belonged, and she'd be alone in the house again. Oh, she could handle it, but deep down, she knew she didn't want to. She was tired of living alone, tired of having no one to sit with when the 10 o'clock news came on, tired of having to be responsible for every little facet of her life. The past few days with Annie had reminded her of what she had lost, a knowledge that had taken her years to bury. "Well," she said, shaking off the slow throb she sensed building in the back of her head, "let's get to it," and hurried Annie out of the car and toward the building.

Annie looked around the parking lot which was completely empty except for two cars near the side door. The sun just barely poked over the mountains to the east of them. "I like to sing." She felt it necessary to explain. "I'm sorry we had to get up so early, but singing makes me . . ." she considered what she wanted to say with care. "It makes me feel . . . safe," she concluded. "Like I belong somewhere," she finished lamely.

Ramona felt a sudden punch to the stomach. "Oh, Child." She reached out and hugged the girl tightly. "You belong with me as long as you need me." She was glad Annie's head was down so that she didn't notice the tears of rage which threatened to escape Ramona's eyes at the thought of a family who may have abandoned such a girl without a backward glance.

The building was chilly--the heat controlled by a computer that obviously wasn't programmed for practices this early in the morning. Both Janeen and the accompanist still had their coats buttoned up as they shared the piano bench and conferred over some section of music. They looked up only when Ramona and Annie joined them in the chapel. Ramona was amused to notice they both were focused on Annie; they rose in unison, motioning to her.

"Sit here next to Meryl," Janeen instructed Annie as she moved to the choir seat directly across from the piano. "Let's find out if this singing thing is a fluke."

Ramona glared at Janeen as she slid into a pew on the north side of the room, but Janeen never noticed. Ramona was clearly an unnecessary accessory to the star attraction. Sensitivity wasn't that woman's strong point, or even part of her vocabulary for that matter. Ramona swore under her breath and pulled her own music out of her black folder, turning to the section open on the piano. At this rate, it was going to be a long morning.

Janeen took Annie through an extended round of warm-up exercises directed at both her voice and the cold which permeated the room. "The heat comes on at nine when the rest of the group gets here. We'll just have to suffer till then," she apologized.

Annie's voice, gravelly at first, stretched and opened. By the time Janeen stopped demanding higher and higher scales, Annie had floated over the A an octave and a half above middle C. Pride filled Ramona even as she recognized the futility of her response. Less than a week ago, she hadn't even known this girl, but now she felt like a mother unexpectedly confronted by her child's hidden gifts. She needed to get a grip on herself.

"Don't know where you studied, child, but that voice is a gift from God." Janeen nodded in satisfaction. "Now let's go through the soprano from the middle of page 237."

The murmur of voices, then the piano plunking out specific measures of one after another soprano section lulled Ramona into a light sleep, her head leaning against the outer wall of the chapel. She dozed. It was Annie's voice rising above the accompaniment in a climactic crescendo which startled her, and she awoke with a start. She'd been dreaming about the day she'd brought Ellie home from the hospital. Amos had been so careful as he lifted the child from Ramona's arms to carry her into the house. No car seats in those days. Amos had told her later that he'd never held a baby before, and he was afraid if he jostled her, her tiny foot might fall off her leg. She remembered them both rushing to the cradle next to the bed when the baby woke in the middle of the night and demanded to be fed--Ramona lifting Ellie up out of the bed, and Amos solicitously tucking her swaddling blanket back under those same tiny feet. Tears came to Ramona's eyes again, and irritated, she swiped at them. Twice in one morning, you old fool. "Damn it," she scolded herself at yet another pathetic breakdown. "Get over it. She's been gone too long; she's not coming back."

"No, Annie, you've got to hold that note for four full counts. Otherwise, the piano sounds like it's gone off by itself and decided to ignore the singer," Janeen's tone was demanding and impatient. Half-rising from her chair, Ramona intended to give Janeen a piece of her mind about bullying Annie, but she lowered herself back down when she saw that the girl didn't seem upset and obediently sang the phrase again. Ramona sighed. She knew she was already way too attached to the girl. "This has to stop," she ordered herself firmly.

By nine, the room was full of choir members ready for their Saturday morning rehearsal. This time it was Annie alone who sang the "I Know That My Redeemer Liveth" solo. Mildred, her leg in a Velcro cast, didn't appear in the least upset by the youngster usurping her moment in the limelight. "That high A was a stretch for me anyway," she confided to her seatmate.

Already the choir accepted the young girl as a soloist, and the way many of the sopranos leaned forward in their seats as Annie's voice soared to the triumphant conclusion made it clear that they, like Ramona and Viola (who'd arrived late with a touch of flour on her nose), had accepted Annie as one of their own.

By 10:30 the entire choir was restless and impatient to get home to the Saturday morning routine of grocery shopping, washing cars, and cheering their kids on at season-opening Junior Jazz basketball games. "All right Group, that's IT for Today." Janeen didn't sound happy about the quality of the rehearsal, but then, she seldom was happy about anything. "Remember!" she commanded. "It's almost DECEMBER! We only have only a couple of weeks until the performance. I expect you here early Wednesdays and Saturdays. ALL OF YOU. Dress rehearsal is Friday, the 20th at the high school auditorium. I don't care how important you think family Christmas parties are, there are no excuses for missing it. PERFORMANCE is the 22nd. THE SATURDAY BEFORE CHRISTMAS." Since she'd been repeating the same information every week since rehearsals began right after Halloween, most of the choir members ignored her as they reached for coats and hats. "And I'd BETTER not see any stragglers trying to sneak in after the opening announcements—YOU know who YOU are, Rachel Belowitz." Janeen glared directly at the always tardy second soprano. Rachel never noticed the admonition; she was too busy whispering to her seatmate about the tear in her brand-new loveseat--"only three weeks old, mind you."

From the double doors on the side of the chapel opposite Ramona and Viola, a voice called out, "Can I have a minute, Janeen?" A short, muscular woman elbowed her way past tenors and basses and up the aisle toward the microphone.

Ramona turned and exchanged a knowing look with Viola. "Here it comes," she said.

The woman nudged Janeen out from in front of the microphone without bothering to excuse herself. "For those of you who don't know me," the microphone squawked at the volume of her voice, "I am Jesse Simpson, Mayor of Douglas Valley and chairperson of the Town Council."

"As if she'd let anyone forget," Ramona whispered to Viola in disgust.

Simpson paused a moment to let the audience settle back down and pay attention to her critical message. "We have a special study session coming before the Council next Tuesday night that has the potential of improving the quality of life for every citizen in Douglas Valley. I want to invite you all to come to our regular meeting at 7 PM in the Field House at City Hall." She smiled, careful to show a narrow section of her upper teeth as she had practiced to so often in the mirror. "Your Douglas Valley Town Council has some big plans for the future of our downtown area, and you all must come out and hear about them."

The mayor's smug satisfaction with her message grated on Ramona, and she snorted— her automatic reaction to everything that came out of Jessie Simpson's mouth. All around Ramona, choir members who had stopped what they were doing to listen, nodded obediently, relieved to escape what they feared might be a lengthy speech, a common occurrence when the Mayor spoke.

Rising almost simultaneously, there was a hurried gathering of belongings, and most of the singers were streaming through the double doors at the back of the chapel before Jessie Simpson had made it down the steps of the podium and back to her coat, still draped over the pew near the double doors.

"So, Jesse? You sure Douglas Valley is ready for a hoity-toity mall? Who's going to pay for it? You? The Council?" Ramona's eyes glittered as she confronted Simpson passing the bench Viola and Annie had just exited.

Simpson stopped dead. "Ramona," she said with forced pleasantry. "How nice to see you. And Viola..!" Her smile for each of them never reached her eyes. She zeroed in on the young girl following the smaller woman. "Ah! Annie, isn't it? Your story is all over town. Remarkable voice you have young woman. Must make your guardians here very proud." Without waiting for a reply from the girl who was already flustered by too much attention, Simpson turned back to Ramona. "I assume your concern means we'll see you at the meeting Tuesday?"

"Oh, you can count on it," Ramona replied. "And I'll be speaking to the issue of the Council's attempt to run decent businesses into the ground—businesses which have been stalwarts in supporting every segment of the community, not just the rich and self-important." Ramona's clipped pronunciation emphasized her distaste for the Council's vision of 'an improved quality of life' for Douglas Valley.

"Times are changing, Ramona," the mayor said. "You've been here so long, you haven't noticed what's happening outside this town. Maybe you should get out more." Simpson didn't bother to disguise the venom in her voice. She turned her back on Ramona and headed out the double doors.

Monday, December 2

2:30 PM

MONDAY WAS ALWAYS A LONG DAY. It was a relief for the last bell to ring. Most Mondays after school, Flor dropped in to debrief the weekend after the last bell.

Today she shoved two desks together so that they formed a longer surface which was only slightly arched in the middle, somehow creating an awkward recliner. Gingerly, she lowered her head and back onto one side and draped her hips and legs across the other. Grasping the clump of curled ringlets now hanging off the edge of the contraption, she bunched the long dark hair beneath her head as a pillow. "Damned uncomfortable," she commented and shifted her shoulders slightly.

"Surprising," Carrie Jane said dryly.

"I'm tired," Flor shot back, "and I need a few minutes to unwind before I dive into those quizzes on dependent clauses." She thought about the prospect for a minute. "Most sophomores think a 'dependent' clause is related to some kind of not quite grown-up Christmas elf."

"Then you ought to have an interesting afternoon," Carrie Jane laughed.

"What's on your docket for tonight?"

"Not much. I have a meeting with Eduardo Caballero's father in a little while, and then an appointment with my laundry and a Hallmark movie."

"Nice. A prospect no woman could resist."

"Yep. Another exciting evening," Carrie Jane agreed. "It's the New-Christmas- Movie-Every-Night season." She grinned. "At least I know there'll be a happy ending. How 'bout you?"

"I'm headed for a bowling date with the guy who handles the Pepsi vending machines in the gym."

Carrie Jane eyed her speculatively. "Hot? Rich? Tall?"

"Nah, just nice. He lives in the apartment directly above mine. We talk sometimes at the mailboxes. And he's promised me all the free Pepsi I can drink."

"Bonus."

"Yep." Flor sighed contentedly. "He's relaxing." She rolled onto one shoulder and leveraged her weight off the desk, untangling her limbs into a standing position. "Well, I'm out of here. Good luck with your parent meeting. Let me know how it turns out."

More than half an hour passed before Carrie Jane heard footsteps in the hall. A man of medium height with dark hair streaked white at the temples and dressed in jeans and a T-shirt leaned into the doorway. No paunch, she noticed. Impressive.

"*Señorita* Plunkett?" Eduardo's father stretched her last name into something that rhymed with 'parakeet'.

"Mr. Caballero?" Carrie Jane rose from her desk, shook his hand—his grip firm and confident—and gestured to Eduardo's father to take the chair she placed beside the desk. "Thanks for coming."

His whole face lit up as he smiled at her. "Eduardo did not mention that his English teacher was so lovely." His English was excellent, only a barely discernible accent flowing through his words.

Carrie Jane's dimple peeked out. "It's a pleasure to meet you," she responded. No wonder Eduardo's so good looking, she thought.

"Thank you for caring about Eduardo. He has spoken about things you discuss in your class. He told us about the church that carries protest signs across the street from the funerals of soldiers, and the states that are allowing their citizens to use marijuana."

Carrie Jane was astonished. "He talks about our class discussions? He never says a word in class, and he usually seems bored with the whole thing."

Mr. Caballero sighed. "I look at his grades once a week on the computers at the library. I do not understand why he does nothing. When he was young, he loved school, but now he has changed. He is angry all the time."

Carrie Jane nodded. "He's a bright kid," she agreed. "But he is not going to be able to graduate if he fails this quarter, too. He simply won't have time to make up another English credit."

Mr. Caballero nodded. "I understand," he said.

Carrie Jane turned to the grade sheet open on her computer, studying the record of Eduardo's classwork, shaking her head in frustration. "To be honest, Mr. Caballero, I just don't get it." She twisted the screen so that he could see it and highlighted Eduardo's grades. "Look," she said. "Nothing. Nothing at all." A string of zeros marched across the page. "What happened? When did he quit trying?"

Mr. Caballero's eyes closed in concentration. "My son . . ." he began, then lapsed into silence for a moment. "His life . . . has not been easy. His mother died before he was two years old. It was a difficult time. When he was 10, I married again. She is a kind woman, and she has grown to love Eduardo. I believe he loves her--and his younger *hijos* also. But he is almost a man." He sighed. "For us, the future is always difficult."

Carrie Jane didn't ask, but she suspected Mr. Caballero was not speaking of his family alone. She said nothing.

"Even when he was young, Eduardo was different. His friends loved the football, er . . . soccer," he corrected himself. "He loved books. Because of my work at the garage, he was with his grandmother. She has never learned much English, but he watched television, and he learned. There was a library not far from the apartment. He would beg her to go there and sit on the floor in the part that had books for children. Once when the library lady was not busy, she sat by him and read him the story. When the time for his fifth birthday came, he was already reading by himself." There was pride in his voice. "But now, he reads nothing. After school and then his job with me in the garage, he goes to his room and listens to his music. Even while he is eating with *la familia*, he is alone. When I try to talk to him, he says, '*Padre*, I love you.' But he will say nothing more."

Carrie Jane's eyes glistened with unexpected moisture. "I'm sorry," she apologized as she reached for a Kleenex. "I don't know what's gotten into me."

Mr. Caballero's eyes softened. "You care about my son," he said. "Thank you," he said simply.

"How can I help him?" she asked as she dabbed at her nose.

"Perhaps it is time for both of us to ask him. I have treated him as a child for too long," he said thoughtfully. "Now is the time for me to speak with him as a man. *Quizás* you too could speak to him. Show him what you have shown me," he gestured to the computer screen. "He is proud. He does not like to fail. Let us remind him of what is true. He must decide what to do."

Carrie Jane sat without moving for a long time after Mr. Caballero left her room. She felt an overwhelming sadness for the boy and his father. That was the difficult part of being a teacher. Sometimes she spent more time with her students than their parents did. She listened to them, read their papers filled with both their hopes and their pain, shared with them the exhilaration of new ideas, watched them build—and sometimes destroy--friendships, and grew to love them. But she was not a parent; she had so little leverage to ease their burdens.

It was quiet in the building now. Most of the other teachers had either gone home or were at their desks grading papers and planning tomorrow's lessons. Carrie Jane listened to the silence, then she bowed her head and said a quiet prayer for Eduardo and his father.

Monday, December 2

4 PM

DOWNSTAIRS EDUARDO CABALLERO LEANED AGAINST the wall just inside one of the double sets of doors which formed a small barricade against the usually fierce Douglas Valley winters. The little breezeway that separated the two sets of doors was empty now except for the boy. School had been out for some time. He didn't have to work tonight, but he didn't want to go home either. There was nothing there anyway but noisy kids and chores. He was tired of his father hounding him about homework. Who cared what dead authors said about moral responsibility, or what the atomic number of plutonium was? He brushed them out of his mind without a second thought. For a moment he struggled with himself about whether or not he should make the call. He knew it was stupid, but he hit speed dial before he was even aware of it.

A male voice answered, "¿Hola?"

Eduardo hung up abruptly, disgusted. Of course, he wouldn't let her answer. He wouldn't let her do anything.

He leaned against the brick wall and closed his eyes. For the ten-thousandth time, he agonized—what was he going to do? What were they going to do?

"Eduardo? I'm surprised to see you here this late? You waiting for a ride?" Miss Plunkett shifted the long strap of her briefcase to her left shoulder as she pushed open the door with her right arm.

"No."

She frowned. "Can I help you somehow?"

"No," he said shortly, then added, "thanks," when he realized how rude he must have sounded.

Eduardo didn't welcome conversation, but he could see she had something she wanted to say. Might as well let her get it over with. He figured he owed her after his dig at Ollie in class today.

"You know you are probably my brightest student," she began.

He looked directly at her for the first time. "Yeah," he nodded. Why beat around the bush? He'd known that for a long time. But as far as he could tell, being smart had just made him angrier at the stupid people around him.

"Why is it that you are failing? I talked to your dad. We have agreed that this is your problem."

With some effort, he kept his face impassive. She talked to his father? Crap!

"You're an adult now. What are you going to do about graduation?" Her voice trailed off, waiting for a response

"Who cares?" he answered shortly, staring out the heavy metal security doors into the parking lot.

She didn't let him bait her. "Mr. Ruggers told me you're failing physics, too. He says you never miss a class; you just don't do anything." She didn't sound upset, just concerned.

"So?"

"You know you can't support a family without a decent job. That usually means some kind of post high school training."

Surely, she couldn't know, he thought. No one knew.

"Are you going to try college?"

Comprehension dawned. She meant what was he going to do after high school? He breathed a sigh of relief and answered, "Why bother?" The truth was he liked Miss Plunkett. She was a good teacher. She made them write every day which was a pain, but he had to admit he was getting better. And he liked listening to the class discussions about "current issues of national discourse" as she called it. No other English teacher he'd ever had mentioned anything at all about what was going on in the real world. All they were interested in was where to put commas and what the secret meaning of a poem written 200 years ago was--200 years! Gimme a break.

He'd had enough. "Look," he said abruptly. "I gotta go." And he pushed open the outer door, leaving her alone in the breezeway.

The door slammed behind him. His long legs broke into a trot. He didn't look back. It had been the longest conversation he'd had with Miss Plunkett since he'd joined her class in September. He knew she was watching him as he weaved through the cars in the parking lot and headed toward the street.

By the time he passed Ollie's Cherokee, he'd already forgotten the teacher. He slammed his fist down on the hood, the combination of worry and anger getting the best of him. He never even owned a decent bike, and Ollie's ride must have cost a fortune. America certainly was the land of equality, he thought savagely. Ducking his head to hide his turmoil, an expletive exploded from his mouth. He didn't bother to check to see if he'd dented the hood. Escalating fury propelled him from the parking lot and onto the nearby street.

Without even thinking, when he stopped long enough to look around, he found himself on the corner of her street. It wasn't that he'd meant to come here. He'd been stewing about Miss Plunkett's warning. He knew she was right. He already had a minimum wage job he disliked. The odds of finding a career without a diploma were poor. And suddenly, there was her house.

He slowed down. Eduardo was pretty certain she must give off some kind of magnetic resonance like Temp talked about in physics--that she called to him through some secret, undiscovered force which he was incapable of resisting. And he didn't want to resist. He loved her.

There was a break in the fence of the little home next door to her house. Under the cover of a huge, untamed Russian olive tree which had long ago invaded her father's side of the weathered wooden posts, his arrival was virtually undetectable.

Her room was at the back. He could see her shadow moving around though the curtain was drawn; her enticing silhouette showed the basketball-sized bump that was growing where her waist had been. When her father discovered she was pregnant, he'd forbidden her to leave the house, but he hadn't been able to force her to tell him who the father was. Eduardo knew he had to get her out of there soon. She needed him to take care of her. Once again, he raged at the unfairness of their situation.

Months ago, he'd found that if he stood on the water meter, he could just reach the edge of the windowsill. She heard him immediately. She could always sense when he was near. She pulled the window up and leaned down toward him. "Wait," she whispered. It was freezing. She ducked back into her room, grabbing a blanket to wrap around her shoulders. She leaned back out the window, reaching down to touch his face tenderly. "You shouldn't be here."

Her long dark hair fell over her shoulders and onto his hands. He let the sleek strands slip gently threw his fingers. Lifting the silken tresses, he pressed them to his nose and inhaled the scent. She always smelled like gardenias. "I didn't mean to come," he said. He looked up at her, anxiety dissolving at the soft expression in her eyes. "I had to see you. Are you OK? How is the baby?" He caressed her hand resting on the windowsill.

She trembled involuntarily in response.

"How are you feeling?"

"Fatter." She smiled at him. "The baby is getting so big; it is harder for him to move around. He doesn't kick as much. The doctor says he must be a rebel to kick his mama," she shared the old obstetrics joke. "Maybe he just takes after his father." She laughed out loud, instantly twisting in fear to check the door for a reaction from her father in the next room. Something smacked against the far side of her bedroom wall, and they both started. "You must go," she whispered.

"I love you," he said and reached up to touch her cheek. "I'll figure something out. I promise."

"I know," she said. "Now go." She pulled the window sash down as quietly as possible and turned away, the curtain falling back into place and blocking his last possible vision of her.

Eduardo stepped down from the water meter and stood still for a moment.

Then he turned, slipped back behind the Russian olive, and headed out of the neighborhood toward home.

Tuesday, December 3

1 PM

DETECTIVE GIFFORD HELD THE LITTLE evidence bag with the red plastic heart Temp had returned Friday morning and absently wove it back and forth between his fingers, a habit so old he'd forgotten that he even did it. He stared straight ahead through his windshield, but his mind was elsewhere trying to figure out how this small piece of evidence was tied to the Jane Doe, Annie—he reminded himself—that Mrs. Z. had found behind the bar. Temp Ruggers hadn't been able to tell him much about the printing which had been the original purpose of the little heart, just that the ink was the cheapest variety available and that it appeared that someone had apparently used the disc as a talisman, rubbing a finger or thumb across it so frequently that it had worn a groove right down the center of the plastic, not just smudging the letters, but eliminating whatever had been there all together. No fingerprints either. Could have come from any business in the valley. Just not enough information to tell.

Temp had more to say about the paper. It was heavy-weight linen. Not something he'd ever seen before. He'd tested a tiny corner with several kinds of chemicals. It didn't absorb water; didn't dissolve when exposed to several mild concentrations of acids; didn't wrinkle--not even after Temp had taken the whole sheet, folded it in half, then stacked a couple of chemistry books on it overnight. Seemed imperious to every test he tried. "Oh, and the gold border? Genuine gold leaf, not fancy ink. I don't know where the guy who gave that paper to the girl found it, but the formula must be worth a fortune," Temp concluded.

Doesn't make sense, Gifford thought. Why give a kid you don't know an invaluable piece of paper and then just disappear? And why that girl? Maybe the guy knew she'd lost her memory and figured she'd be a safe place to stash the paper because no one would be likely to believe her story? He unconsciously shook his head back and forth. Not likely. This Annie thing might be a lot more complicated of a problem than he had originally thought.

The next step was tedious. Start knocking on doors of local businesses to see if anyone recognized either piece of evidence. He resigned himself to a long day. It would sure save some time if Annie happened to have remembered who she was. He brightened at the thought of another round with Mrs. Z.

Ramona opened the door and pulled him inside. "Stupid wind," she muttered as she forced the door shut behind him. "Your lucky you didn't come earlier. I've been over at Viola's. Annie's still there helping her begin her annual onslaught of cookie making. Last year it took Viola a week just to clean up the mess. 'Course I have to admit, I must have eaten a couple of dozen chocolate frosted ones myself," Ramona chuckled. The two were seated at opposite ends of Ramona's couch, Gifford's long legs stretched out in front of him, filling up half the room.

"Well, other than showing an interest in cookies, has Annie given any sign she might be remembering who she is?" Gifford steered the conversation back toward the purpose of his visit.

"No memories at all, as far as I've been able to tell. She knows her way around the kitchen which suggests some good training at home, but she can't remember any favorite recipes or even whether she prefers Chinese to burgers until she tastes one or the other. . .. There is one odd thing though." Ramona told him about the visit from Marisa the day before. "Annie apparently speaks Spanish. At least some. She could understand what this little girl we met was saying, although when we talked to the girl's mother, Annie said her speech was too rapid—or maybe it was vocabulary—anyway, she could only sum up what the mother was saying."

"Spanish?" Gifford was astonished. Annie certainly didn't look Hispanic, and he wouldn't have thought the girl was old enough to have studied a language in school. Maybe she learned it at home—or from a friend or neighbor. "Anything else, Mrs. Z?"

"No—oh wait. She sings—well, you wouldn't believe the sound that comes out of that slight body. And she has sung at least parts of the *Messiah*." Ramona looked at him out of the corner of her eye to judge his reaction to this information.

Gifford pulled his phone out of his pocket, making notes and shaking his head simultaneously. Annie was starting to sound like a character in an Elizabethan novel—'very accomplished, indeed'. He smiled inwardly as he admitted to himself that he had to credit Mrs. Z for knowing what that phrase meant.

"Any idea where she got that little plastic keyring?" he asked. "Might help us figure out where she'd been before you found her."

"I asked that. She said it was under a couple of those boxes she'd had to move to get out of the rain. Didn't even remember it was in her pocket." Ramona shrugged. "Now what? Doesn't seem like you have much to go on."

He grimaced. "Well, I guess I start asking questions from folks who might have seen her the night she appeared. Give me a call if you stumble across any more little unexpected talents!" He studied his list. "Hard to believe someone hasn't called the department about a kid like this."

It took Gifford only ten minutes to make the trip to the Seaweed Bar and Grill to check whether the owner had noticed Annie outside a few nights before. Willy Nelson, not the famous one—the guy he'd known since second grade was behind the counter wiping down the bar. "Hey, Giff what's happening? Drink? On the house?"

It was a long-time joke between them. Giff didn't drink. During his basketball years, the coach would have thrown him off the team if he'd ever had alcohol on his breath, and after that, he'd investigated way too many accidents to find anything about drinking appealing.

"Thanks, Willy." Gifford did a quick once-over of the room through the mirror behind the bar where a wilted Christmas wreath was the only sign of the coming holiday. The room was dark, barely enough light to see the half-dozen empty tables. A solitary customer sat alone at a table against the wall. "Kinda slow today?" Giff said. "Just need a little information."

"Yeah, it'll pick up around four or five when the after-work crowd starts trickling in."

"How's business now that Christensen's closed down?"

A pained expression crossed Willy's face. "Nobody left but Ada, me, and a couple of rundown shops selling cheap stuff from Mexico. Makes the whole block less appealing, ya know? Boarded up windows and peeling paint." He shook his head in disgust. "Town Council's making noises about declaring the whole area blighted and bulldozing the block. They've got some crazy idea that what people really want is a new mall with fancy stores. Who's gonna want to wander in and out of 'fancy-schmancy stores' when the weather is five degrees and there's six inches of snow on the ground?" He looked out the smoked glass front window at the rain now cascading down the pavement in front of the bar. He grinned in genuine amusement, showing off his less-than-stellar dental hygiene. "Well, maybe next year. . .. Nobody in Douglas Valley has that kind of money anyway. What's the point?"

Gifford had heard a rumor or two about the Town Council planning a downtown renovation. "Sorry, man. You've been here a long time," he sympathized absent-mindedly. With a bit of guilty relief, he admitted to himself that the slow business climate meant there'd be fewer witnesses to ask about Annie.

"So, what's the reason for this little get-together? I assume must be business seeing as how you don't usually hang out in bars."

"We found a girl out back of the building Tuesday night. Doesn't seem to know who she is or how she got there. Were you around that night?" Gifford knew the question was unnecessary; Willy was always around. He kept a close eye on his investment. He'd been stung once when somebody had had too much to drink, picked a fight with a guy he didn't even know, and torn the place apart. Gifford had investigated the incident, and Judge Callister had seen to it that the drunk had paid some of the damages and spent a month in jail. Willy had been very grateful.

"We don't get many single women in here. What'd she look like?"

"No, not a woman. Just a kid. Maybe 12 or 13? We're not sure. Fair-haired, small-boned, big eyes. Pretty. Anyway, she was hiding under some boxes out back; she says she talked to a guy on the sidewalk in front of the bar--an old guy with totally white hair. Almost down to his shoulders, she said. Either the girl or the fellow ring a bell?"

Willy thought for a minute. "You know I'd run a kid off if I saw one hanging around. But the guy? White hair? A couple of regulars are salt and pepper types, ya know, but white hair? Most guys that old'd need a walker to get in here. It's probably easier for them to get the wife to buy the stuff at the state liquor store and drink at home." He laughed. "Nah, nobody comes to mind, man."

"Anybody else in here that night that might have seen her or him?"

Willy thought for a minute. "It was a slow night. Middle of the week. Rainy." He gestured at the weather outside. "Only two or three guys around. Ya know George Vogel? And that guy they call 'the Moose.' Big guy. Works for the power company on line jobs in the mountains. He comes in once in a while when he's in town. Don't remember anybody else specifically. Sorry, Giff."

Gifford entered the information into his phone and emailed it to his desktop. "No problem. Thanks, Willy. I'll track down these guys, anyway. Maybe they remember something.

Outside he pulled the collar of his coat up around his ears, trying to recall if he'd even seen the sun in the last week; it was weird weather. Not quite cold enough for snow—but damp, windy, nasty. Gifford didn't like rain. In his business, it seemed to bring the crazies out.

A little bell rang when he pulled open the door of Ada's shop. The place looked deserted, but he could hear the low, rhythmic sounds of machinery spinning in the background. A voice hollered, "Hang on. I'm coming."

Ada pushed back the drape she used to separate the front desk from the working area. As long as he'd known her, she'd worn her hair in a bun at the back of her neck. In the old days, it was a lush, deep brown; now it was completely silver. Judging by the size and weight of that bun, he figured her hair must be long enough to brush her waist. Her face was still smooth, without noticeable winking, the result of spending her days in all that humidity, he'd always thought. She was 65 or 70 now at least, Giff figured, and her lean frame was nearly as slender as she had been as a young woman, though she moved slower now than she had the day the seven-year-old Giff had tried to rip off a handful of suckers she kept on the desk for the fussy babies of customers who had to wait a few minutes while she found their orders. She'd darted out from behind the counter faster than he'd believed possible, grabbed him by the ear, and encouraged him to return her property or call his mother and admit his crime. A single mom, Giff's mother didn't look favorably on petty theft. It was an easy decision. He'd put the suckers back in the jar and promised to come in every day for a week to sweep the sidewalk in front of the shop—no small task in the days when smokers were more common, and Ada's business boasted a wrought iron bench out front where people liked to congregate and visit.

"Giff!" Ada's voice reflected her pleasure at seeing him. She came around the desk and hugged him, a routine of which he never tired.

."Ada," he looked down at her with equal delight. "How's business?"

"I manage to keep the doors open. But if we don't figure out a way to get a few more shops around here, I may have to close up. It's just too much trouble for people to make a special trip downtown to leave their laundry when they can go to the neighborhood Albertson's and drop it off before they do their grocery shopping." Her voice was matter-of-fact. Ada had seen almost five decades of the ebb and flow of business, so she was well aware that nothing stayed the same forever.

She eyed his empty arms. "No laundry? I take it this is a more professional visit?"

"Guilty," Giff responded. "Ramona Zollinger found a girl out behind the Seaweed Tuesday night. Kid can't remember her name or anything about her life. Doc Ferguson checked her out and says she hasn't had a concussion or any obvious injury, so we're trying to find out where she might have come from until she remembers something useful. Says she talked to a guy with white hair in front of the bar—we think somewhere around 9 o'clock. Were you still around then? Any chance you saw her?"

"I was here. Probably in the office, finishing up the books." She thought a moment. "I left about 9:30, but I don't remember noticing a youngster around. It was a miserable night," she recalled. "I climbed into the truck and headed home as soon as I locked up. I kept thinking that the rain would be turning to snow, and I'd better get home before the highway iced over." Ada lived five miles outside of town on a couple of acres she and her husband had turned into one of the most prolific kitchen gardens in the valley. Her husband had died in a farming accident when he was still in his 50's, but Ada employed a couple of high school kids to help her with weeding and watering during the summer months.

"Yeah, I figured that might be the case." Gifford felt a stab of guilt that he hadn't been by to visit in quite a while. He knew she was lonely. He made a mental note to do better. "Either of these things mean anything to you?' Giff handed over the two evidence bags from his inside jacket pocket.

She looked first at the parchment in its protective bag, turning it curiously from front to back a couple of times. "Nice," she commented, intrigued by the light which flashed across her face when she fingered the parchment. Then she shook her head and handed it back. She lingered longer over the second bag. "Can I take this out?"

He pulled a plastic glove from another pocket. "Use this," he said.

She laughed, obviously delighted to get to play CSI, and rammed her hand into the glove. Opening the bag with care, she lifted out the small plastic heart. "Hmmm," she said. "Only a couple of businesses around here use something like this. Nothing in Douglas Valley that I know of, but there's a bookstore in Newman that was handing out heart keyrings advertising at the Chamber of Commerce meeting a couple of months ago."

Giff's ears perked up. He'd written off the little heart as a lost cause when Temp hadn't found any information about it. "You know the name of the place?"

"Linford or Langford Books and Paper. Something like that. Fairly new. Maybe they know something about the paper, too. I think they're located in that new little strip mall on the east side of the highway, a block off Main in downtown Newman." Though the two communities were least then 20 miles apart, Newman was an upscale tourist attraction located at the entrance to Brigham National Forest. Taking out his phone, he added the information. "Thanks for the lead, Ada. I'll check it out."

"How come you don't bring in your uniforms for cleaning anymore?" she chided him. "They added a nice little sum to my balance sheet," she teased.

"Wash and wear. Everything's wash and wear nowadays. Besides, I'm a detective now. We don't wear uniforms."

"Big shot! Who knew the little snot who tried to steal my suckers would turn into the 'fuzz?'"

6:30 PM

Fully a half-hour early for the weekly Town Council meeting, Ramona pulled the car into what she considered her parking place next to the Mayor's designated spot at the VIP parking lot in front of the Town Hall. Her Prius was so familiar to the Town Council members that most just assumed Ramona had been assigned the parking place by some long-

71

retired official in the mythical past, and they parked their cars elsewhere.

Legend had it that a hapless secretary, not long after she was hired, had once pulled into the spot to avoid the assault of hail from a particularly nasty thunderstorm, and Ramona had had her car towed. It was a story Ramona didn't bother to refute.

"Now, Annie, tonight you're going to see democracy in action," Ramona grunted with satisfaction as she headed for the wide staircase at the entrance of the courthouse.

"Well," Viola clarified, looking sidewise at her friend, "At least you're going to see Ramona in action."

Ramona didn't deign to respond.

Earlier in the day, the wind had picked up again, and now it whipped their scarves around their faces as they huddled together and climbed the steps of the building. Looking up into the dark sky with clouds rolling across the moon, Ramona wondered, cold enough, but where's the damned snow?

"Isn't this where we met with Judge Callister?" Annie yelled over the rattling of the last dried leaves whipping against their branches. She braced her body against the heavy wooden door which Ramona had forced open. The wind banged it shut behind them the moment the slight young girl let go of it and stepped inside.

"Yep. Town Council meets in the big room over there." Ramona pointed to the wide double doors now open to an auditorium across from them, which someone long ago had dubbed the Fieldhouse. At least three dozen rows of padded chairs lined the hall, and the women could hear someone out of sight fiddling with the sound system. "Courtroom's upstairs—police station on the other side of this floor. Giff's office is down that hall and left." She gestured to a dark corridor on her right lit only by a neon EXIT sign with an arrow pointing toward the doors they had just entered.

Ramona led the way into the hall and chose three seats center front. Since every seat was currently vacant, it wasn't a difficult choice.

"She likes to be sure the Council knows she's here," Viola said. "As if they wouldn't notice her even if she sat all the way in the back."

"Need to keep the Council on their toes. Otherwise, they'd steal the ground underneath our feet," Ramona pointed out matter-of-factly.

Annie looked down at the alternating squares of polished black and white marble she was standing on. "Oh," she said, although she clearly had no idea what Ramona was talking about.

While Viola helped Annie out of her coat and settled her on one of the chairs, Ramona bundled up their coats over her arm and carried them to the racks at the back of the hall. "Henry," she greeted the fellow plugging and unplugging a computer link-up at a desk just to their left.

"Miz Z," he acknowledged her without looking up.

Annie studied the long table on a raised dais directly in front of her. The name of each council member was neatly carved into wooden plaques resting on the table in front of five worn leather chairs--Jesse Simpson's name in the center and two members on either side of her.

"Isn't anyone else going to come?" Annie asked, looking over her shoulder at the rows of empty seats.

"They'll be along," Viola assured her. "Town Council meetings have a bigger draw than soap operas in this town."

By five minutes to the hour, the hall was filling in with people jockeying one another good-naturedly for a position closer to the microphones Henry had attached to two steel stands, one on each side in front of the audience. Several glared at Ramona and Viola or looked at Annie curiously. Word of the 'girl with amnesia' had spread through the community like a flash flood, but only a few folks had the temerity to gawk at her in open speculation. Ramona gestured impatiently for one after another onlooker to move on, and one glance at her face convinced them that it would be prudent to find a seat somewhere else. The decibel level rose as folding chairs scraped against each other, and parents shushed their young children for whom they'd been unable to find babysitters.

At precisely 7 PM Jesse Simpson led her counterparts single file into the auditorium, settling herself into her "throne," as Ramona whispered to Annie.

Simpson leaned into the microphone and demanded, "Silence. Silence, please," while she tapped the mic to be sure it was working. She paused for a long moment to allow the crowd to turn its attention to the podium, then struck her gavel to declare the meeting officially open.

The crowd rose obediently for the posting of the colors and repeated the Pledge of Allegiance; an older woman just behind Annie sniffling audibly. When Annie twisted around to see if the woman needed help, Viola whispered, "She cries at McDonald's commercials, too; just ignore her."

"Thank you," Mayor Jesse said. The loudspeaker buzzed with an annoying electrical shriek which startled half a dozen babies and set them screaming. Henry rushed over to double-check wires until he unplugged the culprit and the feedback noise ceased. "We appreciate all you folks who are interested enough in your community to come and participate in these meetings. Tonight's agenda is projected on the screen behind me for those of you who are interested. We'll start off with patron comments. Several of you signed up to speak, so" she consulted her notes. "Apollina? Looks like you're first up."

A heavy-set woman with a worn wool coat still buttoned tightly over her ample chest came to the microphone on the left side of the auditorium.

"I wanna complain about the amount of money just sitting in the budget for snow removal. Since there's no snow, why haven't you all diverted some of that cash into doing somethin' about those goats Jamison Farber keeps in the field across from me? They're always sneaking out of their fence an' chasing my cats. Stupid critters cornered Lancelot up a tree. Had to call the Fire Department to come get him down."

"Yes, we heard about that, Apollina. That little visit cost the town a couple of hundred dollars. Next time, get a ladder." The crowd laughed as Apollina stormed back to her seat.

Once the patron comments were finished, Simpson read a list of budget items that required approval. The Council voted in favor of three and in opposition to one. "OK, next on the agenda is a discussion of the possible conversion of three blocks of the downtown area into a state-of-the-art mall complex. As most of you know, the Council," she emphasized the word to remind the crowd of the importance of the assignment, "appointed Stuyvesant Harker to draw up a proposed design, and he's here tonight to give us a look. The Chair turns the meeting over to Mr. Harker."

A tall, urbane gentleman with incongruously spiked white hair and a three-piece suit reminiscent of a fashion more popular twenty years before took over the microphone on Simpson's right. "Henry, if you will please," he said as Henry punched a couple of buttons and launched a PowerPoint presentation onto the screen. "Thank you," Harker said. Pushing a button on his remote, the screen behind Jesse Simpson lit up with a panoramic view of Main Street.

All eyes riveted on the architectural drawing showing a graceful two-story grouping of commercial structures spanning most of the three-block downtown area and surrounded by lush landscape sitting in the place of what was currently boarded windows and weed-broken sidewalks. The crowd murmured its approval. Somewhere behind Ramona, a man's voice lifted above the nodding heads. "Look at that, LaVonne. Now that's something, ain't it?"

"Sure is," Ramona said under her breath in disgust.

"As you can see, this proposal includes diagonal parking hugging the storefronts on both sides of a landscaped walkway which features trees, wild grasses, and, of course, flowers during the warmer months. The mall itself houses thirty-five spaces for commercial use, an anchor department store, two magnet restaurants, a fast-food court, room for several kiosks, and ample benches along the length of the center parkway for families to relax as they shop. Plus," Harker paused to give his audience a moment to anticipate the pièce de resistance, "an over-arching glass ceiling which covers the walkways and is retractable during pleasant weather in the warmer seasons."

The crowd "oh-ed and ah-ed" in response to a slide which demonstrated the flexibility of the glass arch which covered a central gathering area dotted with chrome and glass tables and chairs.

"What about more parking?" someone from the back called out. "Those strips in the front can't handle the kind of traffic something like this might draw."

"Exactly right," Harker agreed. "Excellent comment. These plans include an underground parking lot which can be entered from 100 North on the opposite side of the block." He smoothly shifted to the next slide--a two-level rendition of additional parking which included escalators to the ground floor.

"What's it going to cost?" an old man sitting on the last row yelled. "Hope you're not planning to raise my taxes to build that thing."

Around him a few voices of agreement caused people to shift in their seats, several animated discussions breaking out.

Jesse Simpson inserted herself into the conversation, rapping her gavel on the desk to bring the crowd back to order. "Now, Spencer, give the man a chance to finish his presentation. Then we'll talk about money."

Harker's last slide was a view of a black and white photo of the downtown area as it currently appeared juxtaposed against the pleasing pastels of the architectural rendering of the future plans. The crowd watched in silence.

He explained the advantages of replacing the current blighted downtown area with a public investment which would "draw shoppers from communities around the area. The increased property tax alone would revitalize this area," he concluded and then sat down to enthusiastic applause led by members of the Town Council.

"There you have it. Think about what our downtown looks like now," Simpson instructed, "then compare that to what Stuyvesant has just shown you. Imagine your family shopping at a Gap store or REI instead of having to travel clear to Salt Lake for specialty items. This mall would make Douglas Valley the regional center for commerce. That means dollars in every one of our pockets." The screen above her head shifted and a spreadsheet with several columns appeared. "We've asked the County Budget Officer Owen Hainsworth to spend a few minutes talking about financial options."

Hainsworth wore his customary rumpled suit and bow tie—this one bright green with blue stripes. He impatiently brushed out of his eyes the shock of sandy hair that insisted in creeping across his forehead, cleared his throat, and took a deep breath. "Folks. I'm sure you can guess that a project like this isn't going to be cheap. Somewhere in the neighborhood of 280 million dollars." He used his laser pointer to highlight the first column. A collective gasp when up from the audience, most of whom had annual incomes of considerably less than six figures. "Now don't get all riled up. The Town Council has found a consortium of business people who are interested in seeing Douglas Valley take its place among our more prosperous neighbors. They're willing to put up half the capital if you folks are willing to pass a bond to raise the rest?" He walked the audience through the numbers and concluded with an opportunity for questions from the audience.

Ada Apodoca was first in line. "Madam Mayor," she addressed Jesse Simpson from the microphone on the right of the hall. "What's going to happen to my business if you bulldoze my block?'

"Well, Ada, of course we'll give you fair remuneration for your property. And as a longtime member of the business community, you'll have first choice of a new location in the mall if you decide to improve your business prospects there."

"Great. Then I can become the proud owner of a lease which triples or quadruples my current one. My business can't support that kind of increase. You know that. And I'm not the only one. Willy's bar, the Arco station, the cosmetology school, and a half a dozen others on those three blocks, not mention the shops that support a couple of Hispanic families down the road from me. What about them?"

"Now, Ada. This is just a preliminary look at our plan. I'm sure we can work together to find a satisfactory solution," Jesse Simpson soothed. "Next!" She dismissed Ada with a nod and signaled to the person waiting in line to speak after her.

Ramona leaned across Annie to Viola, fuming. "A 'satisfactory solution' means that Ada and the others just have to close their businesses and find something else to do. The downtown will be pretty, but there will be a lot of casualties in the rubble."

"Ramona," Viola could see a storm brewing. "Even you must admit that something has to be done about downtown. Every block has boarded-up windows--if they haven't been broken out already by vandals. Driving through there at night is getting downright scary. Besides," Viola pointed out, "I haven't heard you come up with any other ideas."

Ramona ignored her as she headed for the microphone with the smallest line, glaring at Jesse Simpson as she went. The two people at the front of the line saw her charge toward them and wisely scuttled back to their seats out of her way.

"Mayor," Ramona began, her tone decidedly less than respectful. "Three hundred million dollars is a whole lot of money. What kind of increase is that going to add to the amount of property tax my neighbors and I pay?"

Hainsworth stood up. "If I may, Mayor? Ramona, we're looking at about an additional $7.83 per hundred thousand dollars of property value a month over the course of the bond for the average taxpayer."

Ramona did a quick calculation in her head. "For my house, that's around $200 more taxes a year." She turned to the crowd. "You all got an extra $150 or $200 a year? I sure as hell don't."

"Ramona!" Viola hissed across the room. "Watch your language!" Sporadic chuckles broke out from the audience.

"Ramona," Jesse Simpson's stern voice rose over the laughter. "I believe your three minutes are now up."

Ramona ignored her.

"Hey, let her finish!" someone halfway back of the room called. "Lot of us want to hear what she has to say."

"Members of the Town Council, we all agree that the downtown area needs some attention. The problem I have with your solution is that it displaces businesses which have provided dependable services for a lot of years for the people of this town. It seems to me that booting them out is both disloyal and unfair. I submit that we need to rethink this proposal and look at other options."

"Yeah," "Amen," "Go, Ramona," came from a few equally dissatisfied residents in the surrounding area. About half the crowd applauded as Ramona took her seat.

"Proud of you, Ramona," Viola patted her hand while Ramona lowered herself carefully back into her chair. Viola's shrewd eyes watch the process. "Your knee bothering you?" When she got no response, she went on, "Your point about ignoring the situation of current business owners apparently struck a chord. Lotta folks will be thinking about that one."

Annie looked from the one to the other, her eyes wide.

Ramona gave her a squeeze and whispered under her breath to the girl, "That ought to give the Mayor a little heartburn!" Annie frowned as she tried to figure out what health had to do with Ramona's comments.

There were angry looks and catcalling from at least half the audience. The other members of the Town Council shifted uneasily in their chairs, glancing at Simpson for some sort of clue about how they should respond to this insurgency. Finally, Brady Iverson, owner of the Iverson's Ranch Feed and Equipment Store and generally accepted as Simpson's chief deputy, spoke up.

"Y'all know my business attracts ranchers and farmers from all over the county. It'd sure be nice if when they came to buy a saddle or a feed trough, there was a shopping area for them to get school clothes and all them accessories that magazines tell women they need." The men in the audience rolled their eyes appreciatively. "This new mall would give them that option. Think what would happen if they left my place and spent the rest of their paycheck in our town instead of some fancy store in the city where you have to pay to park." Nods of approval greeted this scenario. Every business owner knew the value of getting a customer in the door. An increase in gross sales almost always followed.

The meeting droned on for about another hour as residents took advantage of their time at the microphone to express their opinions. Mostly Ramona sat in stoic silence, but Lehi Alger's impassioned plea not to dislocate his small engine repair shop caused her to shake her head in annoyance. "Mayor Simpson," Lehi pointed out with tears welling up in his eyes, "You were my Cub Scout leader. How can you do this to me?"

"That boy says the same thing every time he disagrees with something. I taught him to make a better argument than that, but he never really got the message," Ramona whispered to Annie. "See that you remember that."

Annie nodded dutifully, but she could not imagine whenever she'd ever be forced to speak to so many people at once.

Ramona and Viola chatted with five or six people on their way out. The three were on the verge of exiting the building when a voice called out from the stairway. "Ramona, hold on a second."

Judge Callister was descending the steps, his dark wool overcoat folded neatly across one arm and his briefcase in the other hand. They waited while he crossed the hallway toward them. "I just wanted to confirm how the foster care is working out? Has Detective Gifford discovered any clues to Annie's background?"

Unaware of what she was doing, Annie backed a step farther away from the Judge and edged nearer to Ramona.

"Nothing yet," Ramona reported. "But Annie's doing fine with us."

"We're like a couple with an amicable divorce settlement—sharing custody," Viola chimed in.

The Judge looked at Annie. "What about it, Annie? You OK?"

Annie nodded without reply.

"Good. Very good. Let me know if there's any change in the situation," the Judge said, setting his briefcase on the floor and slipping his arms into his coat. "Ladies," he tilted his head in their direction and headed out the front doors of the Courthouse into the wind.

Thursday, December 5

2:30 PM

IT TOOK A COUPLE OF days for Gifford to track down and interview both the men Willy said he thought were in the Seaweed the night Annie appeared. He wasn't surprised that George Vogel didn't even remember being in the bar, let alone yelling at a young girl or noticing a guy with the "white hair" Annie had described. George had spent many a night on a cot in jail while he slept off his daily binge. Ironic, Giff thought. George's wife and two children were killed by a drunk driver on I-15 as they were returning from a visit to her sister down south. Now George was the drunk. But he walked everywhere. As far as Giff knew, he'd never gotten into a car again.

Gifford had left a note with Willy to give the other possible witness if he showed up again at the bar. He'd turned up today at the station on his way to another job in eastern Colorado. His nickname, 'the Moose', didn't do him justice. He was at least 6' 6" and weighed maybe 280. He looked like every pound was muscle. Giff wondered aloud if he'd been a serious candidate for the NFL.

"Nah, I don't like games. Too many other guys to get in the way of a good fight," the Moose had answered with disturbing candor. The Moose, whose legal name was Curtis Lyons (apt, Gifford thought), did remember being in the Seaweed the night Annie was found. In fact, it turned out, he remembered it in great detail. "Yeah, I know the night ya mean. I was in town looking for an old buddy who used to be a regular at the Seaweed when he worked around here. But he wasn't in there that night, so I just had a couple of drinks and headed back to the job."

He paused a moment, considering. "It was raining." His eyes hardened. "I hate the rain. Makes mud, ya know. Working in mud slows everything down. What's the matter with the weather around here? Ain't you folks supposed to have snow in December?"

Giff steered him back to the night in question. "So, we've got a lost kid, a girl who says she talked to a white-haired guy in front of the bar that night. Ring any bells?"

The Moose nodded. "Yeah. Sure. I saw 'em. I was sitting up front next to the window. They were talking under that streetlight on the corner. I figured he was her grandfather or somethin'. She was wet, really wet. I thought maybe he was scolding her for being out in the weather, but he didn't look upset; now that I think about it, he didn't even look worried."

"Can you describe him?"

"Little guy. Maybe 5' 7". Had long white hair, almost down to his shoulders. It was weird though. He handed the girl something, and when he turned into the light, his face didn't seem to have any lines. Guy with white hair, ya expect to look old. But he didn't look over 40. Had on a cashmere overcoat. And nah", he held up his hand to stop Giff from asking, "I'm not sure it was cashmere. I like lamb's wool myself, but it looked expensive, and he must not have been outside very long 'cause the coat didn't look wet."

"You ever seen the guy before?" Gifford asked.

"Nope. Just a guy, ya know?"

"Could you see what he gave the girl?"

"Yeah. Looked like some sort of note. He handed it to her, said something, and left her standing in the rain. Poor kid, she musta been freezing. What kind of guy leaves a kid alone out in the weather?"

"You did," Gifford pointed out. Moose had the grace to look uncomfortable.

Rather than heading back to the office, Gifford folded his tall body into the seat of his unmarked car, pulled the door closed after him, and double-checked to be sure he had the evidence bags with the paper sample and the plastic key ring. He didn't want to make a trip to Newman only to discover he'd left the reason for his visit back at his desk in the office. He chuckled to himself, remembering the early days of his rookie service. He spent half his time the first couple of months retracing his steps to finish some form he'd forgotten or find a folder he'd buried in the stacks on his desk which had quickly threatened to engulf the tiny workspace he'd been assigned. Later he found out that the other guys had been taking bets on when his precarious tower of case notes would exceed the angle of repose and carpet the station with scattered papers, which triggered the memory of the teacher he'd bumped into outside Temp's office. He wondered if she was dating someone?

Not today, he thought reluctantly, forcing his mind back to the task at hand. Annie had been found more than a week ago, and no one had registered a missing child. It made no sense. How could a child, especially one as unusual as Annie, simply appear out of nowhere? Even the feelers the department had sent across the country had generated no response.

As he glanced at the evidence bags on the seat next to him, it occurred to him that he hadn't read the actual official copy of the evidence report Temp had done for him. Maybe there was something else in the paperwork that might prove useful. He checked his watch. Easier to stop by the school than retrace his steps back to the office. Besides he owed Temp a six-pack.

Stopping at the 7/11 on the corner next to the high school parking lot, he grabbed a six-pack of Diet Coke for Temp and a 64-ounce Root Beer the size of Texas for himself, then rolled his car into the small faculty lot behind the science department. Through the large north windows, he could see Temp still at his desk, a stack of papers next to the book he was reading.

"Since when does a teacher have time to read a novel," Gifford greeted Temp as he slipped through the lab doors and into Temp's office.

"Hey, I'm just studying the future of science!" Temp grinned and held up the lurid cover of the paperback—robots appearing to overrun the frantic residents of a dying Earth. "You know the reason good science fiction is harder and harder to find? Cause science is catching up to imagination. Predicting a distant future is pretty difficult when it is nipping at your heels."

Temp rose and grabbed Gifford's hand in a warm greeting. "So, another assignment from the Sheriff's Department?"

"Nah, I figured I owed you this." He handed Temp the icy six-pack of Diet Coke.

"Excellent." Temp acknowledged the debt. "Thanks." He pulled one from the plastic holder and set it next to his book. He opened the little fridge behind his desk, putting the other five on a shelf next to a rack of test tubes filled with something that appeared to be fermenting.

Gifford wrinkled his nose. "That looks like it might have been in there since I was at school here. You ever gonna clean that fridge?"

"I make my aide do it once a semester—it's her favorite job."

"I bet." They grinned in shared appreciation at the picture.

Gifford moved a stack of books off the only other chair in Temp's office and sat down. "Just wondering if you have a copy of the official report you did on that missing girl evidence last week. I'm too lazy to go back to the station and grab a copy."

"No problem," Temp said. In less than 30 seconds he had pulled up the file on his laptop and had the printer running a copy for Gifford. It was one thing he really admired about the teacher. His mind was as ordered as the scientific method. He made it easy for students to learn because he moved step-by-step through a hypothesis, giving kids the pattern and letting them walk through it themselves. It was something most never forgot.

"Thanks. I'm just on my way to check out what you told me about that keyring. Turns out there's a new bookstore in Newman that uses those little rings for advertising."

"Let me know if something turns up."

"Sure thing."

Gifford was just clicking the unlock on his car when a voice behind him said, "So, Detective. You here to stave off a crime wave at the high school?"

He turned to find brown eyes and a sprinkle of freckles laughing at him.

"Miss Plunkett, isn't it? A pleasure to see you, too." He hoped his voice didn't sound too eager. "You always hide your car out here? It's a long way from the English department."

"True," she agreed. "Last year some smart-aleck seniors picked up my little car," she gestured to a battered Fiero a couple of cars down from his, "and carried it over to the flagpole, blocking the whole front entrance of the school. Thought they were hilarious. I cracked the concrete driving it off, so now I park back here. Less temptation."

"I could arrest those vandals for you," he offered.

"The ring-leader is in Afghanistan. Might be a lengthy investigation. So, what brings you here?"

"Got a minute?" he asked. When she nodded, he told her about Annie. "You hear any rumors about a runaway or a family that has some serious trouble?"

"Staying with Ramona Zollinger, isn't she? I met her at the *Messiah* practice last week. She has a voice about three times as big as she is." Her eyes looked thoughtful; then she shook her head. She leaned against his car, resting her briefcase on the hood. "Nobody's claimed a kid like that? What's wrong with this picture?" she furrowed her brow. "No clues about where she came from?"

"Just these," he said opening the driver's side door and depositing the report Temp had given him. He pulled the evidence bags from his pocket and handed them to the teacher.

She studied the notepaper, turning the bag over a couple of times, the gold shimmering enticingly through the clear plastic. She shook her head. The red keyring was more familiar. She held it up to her face, studying the faint impressions. "Hey, I've got one of these. At least one similar. Came from a bookstore in Newman." She batted her eyelashes at him. "I may have a small" she held up two fingers separated by an inch or so, "addiction to books. Probably didn't know I was that kind of girl, did you?"

"I might have guessed," he said, laughing at her. "I am a detective after all. Linford's in Newman, by any chance?"

She looked up in surprise. "Yeah. A college roommate renovated a defunct drugstore and built a shop that specializes in women's literature. I've already spent too much money at the place."

"So, what's this roommate's name?"

"Kyra—used to be Kyra Whatcott—now Linford. Her husband grew up in Wyoming and got a job at the Dodge dealership in Newman— specializes in vehicles for ranch use. I guess he's done quite well because bookstores aren't usually a high-volume enterprise, so he's probably subsidizing Kyra, but he seems happy to have her doing something she loves."

Gifford thought for a moment. "Tell you what. I was headed that way next--you come with me and introduce me to this roommate, and I'll buy you dinner at the best burger joint in the state."

"Hmmm," she laughed. "You or a stack of essays?" Her hands balanced the invisible scale. "Tempting, but I do love a session with the red pencil," she gestured to the briefcase atop his car. She pretended to analyze the situation. "In order to make an informed decision, I need facts.

How do you know which the 'best burger joint' in the state is?"

"Years of thorough investigation. That and my grandma's sister owns the place. Used to work there weekends in high school. The secret is onions, lots of onions."

She exaggerated licking her lips. "Well, that settles it. Lead on, McDuff."

Newman was only a 20-minute ride away, but Gifford couldn't remember a more relaxing conversation." Do you always take dates to interrogations? Pretty nifty way to pick up girls," Carrie Jane pointed out.

"Only the ones who make me laugh," he answered.

"That's with, not at, I hope."

5 PM

Unlike Douglas Valley and its agricultural base, Newman's economy rested on its location at the entrance to Brigham National Forest. The town had more in common with Park City, Utah's Olympic ski venue, than it did with the neighboring farm and ranch communities. Newman boasted more than two dozen motels, most of which catered to tourists--largely families--who came to camp and fish in the pristine lakes and rivers which riddled the mountains just east of the town. Alpine architecture was the dominant influence. Even City Hall was constructed of giant logs hauled down from the mountains during the Depression. Here the air almost always had a pine-flavored breeze blowing down the long canyon that greeted visitors at the entrance to the forest. Linford's was prominently located at the corner of Center and 1st East, only two miles from the gate to the federal territory run by the National Forest Service.

"You can take 1st down to a parking lot behind the store," Carrie Jane instructed. "Kyra has a dozen spots reserved for customers back there."

They used the store's back door, passing through a long, narrow hallway bordered by floor-to-ceiling bookshelves filled with used paperback books sorted into categories—mystery, romance, western, etc. Attached to each shelf was a card that advertised the prices of the groups of books there. Nothing over a dollar. One entire set of shelves was labeled "take one, give one"—a free book exchange.

Gifford noted what appeared to be a work area visible through a half-open door on his left. The room was stacked with boxes, some with the tops neatly sliced off, some with their contents spilling onto a sizeable table in the center of the room. Packing tape, labels, mailing, and advertising flyers littered the surface. Rounding a corner, Gifford was pleasantly surprised as the hall opened into the heart of the store.

A spacious room spread out before him--shelving arranged in an unusual octagon format around its outside borders. Waist-height shelves filled in the area closest to a central open space making the room seem less cluttered than most bookstores he'd been in. A multi-colored oriental patterned rug anchored several easy chairs with cheerful Victorian era upholstery. At opposite angles of the room, a couple of over-stuffed couches were obviously designed to let readers relax and take their time browsing the hundreds of brightly patterned books lining the shelves. Six or seven customers, most young women in jeans and t-shirts, filled the available seats, although Gifford noted a man and a teen-aged boy in the mix. On one side of the room, a mother was sitting on the floor quietly reading a picture book to what looked to be young twin daughters. The smell of coffee permeated the air, and Gifford sniffed appreciatively.

"There's a nook next to the desk with hot drinks and a soda bar. Kyra has fresh cookies from a bakery down the street delivered a couple of times a day."

"Sounds expensive. How does she make any money?"

"I think it was tough at first, but she had this dream of making reading an irresistible temptation—like chocolate. She wanted her customers to cherish books the way she does. She says 'a nibble and a sip' encourage customers to relax and stay awhile. The longer they stay, the more books she sells."

"Carrie Jane!" a voice from the front of the store rang out. "What the heck are you doing in Newman on a school night? I thought you were chained to your desk at work." Most of the readers didn't even look up at the newcomers or at Kyra as she appeared out from somewhere near the front window, arms spread wide to engulf Carrie in an energetic hug.

"Haven't seen you in way too long." A woman no more than five feet tall, and almost as wide, grinned at her friend and drew her toward an empty couch.

Gifford was then left standing alone. He wasn't sure whether to sit down or back into a corner. There are a lot of women in this little store, he thought uncomfortably.

"Who's your friend?" Kyra looked up and eyed Gifford speculatively.

"Detective Gifford, this is Kyra Linford, bookshop proprietor, and purveyor of fine quality writing materials," Carrie Jane announced formally, her dimples peeking out from her cheeks.

"I think she must have read that in a Dickens novel, and she loves to show off whenever she can." Kyra looked up at him. "Take a seat," she ordered, patting the cushion next to her. "Don't want a member of law enforcement to intimidate my customers." The teenaged boy looked up, momentarily alarmed. When Gifford didn't seem interested in him, the boy went back to his book—The 10 Most Grisly Crimes of the 19th Century.

Gifford looked around. He saw lacy ferns poking their heads out between lines of books; a computer and cash register were visible on the front desk through a break in the shelves. A display of antique teacups and coffee-table books about Victorian England were interspersed between the business machines. On the wall behind the counter, a couple of intricate quilts in muted colors contrasted with a display of the latest thrillers, and one of the shop's front windows was filled with flowered stationery and leather or clothbound journals boasting parchment-like pages intended to tantalize readers to jot down their reflections at the end of the day. Overall, there was a sense of serenity that slowed Gifford's breathing and caused him to stretch his legs out on the carpet in front of him. "Nice place," he acknowledged. "Kind of feminine, but I like it."

Kyra grinned at her friend. "Seems pretty normal for a cop."

"Now be good. He offered me food if I introduced him to you."

"Ah," Kyra nodded sagely. "Food. Now I understand." Turning to Gifford, she informed him, "Carrie Jane will do anything for a meal she doesn't have to cook."

"Hey," Carrie Jane protested. "I'm a good cook!"

"Now-w." Kyra drew the word out, making it more than one syllable. "Not so much when we lived together. May I mention the words 'Kleenex tomatoes'?"

"Humph," said Carrie Jane. "I recognized my weakness and made it a strength."

Kyra raised an eyebrow. "While the rest of us suffered."

"Kleenex tomatoes?" Gifford asked, confused.

"Ignore her." Deftly, Carrie Jane changed the subject. "Detective

Gifford has something he wants to ask you about."

Kyra's eyebrows rose. "Official?"

Gifford nodded.

She looked around at her customers, all apparently disinterested in their conversation. "Let's go to my office," she suggested. "Less distracting." Rising, she led them through a small latched gate next to the sales counter and into another narrow door. The office was a stockroom that had been walled off by a highly polished antique door, complete with a peep window and an intricate pewter doorknob, an ornate key protruding from the lock. Small and compact, it held an old-fashioned roll-top desk, a modern ergonomic chair upholstered in leather matching the deep cherry of the desk, a set of wall-mounted shelves, a file cabinet, a reading lamp, a laptop computer, and a stack of eight or ten books perched randomly atop each other. Kyra gestured at the pile. "This week's reading," she explained.

"And I thought I liked my job," Gifford muttered.

Kyra unfolded a couple of folding chairs stacked neatly behind the desk. "Have a seat," she invited. "So, Detective Gifford—isn't it?" He nodded, and she continued, "What can I help you with?"

Gifford pulled the small evidence bag holding the worn key chain token out of his shirt pocket and handed it to her. She studied its contents, turning the bag back and forth. "It looks like one of mine," she said. "I have a little basket of them by the cash register. Never hurts to have the shop's name out in public. Where'd you get this?"

Gifford told her about Annie, about her memory loss, and his efforts to find out where she belonged. "Nobody seems to know anything about her. She just appeared in the rain one night. No memory as far as I can tell. On the other hand, she's a great kid, the kind someone would worry about if she turned up missing. I can't figure out why no one has come forward already. Unless they can't." He looked at Carrie Jane, unspoken worry lined his face.

"Accident, maybe?" Kyra spoke mostly to herself.

"Or worse," Gifford said shortly.

"Can I take it out of the bag?"

"Sure. We already checked. No discernable fingerprints. We think it must have been lying in a puddle of alcohol or something. Then it spent an hour in the laundry."

Kyra pulled a small magnifying glass out of one of the cubbies on her desk. At Gifford's look of surprise, she said, "Use it all the time. Especially for old books. Having some accurate provenance raises their value." She studied the keyring carefully. "What does the girl look like?" she asked without looking up.

Gifford pulled out his phone. "Here's a picture of her the day the Judge assigned her a set of foster guardians." He handed Kyra the phone.

"Must brush her hair constantly. Look how it glows." Kyra mused as she passed the phone to Carrie Jane, who also studied the picture with more care than she had done when Gifford showed it to her earlier. Kyra shook her head. "Don't think she's ever been in here," Kyra apologized. "A memorable face. You'd think someone would claim her."

"Exactly," Gifford agreed.

Kyra's attention went back to the little keyring. "Somebody almost wore this thing out," Kyra said, rubbing her thumb over the depression in the plastic which had obliterated most of the writing on it.

Handing the phone back to Gifford, Carrie Jane reached for the keyring. "Let me see it." She held it for a minute staring at the indentation. "I have a student who does this. Rubs his thumb unconsciously back and forth across whatever he's holding. The other day he actually snapped a pencil in half from the pressure."

"My brother plays with the change in his pocket like that. Whenever I'm trying to talk to him, there's this annoying tinkling sound in the background. He doesn't even notice." Kyra said in disgust. "Drives me crazy."

"Unfortunately, even if this is someone's tension-reducing token, we are left without a clue," Gifford concluded. "We all have our little quirks, but as far as I can tell, this one is impossible to trace."

"Well, let's see if anybody in the store recognizes the girl. Some of them are regulars. If she's been around, one of them might remember her."

Back in the bookstore proper, Kyra asked for everyone's attention. "Sorry to interrupt your reading," she said, "but this is Detective Gifford from the County Sheriff's Office," she looked at Gifford to confirm her assumption. Gifford nodded. "He's hoping someone here might recognize this girl." Gifford passed around the picture on his phone.

"What's she done?" The teenager asked, eager to participate in a real-life crime.

"Nothing." Gifford addressed him. "She has amnesia. We're trying to find her family."

"Oh," said the teen obviously disappointed.

"How old?" asked an athletic twenty-something girl in cargo pants and hiking boots, who was improbably engrossed in a non-fiction book about an early Roman emperor.

"We're not sure. I'm guessing 13 or 14, maybe as young as 12. She doesn't remember."

"Let me look again," said the girl, apparently stricken by Gifford's answer. "She has nice eyes," she said shaking her head again. "Sorry. I've never seen her."

"Anybody else?" Gifford asked.

No one answered. Conceding defeat, Kyra handed the phone back to Gifford. He pulled his card out of his back pocket. "If you think of anything or hear about something from one of your customers, let me know."

"E-mail the picture to me. I'll put it up front. Maybe someone will recognize her." Kyra suggested. Shaking her head, she echoed what Carrie Jane had said earlier. "Something wrong with a society that loses children."

Their visit over, Kyra hugged Carrie Jane again and reminded her about their approaching lunch date to celebrate the end of the semester.

Once they were back in the car, Gifford headed straight for his great aunt's place. "Don't let the name throw you. It's called Grandma's Burgers and Shakes. My aunt had her first grandchild the year before she opened the store, and she wanted to make sure everybody in town knew it."

Like most other businesses in the area, the burger place looked like it belonged in a village in Switzerland. It had a tall pitched roof and two dormer windows behind which Gifford knew, from the dozens of times he had climbed those stairs every day, there was an attic stacked with Styrofoam paper products and the odds and ends of equipment left over from the constant remodeling which was his aunt's hobby. "Other people change the furniture around in a room; Sally changes out the milkshake mixer or the straw dispenser. Drives her employees to distraction trying to keep up with the machine-of-the-month," Gifford explained affectionately.

They ordered deluxe burgers, shakes, and what Gifford proclaimed to be the best onion rings this side of Denver. "Not much of a competition, considering the Rocky Mountains are the only geography between here and there," Carrie Jane commented dryly, but she had to admit, Gifford was right. It was a great hamburger. She liked that it wasn't so large she couldn't get it in her mouth and that it was dripping with sautéed onions, not to mention cheese and plenty of all the usual fixins'.

"Delicious." she decreed.

"I told you." Gifford didn't bother to disguise the smugness in his voice. He added, "Thanks for introducing me to Kyra. Even if she can't help with the investigation, I think I may have to make another trip or two to her store. I saw a couple of books which looked like Christmas presents to me."

Carrie Jane beamed. "You liked the store! Chick books and all!"

Sheepishly, Gifford agreed. "I've got two sisters and half a dozen nieces and nephews. They're all kind of wild little kids. I can't imagine where they get it." Mock innocence played across his face. "Their moms have trained them that bedtime means a bath and a story, so new books are very popular at their houses."

Carrie Jane grinned. "I'm guessing you're not one of those people who finish up their holiday shopping in July."

"I love Christmas," Gifford admitted, surprised at himself. He was usually very careful not to reveal personal details to anyone outside his immediate family. Nothing good came from appearing soft. "I know it sounds like a chick thing," he plunged on," but I love Christmas music—even sing in the choir at church sometimes." For just a moment, he sounded bashful. "I like glittering trees, red and green decorations, the whole ballgame. . .." He'd come this far, he supposed he might as well go all the way. "I guess it's tied up with getting to buy presents for people I care about." The words came out in a rush. He studied the remainder of his burger and avoided her eyes.

But Carrie Jane seemed charmed by his reluctant confession. "Why, Detective! A tough law enforcement type who has a heart of gold. Sounds like a novel."

"Yeah," he admitted, relieved she didn't seem put-off like his buddies would have been. His eyes twinkling, he slid away from that awkward subject. "Don't let it get out, or I'll never get promoted."

Friday, December 6

6 PM

EDUARDO FIT THE METRIC WRENCH set back into one of the slots of his father's handmade denim tool holder. He carefully folded down the flap and rolled the cloth into a lumpy column, snapping the Velcro fasteners and checking to be sure the smallest wrenches couldn't wriggle out. No school tomorrow. At least he could sleep in; he and his father didn't have to be at work until ten. As he methodically loaded the rest of their tools into two scratched and dented heavy-duty metal boxes, he could see his father's reflection in the small, grime-clouded mirror over the sink of the tiny closet that made up the only bathroom out here in the garage workshop.

At the close of every workday, his father fastidiously scrubbed as much of the grease as possible off his face, arms, and hands. He even changed out of his work coveralls into clean jeans and a t-shirt which he kept stashed in the cab of the truck. "I do not wish to make the house look like I do after work. It is difficult enough for your mother to clean up after the little ones," he often told Eduardo. Personally, Eduardo suspected that his stepmother was waging an uphill battle against impossible odds, but he freely admitted to himself that he appreciated dinner always on the table when they got home from work, and the younger children smelling of Johnson's Baby Magic when they tip-toed in to kiss him good night before they went to bed. Thinking about them brought a half-smile to his face.

"So, Eduardo, what makes you smile? You do not do it often enough," his father called from across the room.

Eduardo shook off his reverie, "Nothing," he said shortly. "I was just thinking about Alejandro."

"Yes," his father agreed. "He is a pleasure to think about." He pulled open the door of the cab of his old Ford and hoisted himself onto the seat, its springs complaining as he settled himself in. Eduardo climbed in beside his father from the passenger side. As always, his father said, "A good day's work makes a man feel useful," while he put the key in the ignition, and the engine obediently leaped smoothly into rhythm.

Eduardo never failed to be thankful that the '89 truck motor turned over without a single protest. His father was a very good mechanic. Eduardo doubted that he would ever be able to match his father's skill. He liked machines well enough, but to him, they were just puzzles that needed all the pieces in place in order to complete the design. To his father, they were living things, the objects of his care and compassion. Eduardo suspected that the day his father died, every machine in the shop and in their house, for that matter, would revolt and refuse to ever come to life again.

Usually, they listened to the radio chatter about the local news on the way home, but tonight his father didn't touch the dials. "Eduardo," he began. "We must speak of your future."

"What future?" Eduardo said bitterly. "Spending the rest of my days working at the garage, and my nights watching reality shows on television?" He winced at the rancor in his voice, but he told himself that he was just stating the same facts they had gone over many times before.

"No, my son. I am talking about the future that you choose for yourself—the future a man chooses. The one your mother wanted for you."

Eduardo turned sharply to stare at his father. It was rare that his father ever mentioned his mother. He had certainly never spoken of her hopes for her son before.

"Your mother was so proud of you," his father began, his eyes never leaving the road ahead. "You were a beautiful child. Even as a baby, your hair was thick and curled over your ears as it does now, and your eyes— she used to say that you had the eyes of the ocean, the coloring changing as the weather. When you saw her come into the room your eyes lit up, and you laughed. You followed every movement she made. She was the center of your life, and you were hers."

Eduardo said nothing. He'd given up trying to remember her face, but sometimes in the night, he was sure he could hear her voice soothing him as he lay awake. There were no discernible words, just a sense of quiet murmurs that eased the worry spinning round and round in his head whenever he thought of the coming day.

"Do you know she read to you every night before she put you to bed, even when you were so small, I could carry you in one arm? She said," his father's eyes gazed at something far away in another time, "she said, 'words were tools'. She believed they would help you find your way."

Eduardo's voice dripped with sarcasm, "You mean like they've done so far?"

His father sighed. "I do not know what she meant. I only tell you what she said. We were very young when you were born, but we were so happy." His face clouded over. "Those days were not easy. We were alone. No one to help us. But when you came, it was as if the angels were watching over us. We had a room over the garage behind the house of a widow. For the rent, your mother cleaned each day. The old woman even put up a small crib on her back porch, so that you could nap while your mother worked. That was when I first went to work at the garage. We could not afford a television or even a radio. At night we would talk of what we had done during the day. And we watched you grow." His father turned to Eduardo--his eyes misty. "She loved you."

Despite himself, Eduardo felt the pressure of his childhood loss threaten to escape the vacuum to which he had long ago relegated it and menace the fragile border of his deepest heart; he forced the tears that sprang to his eyes to retreat. He was a man now. Emotion was a woman's device. Despite his determination never to show weakness, he could not withhold the question that had haunted him since he was old enough to formulate the words. "Why did she leave me?" he asked. "Why didn't she stay?"

For a moment his father considered the road ahead. Then he switched on his blinker and turned off of Main Street, visibly forcing back the long-forgotten sorrow. He threaded his way through the twisted streets of their neighborhood, finally, pulling into their driveway. Switching off the ignition, he turned to his son. "She was very ill. . .. For such a long time. The doctors, they said there was nothing they could do. Her stomach. . .." His voice trailed off. "It was very bad. I thought I would die too watching her suffer."

"At last, I had to let her go, but only because the doctors said it would stop her pain. She was so weak that when she begged to hold you, I had to brace up her arms with my own." His father leaned his head on the steering wheel, avoiding looking at his son. "You didn't cry. You were quiet in her arms. You couldn't have known what was happening, but you cuddled in her lap. It was as if you knew not to move for fear of causing her more pain." He turned to Eduardo, his face awash with tears. "She took her last breath with your head pressed against her cheek."

Eduardo had never seen his father cry before. The silent shaking of his father's shoulders was so painful to watch that he squeezed his eyes shut to block out the vision.

For several minutes neither spoke, each alone in his thoughts. Then Eduardo's father's voice penetrated his son's memories. "After she died, I stopped living. Every morning I went to work, leaving you with your *abuela*. When I came to pick you up at night, you heard the door open and tottered toward it. Always you looked up, staring at the space behind me, waiting for her. When she didn't follow me in the door, only then would you go back to your toys. You never cried. You were so little to lose so much." His voice was quiet.

"Now you are a man." His father studied his face. "You have so much of her in you. The eyes, the love of the books, the learning. I do not understand what has happened. This week I speak to your teacher of English. She tells me that you are not passing her class—she says that you are the smartest, but you do nothing. What has happened, my son?"

For a moment Eduardo was tempted to tell his father about Belen, the baby, the burden of worry that he carried every waking moment. But he could not. His father bore too much already, scrambling each day to earn enough to pay for food and rent and still the bills to the hospital for Alejandro's birth. His father was right. He was a man now. A man dealt with his own problems; he did not run to his parents. So, he said nothing. He would have to find another way.

10 PM

At ten o'clock the house was silent at last, even the baby snoring lightly in the crib across the small room Eduardo shared with his younger brothers. He lay on his top bunk bed, still fully dressed staring at the ceiling. It was the only space in the house that was solely his. The younger boys, who shared the lower bunk, knew better than to crawl across the bed he carefully made each morning before he left for school. And when he came home, his headphones in his ears, it was a refuge from the chaos in a household of the four younger children. Tonight though, worry raged through his head like a violent storm. No matter how loud he turned the music, it faded into the background of his thoughts which raced helter-skelter across his mind, slamming into each other like tidal waves that threatened to drown him with anxiety.

Finally, he could bear it no longer. He carefully unplugged the earbuds from his phone and slipped them into the small case suspended from the post of his bed. It had taken him almost six months to save enough to buy a smartphone—he didn't intend to have to replace it. His fingers texted the letters without even looking. "Meet me at our place as soon as you can." Quietly he slid down to the floor, his stocking feet barely making a thud as he grabbed his shoes and opened the door, one hand pressed against it to deaden the sound. Even that slight rustle caused Alejandro to open his eyes and lift his head, smiling sleepily at Eduardo. Then the baby settled back onto his mattress, sucking contentedly on his middle three fingers and closing his eyes again.

It was bitter cold, the sky clear of the clouds the wind had whipped through the valley earlier. Stars lit his way down the block and out of the housing complex. He jogged, tugging his jacket more tightly across his chest until the motion of his legs warmed the rest of his body. It was less than 15 minutes until he was in the alley behind the old Christensen's Department Store, a solitary light flickering from a window at the back of the building. She is here already, he thought and the tension in his body drifted unbidden down to his feet, then seeped away entirely.

His fingers found the tiny gap he and Belen always left at the bottom of the window next to the loading dock, and he raised it as quietly as he could, its hinges complaining at the unexpected stress. One leg and then the other dropped onto the floor inside, his cell phone clattering from his pocket, dropping off the edge of the concrete and into the alley. He swore softly under his breath. It wasn't the first time he'd lost something out of his back pocket while climbing through that window. A couple of weeks ago, he'd had to crawl around scooping up the change and random odds and ends when he'd brushed the edge of the sill and knocked the stuff out of that same pocket. He never did find the free Big Gulp coupon he'd been hanging onto as a treat for Marisa. It had been raining so hard that night, he figured the coupon must have washed into the little river that had formed in the alley and disappeared across the side street into the alley behind the Seaweed Bar. He had been already soaked; it wasn't worth the trouble to go after the coupon and whatever else had escaped his pocket with it.

Now he untangled his legs from the window, reached down and grabbed his phone, tucked it deeper into his back pocket, then climbed back through the window. There was the faint sound of music coming from one of the long-abandoned dressing rooms. He stopped for a moment to listen; then he smiled. She was playing their song—an old one his grandmother used to sing to him as she rocked him to sleep each afternoon when he was just a little boy. It was probably the only song the old woman knew in English. Her aged voice always wobbled as she sang, but the love she had felt for him had always permeated the words. Blue Moon, I saw you standing alone/ without a dream in your heart/ without a love of your own.

Belen was waiting in the doorway, her long satin hair hanging down over one shoulder. The light from the candle she had lit silhouetted the soft curves of her now swollen body. He stopped breathing, and for a moment, he just stared at her.

"Eduardo," she whispered his name. "Oh, Eduardo."

He rushed towards her, wrapping his arms around her and burying his face in the sweet smell of gardenias. Neither said another word.

The music in the background stopped, waiting for the next command, but Belen and Eduardo didn't notice. Unexpectedly, he felt the baby kick him hard in the abdomen. "Oomph!" he said, laughing out loud, "So Little One, you know who I am?" and he backed away from Belen, touching her belly gently. "And how are you today?"

"He has the hiccups," Belen said, amused. "He usually gets them about bedtime, so that I cannot sleep." A shadow of worry swept across her eyes.

"What?"

"I am sorry to have put us in this position. The baby."

Eduardo bent down and lowered himself to the quilt she had spread out on the floor; he pulled her to him, his body making a backrest for her to lean against. She relaxed at his touch and nestled her head against his neck.

"Never be sorry," he said. "The baby will look like you, and I will see your face every morning when I lift her from her crib. She will be a sign of my love for you."

"What if it's a boy?"

"Then he will be very pretty," Eduardo teased. "Like his mother." He lifted her hand to his lips and kissed her palm. "The baby is sent from heaven. My father says special angels are assigned to watch over each child." He looked into her eyes, "Especially ours," he added. You are my angel, he thought, but he did not voice the words.

She touched her phone, and the music began again. They sat cuddled together, saying nothing, content to be together, listening to the music for so long a time that the candle flickered and threatened to die. Outside stars began to arch toward the horizon in the dark sky.

His back ached from cradling her for what he knew must have been several hours, but he ignored his stiffening muscles. With his eyes closed, he could pretend that he could hold her close to him forever. He must find a way for it to be true.

She stirred and glanced at her phone. Soon it would be light. "I must go. My father will be waking to prepare for work. It is already morning." She turned her head and touched his lips with hers. "I love you," she whispered.

He helped her fold the quilt and pack it into her bag with the phone and the remnants of the candle. "I love you, too," he replied. They walked arm in arm down the dark hall toward the faint light now appearing outside the loading dock window. Tenderly he lifted her body in his arms, resting her head against his shoulder. He carried her to the open window. With great care, he lowered her through the window and onto the other side of the sill until he felt her feet take her weight. Then he followed her out and onto the loading dock, pulling the window shut but careful to leave a tiny gap at the bottom.

The moon had traveled across the sky and was sinking toward the mountains whose peaks were outlined in a faint gray glow. Another day had begun.

Saturday, December 7

Noon

VIOLA WIPED THE LAST DISH in the drainer and put it in the cupboard. She had a fetish about counters being clear of clutter, but the past few days had challenged that notion. She and Annie had finished the last batch of cookies at midnight. Except for the interruption of this morning's choir practice, they had worked steadily to assemble the ½ dozen varieties and hundreds of cookies into neatly packed gift bags. Cellophane bags covered with Christmas bells and holly marched across Viola's prized granite counters. Red and green curls of ribbon dripped from each package. Now every flat surface was filled with them--103 to be exact. Viola believed it was the details that measured the quality of the project. Once again, the bake-a-thon was a success.

Rows of homemade treats were ready to be delivered to "practically everyone in town" an exhausted Annie declared, falling into the nearest kitchen chair. "So, now that we're finished, what do we do next?" Annie was hesitant to even ask the question. She knew all those cookies had to go somewhere. "Maybe lunch?" she hinted. "Bacon and tomato sandwiches?"

"Girl, if you keep eating like this, we're going to have to get you a bigger bed!" Viola chided.

Annie's face allowed a half-smile to appear. "It's the bacon. I like bacon," she admitted shyly as she opened the fridge and rummaged around for the ingredients to her favorite sandwiches.

Viola didn't even try to stop the girl. She was an expert at consistency in parenting rules, but she was finding it impossible to deny Annie anything. The child was different from any kid she'd ever known. She'd been alternating nights between Ramona's house and Viola's for more than a week, and she had yet to disobey a rule, leave a chore unfinished, or even grumble when Viola told her it was time for bed. It wasn't normal, which worried Viola more than she cared to admit--even to Ramona. Viola had spent a lifetime studying childhood age markers. Annie didn't fit in any of the charts. More and more Viola worried that Annie was covering something ugly in her past, something she'd buried so deeply that she may not even be aware it was there. Viola speculated that perhaps years of emotional abuse—or please, Lord not something worse--had made Annie hyper-vigilant, careful to anticipate Viola's unspoken expectations and fill them even before Viola had a chance to give them voice. And what if she had to send Annie back to a dangerous past? What then? She didn't think she could bear it. Not again. She took a deep breath and managed a cheerful face. "Next," she announced. "We deliver cookies!"

Annie looked around, alarmed. "All of them? Today?"

"I have a list. I've laid it out so that we deliver the nearest ones first and then fan outward."

"Are there any extras?"

"Why? Are you still hungry?" Viola teased. "Surely you can't eat another cookie?"

"It's just that . . ." Annie stopped, unsure of what to say next.

"It's all right, Child. Tell me," Viola could see the apprehension in Annie's eyes. "I'm sure we can find one or two leftovers," she said.

"I just thought maybe we could give one to that judge, and maybe the detective who is trying to help me. Oh, and that little girl who came to the door asking for money."

Viola swallowed. "Oh." It wasn't often that Viola was struck wordless. Adolescents were supposed to be too self-absorbed to be kind without prompting. "Well, I'm sure we can manage that. I'll add them to my list." Perhaps Annie wasn't as afraid of the justice system as Ramona had feared. But what else could it be?

They started next door at Ramona's house. They really didn't have to take her cookies, since she'd helped frost and bag them, eating several of the double chocolate ones in the process, but Viola wanted a chance to speak to her privately.

Ramona was on the phone when they walked in. Viola motioned Annie to a chair at the kitchen table and started unloading the dishwasher. She wasn't one to sit around and wait.

"OK, Janeen. We'll be there. See you then." Ramona slipped her phone in the pocket of her jeans and turned to Annie. "Janeen wants you to come to an extra rehearsal she's called for the soloists before practice next Wednesday. Is that OK with you?"

"Yes, ma'am," Annie agreed. "Viola, too?"

"Well, technically it's just you, she wants. But I was thinking we could head over to Leatherby's for a hot fudge sundae after the rehearsal. Been a long time since I've had enough chocolate."

Viola grinned. "Two or three weeks, maybe?"

Ramona looked sheepish. "Annie's never been there," she defended herself.

"Give her the cookies." Viola instructed the girl and explained to Ramona, "Annie wants to pass out a few bags to people on her list. I thought we'd do that first."

Ramona looked up sharply. "Her list? "She sat down next to Annie at the table and leaned toward the girl. "Do you remember someone?"

"No, ma'am. But it's Christmas. I just thought maybe I could say thanks to a couple of people I've met."

Voila looked over Annie's head at Ramona. We need to talk, she mouthed.

"Well, maybe I'll go with you for a while. That sounds better than mending that old bedspread for the hide-a-bed in the office."

"Phtttt!" Viola dismissed the mending. "That old thing isn't good enough to give to Deseret Industries," she said under her breath.

"Annie," Ramona glanced up at Viola, "would you mind fetching my coat out of the hall closet—the fleece jacket, not the Sunday one."

Annie nodded, rising and heading down the hall.

"Ramona," Viola leaned toward her friend as soon as Annie was out of earshot. "She wants to give cookies to Judge Callister and Giff! Wouldn't she try to avoid them if she was afraid of law enforcement? But then if she's hasn't had a run-in with the law, why does she jump every time Giff shows up? Speaking of which, have you heard anything from him? Is he making any progress?"

"Nothing, but what I told you yesterday. He's still checking out that stuff I found in her pocket. So far, no luck."

"Maybe someone will recognize her when we're out today."

"Here you go, Ramona," Annie interrupted as she walked back in the room, handing over the worn purple fleece.

"I know," Ramona headed Viola off before her friend had a chance to bring up an aggravating ongoing subject. "I know I should buy a new one," she defended herself slipping an arm into the jacket, "but at my age, it just doesn't seem like a priority. This jacket and I have been together a long time; can't let go of something that loyal." She straightened the collar and patted the jacket affectionately.

Viola rolled her eyes. "Let's go, Annie, before she decides to wear that housecoat she insists on patching up every couple of years."

For a change, Ramona got the last word. "Don't knock it. Being cheap means I can splurge for the ice cream Wednesday."

The three of them spent most of the afternoon taking turns knocking on doors and passing out the cookies. Whenever it was Annie's turn, Ramona or Viola had to introduce her. Most of their choir friends had seen and heard Annie at rehearsals; they almost universally had assumed she was a niece or friend of one or the other. When they heard of her discovery behind the Seaweed Bar, they all had opinions about her past. A couple of them were pretty far-fetched. "Maybe Annie saw a mob hit and got a concussion from the assassin hitting her on the back of her head with his nine-millimeter?" Ramona stared that idea down.

"Maybe her brother knocked her down the stairs, and when she came to, Annie wandered away." Viola raised an eyebrow.

"Maybe she was bullied at school, and she's hidin' out."

"Really?" Ramona said. "That's all you can come up with?"

But no one admitted to having ever seen Annie before or even having heard about a lost child. Viola managed to whisper to Ramona while Annie finished a cookie delivery, "It's weird. Gossip in Douglas Valley is our most popular form of cheap entertainment. How could Annie have just appeared without somebody in town having an idea of who she was or where she came from?"

They had distributed cookies to more than 30 families, and thus far, no one had a single connection to Annie. It was discouraging.

By the time they got to Marisa's duplex, it was late afternoon and the temperature had dropped with the sun disappearing behind the mountains. Before they got out of the car, the little girl had thrown open the door and was racing down the steps toward them. "*Mamá,*" she yelled, "it's the Annie-girl. She came back to see me like she promised." Marisa jumped at Annie as she climbed out of the back seat. Annie lost her balance, laughed, and fell back into the car with the little girl in her lap.

Luz scolded her daughter even as she came out the door to greet her visitors. "*Marisa. Bajar a la chica. ¡Déjala ir!*" She turned to Ramona and Viola, toning down her exasperation at the little girl. "Please come in. I am afraid my Little One doesn't have many friends."

"That's hard to imagine. Seems like that child has enough personality to share with dozens of friends," Viola observed.

Luz laughed. "It is true," she agreed. "Even the man who reads the machine for our water bill knows her name."

While Ramona introduced Viola, Annie and the little girl held hands as they skipped up the stairs and settled onto the living room couch. "I brought you a Christmas present," Annie said holding the gaily wrapped package just out of the little girl's reach.

Marisa eyed the package. "*¿Para mí?*" she feigned surprise, taking a smug peek at her older siblings who stood silent next to their mother.

The baby dropped the blocks he was stacking and studied the visitors suspiciously; then he scooted on all fours across the room and pasted himself to his mother's leg, ducking his head against her calf. The two older boys made no effort to conceal their keen interest in the package from across the room.

Annie handed Marisa the package. "It is for you, but you must share with the others. There are plenty for everyone."

Marisa was already untying the red bow that encircled the bag. "It's cookies! With sugar on top!" The other children leaned forward in anticipation. "I will choose one for each of you," Marisa decided. She looked down into the bag. Climbing down off the couch and hurrying over to her mother, she added, "Cookies that look like little people!" She turned back to Annie. "You made these people?"

Annie nodded. "They're called Gingerbread Men. We put extra ones in that bag so you all could have one. There is one girl for you and three boys for your brothers."

"What about Eduardo?" Marisa looked to her mother in alarm.

"I am sure Eduardo will be pleased with any one of the others," Luz soothed her daughter.

Marisa seemed satisfied. "*Que rica!,*" she decreed to the women on the couch. "We are very happy."

This time all three of the women laughed together. "Always the princess," Luz beamed in affection as she hugged Marisa.

Solemnly the little girl reached into the bag and handed a cookie to each child, the baby grabbing for the curly ribbon discarded onto the floor next to him.

"Marisa?" The little girl glanced at her mother and saw the instruction in her face.

"Thank you," Marisa said to her visitors. "We are very happy to have these wonderful cookies." She bit into hers, her eyes widening as she tasted the sharp sweetness. "Oh!" Surprise washed across her face. "It makes my mouth dance!" she exclaimed. "I like these happy cookies!"

Judge Callister wasn't home when they went by his house to deliver Annie's gift, but the housekeeper agreed to see that he got the cookies as soon as he returned.

Detective Gifford answered the door of his condo on the first knock. "Mrs. Z, Viola, Annie? Something happen?" he asked in alarm.

"It's Christmas, Mark. Can't we bring you a little gift without an ulterior motive?" Ramona scolded.

Gifford looked at her with suspicion. "I've known you for more than 15 years and you've never felt the need to add me to your list before."

"Don't be so difficult," she ordered. "Annie just wanted to thank you for helping her."

"Yes, sir," Annie said formally. "Thank you for trying to find out who I am. Even though you haven't found out much, I appreciate it," she said as she handed him the gaily wrapped bag.

Gifford acknowledged the left-handed compliment with a grin aimed at Viola and Ramona. "She's starting to remind me of you two," he said. Turning back to Annie, he said, "It's my job, Annie, but I'm happy to do it for you, especially." He emphasized the last word, looking into her guileless blue eyes. "I'm glad to see you are beginning to warm up to me a little." He gestured to them all. "Won't you all come in for a glass of milk to go with those cookies?"

"Sure," Viola answered without consulting the others. "We've delivered more than 40 bags of those things, and I'm about to fall over. All that getting in and out of the car isn't good for us old people."

"Speak for yourself," Ramona shot at her, but she settled into an easy chair in Giff's surprisingly comfortable great room with a sigh of relief.

"So, Annie, how are these two treating you? Can't be easy for a youngster like you to live with a couple of 'old' ladies?"

Viola gave him the evil eye. "Watch it," she said. "It's OK for me to call us old, but you had better pay attention to your tongue!"

Gifford laughed.

Annie relaxed visibly. "I like them," she confessed. "Even if they are old." She glanced at her guardians. "We made the cookies ourselves."

"So there!" Ramona added, then shifted the conversation to another topic. "Any news on the investigation?"

Gifford reached in the bag and dug around until he found the chocolate cookie with chocolate frosting. He took a bite, chewing it with obvious enjoyment. "Good," he said smiling appreciatively at the cookie. "Really good."

He answered Ramona, but he looked at Annie, sympathy evident in his face. "I have a couple of leads. Had an appointment with a guy who saw you and the old man at the bar before Ramona found you, and there's a store in Newman which gives out key chain attachments like the one in your pocket that you said you found in the alley. I'm hoping someone there will recognize your picture."

Viola saw Annie stiffen slightly as Gifford spoke, and she moved closer to Annie on the couch, putting her arm around the girl protectively.

Letting out a deep breath slowly, Annie braced herself as she asked, "What happens if you can't find out who I am and where I belong? What if nobody cares that I'm lost?"

Instinctively, Ramona leaned across her chair to the couch and reached for Annie's left hand. Viola on one side, Ramona on the other—the two women a formidable fortress protecting Annie from any further harm.

No one spoke. Gifford was surprised to find himself engulfed with an unexpected sense of profound sadness. He had always prided himself on his ability to stay focused on the assignment and not get bogged down in the complexity of emotions brought on by the human condition, but this young girl with her unexpected kindness and her wide, unguarded eyes stirred something in him that he couldn't quite put his finger on. "Oh, Annie," he said. "I know someone misses you—maybe many people. I'm sure of it." He took another bite of cookie. "We'll find them. I promise." He hoped to heaven that was a promise he wouldn't have to break.

No one said anything while Gifford finished his cookie. Then

Ramona interrupted the silence with a reminder that they'd better get moving. "A lot of cookies left out in that car."

Tuesday, December 10

7 PM

THE FOLLOWING TUESDAY RAMONA SLIPPED into a back seat just as Jesse Simpson was reciting the date, time, and attendees of the regular Tuesday Town Council meeting into the audio recorder. Ramona doubted that there were more than five or six people in the whole county that bothered to listen to the record. If they didn't care to show up to the actual meeting, why the heck would they want to sit in front of their computer for a couple of hours and be bored to death?

The crowd was sparse. Ramona figured interest in the last meeting before the New Year was superseded by the calendar's downhill rush toward Christmas. Jesse Simpson cast a fleeting look at Ramona as her eyes surveyed the audience. Ramona smiled pleasantly in response. The mayor ignored her. Ramona's grin widened. She found a certain satisfaction in raising the Mayor's annoyance factor.

Ramona didn't intend to say a word tonight. She knew she'd unloaded all her ammunition at the last meeting. Tonight, her presence would be a reminder that someone was paying attention to whatever the Town Council was up to.

Judge Callister slipped into the seat next to Ramona as the Council was voting on the consent agenda. "Judge," she acknowledged, then turned her attention back to the meeting.

"Ramona," the judge whispered back. "You can call me John when I'm not on official business."

"And exactly how would I know that?" she said with asperity, not bothering to turn her head in his direction. "This is the Town Hall, and you are a judge."

He sighed. "Never mind."

Because additional discussion about the proposed mall wasn't on the agenda, the Council moved along rapidly, approving a $60,000 purchase of upgraded software for the town offices and discussing two zoning changes, neither of which involved developed residential or commercial property, so no one had signed up to speak for or against either. All in all, it was every bit as boring as Ramona expected, which suited her just fine. The last three weeks had been crammed with upheaval—even before she discovered Annie behind the bar. Christmas was like that.

Jesse Simpson hit her gavel against the table and declared the meeting adjourned.

Wincing as she moved her stiff muscles and gathering up her coat, scarf, and purse, Ramona was ready to be done with local politics for a day or two.

"Have you got a minute?" The judge asked.

Ramona was irritated. "What is it, John? I'm tired, and I want to go home."

"I've been looking into this new mall idea. I think there's a real possibility that the Town Council intends to declare the whole area 'blighted'; then they don't have to pay business owners the prices their properties are currently worth. It's legal, but it's as immoral as hell." His increasing volume attracted the attention of a couple of other spectators just exiting their aisle.

Ramona stopped open-mouthed. "Now that's the John I remember from high school!" she approved. "I suspected there was something fishy about Jesse Simpson's assurance that the town could acquire all that land without any trouble."

"It's the money. Pretty difficult to overlook the glint of gold."

Ramona nodded.

"You up to a late dinner at Denny's? Maybe it's time we joined forces."

10:30 PM

Sometimes it just didn't pay to go to those damn meetings, Ramona fumed as she settled into her rocker to read the front-page editorial from yesterday's edition of the Douglas Valley Weekly after her dinner with the

Judge. The newspaper had come out in support of the Town Council's plan--Jesse Simpson's plan, Ramona amended--to renovate the downtown area. Nobody seemed to be considering the consequences of the increased tax burden alone, not to mention the implications of a ½ dozen businesses closing their doors. Exasperation emphasized the age lines around her mouth.

She and John had talked for a couple of hours about how they could marshal enough political clout to stop 'Queen Jessie', as Ramona dubbed her. Support for the new mall meant pretty buildings with fancy landscaping—that was as far as most citizens got when they thought about the Mayor's proposal. Ramona slammed the newspaper pages together, forcing the paper into uneven folds, and dumped the mess onto the floor next to her chair. "Idiots," she said aloud.

"Ramona," Annie's voice carried from the guest bedroom. "Is everything all right?"

Ramona was instantly contrite. "I'm sorry, honey. I was just reading the paper. Didn't mean to bother you." She rose stiffly from her chair and padded down the hall to Annie's door. "I thought you'd be asleep by now."

The lamp next to the bed made Annie's eyes glow with concern. "I was just--"

"Worrying," Ramona finished for her as she entered the bedroom and gestured for Annie to scoot over. She lowered herself onto the bed next to the girl, her back resting against the headboard. Gently she reached over and smoothed Annie's hair behind her ear. "We'll figure it out," she said.

The house was quiet, even the creaks common to old homes had settled for the night. There was a peace here Ramona hadn't felt for a long time. "Do you believe in angels, Annie?"

The girl's body twisted toward her, her hand reaching for Ramona's. "From heaven?" She considered the question. "Yes. I guess I do."

Ramona absently ran her fingers across the girl's palm. "When my daughter was frightened in the night, I used to tell her about her guardian angel—the one assigned by heaven to keep her safe from harm." Ramona felt the girl relax as she snuggled closer to the older woman. "You have one, too. Someone who knows your path back home and is assigned to help you get there." Ramona shifted a pillow under her back. "Sometimes when life is so difficult or unfair or painful, and we don't believe we have the strength to keep going. . ." Her voice trailed off. Memories invaded the silence. Even after all these years, they were almost more than she could bear. Ramona shrugged off the melancholy which had overtaken her. Stop it, old woman. Your troubles are nothing compared to those of this child. She pulled the quilt up over Annie's shoulders and tucked it around her. "Annie, try to remember. Maybe there was a time you felt that Someone was watching over you?"

Annie nodded. "Like you and Viola," she said. Her eyebrows furrowed as she considered the idea. "Only I guess I'm lucky because I can see you and talk to you."

Ramona's breath caught as she looked down at the girl. No one had ever called her an angel before. A devil more than once, but never an angel.

When she spoke again, Annie's voice was soft. "Where's your daughter, Ramona? Does she live far away?"

There was a long pause. Ramona gathered her emotions. "I don't know," she said. "She's lost, just like you, and I can't find her."

Annie was completely still, her attention focused on Ramona, waiting for the rest of the story.

"A long time ago," Ramona began, "my daughter did something that made me angry, very angry." Seared into her memory, Ramona had relived those days in her dreams for twenty years. "It was a boy. I didn't like him. He was headed nowhere. No job. No skills. No ambition. His family dragged him here to the states when he was a kid. From some country down south." Even now the words were bitter in her mouth. "Oh, he was handsome. I'll give him that. But Amos and I," she paused and bit her lip, "Amos and I couldn't have more children. Everything we did was for her."

"And all she could see was that pretty boy. Wanted to dump college, ignore all our plans for her." Anger seeped into her voice. "We tried bribing her with a car if she'd stop seeing him. Then we grounded her for weeks on end. We even resorted to begging. We just made her want him more. Snuck out to see him after we went to bed. Sluffed school to meet him. It was like an addiction." Her voice hardened, reliving the events. "We fought about him constantly."

"What was he like?" Annie asked.

Ramona caught her breath and stared into memory. "I have no idea," she admitted. "We refused to meet him. I guess we hoped if we paid no attention to him, he'd go away." She looked directly at Annie, but her eyes were riveted on the past. Sorrow washed across her face. She released a deep sigh. "Then one miraculous day, she quit arguing. She just shut down. Never mentioned him again at all. Her father and I breathed a sigh of relief. We had the daughter we remembered back—thoughtful, dependable, hard-working. It was finally over."

Ramona squeezed Annie's right hand so hard the blood drained from it. "I remember that night as if it were yesterday. We were doing the dishes. I was washing; she was drying and putting away. I said that I had been worried that if she hadn't stopped seeing that boy, I would have had to tell her she couldn't live here anymore. She didn't say a word, didn't raise her eyes, just she just kept wiping that stupid platter—we'd had fried chicken for dinner." Ramona's other hand clenched the butterfly quilt under her fingers into a tight knot, but her eyes never left Annie's face. "I told her how much I appreciated her finally coming to her senses. When I got up the next morning, she was gone. Her clothes, everything. I . . . .." Now Ramona's voice was flat, matter-of-fact. "I went straight to the cupboard, yanked that cursed platter from its place on the shelf and shattered it on the kitchen floor."

Annie reached out and covered the older woman's fist with her other hand. "Oh, Ramona," she said, tears glistening in her eyes.

Ramona sat silently, trapped in the past. At length, the tension in the winkled fingers beneath the young girl's palm faded.

"What's your daughter's name?"

Ramona dragged herself into the present by the empathy she heard in Annie's question. Making a visible attempt to shake off the grief which had threatened to overtake her, she answered, "Elinor. I named her after a character in a book—I hoped she'd grow up strong and independent like that Elinor." Ramona's eyes saw something a great distance away. "She did."

"Don't worry," Annie said softly. The girl pulled Ramona's hand close to her face and kissed the back of the aging skin. "Her angel is watching over her."

For a long time, the girl and Ramona held onto one another, neither speaking. Eventually, Annie's breathing slowed and took on the steady rhythm of sleep. Ramona disengaged her hand from the girl's, rose from the bed, tucked the quilt up under Annie's chin, and tiptoed from the room, one lonely tear glistening on her cheek.

Wednesday, December 11

4:30 AM

THAT NIGHT HER DREAMS WERE filled with fractured memories of Ellie and Amos alongside students from her classes whom she hadn't thought about in years. It was a reprieve when she woke up early the next morning to the sound of hail beating against the rain gutters outside her window. Wind whipped the small stones of ice into a frenzy and slammed them into the panes, shaking the frames and threatening to break the glass. The sky outside was uniformly black, no stars visible, just the wind and the noise. Oddly enough, she found it comforting. Something about the sense of being closed in, safe from the assault of an unpredictable world-- if not the weather, she thought in momentary wry amusement.

The clock on the small table next to her bed read 4:30 AM. She sighed. She'd imagined that now she was retired, she could sleep in until eight every morning, but her body had been programmed to rise before dawn and get ready for school. Apparently, it was frozen into the pattern of too many years. She turned over and stared at the ceiling. Some mornings she could fool herself into believing that she didn't feel well and trick her body into going back to sleep for an hour or so. It did not appear that that would be the case this morning. The wind seemed to howl even louder. Better check on Annie, she thought, pulling on her robe from the end of the bed. But the girl was sleeping peacefully, oblivious to the clatter of hail on the roof.

She turned the handle of the girl's bedroom door carefully shut and walked down the hall to stand in front of the living room window, watching the hail pile up on the brown grass and then spill off the edge of the overhang on the roof. The glare of the ice on the ground reflected the porch light's glow, and the pool of white ice crystals forming on the yard mesmerized Ramona. One thing she loved about Douglas Valley was the unpredictability of the weather.

Her thoughts roved over her agenda for the day. This evening was a rehearsal for the *Messiah*. Janeen had asked Annie to be there ½ hour early with the other soloists to warm up. Now that the conductor was convinced Annie's voice wasn't a fluke, Janeen was positively euphoric. "I've already heard rumors that Annie's performance is going to draw the largest audience we've ever had before."

Ramona suspected Janeen's enthusiasm was largely delusional. People who loved music came to concerts. People who didn't, didn't—no matter how talented the performers. On the other hand, it wouldn't hurt Ramona's feelings if they did have a large crowd. It was exhilarating to sing to a hall packed with an appreciative audience.

There was a sudden crack of lightning, and for an instant, the sky was bright enough to read by. It was followed by a distant boom of thunder. The porch light and all the streetlights on the block went dark. A startled cry came from the guest bedroom.

"It's all right, Annie. Just a storm. Go back to sleep," she called to the other room. In the distance, Ramona heard the wail of sirens. "Must have hit a power line," she muttered, heading for the kitchen to make herself a hot chocolate. She swore under her breath as she automatically flipped the switch for the kitchen light, and nothing happened. Crap. No microwave. No chocolate. No more newspaper. Might as well go back to bed.

The sirens blared for a long time.

6:00 AM

The insistent ringing of the phone next to her rocking chair startled Ramona. It took a moment for her to remember that instead of the bed, she had rested in her favorite chair to watch the storm after the power went off. Her neck was crooked at an odd angle, and it complained when she reached over to answer the phone.

Janeen's voice was even more strident than usual. "Ramona. We've got a BIG problem. I'm calling a meeting of a few choir members from each section to show up this morning for a meeting." Her voice rose higher as she spit out each sentence. "We might have to CANCEL the concert! I just don't SEE what else we can do. I need you at the church at 7:30 AM." Janeen paused to take a breath.

"Wait a minute. What on earth are you talking about?"

"The high school! The auditorium is so BADLY damaged, the Fire Chief says we can't HOLD the concert there."

Ramona shook her head to force it to focus. She must still be asleep. "What the heck's wrong with the high school?" she demanded.

"The fire!" Janeen said as if explaining to an idiot.

"What fire?" Ramona's head cleared instantly. She saw the long halls filled with kids and her teacher friends. Horror grabbed hold of her, and she clenched the receiver. "Janeen," she ordered. "Stop. What happened?"

"It burned. The auditorium. Lightning struck the bell tower and that whole section of the building went up in flames. Didn't you hear the sirens?" she asked incredulously.

"Oh, my God, Janeen. Was anyone in the building? Was anyone hurt?" Shock whipped through Ramona's whole body. Janeen's shrill voice faded. She looked at the clock. Only 6:00 AM. It was still dark. She must have dozed for only an hour or so. Relief poured through her. Way too early for most kids to be in the building. Basketball team? Cheerleaders, maybe. Orchestra practicing for the Christmas concert? Probably a dozen groups that scheduled early morning practices. But if the fire started right after the power went out, then maybe they couldn't get in. Who else? Nobody there that early except--Henry. She pictured his face as he leaned into the courtroom the morning she took Annie to see the Judge. He had worked nights at the high school for years. "Janeen!" Ramona interrupted the steady stream of rising panic on the other end of the line. "Janeen! Is Henry all right?"

"Henry? How should I know? There were a couple of ambulances in the school parking lot," Janeen dismissed Ramona's attempt to divert her attention to inconsequential details, "but WHAT are we going to do ABOUT the CONCERT? That's the PROBLEM!!!!"

"Janeen!" Ramona was appalled at the woman's incomprehensible lack of concern. "Was. Anyone. Else. In. The. Building?" Ramona demanded. "When did it happen? Are the classrooms OK? The library? The books?"

"I don't know!" The choir director snapped. "Aren't you listening? OUR CONCERT may have to be CANCELLED! CANCELLED!" Her voice took on a note of hysteria. "I've got other people to call. Just BE there. Seven-thirty!" The line went dead.

Ramona dropped the phone to the floor just as Annie rushed out of the bedroom toward her.

"What's happened?" She read the distress Ramona's face. "Is Viola all right?" The girl leaned toward the front window trying to get a glimpse of Viola's house next door.

"Viola's fine," Ramona left the rocking chair and put an arm around the girl. "It's the high school," she clenched her teeth to hold back her fear. "Apparently there was a fire. I need to get over there. Where's my coat?" She cast about looking for the worn wool coat as if it would magically appear.

Annie stopped her. "Ramona! Stop! You're not even dressed. It's freezing outside. Wait a minute. I'll get ready and go with you," the girl ordered.

Taken aback by Annie's authoritative command, logic returned. Ramona pictured the pandemonium which must surely be surrounding the school--the chaos of fire trucks, police vehicles, ambulances, water lines strewn across the parking lot. Probably dozens of kids wandering around.

"You're right," Ramona acknowledged, grabbing the phone from where she had dropped. "We'd both be in the way. But, Viola. Viola will know." Ramona used to believe the woman had to be psychic. Now she understood that Viola knew random people in every segment of society from parents she'd helped adopt children to the drug addicts that she'd found placements for in addiction programs. Some years ago, the Fire Chief's oldest daughter had been diagnosed with leukemia. Viola had been assigned as the intermediary between the medical personnel, the hospital, the school district, and the rehabilitation program. If the Chief had spoken to any civilian, it would be Viola. Annie watched anxiously as Ramona hit speed dial.

"You heard about the fire?" She didn't bother with a greeting; forcing the panic to the back of her mind, she held her voice steady.

"Yeah. I was just going to call you." Viola was wide awake, her words crisp.

Ramona didn't question that her friend was already analyzing the disaster and making a mental list of what help would be needed. Emergencies had been her business.

"Anyone hurt?"

Viola answered the unspoken question. "Henry's OK. Some burns on his hands trying to put out the flames before the Volunteers got there, but nothing more. Chief was interviewed on the news a little while ago. Doesn't appear anyone else was in the building, although two Volunteers suffered a couple of broken bones when a steel support shifted and trapped them between it and some equipment backstage. Chief says they'll be OK. Not much left of the auditorium. School's canceled till the Board meets and figures out what to do now. Good thing the fire happened early this morning. No kids in the building."

"Thank heaven." No students hurt. One of her greatest fears when she had been working was that at some point, she might have to explain to a mother why her child had been hurt, or God forbid, died under her care. She knew what it was like to lose a child; it went against the laws of nature. Children were supposed to grow up and continue on long after their parents were gone. Ramona made a mental note to check on Henry later in the day. She knew he lived with an adult daughter. It sounded like he was probably going to need a little help.

Viola answered her next question without her having to ask. "Chief requested on the air that people stay away from the school. It'll take several hours to be sure there are no hot spots left. We'd just be in the way. You'd probably be the most help later when the district has to decide how to rebuild."

Ramona nodded, unconscious of the fact that Viola couldn't see her. As an afterthought, she added, "Janeen's hysterical about canceling the *Messiah*. Wants to meet at the church at 7:30." Ramona's disgust echoed on the line. "High school burns, and all she can think about is singing."

Viola was practical. "Might as well deal with that problem and get it over with. Besides Carrie Jane and Flor probably need a little support this morning. Maybe we could invite 'em over a late breakfast after the meeting?"

"Good idea," Ramona admitted grudgingly. Sometimes Viola could be maddeningly intuitive. OK, more than just sometimes. That's why she had been so good at her job. Ramona felt a pang of conscience. Her young friends' reactions to their losses from the fire hadn't even occurred to her. She dismissed the thought. Pretending she'd been on the same wavelength, Ramona said briskly, "I'll call Carrie Jane now."

The church parking lot was almost as full as if there were a full rehearsal at the 7:30 meeting time. Perversely, the weather had cleared, and the blue sky bore no apology for its violence earlier. Viola scanned the scene as she climbed out of Ramona's car. "Looks like the entire choir showed up."

"They must be worried about the performance," Annie said.

"More likely, they need to share a little gossip. Trouble really brings out the spectators in this town."

Ramona pulled open the door to the building, and they were assaulted by the chaotic noise of dozens of voices. The chapel was jammed with singers. Threads of chatter wove in and out of their progress toward their accustomed seats.

"I heard the fire's not all the way out. Maybe more damage later this afternoon."

"That's ridiculous. Of course, it's out."

"My kid is thrilled he doesn't have early morning band practice. Guess this means no Christmas concerts."

"I heard Jason has two broken ribs. Black and blue all over his left side."

Edging past several sopranos who were so engaged in conversation they didn't bother to greet them, the three had to squeeze together at the end on a bench. Ramona shot a look of annoyance at Viola and Annie.

Viola shrugged her shoulders. "Helps them deal," she said.

Janeen stepped to the podium and tapped the microphone a couple of times. "Is this working?" she mouthed to the singers on the back row. When they nodded, she said, "OK, PEOPLE. PEOPLE!!"

Ramona rolled her eyes. Even genuine misfortune was reduced to melodrama in Janeen's mind.

"QUIET!" Janeen demanded, confirming Ramona's opinion. "WE'VE A LOT TO DO THIS MORNING. By now you all know about the TRAGEDY at the high school." She gave her audience an accusatory stare as if they were all to blame for the choir's current dilemma.

Moroni McGraff in the back row of basses didn't wait for Janeen to finish her explanation. "What happens now, Janeen?" he called out. "Where are we going to find a venue big enough to hold all 200 of us and an audience too?"

"Exactly," his seatmate nodded.

"Yeah, there ain't another place big enough in the whole town." Old Man Jerome added.

An alto raised her voice to be heard over the low murmur of choir members dissolving into conversation with their neighbors. "What about that business convention center in Newman. I hear it's pretty good-sized?"

Janeen leaned into the microphone. "PEOPLE! PEOPLE! Try to get a GRIP!! RAISE your HAND if you want to say something. PLEASE!" She pointed at Moroni. "You're right. That's the PROBLEM. We're here today to SOLVE it." She looked at the alto who suggested the convention center in Newman. "Unfortunately, that place is booked clear through the next two weeks. It is CHRISTMAS, YOU REMEMBER! I CALLED as soon as I HEARD about the fire. Got the HEAD of the Chamber of Commerce out of bed."

"The reason we have the concert at the high school is that there isn't another place within 20 miles that's big enough. This is a waste of time," Ramona whispered to Annie in a low voice.

"Does that mean we won't be singing at all?" Annie's eyes widened at the possibility.

Bishop Marlin, whose congregation loaned the choir this building for rehearsals, suggested, "Why don't we have the concert here? Open the folding doors to the Cultural Hall. Seat the choir down the center of the whole room and put the audience on both sides? It's not as big as the high school auditorium, but there's probably room for a couple of hundred people."

Janeen considered the idea. "That might work. We'd have to have some kind of LOTTERY for tickets like the District does for graduation. There wouldn't be room for all of us to have our WHOLE families come, but MAYBE a spouse and a child or two."

A voice from somewhere behind Ramona yelled, "Well, my in-laws are flying out from Chicago to hear the performance, so I'd need tickets for them and my wife. Could I get that many?"

"Aw, Jonesy. I've met your mother-in-law. It'd be OK if she didn't come," his neighbor from the farm next to his land commented. A hoot of laughter broke out.

Suggestions flew around the room for another 20 minutes, but no solution seemed seriously viable. Finally, Amy Holstrum, last year's choir president stood up. The audience quieted immediately. "It doesn't seem like we've made any headway at all thus far. I suggest Janeen have the section leaders meet with her tomorrow afternoon. By then we'll know more about the damage and the repair timeline. They can let us know what they decide through the calling tree. Since it looks like most of us are here, if we're still going to try to hold the concert, then let's use this time for practice. That way, should the committee find a solution, we'll be ready to perform."

A few of the members muttered in disgust about practicing when there wasn't a chance of finding a place for a concert, but general approval of the idea spread through the crowd.

"Hallelujah!" Ramona said. Viola grinned at her unexpected pun. "Let's get this over with."

An hour and a half later, Carrie Jane and Flor, along with Leon and a couple of other teachers in the choir, followed Ramona out of the parking lot and headed for her house.

As they all crowded into her kitchen, Ramona directed Leon to the hall closet where she kept four folding chairs for just such an occasion. By the time they were all seated around the table, they were shoulder-to-shoulder, but no one seemed to mind.

"Have you all been over to the school to see the mess?" Viola addressed the teachers. "Is there a lot of damage in classrooms?"

"Lots of water damage," Ellen Wrensetter said. Head of the Social Studies department, she'd come directly from the school only a few minutes before the rehearsal ended. "When the sprinklers went on, they activated all over the building. I guess there's no way to control the water in different sections of the school. Looks like most of the classrooms got doused. And all my maps on the walls are destroyed.

"Of course, we haven't seen inside the whole front half of the building yet, just the classroom wings and the media center. Chief said it would be at least tomorrow before he can assess the rest of the damage."

"Clyde arrived minutes after the first alarm when off. I bet he never imaged this kind of problem when he took the job as superintendent," Flor interjected. "He says the computer labs are mostly gone. He was on the phone with the state risk control people when I left the school and headed to the meeting."

"Quite a few teachers had all their curriculum stuff on their laptops which they usually take home, so those may be OK. It'll take a while to assess the damage there." Leon added. "For many of us, it'll be like starting over. And I'm guessing the school district can't afford to pay us to reproduce all those lesson plans and handouts. It's going to be ugly." The other teachers at the table nodded in agreement.

"It won't be any help to some of you, but I have 40 years of English lesson plans in the file cabinet in the other room." Ramona gestured across the hall to the bedroom she'd commandeered for an office years ago. "It's open season for anyone who wants it."

The true scope of the problem began to sink in.

"New subject," Carrie Jane decreed. "This one's too depressing." She looked across the table at the young girl who seemed a little overwhelmed by the number of people in Ramona's small kitchen. "Annie, I had tears in my eyes when you sang today. Handel must be pleased if he's up there somewhere," she pointed upward to a spot somewhere beyond the ceiling.

Annie smiled shyly. "Thank you," she said and ducked head down a little, uncomfortable to be singled out for such praise.

"Amen," Flor chimed in agreement. "When you get to high school, I want you in my class!"

"She always wants the best students," Leon complained. "Doesn't care a wit about the rest of us. Just takes the cream!" His mock resignation brought a smile to the rest of the group.

"So, Ramona. Do you really think there's any chance that Janeen's committee can find a place big enough for our concert? Seems like most of the possibilities were discussed and discarded for one reason or another." Carrie Jane looked up at Ramona who was handing the bagels she'd just heated in the microwave to Viola.

"Annie," Ramona requested. "Could you dig out the cream cheese and fruit tray from the fridge?" She turned back to Carrie Jane. "In answer to your question, the truth is, I don't think it looks good. There just aren't more than one or two buildings in the whole county big enough for us, plus an audience. This may be the first year in the last 30 that we don't perform the *Messiah* for Christmas."

"Well," Leon winked as he looked around the room. "We've got all the parts represented here and one of the soloists." He beamed at Annie. "Maybe we could do a concert in your kitchen." He burst into a rousing rendition of the bass part from the Hallelujah Chorus. No one joined in, but Carrie Jane lifter her hands up as if to say, see what we have to deal with? After half a dozen measures his voice trailed off. "Spoilsports," he complained, exaggerating his dejection.

Annie laughed out loud. Both Ramona and Viola stared at her. What a difference a few days and a few friends had made. Still smiling, Annie asked Ramona, "How big do you think the building has to be?"

"Concert usually attracts several hundred, so maybe 800 to 1,000 including all of the choir members. There just isn't a hall that big anywhere in town," Ramona explained, mixing hot water and Stevens Cocoa into cups and passing them around the table.

"What about that old empty building on the block next to the bar where you found me? It's pretty big." Annie suggested.

"Christensen's?" Viola scoffed. "That building's been empty for more than five years. Place is a rat trap. Sheriff says kids crash in there when they're running from their parents or hanging out with friends. Wouldn't be surprised if the place isn't littered with beer cans and drug paraphernalia. Through cracks in the plywood covering the entrance, you can see the ceiling's come down in a couple of places, front windows boarded up. Spray painted gang symbols on the walls. The whole place needs to be torn down." Viola bit off the last statement as she stole a look at Ramona to see her reaction. Tearing down Christensen's was a touchy subject since the Town Council meeting.

"Hmm," said Carrie Jane. "It is big enough. But, Annie, cleaning up a place like that would require hundreds of hours of work. It's only ten days till the concert. And besides, I think the mayor would be very unhappy if we cleaned up the place just as she was trying to get enough political support to tear it down."

Leon chewed his bagel thoughtfully. "Wonder how much money it would take to paint the walls?"

"You plan on taking that on as a side job?" Flor laughed.

"No. But think about it." Leon looked serious for a change. "We have a week and a half before the concert." He enumerated his arguments on his fingers as he went on. "We have several hundred students who are going to be roaming the streets at loose ends because school is closed. We have an empty building large enough to house a concert. All we'd need is some startup cash, and the student council to back us by rounding up volunteers."

Everyone at the table stopped eating.

"Well, what do you know," said Viola.

1 PM

That afternoon Annie, Viola, Leon, and Carrie Jane planned to drive over to Christensen's and take a hard look at the possibility of holding the concert there. Flor begged off, mentioning something about a date with a vending machine.

Ramona volunteered to take on the task of finding some funds for paint and repairs should the plan seem feasible. Her first thought was John Callister. No one answered his phone, so she left a message. "John," she said without preamble. "I think I've found a way to put a little hitch in the Mayor's plans." She was headed out the door when she was startled by the appearance of Detective Gifford on her front porch.

"Good heavens, Mark," she sputtered. "You scared the hell out of me."

"Sorry, Mrs. Z. Thought you might like to see this report about the fingerprints I had the State Police analyze for me. I was hoping you might have some ideas about the results."

Ramona's eyes narrowed. "You want me to look at a police report. I thought that was a 'no-no'? And why aren't you over at the high school spending the taxpayers' money trying to figure out if some kid managed to help the lightning extend his Christmas vacation?"

"I don't do fire investigations. I just look for lost kids." He chided her. "Like Annie, for instance." His face was impassive, but she recognized the rebuke.

"I'm sorry, Mark." Ramona was embarrassed. "I'm not thinking very well this morning. It's the fire." She gathered her thoughts. "Of course, come in." She gestured to the couch and sat at the other end opposite him. "I take it this report sheds some light on Annie's history. Have you found her family?" A pang of loss accompanied her words. Without any effort at all, Annie had become the key to a place in her heart that she had kept locked for a long time.

"No. I haven't found her family. At least . . ." His eyes clouded. "At least I don't think I have. But something very strange has happened." He pulled a folded paper out of his inside pocket. "I sent Annie's fingerprints to the State Crime Lab to see if there were any hits—before I knew her, I thought maybe it was possible she had some kind of petty crime record. Anyway," he continued. "The computer system came up empty, so someone with too much time on his hands at the state lab decided to check through the old files which haven't been transferred online yet. The report came this morning. It took a while, but the lab identified them. They're an 89% match for a girl named Charlotte Eagleston." He paused, not certain how to explain the problem. "She died in 1968. Gunshot. Salt Lake City. She was 13 years old."

Ramona eased herself deeper into the couch with exasperation. "Some idiot made a mistake. Not surprising since most employees are like the B-/C+ students I used to have—do the minimum and don't bother with doing the job right." It was an old theme with Ramona. She'd never had much patience with mediocre students. Just too dang lazy, she always said.

Gifford had heard it before. Ramona had never bothered to keep her opinions to herself. Not even during school hours. "The police report says this Charlotte was walking her little sister home from school. She always took a short-cut through the backlot of a movie theater. Apparently, a couple of guys were in a neighboring yard cleaning their rifles in preparation to go pheasant hunting. One of the guns went off, ricocheted off the pole of a chain-link fence, and hit the girl in the chest. She died at the scene."

"My God," Ramona said, appalled by the idea of another mother losing a child. When did it ever end? "But how does that connect to Annie? Is that some relative or something? I don't understand."

"Exactly. There's the problem. How could Annie's fingerprints be so similar to a girl who died almost 50 years ago? I did a little checking. Dad abandoned Charlotte's family years before. Mom had been on track to become a concert pianist but had to quit school to support the two girls. Taught piano lessons—even sponsored a group class on Saturdays for mostly Hispanic kids whose parents could never have afforded music lessons for their children. Seemed to be loved by everybody in the neighborhood but disappeared after Charlotte's death. No connection to Annie at all as far as I can tell. To be frank, Mrs. Z., fingerprints don't lie, but it makes no sense. I was hoping maybe Annie has said something that might give us a clue about what to do next."

"Well," Ramona considered, "Annie obviously didn't die 50 years ago. I don't know much about fingerprint procedures, but that was a long time ago. No computer scanning back then. I assume that means all the work must have been done by hand?"

"Most likely."

"Like I said, somebody made a mistake."

"Possibly. But fingerprinting has been pretty accurate since the time Sherlock Holmes invented it."

Ramona raised an eyebrow. "Sherlock Holmes?" she couldn't resist. "See, I told you that life imitates fiction!"

Gifford ignored the I-told-you-so. "Annie hasn't remembered anything about her past at all? Nothing?"

"The only reference she's made about her life is that a little Hispanic girl reminded her of someone, but she had no idea of who."

"That little girl about kindergarten age?" Gifford asked sharply.

"Younger," Ramona replied. "But bossy, very bossy. Still, if you think about it, we actually know quite a bit about Annie's background. Approximate age; some kind of voice training; excellent vocabulary; unusually good manners suggesting strong family influence; a smattering of Spanish—all those imply an upwardly mobile framework. And don't forget creative." She told him about Annie's idea for the choir concert.

Gifford shook his head in frustration. The image of Annie handing him a bag of Christmas cookies leaped into his head. Experience had taught him that kindness was a behavior that didn't just spring from the gene pool. Someone had patiently modeled it for the child. And she appeared to have learned the lesson well. "The whole thing just doesn't make sense. I asked the Crime Lab if they had any pictures of this Charlotte or the family. Maybe a distant relative or something? They'll email them to me if they find anything." Gifford didn't believe in coincidence. There had to be a connection. Got a guy in the capitol looking into the whole mess for me. It's possible he'll have something for me in a couple of days. What I can't figure out is why someone hasn't reported Annie missing. A kid like that? She must matter to someone."

"She matters to a lot of people," Ramona said. "A lot of people," she repeated.

Thursday, December 12

2 PM

RAMONA'S PHONE CALL TO JANEEN the day before about Leon's idea hadn't gone well.

"You've GOT to be kidding," Janeen had barked. "We are not holding the concert in that DUMP downtown. We are talking about a SERIOUS musical presentation here, not some sort of CARNIVAL sideshow. ABSOLUTELY NOT."

The sectional leaders' meeting on Thursday afternoon was more positive. The deciding factor was Amy Holstum. "I think it's a wonderful idea. We can get the whole community involved. It's been a long time since people in this town cared about what was happening to the downtown. Let's give them a reason to pay attention."

Janeen howled, but ultimately, she gave in, largely because the idea of having to cancel the concert was so repugnant. "It's TRADITION, people!" as she had pointed out at least 15 times during the meeting.

"Well, it may be tradition, but renovating that building so it's useable is going to require all of us to donate some considerable time," reminded Nephi Henderson, the current choir president. His wasn't the strongest voice in the choir, but his down-to-earth practicality and common sense often swayed the opinions of the larger group.

Ramona spoke up. "The kids will show up. When I was teaching school, I could always depend on them—it was their parents who weaseled out of volunteering." She cast a withering glance at each one in the room.

"What about money? It's going to cost a fortune just for enough paint to cover the walls."

"I have an idea about how to jump that hurdle," Ramona said. "I'll get back to you."

6:30 PM

John Callister met Ramona at the Seaweed Bar and Grill. He'd suggested they might as well have dinner while she explained her proposal. Privately, Ramona thought it was a less-than-appropriate place for a man of John's prominence in the community, but he'd brushed aside her complaints.

"I like Willy," he said. "The food's good, and he needs the business."

She couldn't argue with that. And, she admitted, it had the advantage of sheltering them from the prying eyes of the Town Council, whose political ambitions depended on a wholesome 'family image'. A place like the Seaweed wouldn't be good for their reputations.

Willy had greeted the Judge like an old friend and seated them at a corner table near the back of the bar. "Only the best for the Judge," he said.

Ramona wondered what prompted that kind of deference from Willy, but she didn't ask. Some things were best left undiscovered. And John was right. The food was excellent. Her jumbo shrimp was light and crispy, and she loved the coconut mango sauce Willy provided as a dip. As far as she could tell, there were no sloppy or angry drunks hidden in the shadows. Who knew? She might have to bring Viola and Annie here someday for lunch.

"So, what's your plan to throw a chink in" he looked around to be sure it was safe to be politically incorrect 'Queen' Jesse's agenda?"

Ramona filled him in about Annie's idea to use the old Christensen's building to house the concert. "Here's the deal," she summarized. "If we can pull off a concert there and make the place look presentable to the audience, we have a lever we can use to convince voters that demolishing the downtown is unnecessary. We can argue that restoration is a better plan—not to mention a lot cheaper."

Callister rolled the idea over in his mind, nodding as it unfolded. "I like it," he agreed. "I assume you're planning to use a magic wand to transform the place overnight? It needs some serious upgrading just to make it safe."

"Viola took Harold Elliot over there to look around this morning."

Ramona knew dropping Harold's name was an argument in her favor. He was the retired zoning commissioner and well-respected by virtually everyone in town—even Queen Jesse Simpson. "He says most of the problems are cosmetic. Except for some wallboard replacements in the ceiling and walls, he thinks it's still up to code. It just needs a lot of man-hours to make it look presentable. The front windows will have to be replaced, which is going to be the biggest cost. And convincing the city to turn on lights and water for a week will be a problem. On the other hand, it has plenty of room for our audience. We'll have to ask the high school if there are enough undamaged folding chairs left to seat a crowd that large. I'm sure the schools' stage crew could rig up a sound system for us with Henry's supervision." She paused. "I think it has real possibilities, and I'd love to see Jesse Simpson's face when we light up that building and invite the town in." Her look of self-righteous satisfaction was all the convincing John Callister needed.

"Now I see what you're really proposing. It would certainly take down the Mayor's plan a notch or two." He dipped another shrimp into the sauce and chewed as he considered the option. "But if Harold thinks it can be done, maybe it can." Wiping at an errant drip next to his plate, he asked, "Where do you plan to find the numbers of volunteers you'll need to make this happen?"

"That's the beauty of it, John. We use kids from the high school. The carpentry and construction class can do the drywall. Their teacher is contacting them as we speak. And the painting? Practically any kid can hold a brush. The big problem is money. It's going to cost a bit, especially replacing those front windows, and we can't wait for donations to pour in. We needed to start yesterday to finish by a week from Friday's dress rehearsal. That's where you come in."

"You want me to back the project?" He asked in disbelief. "You must have an inflated idea of what judges in small towns make."

"No. I don't want your money. I want you to convince the County Bar Association to provide the funds. They sponsor those charitable grants that are targeted at community improvement." She finished in triumph. "What better way to improve the community than to invest in a project that creates volunteer work for teenagers and lets them see how a small group of people can change the world!"

Callister's eyes twinkled. "Now I get it. You aren't really interested in me at all. You're just going to use me and cast me aside after you get what you want." He struck a judicial pose. "Well, this is going to cost you." He paused a moment to think. "OK. Here's what I want. If I get the Association to front the money, you must have dinner with me one evening a week for a month. And," he held up his hand to stop her from sputtering. "And you have to enjoy it—without complaint. Of any kind," he emphasized.

"Good grief!" she said. "You aren't any easier to get along with than you were when we were in high school. No wonder I picked Amos instead of you."

Friday, December 13

8 AM

Belen opened her eyes. Her room was still dark. There was no sound from her father's room down the hall from hers, but something had awakened her. She lay still listening. The house was quiet; no wind for the first time in what seemed like weeks. She closed her eyes. Without warning her stomach tightened painfully for a long moment, then released. Her back ached, and she shifted position, curling into a little ball to relieve pressure on it. That felt better. She dozed.

When she awoke again, sunlight was streaming in the window. For the first time in a long time, she felt lighthearted. She looked forward to her weekly walk to the library. For a change, she wouldn't have to clutch the hood of her wool coat around her head as protection from the icy wind. As always, her first thought was of Eduardo. She rubbed her stomach affectionately. The baby moved beneath her hands. "So, Little One. You think of him, too."

****

A few blocks away Eduardo was lying on his bed staring at the ceiling. His little brothers were attempting to lift Alejandro out of his crib, but now that he was almost one, he managed to wriggle out of their grasp. The fact that they were both barely taller than the railing of the crib didn't help. Eduardo laughed. But he sobered instantly when he remembered that soon he would have a baby to lift from the crib each morning. He took a deep breath. The weight of his worry descended on him again.

Without warning Marisa bounded into the room, slamming the door against the wall with a thud. Her pajama tops and bottoms were mismatched, and her ponytail was limp, crushed, and hanging over her left ear from the constant twisting she did in her sleep. Eduardo had learned early that laying her next to him for a nap meant she would eventually go to sleep, and that he would have bruises in the ribs where she kicked him as she dozed. The younger boys eyed her warily.

"Mama says breakfast is ready," she announced. "*¡Vamos ahora!*"

The little girl's assumption that she was in charge had long ago overcome any resistance the boys had to her bossy attitude, though it infuriated his younger brothers and amused to Eduardo. They obediently headed for the kitchen, Eduardo lifting the baby into his arms as he went. Already at the table when they entered the kitchen, their father passed each a glass of milk.

"Eduardo, you will work at the shop again today?" His father asked.

"Yeah. Probably." Eduardo answered as he slipped Alejandro into the highchair and secured the tray. The baby looked for his mother and wailed for food. Eduardo automatically grabbed a box of Cheerios and sprinkled a few on the tray. The baby stopped mid-yell, grabbed a handful and crammed them into this mouth.

Eduardo and his father smiled in unison.

"Mr. Cisneros told me he has several oil changes scheduled today. Kids with cars are bringing them in since there's no school." Eduardo concentrated on buttering the toast and passing slices to his younger siblings, hoping his father didn't notice the envy that he felt every time one of his classmates handed him the keys to a car for a lube job in the garage.

Luz finished stirring the sauce at the stove where she was cooking huevos rancheros. She stared at him thoughtfully as she carried the pan to the table and spooned eggs onto the plates. "Do you have something else to do?" she asked.

"I thought I might go over to the library a little while this morning." He was careful to keep his eyes on the plate in front of him. His stepmother wasn't easily fooled.

"School is closed, and the first thing you want to do is study?" His father asked in disbelief.

"Not study. I need to use the internet." He focused on spooning the spicy eggs his stepmother had ladled onto his plate into his mouth as if he had no other concerns. "I want to do some research about . . . college." It was what his parents wanted to hear he recognized with a pang of guilt.

"Ah," nodded his father approvingly. He settled back into attacking his breakfast. "It is good to consider the future."

Eduardo kept the relief out of his voice. "Maybe I could come over to the garage later?"

Once he had finished eating, he rose--automatically grabbing a wet wipe and sponging off the faces of three-year-old Jesus and the baby. Somehow Alejandro had managed to get salsa between his toes. Eduardo caught his stepmother's eye. She shook her head in mock horror. The baby giggled and grabbed for the wipe as it tickled his feet.

9 AM

Though he had no intention of doing a college search at the library, Eduardo grabbed his backpack. He checked the bottom of the zipper pocket to be sure the silver charm bracelet he had bought Belen for Christmas several weeks ago was still inside. It had taken him three visits to the little boutique next to the cosmetology school to find exactly the right charm—the tiny heart with the words "*nuestros tesoro*—our treasure" now hung from the delicate silver filigree chain, both their initials engraved on the back. He pictured her delight when she opened the gift and read the inscription. Adding a charm for each year of the baby's life, he intended the bracelet to be a visible reminder of his love for her and the coming child. Today, because they had time to spend a few hours together, he would give it to her—an early Christmas present.

He slipped out of the house and stopped on the front porch to text her that he would meet her at their table near the back of the non-fiction section of the library. Her father allowed her a regular trip every Friday to choose several books to read in the long hours she spent cloistered at home. Belen saved those precious hours until Eduardo could join her.

"Eduardo?" His stepmother opened the front door and pushed the storm door wide. She wiped her hands on her apron as she momentarily shivered in the cold without her coat. "Eduardo. Can I help you?"

"What?" Startled, he turned toward her, shoving his phone into his pocket.

"It is not difficult to see that you have worry. I would like to help if I can."

She took a step toward him, putting her hand gently on his arm. "You are my son," she said. "It makes me sad to see you unhappy."

For a moment he could think of nothing to say. The tenderness in her voice almost dissolved his resolution. He struggled with his instinctive reaction to tell her everything and let someone share his burden. But he would not. She was not his mother, still, he knew that she had loved the silent, solemn boy he had been from the moment his father had first introduced them. It was she who bandaged his knees when he insisted he didn't need foam pads as he learned to skateboard and soothed his nightmares when he woke in the dark. I am fine," he assured her. "It's just weird that I don't have school today, I guess." He knew it sounded lame, but she accepted his excuse without comment.

She studied his face. "I am sorry that the little ones take up so much of my time. You are strong, so strong. But you are still young. Perhaps there are burdens you do not share with us? Let us help." She paused. "Remember you will always be our child."

Eduardo twisted away from her, fearing that he would not be able to resist the genuine concern in her voice. When he turned back, he placed his hand over hers still resting on his arm. "We are all lucky to have you," he said, and he kissed her lightly on the check. "You're cold. Go back inside. I will be home after work." He held the door open for her to go back inside, thinking not for the first time, what a fortunate man his father was.

When he arrived at the library, he ducked into the stacks and headed for 'their' table to wait for Belen. Months ago, when they had first realized that she was pregnant, he had borrowed his father's truck, leaving work after complaining of stomach pains. He arranged to meet Belen at the 7/11 down the street from her house. They didn't dare go to the library or a local store. Too many classmates to see them and wonder. He'd heard about an out-of-town bookstore which specialized in women's books. Belen knew nothing about having a baby. In fact, because of four younger siblings, he knew more than she did, but it wasn't enough. Together they had driven to Newman in search of information. That was before. When he still thought that knowledge mattered.

He had parked right in front of the bookstore so that he could see Belen as she walked in alone. Considering what they were planning on buying, he didn't want anyone to notice they were together. Through the front window, he'd watched as she browsed the shelves, occasionally smiling at him as she stole a glance over her shoulder. Their plan was simple. She would pretend to be browsing through the health section and locate the book they'd read about on the internet. She'd casually leave it on the end of a shelf where it would be easy for Eduardo to spot. Then she'd head back to the truck; he'd go in, grab the book, and pay for it. They'd debated whether it would be better for him to just go in and buy it, but she insisted that if they were going to spend that kind of money, she wanted to be sure the book was exactly what they needed. He finally gave in. Not because he agreed with her, but because he couldn't deny her anything. He wasn't sure if he would ever be able to.

He watched as she browsed through what looked like a whole section on pregnancy and childbirth, going from one text to another, reading the tables of content, examining pictures. Finally, she settled on a book and purposefully placed it on the end of a shelf where he could clearly see it. Then she wandered out of the store as if she hadn't found anything that interested her.

Once she was back in the truck, he slid out of the driver's seat, brushing his hand against hers as he left. Heading into the bookstore, he pretended to look around nervously. "Have you got any books about having babies," he asked the plump, short woman at the cash register.

"You having one?" she asked him cheerfully, tactfully ignoring his obvious youth.

"No. It's my mother. She's remarried, and now she thinks she's pregnant. It's been a while since she had me, and she's throwing up, so she sent me down here to get a couple of books on babies." He shrugged his shoulders in a gesture of annoyance as much as resignation.

"Sure," she said in obvious sympathy to his apparent discomfort. "Right over here." She led him a large section of colorful books which touted the wonders of having a baby.

After she headed back to the front of the store, he sorted through the shelves and, when he was sure no one was looking, picked up the book Belen had left at the end of the shelf: What to Expect When You Are Expecting. It wasn't cheap. One more thing to deplete his meager income, but he figured they didn't have much choice. And once she told her father, Eduardo suspected that going to the doctor together was going to be out of the question.

"Here you go," the woman said as she handed him the package after he had paid for the book. "And here's a little reminder for you when you need a book on potty training." She laughed at her own joke as she handed him a small red plastic heart attached to a key chain. It was stamped with an old-fashioned feather pen atop a small inkpot and the words Linford Books in bold letters.

Eduardo remembered his anxiety after he had dropped Belen off at home that day. Would his father figure out that he hadn't gone straight home to bed? Perhaps he could say he'd had to stop at the school to pick up homework? But no one had seemed the least bit concerned, even if they had noticed the time-lapse. When he got home and told Luz he didn't feel well, she clucked over him, checking his temperature and putting him to bed with a glass of 7-Up to calm his stomach.

The next day he had taken the book with him to the county library and placed it incongruously on the shelf between a stack of heavy tomes about Utah history. Weekly when he met Belen secretly at the library, they poured over the book, reading details about the progress of the fetus and the mother's body changes. They were pretty sure they were becoming experts on having a baby.

Waiting now for Belen, he pulled the book off the lower shelf where it was hidden and randomly began to read.

He caught the scent of her perfume even before she rounded the corner and came into view. She winced and held her hand protectively over her belly. "It is the contractions—the practice ones it talks about in the book," she explained gesturing to the book he was reading as he jumped to his feet to help her. "They come more often now." She settled into the chair next to him, breathing heavily. "The Little One is getting impatient."

He glanced in both directions, making certain no one was nearby, then he put his arm around her shoulders and drew her to him, her head resting against him. "What does the doctor say?"

"She says the baby is right on schedule. My father is taking me every week now. Soon my pregnant clothes won't fit. I shall become a whale, and you will think I am too ugly to love."

"That day will never come." As proof, he dug into his backpack and pulled out the tiny package. "Here I have brought your Christmas gift. It is early, but . . ." his voice trailed off. He had no excuse. He just wanted to share it with her. Now. Today.

She smiled. I love you, she mouthed as she unwrapped the small box and lifted the lid. The intricate, silver filigree bracelet lay spread out on a bed of soft blue velvet, its single charm glimmering in the light of the reading lamp next to her. "Oh," she exhaled. "It is so lovely." She gently turned his face toward her. Kissing his cheek, she said. "I have never owned anything so beautiful." She lifted the chain and held the small heart up to read its inscription. "It is for the baby," she whispered, and she started to weep.

"No, no," Eduardo said alarmed. "I didn't mean to make you sad. I wanted . . ." he tried to explain, but no words came.

She put her finger on his lips to stop him. "We love it. You could not have chosen a finer gift. Here, help me put it on." She held her wrist up to him.

A bolt of electricity went through him when he touched her. His fingers fumbled with the clasp, but he managed to attach it to her wrist. He wasn't sure he had the strength to let go of her hand. Determination swept over him. Enough of this hiding and the endless secrets. He could do it no longer.

"Belen," he said. "It is time for us to be together. I will talk to your father. He will understand."

Instantly she was frantic; she looked at him with dread. "My father . . ." she began. "He is getting worse. You do not know him. He will not understand. Never." She bit her lip. "My mother left us when I was seven. One day she walked out the door and never came back." Eduardo already knew the story; she had told him many times. "After that, he was different. We stopped going anywhere with friends or even to the church. He believes that someday I will try to leave him too. And he will stop me." She touched his face tenderly. "If he finds out who you are, he will take me away." Her eyes pleaded with him to reconsider. "I could not live without you. And the baby."

His certainty wavered. "Then I will speak to my father. Our house is very small, but we will find a way. Perhaps the baby can have Alejandro's crib. He is almost too big for it anyway." He fingered the bracelet as he held her hand. "Mr. Cisneros would hire me full time, I know it." He hoped it was true. "I can quit school--there is nothing there anyway. I will work, and we will get a small place like my parents did." Unbidden, the memory of a tiny sitting room with a rocking chair and a worn futon came into his head. Perhaps the old woman still lived and would be willing to rent to another young couple with a baby? His grandmother would know.

In his mind, it was decided. His determination brought a sense of finality. It was what a man would do. It was time.

Saturday, December 14

9 AM

ACROSS TOWN, HENRY MET RAMONA, Viola, Annie, a half a dozen teachers, and 25 or 30 kids at the front door of Christensen's with the keys. "Judge got 'em from the real estate office," Henry explained, holding the keys awkwardly in his left hand because his right hand was still swathed in bandages. "He said breaking and entering was not an 'aus-pi-cious" he was careful to sound out the word exactly as the Judge had pronounced it, "way to start."

Ramona patted Henry on the back, whispering as she did so, "I was so worried that you were caught in the fire. Thank goodness it wasn't worse." Then she straightened, raised an eyebrow at him, and commanded, "Well, let us in already."

Viola shook her head in disapproval. "Nice, really nice," she muttered.

Henry pulled open the double doors, and the group crowded in. The hall was dark and smelled faintly of urine. Though most of the larger fixtures had been sold off, there was rubble everywhere. Chunks of wallboard hung randomly from several spots on the lofty ceiling. The expansive space was covered with mangled metal clothing racks, boxes overflowing with cheap plastic hangers and pricing paraphernalia, litter from local fast food joints, even rocks and old newspapers which had been balled up and thrown through the windows by vandals sometime in the past. Not only that, but the room was also freezing. The sharp winter sun outside was denied access to the room by the large plywood panels which now covered the shattered panes.

The volunteers huddled together in the doorway, most shocked speechless by what they saw. Every eye scanned the chaos. A couple of the smaller students wrapped their arms around their chests and shivered with the cold. An older girl pulled off her sweatshirt and handed it to her younger sister.

"I didn't know it would be this bad," Annie began. "Maybe I made a mistake?" she beseeched Ramona.

"Nope," interjected Leon cheerfully. "There are enough of us that it should only take us a couple of hours to clean up the trash. There's an old dumpster out back that hasn't been used since the store closed. I brought a box of trash bags for the smaller stuff. He started handing out the 50-gallon, heavy-duty sacks. "Besides--the harder we work, the warmer it gets. Let's go!"

Several students, used to jumping whenever a teacher assigned a task, detached themselves from the group and started toward the nearest trash. Others followed. Leon's optimism was catching.

Ollie Haverfield, his buddy Tyler, and a couple of other boys from the basketball team scanned the room, spotted the largest piece of drywall fallen from the ceiling, and spearheaded an assault as if it were a rival team member in the way of a game-winning shot. It took all four of them to heft it to their shoulders, but they managed it and disappeared with their burden somewhere through the archway that led to the offices and dressing rooms in the back.

Carrie Jane followed the group as it dispersed into different sections of the room. She was disappointed to see that Eduardo Caballero hadn't shown up, even though most of the other students from her 2nd period English class were there--including Tristen Holyoak. Carrie Jane was amused to see that Tristen was already picking up crinkled advertising flyers and reading them instead of chucking them in the trash.

"Somebody prop those front doors open, and Carrie Jane why don't you and Flor take that crowbar Henry brought and see if you can pull down the plywood across those windows. We need a little light in here," Ramona barked out orders like a drill sergeant. "Everybody else come get a trash bag or start carting junk out to the dumpster." She added, "Kids from the carpentry class will be here later today to start repairing those holes in the walls." Within minutes the huge empty space echoed with the clatter of kids' laughing voices and the scrapping of debris into dustpans and garbage sacks. Ramona and Viola looked at each other. The teenagers obviously thought this was fun, but for the older women, it was going to be a long day.

As the time neared when the carpentry class was expected, a good start had been made on the garbage which students had been gathering up and carting to the dumpster. Now half dozen students were manning brooms sweeping smaller components of rubble into piles for disposal. The combination of the sun warming the air and the physical labor had banished the cold, although the room temperature was still less than 50 degrees, Ramona guessed.

In one corner a couple of senior girls had seen Annie working by herself. She was having trouble lifting a twisted piece of clothing rack out from under a bulky hunk of broken drywall so that she could drag it away. The older girls swooped in to lend a hand. Within minutes the three had become a team, plowing through piles of junk and stacking it for the stronger boys to carry off. Ramona noted with approval that the older girls were neither condescending nor domineering; they accepted Annie without reservations. It was a pleasure to see the young girl interact with people closer to her own age for a change.

By the time Crawford Hyunh and his crew arrived, most of the large pieces of debris had been cleared away. He commandeered several workers to help his students unload sections of scaffolding for the ceiling repair. Before they were finished assembling the structures, a truck from the local Home Depot pulled up in front of the store. John Callister climbed out of the cab and waved Ramona over.

"OK, I got your grant. And I convinced Home Depot to donate a truck to us for a few days to haul all the repair equipment in. Jackson Allred says you owe him big time."

Ramona dismissed Allred's stipulation with a shrug. "Jackson was a smart-alec kid, and now he's a smooth-talking lawyer. Just because he's president of the County Bar doesn't mean he's in charge. Tell him I'll deal with him later."

Callister laughed out loud. "He's going to love having that to look forward to." He headed inside the building. "Couple of you guys wanna help me unload this wallboard?" Several kids dropped what they were doing and lined up to help. At least one of them suspected it was a prudent idea to get on the good side of the judge. You could never tell when that might be useful.

By 4 PM daylight was waning. The light streaming in from the openings which had once housed glass front windows had dimmed to shadows in the back half of the room. The enthusiasm evident earlier in the day had drifted into mechanical determination. Several teens had already left for their shifts at local fast food eateries, and a couple were seated with their backs against the wall checking their phones and listening to music. One or two bored workers had furtively slipped out the back door unnoticed. Now there were fewer than 6 or 8 teenagers left. The labor was reduced to a trickle of effort.

Leon called the workers together. "Hey folks, you've done a fantastic job here. Our light is almost gone, so I think it's time to go home. Home Depot had to special order the windows from Salt Lake, but the Judge says they'll be here by Monday. Tomorrow we finish up the trash and start washing down the walls that don't need patching so they are ready to paint." There was a groan in unison from his listeners. "If you can, bring a bucket, a couple of rags, and something like 409 or dish detergent. Oh, and bring a friend." His audience looked dubious. "If you need help convincing them to come, Ollie and his buddies would be happy to come over and exert a little tender enforcement."

Ollie preened and flexed his muscles. His buddies nodded in approval.

Leon went on. "The more people, the faster we get done." He turned to the construction class crew who were covered from head to foot in drywall dust. "You guys are awesome," he said. "Smart move to bring your superheroes' costumes." The kids laughed good-naturedly.

"Hey, Mr. Westerfeld, this place looks better this afternoon than it did this morning, but there's a ton of work left. Do you really think we can do this, or are we just wastin' our time?" Mason Redfeld pushed his glasses back up on his nose as he spoke. "My dad says this is a dumb idea, and it's never gonna work."

"What do you think, Mason?" Leon countered. "Is your dad right?"

Mason looked carefully around the big hall; all the large junk had been hauled out to the dumpster. Most of the smaller debris was either gone or piled in neat stacks waiting for teams to scoop it up and take it outside. Drywall had been cut to fit and screwed into the largest of the gaping holes that had freckled the walls and ceiling. Even the leftover drywall scraps were stacked and ready for removal. Damp tape glowed along the edges of the repairs waiting for another coat of spackle. Clearly though, the bones of the room were now visible. The whole place seemed more spacious. Not a man to waste words, Mason concluded, "It's good. We did good." The group let go of its collective breath, and a couple of guys near Mason patted him on the back.

"Exactly," agreed Leon.

Sunday, December 15

2 PM

Detective Gifford was at his desk finishing the paperwork on a small burglary ring that had been plaguing mostly Hispanic residents in the area. He signed the report and clipped the file together, happy to have the young thugs in jail. What's wrong with this picture? Kids who think it's OK to prey on the families of other kids? he wondered. The file contained pictures of the wanton destruction the thieves had left behind as they searched for anything valuable enough to be exchanged for drugs. Gifford sighed. Homes of one family after another had been violated; their sense of security defiled because there seemed to be a whole generation growing up thinking only about themselves—not a clue about the ripples their behavior created in the lives of other people.

Unbidden, a sudden vision of his route yesterday past the old Christensen's building popped into his head. When he'd spotted Carrie Jane in the crowd, he'd pulled the car over to see what was going on. Just checking to be sure nothing is happening on the wrong side of the law, he told himself. Huge sheets of plywood had been ripped from the storefront windows and the place filled with teenagers plus a few adults cleaning out the garbage that had piled up over the last couple of years. When Carrie Jane told him about their intention to refurbish the building enough to hold their annual *Messiah* concert in it, he'd been brought up short. Watching the teens tackle what seemed like an insurmountable job—an impossible one, he thought privately--with enthusiasm and dedication reminded him that the kids he encountered were only a very small percentage of the teenagers in this town. It was the reason he stayed in Douglas Valley—good families raising their children so that they could raise good families themselves.

"I didn't know you could sing," Gifford had said in response to the concert preparations, looking down at her face damp with sweat and her hair covered in drywall dust.

"There's a lot you don't know about me," she'd countered absently pushing a wisp of unruly red hair behind her ear. "Maybe you need to investigate more thoroughly," she teased him.

"Yes, Ma'am. Does seem like I've been derelict in that area," he'd agreed.

And before he could arrange a date to remedy the situation, she'd turned and yelled, "Ollie, careful. Look behind you—you almost trampled Annie." Ollie shifted a full sheet of wallboard to his left shoulder and sidestepped the girl just before he knocked her flat. He grinned sheepishly. Sorry, he mouthed to her.

"Now what were you saying?" Carrie Jane looked back at Gifford.

Gifford retreated to safer territory. "That I'll be over tomorrow afternoon when I finish my shift and give you guys a hand."

"A police presence is always appreciated," she's said and unexpectedly reached up to kiss him on the cheek. "That's for being a good guy. Thanks."

Gifford felt like he'd just been awarded a White Hat. As soon as this workday was over, he intended to follow through on his promise. The vibration of his cell phone startled him from his very pleasant daydream. But it wasn't Carrie Jane. It was Ramona.

"Mark," she said without greeting. "Get over here to Christensen's. Annie saw the white-haired man again." Then the phone went dead.

Gifford took off at a run, rolling out of the police parking lot and shoving his flashing light on the roof as he sped toward downtown. He had a lot of questions for the white-haired guy, and he intended to get some answers.

Gifford maneuvered his unmarked car in front of the fire hydrant, the only parking space left on the street by Christensen's. He was out of the vehicle before it had rolled to a complete stop. Ramona waited for him on the curb, her arm around Annie---who looked like a deer in the headlights. Viola stood next to them--a sentry protecting her village from attack. The young woman and the two older ones greeted him with obvious relief.

"Where is he?" Gifford demanded, surveying the work crowd who had abandoned their jobs and were now gathered in front of the store.

Gifford had a fleeting impression of a much larger group than yesterday.

"Where is he?" he asked again, scanning the area for any sign of shoulder-length white hair.

"Around the corner," Annie pointed to the end of the block.

Gifford sprinted down the side of the building and swung into the alley. The long narrow lane wove behind buildings for several blocks in either direction. There was nothing moving either east or west as far as Gifford could see. Calling the dispatcher for backup as he went, Gifford headed west toward what was the more commercial section of town. He checked with the clerks of the only two viable businesses next to Christensen's—a TruValue store and a beauty supply. Neither had seen a white-haired guy, and no one had entered either store from the back. From there the alley opened onto a side street; Gifford sprinted across to the Seaweed Bar and Grill. Willie was washing the front windows, and the clean glass reflected the sun so brightly that it was impossible to see inside.

"If that guy had come this way, I'd have seen him," he told Gifford. "The whole street has been dead today. Not even one customer yet," he added in disgust.

Gifford noted the irony that no one was drinking yet. From his point of view, that was good news. "Thanks, Willie. Let me know if you spot him."

"Sure, Giff." Willie set his bucket down, intending to visit a few minutes, but Gifford was already headed back the way he came.

"You ever find out who that girl was?" Willie called out. Gifford was too far away to hear.

A black and white police car came barreling along the street past Willie, its lights flashing and siren screaming. It screeched to a halt alongside Gifford's car a half a block up.

The patrolman was already out of the car and talking to the two women when Gifford jogged back up to join them. "Detective Gifford," the patrolman acknowledged his superior's arrival without moving his concentration from the girl he was questioning.

"Shaloe," Gifford returned, his eyes already scanning the crowd for any sign of the white-haired man. Sometimes suspects were so enamored of the upheaval they caused, they couldn't resist watching the fallout from an inconspicuous spot in a crowd, but none of the faces surrounding him sported white hair. Even Ramona and Viola, probably the oldest people in the group, had varying shades of gray, not white, frosting their former vibrant hair colors. He shook his head in frustration. "How on earth did he slip away?" he said to no one in particular.

Patrolman Shaloe looked up. "Should I start a door-to-door, Sir?"

Gifford nodded. "Let's finish hearing the details first, but then we'll split up and canvas the street."

Carrie Jane and a couple of other teachers nodded in Gifford's direction but said nothing. Most of the kids were so intent on listening to the conversation that they'd pulled the headphones out of their ears. Unconsciously, they had formed a semi-circle around Annie and her guardians.

"There was still a lot of glass on the sidewalk out here. I was sweeping it up when he came around the corner," Annie began, clearly shaken, but Gifford registered a moment of relief when he realized she hadn't retreated to the frightened stranger she had been when Gifford first met her.

"I didn't notice him till he talked to me. I had my back toward him," she explained, "and out of nowhere this voice asked me if I still had the paper he gave me?" She looked at Ramona. Her voice wavered. "For a minute I was really scared, that's why I screamed for you."

"You did the right thing," Ramona assured her, wrapping her arm tighter around the girl. She addressed Gifford. "By the time I got out here, all we saw was a glimpse of white hair headed into the alley. Then I called you." She glanced at Viola. "We're a little past the age of tracking suspects all over town," she apologized.

Privately, Gifford wished more of the residents of Douglas Valley would adopt that attitude. As if to contest his unspoken thought, out of the corner of his eye, Gifford saw half-a-dozen unusually tall boys appear from the east end of the block. He recognized a couple of them from the high school basketball games he occasionally attended. They slowed their pace as they arrived, shaking their heads at Annie as they came.

"We couldn't find him," the obvious leader of the boys said. "He must have been moving fast 'cause we couldn't have been more than a minute or so behind him after you screamed, but he'd just disappeared. It was kinda weird." He searched his buddies' faces for agreement. They nodded their heads. "I mean he had white hair. How could an old guy like that have moved so fast?"

"And you are?" Gifford questioned.

"He's one of my students," Carrie Jane called, moving to the front of the crowd. "Oliver, Oliver Haverfield."

"You guys chased this 'white-haired' man? Did it occur to you he might be dangerous, maybe even armed?" Gifford spit out the words. "This guy isn't some ballplayer trying to show off his machismo. He could be stalking a future victim. You guys," his look included the half dozen kids with Ollie. His voice steeled, "You guys stay away from him and let us do our job," he ordered.

Ollie looked startled. "That old guy? We," included his buddies in his gesture, "we could have taken him. No trouble," Ollie he answered confidently.

Gifford stared at the boys until one by one, they lowered their eyes.

"Mark, they were just trying to help," Carrie Jane interjected.

Gifford nodded and changed the subject. "Annie," his face softened, "what was he wearing? Did you notice anything different about him? How tall do you think he was? Taller or shorter than me?"

"Shorter," Annie said promptly. "A little taller than Ramona. He was wearing that same coat, but it wasn't buttoned-up, so I could see he had on a white shirt. And white pants." She appeared genuinely confused. "Who wears white pants in the cold?"

"White?" repeated Gifford, raising an eyebrow. He turned to the young patrolman. "Any businesses around here use white uniforms?"

"Bakery down on 4th," Shaloe answered promptly. "Maybe the guys who work out at the dental supply warehouse on this side of Newman. Nobody else I can think of offhand, Sir."

Gifford focused on Annie again. "Did he say anything else? Anything at all?"

"Yes," Annie answered. "He told me I'd need that paper. I asked him 'why'? But he was already moving around the corner toward the alley."

Gifford was relieved to note that she seemed more puzzled than upset. On the other hand, Gifford was upset--very upset. He didn't like people who tried to manipulate kids. He intended to find this guy and see what the hell was going on.

"Detective Gifford?" Annie's voice was tentative. "Do you still have that paper he gave me?"

Gifford nodded. "It's in an evidence box at the station. Don't worry; it doesn't go anywhere until we find out what this is all about. And where you belong." He added in response to the automatic protective instinct that arose in him whenever he interacted with the girl.

Ramona and Viola looked at each other in unspoken agreement. She belongs here, they thought simultaneously.

Tuesday, December 17

9 AM

EDUARDO SAT AT THE KITCHEN table making a list; he glanced around occasionally to be sure no one could slip up on him and peer over his shoulder. The baby was down for a nap in his *abuela's* back bedroom. He'd delivered the two younger boys to play at the neighbor's house and assured his stepmother that she and Marisa could do the grocery shopping without concern about the little ones. He stared at the classified ads in the free advertising brochure he'd picked up from the 7-11 across from the high school the week before. The ink had worn away at the creases because he'd unfolded and then refolded the pages so many times in the last few days. Staring absently at the stove, he rubbed a pencil back and forth between his fingers as he thought. How could he have been so naïve to believe that he and Belen could find a life for themselves? Just figuring rent and utilities came to more than his entire salary, even if he went full time at the garage. That didn't include food or diapers or gas—for a car he didn't have.

When he'd found out about the baby, he'd opened a savings account at the bank, but even now after eight months, he'd only managed to save $1000.00. Maybe enough for a first month's deposit and rent in some crappy unfurnished apartment that would probably have broken plumbing and cockroaches. He couldn't take Belen to a place like that. And Christmas was only a few days away. He knew his parents were counting on the gifts he would give his younger siblings to supplement the meager offerings they had been choosing carefully all year. But he hadn't purchased a single item. His own problems were weighing so heavily on his mind that he'd barely been conscious of the season, must less the fact that he needed gifts for his sister and brothers. That is until Marisa had climbed on his lap last evening and nestled into his arms.

"Eduardo," she said. He knew that tone. It meant she was about to give him directions. "I want pink ribbon."

"Pink? For what?"

She looked up at him in disbelief. "For my *regalo*! I want it to be pink. With silver," she added. Her fingers traced the hairs on his left arm down to his thumb. She tilted her head farther back so that she could study his face and bat her eyelashes at him. "You have my present, don't you?" she asked sweetly. "I told you what I wanted the day after Thanksgiving, just when Papa said I could." Marisa found it very inconvenient to be limited to a date when she could inform the family about her Christmas wishes. By the time she was two, she had already grasped the concept of acquiring gifts, and since then she had calculated her expectations very carefully.

Eduardo avoided a response.

"Pink is my favorite color," she explained, in case he hadn't noticed.

"Pink it is," he said as he hugged her, hiding his guilt that he somehow had been totally oblivious to the children's anticipation. It was Christmas. How could he have forgotten? And how could he afford presents when every penny spent meant less chance that he and Belen could be together

That night lying awake on his bed, staring at the ceiling, Marisa's face haunted him. She was just a little girl. He knew he was a brute to think of disappointing her. Maybe he could find the plastic Cinderella shoes she had informed him she needed this year? And pink ribbon shouldn't be expensive, should it? By the time morning had lightened his room, he'd made up his mind. What did it matter if he used some of his meager savings? He knew it wasn't enough anyway, no matter how he tried to untangle that financial knot.

Since Christensen's had closed, there was only one other department store in Douglas Valley. Rumor had it that the proprietor was a polygamist whose several wives and multiple children manned the business. Eduardo didn't know if it was true, but the store had a small toy section in the back that catered to families whose budgets didn't allow them to indulge in the more expensive Fisher-Price or Disney products. Eduardo was waiting out front when a woman with long hair piled into a bun unlocked the door for business.

"*Buenos dias*," she greeted him with a smile. "Last minute shopping?"

"Something like that," Eduardo murmured as he headed past her and the camouflage hunting equipment now on sale. Shelves here were closer together than most of the other businesses in town, and they were stacked high with all kinds of random items—housecoats popular with elderly grandmothers right next to fishing gear and small kitchen appliances. When he was little, he had loved to roam the isles looking in amazement at the gadgets his few pennies would have never let him afford, but he'd spent hours imagining how it would be to own his very own Superman kite or a battery-powered lantern to use under the covers when he read late at night. Now he just hoped he could find a knock-off version of Cinderella's crystal shoes.

The toy section display tables were piled with boxes of off-brand, Barbie-like dolls and trucks so authentic-looking that the fire engines even had long hoses wound neatly next to their pump trailers. The toys were not in any particular order, and it looked to Eduardo as if the store clerks hadn't bothered to re-sort the boxes after an entire season of customers pawing through them. They had apparently just picked up whatever had fallen to the floor and balanced those containers in a dozen precarious towers which now threatened to cascade back down to the floor at any moment.

Eduardo sighed and began plowing through the mess, piling the toys he'd examined to his left and grabbing new boxes from his right. He found a small set of brightly colored stacking blocks for Alejandro and sat them on the floor next to him. There were probably two dozen distinct kinds of cars and airplanes out of which he picked a couple for each of his little brothers. He even found a nice set of wooden kitchen spoons for Luz— why they were under a group of bathtub toys he had no idea.

But no crystal Cinderella shoes. Not a single pair. The idea of disappointing Marisa was unthinkable. He pictured her big brown eyes searching under the Christmas tree and then looking expectantly at him, waiting for her surprise. He knew she wouldn't cry; she would just move away from him and curl up on his father's lap, her retreat whenever she was unhappy. The image of the miserable little girl was so disturbing that Eduardo started again through his rejected pile of toys in case he had missed something.

After another 10 minutes, it was obvious he hadn't. There were no dress-up shoes of any kind, much less the desirable crystal ones. He glared at the heap he had left in his wake. Then to add insult to injury, a boxed wooden train fell off the top of the stack, knocking his shoulder as it fell from the other side of the shelves. A voice from behind the heap of toys said, "Oops! Sorry. Didn't mean to bump that down on you."

"No problem," Eduardo responded automatically. Absently, he picked the train set off the floor and moved it to a more secure location. Now what, he wondered? Maybe the gas station on 23rd Street had something? They'd been advertising a "selection" of toys available with the purchase of a tank of gas. Maybe he should check there? There was a Walmart in Newman, but he couldn't imagine the possibility of finding transportation. His father was delivering parts today for the garage, and he had no real friends to speak of. Just Belen. At the thought of her, his stomach tightened. What was wrong with him? Everybody else seemed to manage to solve their problems. Why did he never get a break? His rising anger and self-pity propelled a boxed set of WWI era airplanes to the floor with a swipe of his hand, dislodging a precarious mound of toys which slammed on the floor one after another. In the quiet store, the noise was deafening. He swore under his breath. Stooping down, he began to restack the toys into a more stable pile.

"Hey, son. Something I can do to help?" A man with shoulder-length white hair tied in a knot at the back of his head leaned around from the other side of the toy shelf.

Eduardo bristled. "Nah, thanks. Just can't find a toy my little sister wants for Christmas."

The stranger nodded. Understanding lit up his face. "Sometimes just the right gift means everything to a child." His eyes penetrated Eduardo's rage.

"Yeah," Eduardo replied with disgust. "Sure. But I guess this year, she's out of luck." Unaccountably, his anger receded and drifted away of its own volition. His voice steadied. Taking a deep breath, he thought no sense spoiling someone else's shopping. He swiped at his eyes with the back of his hand. Crap! No matter what he did, it was wrong. He blinked fiercely as he knelt again to bundle up the small stack of gifts he'd separated out for his family.

He sensed the white-haired man staring at him. "Sometimes nothing goes right," he said quietly. "What are you looking for, son? Perhaps I could help?"

"Thanks, but I've already gone through this stack twice." He'd be damned if he'd let this stranger see how upset he was. "My sister wants Cinderella slippers. I guess the store doesn't stock them."

"Mmmmm." the stranger answered. "You mean the transparent plastic kind with the little heels?"

Eduardo nodded. "Yeah. Those."

The white-haired man was already digging into the pile from his side of the shelf.

Eduardo stood there, the toys in his arms balanced awkwardly. "Never mind, Mister. I've already looked twice," he apologized. "But thanks." He wanted to head toward the checkout counter, pay, and get out of there. It was a long walk to 23rd street, but the stranger was intent on sorting through the toys. Eduardo couldn't just head out and leave the old man, so he circled to the other side of the counter. "Here, let me help," he said. He knew it was a waste of time, but the old man was so determined to give him a hand. Probably the only time of year the old guy paid the least attention to some kid's problems, so he set his gifts on the floor, shrugged his shoulders, and began digging through the toys for the third time. A few more minutes wouldn't matter.

He started at the opposite end of the table, once again going through the same boxes. I've seen these roller skates often enough I could do an inventory on them, he thought. Out of the corner of his eye, he saw that the man was carefully moving each box and examining the ones whose contents were hidden from sight to be sure the inside matched the advertising on the cover. Eduardo hurried his own pace. If he left the old man to do all the searching, it might take another half an hour.

Five minutes dragged on. Eduardo finished the toys on his end of the table, but the old man was only 1/3 of the way through the toys on the other end. Enough, thought Eduardo, unable to stifle his impatience.

"Hey, mister. Sorry, I've got to go."

The man didn't even look up. Lifting the lid off yet another boxed train, the man exclaimed, "Bingo!" and held up a pair of exquisite plastic Cinderella slippers. "Look at this." He peered at the tag on the back of one of the shoes. "Size 10. What size does your sister need?"

"What in the world?" Eduardo was stunned. There was no way he'd missed those slippers. His mind flashed to the cheesy holiday song he hated about the kid who spent his allowance on dancing shoes for his dying mother for Christmas. Every time it came on the radio, he changed the station, but here in front of him was as beautiful a pair of Cinderella shoes as he had ever seen, pretty much just like the song. Rhinestones gleamed from the matching bows on the toes of each shoe; the heels curved delicately to suggest a true princess, the plastic unmarred nor scratched. He shook his head to be sure he wasn't daydreaming. When the old man handed him the pair, he stoked their smooth sparkling surface with a touch of incredulity. Was it possible his luck was changing? Maybe that stuff his stepmom was always feeding him about casting his bread on the waters and having good fortune come back to you had something to it? He really didn't care. Relief flooded his body. Marisa will love these, he thought.

"Thought I'd seen a pair," said the white-haired man with satisfaction.

Eduardo couldn't think of a word to say. Finally, he blurted out, "Thank you, so much. You don't know what this means to me. My sister …," his voice trailed off.

The old man stepped toward him, handed him the box, and touched Eduardo on the shoulder. "Remember," he said. "Life is full of good things, too." He added enigmatically, "Even yours."

On the way to the check stand, Eduardo pulled a roll of pink ribbon out from under a bin loaded with red and green spools. The woman with the bun rang up his purchases, stopping to lift one of the slippers out of its box. Satisfied that the bar code on the heel matched the store's, she said, "Didn't know we even carried these." Looking up at Eduardo, she added, "Any more back there?'

"I don't think so," Eduardo said. "Just this one pair."

Wednesday, December 18

Noon

CARRIE JANE DUCKED INTO KNEADER'S, pulling the door shut behind her so that it didn't whip back open. The wind had picked up again in the last hour or so, and the sky was now covered in heavy foreboding clouds. Maybe snow, at last, she thought with satisfaction. The sandwich/dessert shop was filled with last-minute shoppers, mostly women, and laughter muffled the Christmas carols playing over the sound system.

One of the perks of being out of work was that she could actually follow through on her promise to have lunch with Kyra. Carrie Jane spotted her former roommate in a back corner seated improbably at one of the elevated tables, her feet dangling because her legs weren't even long enough to reach the rungs of the chair intended for them. As Carrie Jane surveyed the room, she realized Kyra hadn't picked that table, but undoubtedly had settled on it as a last resort. Every table and chair in the place was filled. She waved at Kyra to signal she'd seen her, then headed to the counter to order her favorite French dip sandwich. She toyed for a moment with the idea of skipping pastry confections displayed prominently in the glass case to the right of the cash register, but convinced herself that sugar was the primary ingredient of Christmas food, and who was she to deny the spirit of the season?

"Add two chocolate éclairs to that order, please," she instructed the young clerk, who grinned in agreement and handed her a number.

"Bring it to your table in just a couple of minutes," he said.

The table Kyra had snagged was in the back next to the window overlooking the street. Traffic streamed by soundlessly, an occasional car filled with teenagers waving wildly to friends inside the store.

"So, how's the enforced vacation?" Kyra greeted Carrie Jane. "Are they still paying you, or do you lose a week's salary?"

Carrie Jane stashed her purse under her chair and pulled the chair closer to the table. The combination of Christmas music and chatter made it difficult to hear. She leaned toward Kyra. "One: the vacation's great. I usually have to rush from school to finish up Christmas shopping and fall into bed too late every night. But this little 'sabbatical' is allowing me to luxuriate in the spirit of the Season. Two: the school district is paying us—there's some sort of insurance clause that covers salaries if the building is not safe for occupation." She grimaced, "Although there are rumors that we might have to go to work a week longer in June to make up the days that state law mandates. Which could be a bummer, but what the heck!" her face brightened. "An extra week off at Christmas is a bonus—especially since the fire was so early in the morning that the school was almost empty. The two or three people who were hurt are already out of the hospital. Thank goodness," she added. Henry was a favorite of hers. Once a couple of years ago, she'd unlocked her classroom door in the morning and found a roomful of brand-new desks—all matching for the first time in her career. Henry had unpacked the replacement shipment the night before and delivered 35 shiny desks to her room first. When she went to thank him, he brushed it off.

"Metal frameworks on the desks are green—school color. Reminded me of you. You like green, I noticed, so there you are." After that brief, slightly confusing response, he'd turned and headed out the door. "I'm off the clock. Gotta go."

Kyra grinned at Carrier Jane. "Everything has a silver lining. What's the school board going to do about repairs?"

"Good question. Last I heard, they were trying to decide if they should raze that whole section and start over, or if it was still structurally sound enough to rebuild."

"Aren't there some classes held in there? And what about plays and concerts?"

"It's going to be complicated; I guess they're looking for another place to hold performances till next school year. Classes like stage tech are going to be canceled for 2nd semester, so I assume the boss will figure the whole thing out somehow."

"Well, I say it was nice of the school board to stretch your vacation, so you'd have time for lunch," Kyra said, amusement lighting in her eyes. "You're usually too busy to hang out this time of year."

"Yeah. Sorry about that." Carrie Jane agreed.

The server interrupted them. "Avocado salad?" He slid it in front of Kyra and scooped up her number. "And French dip." He moved to Carrie Jane's side of the table, carefully setting the small bowl of fragrant beef broth next to her sandwich. At the sight of the éclairs he placed between them, Kyra raised an eyebrow.

Carrie Jane shrugged. "It's Christmas. I had to."

"Excellent. Gotta love the holidays." Kyra leaned toward Carrie Jane in anticipation. "So... the whole reason I called you was to find out how you're doing with that cute cop?"

"Detective, I'll have you know. We educated women don't date lowly cops." Carrie Jane informed her.

"Or don't date anyone at all, most of the time," shot back Kyra. "That's because there are SO," she emphasized the word, "SO many good men out there looking for a wife."

Carrie Jane laughed. "Touché. Actually, we haven't had another date since we showed at your store. But I think he wants to take me out again." She told Kyra about encountering Gifford twice in the last couple of days at Christensen's.

"Wait, wait, wait. You're doing what?" Kyra was flabbergasted. "You think you can turn that trash heap into a concert hall? Whose dumb idea was that?'

"It was Annie's—that girl we told you about. The one with amnesia? And she's right. It's the only other building in town big enough to hold our audience. You should see the place after only six days of work. Drywall up and mudded, trash all gone, front windows replaced."

"Who in town was generous enough to pay for that, for Pete's sake?" Kyra's skepticism showed. As a business owner, she knew firsthand what a window that size was likely to cost. "And if I remember correctly, the whole front was window displays. Maybe five?"

"Six," Carrie Jane corrected her. "Took a half a dozen guys a whole day to set them in place, but boy, do they look great. The real estate owner was salivating with glee when he saw them. I think he increased the price of the property in his head just while he was standing there."

"Yeah, but what about the money?"

"Lawyers, of course." Carrie Jane laughed. "Who else has that kind of money?"

"Wow! Can't believe you talked a bunch of sharks into donating anything. Impressive."

"Apparently, there's a catch though. Viola told me that Ramona had to agree to go out with the guy who arranged the money. Seems they used to be an item in high school."

Kyra's eyes widened. "Ramona! Dating? Holy mackerel. The age of miracles must be upon us. So, who's this guy, or should I say 'man'? I guess at their age . . .." She stopped, speechless. "Who knew? While you and Flor are reduced to trolling the internet for single men, Ramona has one clamoring after her. Unbelievable."

"It's just not right," Carrie Jane chuckled.

"Look on the bright side. Maybe he's got a younger brother. A much younger brother," Kyra amended wickedly.

Carrie Jane gave her a steely glare and concentrated on her sandwich.

"Let's get back to that detective," Kyra said as she forked an avocado slice to go with the bite of salad she already had on her fork. "What do you think of him? He's certainly good looking enough."

Carrie Jane considered the question. "He's funny. And comfortable. We rode all the way over to your place and back, and I didn't have to manage a conversation or pelt him with questions about his life. We just talked. Like friends. It was nice, really nice."

"Hmmm," Kyra said, but she kept her reaction to that information to herself.

Carrie Jane thought it safest to change the subject. "How's business?"

"Booming thanks to your fire. High school kids with nothing to do are coming in all day long, probably for the cookies and hot chocolate, but most of them look around a while and maybe buy a book or two for younger brothers and sisters. I've had to pull extra copies of *Where the Wild Things Are* out of our little warehouse at least twice in the last week.

"When I opened that store," she went on, "the guys at the Chamber of Commerce told me I was crazy--nobody reads actual books anymore, they said. And, of course, electronic books are easy and cheap. It's impossible to compete with them. So, instead, I decided to focus on books as gifts— the kind grandmas might give their grandchildren on birthdays. Now I'm holding my own until a Barnes and Noble decides to move into the area.

Then I'll probably have to close up shop."

Carrie Jane nodded her head ruefully. "I have to believe that books will never go out of style, but almost every kid I assign a novel reads it on his iPad or Nook or Kindle. The only ones who use my classroom copies are too poor to buy an electronic reader. I can't believe there's been so much change in technology just since we left college."

"It's literally a *Brave New World*," Kyra agreed.

Carrie Jane bobbed her head in agreement as she wiped the remnants of her sandwich off her fingers and lifted an éclair out of its paper shell. She bit into the flakey pastry and smiled with pleasure at the smooth, cream-filled center. "Ah" she sighed. "If only these weren't a million calories."

"What I can't figure out is how you stay so slim what with your appetite for tasty food?"

"Essays. Flor assures me that reading a class load of essays burns more calories than walking around the block. Something to do with the energy expended by perseverance being inversely proportional to the brain-fry quotient."

"That's what I like about you. Big words." Kyra tested a bit of éclair. "I accept your hypothesis based on the fact that it avoids any mention of self-control—a phrase I find highly distasteful when it comes to dessert."

"Yep," said Carrie Jane. "That's why we're friends."

5 PM

Ramona was tired. She couldn't remember ever having as much energy as the kids around her obviously did. Her shoulders ached from sitting on the floor painting what seemed like at least 100 ft. of baseboards. Worse, she had only finished one wall. Annie was cheerfully manning a roller and laughing at a story one of the senior girls was telling her about her worse date ever.

". . . so, he spent the whole Saturday night reliving Friday's game (which I had seen, mind you!) with his buddies. I don't think he even noticed when I went to sleep!"

"Hey," Ollie called from across the room. "That was a great game."

Rolling her eyes, the senior girl pushed her paint roller a little faster.

"From now on, I only date boys who talk instead of run."

Ramona wiped her forehead. She knew if she didn't get up off the floor soon, the boys might have to lift her up and carry her home. She looked around with some surprise. At least 2/3 of the walls and all the ceiling were now covered with a coat of what the hardware store called 'eggshell white.' The whole room seemed brighter and more inviting. A second coat scheduled for tomorrow. Day after that they planned to polish the linoleum floor in the morning; then it was just a matter of setting up the risers, hauling in the piano and organ, lining up donations of Christmas trees, poinsettias, and candles, setting up several hundred chairs borrowed from the high school, dress rehearsal Saturday morning, and hope that word had gotten out about the change of venue. Fortunately, the local radio station was managed by one of her former students. He knew he'd be arranging on-air free advertising the moment she'd walked through the door. Good thing she hadn't tabulated that unfinished list before, she thought, or she'd have realized this whole thing was impossible. The concert was still four days away. We might pull this off, she grunted as she rose to her feet. A strident voice over her shoulder caused her to shudder involuntarily.

"Well, well, well. Thought I'd come and see for myself this 'miracle' you people are supposedly producing. I admit the old place is vastly improved considering what a trash heap it was last week," Mayor Simpson announced as she paraded into the store with two of the Town Council members in tow. She wore her customary two-piece suit, her large matching bag over one shoulder swinging in rhythm with her forceful cadence. She headed directly for Ramona.

"I bet you're really proud of yourself. Very impressive, I must say." The Mayor's head swiveled to take in the whole room.

Just for an instant, Ramona wondered if maybe the mayor was going to buy into their project. But no.

Instead, a self-satisfied smirk crossed the Mayor's face as she pointed out, "Too bad we're just going to tear the whole thing down in a couple of months. Lotta people's time and money down the drain." She turned back and challenged Ramona. "How are you going to justify that?" she demanded.

All work in the room stopped, every ear riveted on the conversation unfolding before them. On another day, the teenagers might have enjoyed the sparring that habitually went on between Ramona and the Mayor. But not today. Not when they had already logged a week's worth of labor. And not when the Mayor had just implied all that arduous work was the deluded whim of a bunch of dreamers.

Ramona bit back a whole series of swear words and took a long, deep breath. "Mayor," Ramona greeted her. "Nice of you to drop by. Let me offer you a couple of complimentary tickets to our concert Saturday evening. Bring the family. Nice way to celebrate the holiday." She pulled out of her pocket her own set of the tickets which were allotted to every choir member and held them up.

Annie was the only one in the room who didn't seem to notice the tension. She put her roller on the edge of her paint container and walked over to stand by Ramona. "Do you like music, Mayor?" she asked innocently.

The sincerity in her voice took the Mayor off guard, and she turned to the girl. "Ah, of course, the little singer. Haven't found where you belong yet, huh? Sorry, you have to spend so much time with old people. Can't the DCFS find a more," she searched for the right word, "appropriate placement family for you?"

Annie apparently didn't notice the slur. "I love being with Ramona and Viola," she said simply. "They have been very kind to me."

The Mayor looked unconvinced. "I hear you're singing a solo in the concert on Saturday, assuming you all manage to finish squandering all your time on this futile transformation."

Ollie took a threatening step toward the major, but Carrie Jane grabbed his arm, signaling him to stop with a shake of her head.

Annie's eyes lit up as she looked around the room. "I like working here. It feels good to make something better. And it does look a lot better, don't you think?"

Weighing her options, the Mayor realized she'd have to tread carefully here. Alienating a bunch of potential voters, not to mention the dozen or so adults who were watching her, seemed self-defeating. She turned back to Ramona.

"Perhaps I will take those tickets," she said. "Wouldn't want to miss such a landmark event. Heber," she addressed one of the Councilmen who had come with her, "why don't you bring your camera? We'll document the last episode in the life of the oldest department store in Douglas

Valley. An important footnote in the town history, as it were."

Annie didn't notice Ramona seething next to her. "I hope you'll like our concert," she said. "Ramona says that King George of England was so impressed when he heard the "Hallelujah Chorus" that he stood up during the whole song, and now it is tradition for audiences to do the same. Did you know that? Sometimes when we practice it, I think I hear the angels singing with us, it is so beautiful." Annie's face was radiant.

The Mayor stared at the girl. "Yes," she said slowly. "I remember hearing that story. I haven't heard the *Messiah* in years, now that you mention it."

Too dang heavenly for someone headed the other direction, Ramona bit her tongue before she blurted her thoughts out loud.

But Annie wasn't finished. "We're having a little reception for the choir members afterward. Maybe you and your family could come?"

The Mayor was rendered speechless. She made a visible effort to gather her wits about her, and when she answered, she was startled to find that the spite in her voice had disappeared. "Thank you, child." The perpetual sternness of her expression softened. "We'd love to come. I guess we'll be seeing you Saturday, Ramona." She plucked the tickets from Ramona's outstretched hand and, without another word, she ushered the Town Council members out with her.

Ramona was stunned into silence. She looked at Annie. How did the child manage that? Not even a sharp retort from Simpson. She shook her head. That girl. She shook her head again and picked up her brush. "Guess this means we better make this place look really good," she said to the group, and then she stooped over, grabbed her purse, fished out a couple of Aleve, swallowed them without water, sat back down on the floor, and started again on the long line of unpainted baseboards spread out before her.

Friday, December 20

6 PM

CARRIE JANE BRUSHED A RANDOM strand of hair out of her eyes. "This is more work than dealing with third period," she complained. "I'm pretty sure I've set up ten thousand chairs all by myself."

Flor scoffed as she looked around at the neat rows of chairs marching steadily forward from the large windows at the front of the store. "Good thing you teach English, not math. As I recall, we borrowed fewer than 1200 chairs total."

"Details. Mere details."

"Hey, Dunkett," Ollie called from across the room. "Where do you want these risers?" He and a stream of his buddies were each shouldering a section from the stack they had unloaded earlier in the afternoon to the front of the hall.

"I don't know. Better ask Janeen."

Only the rear end of the choir conductor was visible from where they were standing. Her jeans stretched tightly across a fanny that had seen considerable growth over the years. Masking tape in hand, she was marking the locations of the piano, organ, string quartet, and solo microphones. She appeared to be humming, the sound carrying all the way back to where the boys were working.

Carrie Jane grinned at Flor. "Katy Perry. Who knew?" she said.

"I heard that, Carrie Jane," came the imperious voice. "I happen to like all KINDS of music, unlike some of my STUFFIER counterparts." She twisted her head around so that it looked like it was attached directly to her backside. "Boys," she ordered, "bring those up here. I want them in a semi-circle facing the audience; start about two feet from the acoustic dividers we set up in front of the back wall and give me at least seven rows. More if there's room for them. And MAKE sure there's enough space between each set for choir members to enter and exit without bunching up. NOTHING starts a concert off on the wrong foot as when choir members have to tromp around between rows of risers."

Ollie looked at his buddies and rolled his eyes, but he shifted the weight more evenly across his shoulders and headed toward the choir director.

Flor sat down in the chair she had just unfolded. "I'm bushed," she said. "Good thing the performance is tomorrow. I've lost 5 lbs. in the last week because I've been too tired to eat." She thought about that for a minute. "There's a flaw in my reasoning somewhere, but I'm hungry, so I don't have the energy to figure out what it is."

Carrie Jane sympathized. The last several days she'd fallen into bed without even reading the newspaper, a quantum break in her normal daily routine. "At this rate, Christmas is going to be anti-climactic," she said. "What are your plans for the holiday? Heading up to Salt Lake to see the family?"

"Looks like it," Flor said casually. "I'm taking Orson home to meet the family."

"Orson?" Carrie Jane shrieked, then dropped her voice when she saw the boys up front turn their heads. "Who or what the heck is Orson? Why haven't I heard about this before?" Carrie Jane demanded. "Did you just pick up some stray guy and not bother to tell me?"

"I've been telling you about him all along. The vending machine guy. You knew I'd been hanging out with him."

"When did 'hanging out' turn into 'going to meet the family'? That's kind of a big deal that you haven't bothered to mention, Amiga."

"Yeah, well, he crept up on me when I wasn't paying attention," Flor admitted. "He's such a nice guy, and he lives upstairs, so we didn't have to plan to get together; it just kinda happened. One night we were watching an old movie at his apartment—that one with Meg Ryan and Tom Hanks-- and I just kissed him. Out of the blue."

"What!"

"He kissed me back. A lot." The memory brought a look of smug satisfaction to Flor's face.

Carrie Jane shook her head back and forth in disbelief. Under her breath she said, "Ramona, now you. Who's next, Leon?"

Carrie Jane tried to remember the few details she'd heard from Flor about this man. "He loads and repairs vending machines? What's he like? Age?" She looked shrewdly at Flor. "Is he divorced with a bunch of kids and a ton of baggage? Have I met him some time at school and just don't remember?"

Flor shook her head. "Nope to all the above. I don't think you would have met him. He loads the vending machines at the high school like at 5 AM in the morning. And he doesn't just load them; he owns them." She thought for a minute, tabulating in her head. "Quite a few of them, really. No kids. No ex-wife. He does have a chocolate lab named Parley."

"You hate dogs," Carrie Jane pointed out.

"True, but I love Orson, and the dog is part of the package."

Carrie Jane pulled the scrunchie out of her ponytail and brushed the stray hairs back into a neat bundle. Automatically, she doubled the scrunchie and pulled her hair back through it. Thick clumps of unruly red curls bounced down her back. She stared at Flor, trying to figure out how her best friend could have hidden a budding relationship from her. Or had she just not been paying attention. She sighed. "So, what else about him do I need to know? And what on earth do you have in common?"

"Old movies," said Flor promptly. "And cooking—he's a great cook. He's quiet and doesn't have to always be showing off like most of the guys I've dated. He likes me. ME. Most guys are attracted by the obvious," she glanced down mischievously at her well-endowed figure. "Most of the time they don't even bother to try to talk to me. But he does." The effervescent Flor was suddenly completely serious. "He knows what books I like, and my favorite restaurant, and it's OK with him if I want to hang out with you and leave him home." Flor looked thoughtful. "I guess he's a grown-up, not some boy living in a man's body." Contentment flowed around her. "I'm happy, really happy."

Just as Carrie Jane reached over to give her a fierce hug, there was an earsplitting crash, and a dozen chairs on the row nearest the front windows toppled over in domino effect. Both women shot to their feet, heading for the noise even before they understood what had happened.

Ollie had tumbled onto his rump. He sat amidst a confusion of folding chairs; the section of risers he'd been lifting had fallen askew across both legs and jammed into one shoulder. Apparently, the other end of the riser had slammed into the nearest chair and created a chain of up-ended chairs.

Both women rushed to his side. "Don't move," Flor ordered. "You might have broken a couple of bones. I'll call an ambulance."

Ollie looked sheepish. "I'm all right, Miss Gallegos. I was just so surprised, I guess I twisted funny, and the riser hit that support column and knocked me flat." Gingerly, he twisted his shoulders around so that he could use them to lift the rest of his body upright.

"No, no, no," Carrie Jane said. "Stay put. We'll get that thing off of you." The riser was considerably heavier than it looked. It took both Carrie Jane and Flor to boost it off Ollie's legs and shove it aside.

Ollie shifted his weight. Carrie Jane grabbed his shoulder and kept him from trying to stand up. "You hit the ground pretty hard. How's your head. Did the riser hit it on the way down?" She knelt beside him, looking directly into his eyes for any sign of dilated pupils, her arm still resting lightly on his shoulder.

"Naw, I'm good. Probably have a couple of bruises. No worse than after a hard game." Ollie took her outstretched hand and used it as a lever to pull himself up. "See. Nothing broken." His grin took in both her and the small crowd of his buddies that had gathered around him. "Couple of Ibuprofens and I'll be fine," he said and then winced slightly as he lowered his full weight onto his right leg. He lifted his hands to gesture he was OK. "No problem."

The crowd around him breathed a collective sigh of relief. Without a sign of discomfort, Tyler, who had been hovering nearby, lifted the wayward riser to his shoulders. "Give it a minute, buddy. I'll handle the mess." The other boys nodded and started untangling the other chairs from the pile on the floor, the metal clanging as they pulled them apart.

"What startled you badly enough that you dropped the riser in the first place?" Flor asked curiously.

"That." Ollie turned and pointed out the windows toward the street.

Snow. Huge, silent flakes of white drifted down onto pavements, sidewalks, street signs, trees, and doorways. The pools of reflected light, neatly circling streetlamps and the headlights of passing cars were so bright they obliterated the darkness. The ordinary traffic noise on a Friday night was dampened to a whisper. At least a couple of inches covered the ground already. And there was no sign of the large feather-light flakes stopping any time soon.

Flor gasped; her eyes widened at the sight, mesmerized by the

Christmas card image which was laid out before her. "*¡Dios mío!*" she whispered. She put her arm around Carrie Jane's waist, the boys behind them unloading their burdens and joining them at the window. For a long time, they all simply stood quietly together staring out into the night.

8 PM

"Well, I hope you're satisfied," Ramona looked across the table at John Callister. "I can't imagine what you were thinking when you made me a party to this contract."

John unfolded his napkin and laid it across his lap. "Ah, Ah, Ramona." He wagged his finger at her. "The deal was NO complaints. Just a nice evening with an old friend."

Ramona was flattered despite herself. It had been five years since she'd lost Amos, and the truth was that she missed having someone besides Viola to talk to. She loved Viola, but they'd been friends so long that they could almost finish one another's sentences. John Callister was another matter entirely.

She changed the subject. It was a waste to try to manage social niceties with John. He'd had never had much patience with her attempts at small talk; her pleasantries were generally buried in a flood of one-sided opinions. Even in high school, he'd pointed out that she was too "mouthy" to be included in the popular crowd although she'd secretly suspected that's what he liked about her. When they had been debate partners, he was constantly trying to rein her in. But she knew that tension between them had been a contributing factor when they'd won state championships both their junior and senior years--beating even the teams from schools with squads three times the size of theirs.

Then she'd married Amos, chosen to apply to the local Utah State extension program, and their lives had drifted further apart. While John had gone back east to law school, she and Amos had bought her childhood home, agreeing that Douglas Valley was the place they wanted to raise their children. Or child. She forced her thoughts away from that painful memory. That was the thing about life, she reflected. Good days and bad, and nobody escaped either. Not even John, who had been a federal Third District Court judge until Helen got sick and decided she wanted to come home to die.

"I don't know that I ever told you how sorry I was that you lost Helen," she said sincerely. "She was a lovely person, even to me," Ramona admitted.

Callister smiled. "She liked you, Ramona. She knew you'd tell her the truth even if she didn't want you to. She said you were a busybody and a nuisance, but you were the one who came to the hospital and read to her when she was so sick she couldn't hold a book. And you didn't flinch when she threw up all over you that horrible afternoon just before she . . .." His eyes clouded at the memory.

With her usual lack of tact, she cut through the memories. "Let's talk about something else. Two old people reminiscing about their dead spouses doesn't do the digestion any good at all," she said briskly. "Why am I here, John? We haven't spent any significant social time together in 40 years. Except for the funeral," her voice dropped. More gently, she asked again, "What is it you want?"

Callister had expected the question; it was Ramona, after all. He looked straight into her eyes, purposely making no attempt to pretend he didn't know what she was talking about. "I'm lonely, Ramona. So are you. We aren't kids anymore. We don't have to dance around the truth. And the truth is I like you. I've always liked you. You can make me laugh, and you have a gift for punching holes in my tendency to pontificate. You are pushy and demanding and invigorating. Do we have to have an agenda? Can't we just be friends, again?"

Ramona studied him, weighing whether or not he was sincere. The courtroom had taught him to be a master of manipulation, and she deserved it if she fell into that trap. Still, it would be nice to have a little company occasionally. She knew that John could be very good company when he chose to be. And he didn't require any emotional energy; they'd known each other too long for that. Besides, at her age, the 'drama' of a relationship wasn't worth the trouble anyway.

He waited. Good lawyers learned when to shut up and listen, and he'd been practicing for a long, long time.

"Deal," she said finally. "No strings."

"OK," Callister agreed with a touch of relief. The sticky part of this conversation was over. He changed the subject. "How's the money you strong-armed from the Bar Association's coffers holding out?"

Now that was something Ramona was happy to talk about. After they ordered, she told Callister about the more than 250 kids who'd showed up at one time or another to help ready the old Christensen's place for the concert on Saturday. Because of their combined manpower, the building was cleaned, painted, and polished. "In fact, as we speak, 20 or 30 kids are transporting chairs from the high school and setting them up for tomorrow's morning's dress rehearsal. I assume you'll be at the concert?"

"Do I have a choice?" John countered.

"Good point." Ramona agreed. "You don't. And we, meaning you and me, need every ounce of support we can get to convince the Mayor that she's got a sizeable opposition to her point of view." She swallowed a sip of the excellent fruit puree mixture in front of her. "But it's also true that our choir is enthusiastic, well-rehearsed, and the music is incomparable. Besides, you haven't heard my Annie sing."

Callister raised his eyebrows. "Your Annie?"

She studied him. He'd told her the truth. She respected his honesty. Though she was generally loath to reveal her innermost feelings to anyone, except Viola, of course, Ramona had longed to talk to a third party, someone without a biased point of view, about the fears she harbored concerning the attachment she had formed for Annie. She hoped she could trust Callister not to use that knowledge as a lever when he wanted something from her in the future. "My Annie," she repeated softly. "I keep telling myself that any day now we're going to find out who she is and what's happened to her family, but the truth is I'm not sure I can let her go." Rarely was she at a loss for words, but how could she explain about Annie? She paused, thinking carefully about what it was that made Annie so special.

The waiter brought breadsticks and minestrone, placing the steaming bowls in front of each customer with smooth efficiency.

"I always used to tell my students," Ramona began again, "that one of the characteristics of a 'good person' is the ability to ease the road of people around them instead of becoming obstacles to other people's progress. Annie does that without thinking. It's as if her whole purpose is to make me, others—all of us—just feel better when she's there. And her voice, oh John, wait till you hear her. I can't understand why a child like that is lost. Who on earth could bear to lose her?" There was genuine distress in her voice.

If Callister was surprised at the level of intimacy Ramona's words revealed, he didn't show it. He gave Ramona some time to gather her emotions. "Has Gifford made any progress in his investigation?"

"What he's found so far is kind of weird, actually. Annie's fingerprints are a likely, match to that of a girl killed in a shooting accident 50 years ago in Salt Lake. He asked the Crime Lab to do a little investigating to see if it's possible there's some kind of error. So far, nothing. He says he'll hear from them again next week."

"I wouldn't worry too much. It's not unheard of for a lab to mislabel a piece of evidence. Maybe the original prints were filed in the wrong place. Or misidentified—a very real possibility for ones that old. Who knows? When there are similarities in the print identifiers, it can be difficult to differentiate between older samples especially."

Ramona nodded. "I guessed as much." She broached another track. "Legally, where does Annie stand if no one comes forward to identify her?"

Callister leaned toward her. "Have you considered applying for adoption?"

"I've thought about it," Ramona admitted.

"If she becomes a ward of the state, we look for a permanent foster family. From there adoption is a possibility. What about Ms. Pridgeon? In a case like this, the current custody is given preference. Would she be interested in applying to adopt Annie?"

Ramona thought about it for a minute. "I don't know. We haven't talked about it. I guess it's time we did."

"This case may be particularly tricky because a child is not like an old car. We don't just declare it abandoned and give it a new registration. The legal complications might take years, even if all the parties agree about what the outcome should be. By then Annie would be of age---if we can figure out what age she is—and all the legal hassle may be moot." Callister scraped a spoonful of soup from the bottom of his bowl. "You know, Ramona, I've made a lot of useful connections over the years, and I'll help you however I can. Though it may not seem obvious to the public, the law is intended to improve the quality of life for all its citizens, not just the ones who can afford a lawyer to tilt the court in their favor," he assured her earnestly. "Because children are the most vulnerable members of society, for many members of the justice system children merit the most dedicated protection. Someone in Annie's situation will certainly gain the sympathy of the court."

Ramona caught her breath. It had been a long time since someone had offered to help her. Usually, the reverse was true. She reached across the table and took Callister's hand. "Thank you, John," was all she could manage to say.

Saturday, December 21

6 PM

LUZ WAS SPOONING SPICY-SMELLING beans onto a flour tortilla. "Marisa, tell your brothers that dinner is almost ready, and ask your papa to put a bib on Alejandro and get him in his highchair, *por favor*."

Marisa delivered her message with her usual authority. The boys filed in, scuffling for the chair next to their mother, which meant they'd be served first.

"Where's Eduardo?" Luz asked her daughter.

Marisa looked uncomfortable. "He didn't come when I called him, Mama," she said, her forehead furrowed in as close to a frown of disapproval as a four-year-old could manage. "And he didn't tell me he was leaving!" She announced in exasperation.

"So, my daughter, he must tell you his every move?" Her father laughed. "Did you tell Eduardo the day when you went to collect the Christmas money?" he teased.

Marisa was unabashed. "He wasn't home to tell. And it was a secret."

"Ah," her father said. "Perhaps Eduardo should be allowed a secret now and then?"

The two older boys exchanged nods and grins across the table. Marisa was way too bossy in their opinion. It was rare their father scolded her— even so gently as he did now. Having her put in her place was a source of immense satisfaction to them.

****

Several blocks away Eduardo was sprinting, his breath trailing him in ragged puffs of condensation from the cold. It was almost two miles to the hospital from his house. He had slipped out the door and down the steps without a sound, the only observer Alejandro who was stacking blocks and knocking them over with glee. Once out the door, Eduardo had never slackened the pace of his long legs as he raced down the silent blocks. Passing the duplexes of his neighborhood, his path took him into the older section of town, neat identical brick houses with wide front porches and narrow driveways. Most were lit by the shadows of televisions in the front rooms. Occasionally the curtains had not yet shut out the night, and he could see directly into the kitchens where families were gathered around their dinner tables.

He gave them no thought. His mind was totally focused on Belen and the baby. He knew she must have been terrified to text him while her father was nearby. Eduardo imagined her horror when she felt the water explode down her legs. He guessed that the old man had panicked and forced her to go to the hospital because there was no explanation in the text. Just the words "water broke, lots of pain." He dove across 4th South, barely avoiding a car turning right behind him. He hardly noticed as block after block disappeared, but his pace slowed of its own volition as his lungs protested the strain of the cold and the exertion. Checking his phone for the 10th time to see if Belen had sent another message, he stumbled on a raised crack in the sidewalk in front of the small medical building near the hospital which housed a pharmacy, a physical therapy facility, and most of the offices of the doctors who practiced at the regional hospital. He righted himself before crashing into the pavement, but his legs refused to regain his earlier pace. His breathing became ragged gasps.

Crossing a narrow side street, he finally glimpsed the neon lights of the Emergency Room entrance just a block away. His chest ached from the exertion, and he coughed every time he drew in a breath, but the neon lights announcing the EMERGENCY entrance to the hospital gave him renewed strength. He darted between cars in the parking lot, grateful it was so sparsely populated at the end of the day. He knew that families in his neighborhood often crowded the emergency room in the evening because they couldn't afford to miss a day of work, even for illness or accident, but tonight only a few vehicles interfered with his headlong dash into the building. He bolted past a couple of EMTs guiding a stretcher out of an ambulance, its lights still flashing red and blue. There was blood dripping slowly onto the tiled floor as the stretcher headed toward a set of sliding doors, and an EMT barked orders to a nurse who had rushed out to greet them.

"Hey!" one of them yelled at him as he shoved past them, but Eduardo didn't notice.

By the time he reached the information desk inside the automatic doors, he was bent double from exhaustion. Lifting his head from his heaving chest, he blurted out "maternity?' to the woman. She stared without seeing at his wind-whipped hair and the sound of his uneven breaths, her mind was on the stretcher which rolled in behind him. She pointed over her shoulder to the arrows on the wall across from him, jumping from her desk to assist with the victim now sliding through the entrance and past her.

Eduardo didn't even acknowledge her help. He leaned precariously against the wall for a moment to slow his breathing and then took off, following the green line which led deeper into the hospital. When his family had come to the hospital at Alejandro's birth, they had used the front entrance. He knew maternity was somewhere on the 2nd floor, but everything looked very different from this side of the building. He leaped up two stairs at a time and jogged more slowly down a long hall, only to be confronted by a locked set of doors which announced "Labor and Delivery. Family members only." There was a large red button on the wall to the right of him with a smaller sign that instructed: "Push for Admittance." He pushed.

"Labor and Delivery," said a voice through the speaker.

"Belen Hidalgo?" he asked, his cough overtaking the name.

"Who?"

"Belen Hidalgo," he said more slowly, forcing air into his lungs so that he could articulate the name.

"Family member?" she said.

"Father," he said shortly and realized with a shock it was the first time he had ever said it aloud.

There was a click, and then the doors opened smoothly in front of him revealing a gleaming rounded counter that housed half-a-dozen individual desks which looked out across two hallways forking away from the center to the patient rooms beyond. The ward clerk studied him from behind her desk but made no comment about his age or appearance. "She's down the hall and to the left, B 204. The nurse is checking her now."

Eduardo remembered that the nursery was on the opposite side of this floor near the patient rooms, but he had never been in the area where babies were delivered. He felt a moment of panic. He and Belen had read several books together about the delivery and actual birth. He feared it was not the same as watching it happen. How on earth could he have believed that he was ready for this? And what about his beautiful Belen? What had he done to her? He'd never even been to a doctor's appointment with her. He imagined her screaming in agony, or the baby with its cord around its neck, or what if the doctor couldn't stop the bleeding? What if she was in so much pain that she hated him? Fear, uncertainty, and inexperience jumbled together with his physical exhaustion overtook him. Only his love for Belen kept him moving.

Though he went to Mass with his parents every Sunday, he seldom prayed. But now a prayer came unbidden to his lips. "Oh God, please let her be all right, and the baby, and please give me the strength . . ." He stopped. He couldn't think—strength for what? Dread engulfed him. Reality was way beyond anything a prayer could help. He needed his father. How he wished he'd had the courage to tell him. And now, it would be impossible to explain. His father would be so disappointed in him. He closed his eyes and tried to clear his head. Belen. He needed to focus on Belen. Heading in the direction the clerk had pointed, he read the numbers on the rooms, trying not to hyperventilate. B 204. He took several calming breaths, knocked once, and pushed the door open.

A curtain was drawn across the bed, but he could hear someone asking about her level of pain on a scale of 1 to 10, and Belen's voice murmuring a response. A lower voice interrupted. Eduardo stopped dead. Her father. He had forgotten about her father. He had no idea what to do now. He knew a man would march in and announce that his baby was coming and that he had every right to be here with her, but he shrank from confronting the man he had avoided for so many months. Maybe if he just waited outside?

The nurse leaned around the curtain and said, "Can I help you."

"Wrong room," he muttered and slipped out the door before her father caught a glimpse of him. He leaned against the wall across from her room. I am such a jerk, he said over and over to himself. Jerk, jerk, jerk. He pounded his head on the wall behind him at the repetition of every word. All the talk about being a man and handling his own problems. I am nothing. Useless. Then heard her moan. His self-pity was swept away by the pain in her voice. Belen, he whispered.

He knew she must be clenching her teeth to try to keep the sound from escaping. She hated to appear weak; it was one of the things he loved about her. She had told him once that only with him could she be her true self. "You make me feel safe," she said. "Even when I am sad or frightened, you do not think less of me." She trusted him, and now when she needed him most, he had failed her. Angry tears threatened to escape his eyes. He could not leave her alone with her father. He would not. He straightened his shoulders, stepped back across the hall, and walked into her room.

7:30 PM

Gifford straightened his tie and checked in the mirror to be sure there was nothing caught between his front teeth. He was wearing his best suit with the narrow pinstripes and even a jaunty matching red handkerchief in the breast pocket. He admitted to himself that the handkerchief might be a bit overdone, but it was an important evening. Carrie Jane had agreed to a late dinner after the concert. And anyway, he loved Handel, he told himself. Dressing up was a sign of respect. Not that Handel would notice, he thought, having been dead several hundred years. But still. He laughed at his own rationalization. The truth was that he hadn't felt such anticipation about a date in a long time. And he liked the feeling.

Christensen's was ablaze with light. On the sidewalk outside the store, there were authentic luminarias, hundreds of brown paper bags lining the entrance to the building, each glowing with the light from the real candles inside, each one mounted carefully in small mounds of fresh snow. A team of three or four teens kept a careful eye on the candles, making sure none blew out in the light wind or were the targets of children with incendiary tendencies.

Concertgoers were already arriving, some of the women decked in long, brightly colored holiday dresses they kept at the back of their closets for the rare occasions they were appropriate. Many had badgered their husbands into Sunday attire, though a few men still wore the boots in which they'd walked the snow-packed fields earlier in the day. A couple of young boys chased one another in and out of the arriving guests, and one mother licked her fingers, then tried to smooth the cowlick on her five-year-old's head. Neighbors laughed and wished each other "Merry Christmas." An air of delicious expectation floated among the crowd. Most agreed that Douglas Valley had not seen a night like this in a very long time.

Inside, the choir was warming up behind the acoustic dividers that separated the risers from the small suite of dressing rooms and offices at the back of the store. Janeen had made a fuss about the audience being able to hear the warm-ups, even though they couldn't actually see the choir, but there was nothing to be done about it. There was nowhere else in the building big enough to house the whole group. She had been somewhat mollified when Leon pointed out that at least the choir had room to line up and move onto the risers in an orderly procession.

Chairs in the main hall had been placed in a half-moon shape with an aisle down the center. The string quartet, piano, and organ filled the small hollow left at the front of the room between the risers and the folding chairs. Microphones on either side of the instruments were carefully arranged so that the soloists could step smoothly from their places when it was their turn to perform. Students had abducted Christmas trees from their own living rooms to line the edges of the hall, and the twinkling lights were the only illumination beyond the pools of light provided for the musicians. Concertgoers chatted with neighbors and friends and searched the room for the seats which would likely have the best possible view of their family members in the choir. Anticipation filled the hall.

Carrie Jane peeked around the dividers at the crowd. "Almost a full house already," she whispered to Flor. She could see a whole contingent of students near the back helping families to find seats and corral wayward children. Carrie Jane spotted Kyra and her husband sitting on one side of Mark Gifford. What must be one of his sisters' families was on the other side of him, a child with missing teeth and French braids sitting on his lap. She located several teachers and administrators from the high school and winked at Crawford Hyunh, the woodshop teacher who had spent as many hours supervising kids here in the last few days as she had. Judge Callister's white hair shone in the twinkling lights on the left side of the audience seated next to an older woman Carrie Jane didn't recognize. For a moment she speculated about his appearance with another female when he was clearly interested in Ramona. Fleetingly, she reverted to her default position on men—fickle creatures. Then Ollie and Tyler caught her eye and flashed her simultaneous thumbs up. Who knew that a bunch of kids and some inexperienced adults could transform this derelict building into the scene before her? She turned, wordless, to Flor.

"I know," Flor nodded, her eyes glistening suspiciously. "It's a miracle."

"All right PEOPLE," Janeen's voice was raspy with her unfamiliar attempt to whisper. "Line up for the procession." She spied a tardy choir member trying to slip unnoticed into the clump of altos near the back. "Rachel!" Then Janeen sighed, remembered it was Christmas after all and gave up. "At least you made it."

Out front there was a stirring in the audience and heads turned toward the doors as Mayor Simpson and her husband made an entrance just moments before the concert was scheduled to begin—her actions calculated to attract the maximum attention.

An undercurrent of surprise rippled through the crowd. "Can't believe she'd have the gall to show up here when she's planning to tear this building down in the spring."

"Ain't nothin' that woman won't do to get a vote."

"Didn't know she liked anything but country music."

Spattered laughter accompanied the comments from the audience as the Mayor and her husband were shown to the seats reserved for them on the front row. Simpson waved to the audience and mouthed "Merry Christmas" to them before she settled into her chair.

From behind the curtain Ramona caught fragments of the buzzing undercurrents and realized the Mayor must have arrived. An exaggerated grimace crossed her face, but Annie and Viola were near the front of the line organized by height, so there was no one to pay attention when she muttered, "Idiot," under her breath.

The last stragglers were ushered to their seats just as two boys from Flor's classes silently closed the doors and took their own seats.

At the front of the auditorium, the quartet filed in, shuffled their music stands so each string player could see, and began turning their instruments. From behind the dividers, Janeen gave the signal for the processional. Choir members straightened their shoulders, tucked their black music folders under their right hands, turned their eyes forward, and began to move in unison. The audience quieted immediately, wide-eyed children waving to mothers or fathers as they took their places on the risers. Once everyone was in standing in front of their assigned chairs with their black folders open and ready, Janeen's arms rose and the triumphant opening chords washed through the hall.

8:30 PM

Belen was lying on a hospital bed, her back elevated, dark locks of damp hair plastered around her face. Eduardo pushed the partially open curtain out of the way and walked into the room. A nurse checking Belen's blood pressure turned to look at him with some interest and went back to her work.

"Eduardo," Belen murmured and reached for him, the blood pressure cuff dragging toward him with her movement.

"Hold still," the nurse commanded, realigning the stethoscope just above the inside of Belen's elbow. "I can't get an accurate measurement if you keep twisting away."

On the opposite side of the bed stood a scowling man with heavy muscular arms, his belly protruding considerably above his belt. The small mustache under his broad nose was beaded with sweat. When he caught sight of the way his daughter's featured relaxed as the boy came into the room, his eyes narrowed, and his body coiled itself into a snarl. He reacted instantaneously. "The coward shows his face at last," he said, each word snapping with disdain. "You have destroyed my daughter's life." The man took a threatening step toward Eduardo. "You think you can do whatever you want, take whatever you want," his voice rose. "But never again!" He swore. His face contorted in rage. "Today. Now. You are finished. Get out and do not come back."

"No, no, no Papa!" Belen whimpered. "You cannot. . .. The baby. . .." her words were interrupted with an agonized cry of pain. Short, ragged breaths erupted from her chest. "It hurts,' she pleaded to the nurse. "It hurts so much." A deep groan escaped her lips. She shifted, and a bright red pool of blood oozed onto her hospital gown and made a slow, inexorable path to the sheets beneath and around the girl.

Belen reached out to Eduardo; she gripped his hand so tightly with both of hers that he could see the exposed veins in her wrists rise to the surface. "Eduardo, I need . . ." but her words were swallowed in another gasp of pain.

Alarmed, Eduardo turned wildly to the nurse. "What is happening?" As he spoke, tiny splotches of red began to soak the edges of the blanket which lay atop her legs. "Help her! Help her!" he begged. "Oh, Belen. Belen." Terror swept across his face. "Please," he pleaded with the nurse. "I can't lose her."

The nurse's matter-of-fact voice cut across his voice. "Gentlemen, please step outside," she ordered without looking at either of the men. Her eyes moved methodically from monitor to monitor. "I need to check her and see what is going on." Her calm demeanor was undermined by the sound of Belen's increasing distress. "There, there, it will be right," the nurse soothed the girl as she prepared to lift the sheet. One look at the pool spreading blood around Belen's body turned her voice grim. She commanded the two men. "You need to leave NOW."

"I am her father. I will stay," announced the older man, accustomed to his decisions being law.

"Not if you want to see your grandchild alive," the nurse returned through gritted teeth, lowering the head of the bed simultaneous with pushing its speaker button. "Kristy, call a Code Two and get the doctor. We've got trouble here."

Eduardo was frozen in place. His body seemed physically unable to let go of Belen's hand. She was sobbing now, clutching him with such unyielding strength that his knuckles turned white. How could there be so much blood? "What is happening?" he cried again.

A voice over the loudspeaker repeated, "Code Two, Code Two in room B204. Dr. Timmons to B204, stat."

Only moments later a middle-aged woman with sandy-brown hair and a rumpled white coat strode past open the curtain, ignoring Eduardo and Belen's father. "What have we got?" she asked the nurse as she pulled on gloves and slide a small round stool up to the end of the bed.

The nurse was still elevating Belen's legs onto some sort of clamps and was unhooking monitors as she spoke. "Looks like there's a problem with the placenta. She started bleeding about three minutes ago."

The doctor reached beneath the sheet that now covered Belen's legs, her fingers probing the birth canal. She nodded. "Baby?"

The nurse checked the monitors and put her stethoscope on Belen's enlarged tummy. "Good so far."

Two orderlies and another nurse swept into the room.

"Call surgery to expect us," the doctor said over her shoulder to one of the three. "Let's get her prepped. And get those men out of here. Now!" she barked

Eduardo and Belen's father jumped at the sharpness of the command. Both moved immediately out of the room into the hallway. Neither looked at the other.

Inside Belen's room, the team moved in practiced unison. One unplugged the oxygen and connected Belen to a small portable unit. The other nurse took charge of the IV stand, untangling it from the other cords snaking from the bed to the wall. The two orderlies moved to each end of the bed, one unlatching the brake as he went. The doctor pulled off her gloves and threw them in the medical wastebasket; then washed her hands on her way out the door.

As the orderlies swept the bed out the door and into the hall, the doctor held up a hand to stop the rolling bed. She turned to Eduardo. "You the father?"

Eduardo nodded.

The doctor took a deep breath. They were so young. "Looks like there's a tear in the placenta, the sack encasing the baby," she said, careful to maintain a level voice and keep her explanation simple. "We'll have to take the baby Cesarean. An orderly is on the way with the paperwork." She studied Eduardo's white face, and her focus shifted from the girl to this boy with the dark hair and blue-green eyes. "Chances are excellent they'll both be OK," she assured him. "We know what to do. You can walk with her down the hall to surgery if you like."

As an orderly guided Belen's bed out the door and past the two men in the hall, Eduardo moved alongside it and grasped Belen's hand. "It will be all right," he whispered to her, trying to keep the fear out of his voice. "You and the baby. I will be right outside."

Frantic, Belen turned to him. "Don't leave me! Don't leave me, Eduardo." She clutched at him, grabbing his elbow and pulling him closer as she turned to the doctor and implored, "My baby? Don't let my baby die."

The monitor around Belen's belly began to squeal faster. Frowning, the doctor signaled the orderlies to increase their pace.

Eduardo was almost running to keep up with the pace.

"I'm so scared," Belen gasped as another pain racked her body. "Don't leave me, Eduardo, please."

"We will take care of you and your baby—both of you." The nurse's words from the other side of the bed were intended to reassure the girl, though her eyes never left the monitor flashing the baby's heartbeat.

She addressed Eduardo. "We know what is happening; the doctor has dealt with it many times. She is one of the best at the hospital," the nurse promised as she raced alongside the swiftly moving bed, her stethoscope again on Belen's belly.

Taking the earpieces from her own ears, she held them against Belen's head. "Listen, you can hear your baby's heart. See," she said, "The baby is strong," she smiled reassuringly at Belen, purposely slowing her voice in an attempt to calm the young girl. "I promise. I will give him? or her? to you, the moment the baby is born," she finished.

Brilliant lights pouring out from the swinging doors ahead of them suddenly lit Belen's face. Eduardo took in the words "Surgery. No admittance" as he hurried along next to the bed, his hand still clutched in Belen's steel grip. The orderlies slowed the bed, one slamming the automatic open button.

Putting her hand over Eduardo's, the nurse told him gently, "You must let go of her now." To Belen, she leaned over and pledged, "He will not leave. He will be just outside the door in the waiting room." She looked significantly at Eduardo who nodded in understanding.

He bent low and whispered in Belen's ear, "We are going to meet our baby today." Tears welled up in his eyes. "You and me. Together. Do as the nurse asks. You know that I will not leave you. Ever." He unclasped each of her fingers from his hand, one at a time. He did not want her to see the panic he felt, so he lowered his head, appearing to concentrate on his task. "I love you, Belen," he said as the team wheeled her through a set of double doors and out of his reach.

Through the small window atop each door, he could see the small caravan turn a corner. Here the lights were dimmer, a glow coming from doors at the end of the passage. When they reached them, the orderly guiding the bed halted and punched a button. The doors opened, and the team slid Belen's bed into a large room. Eduardo glimpsed many pieces of shiny equipment, large lights suspended over an empty bed in the center of the room, several trays with instruments, and the doctor now dressed in sterile scrubs, her gloved hands held above her waist to avoid contamination. The team rolled Belen's bed alongside the empty table. Just as the doors whished closed, Eduardo head the nurse say, "Ready, one, two, three," and saw Belen repositioned onto the new bed. Abruptly the bustle and clatter ended.

Eduardo was left in the silent hall. He felt a wave of grief so strong it was almost palpable. There was nothing he could do. These strangers did not know Belen. They did not understand that her very existence allowed him to breathe. What if she didn't matter enough to them? A single stark realization slammed into him. All that he cared about might very well be lost in the next few minutes. Then he would truly be alone. He gave a shuddering sob, dropped to his knees, his back sliding down the wall until he was crouched next to it. He covered his face with his hands and fought to stop the agony. He made no sound, but great convulsions of air exploded from his chest, and his whole body trembled with each gasp. It was as if all his strength was seeping away until there was nothing to hold him together—a straw casing without substance. He was afraid he had become so weak he might never be able to stand again.

"Go ahead and cry, you 'pretend' man," a harsh voice assaulted him from down the hall. Seconds later a rough hand dragged him to his feet. "You think your world is ending, but I know the truth. You will walk away like every other coward who can see nothing but himself." Belen's father was consumed with fury. "You did this to her. If she dies, you will carry the blame. And I will never let you forget. Every waking moment I will make you suffer." He looked up into Eduardo's face, holding the boy's shoulder in an iron grasp. "Leave here. Leave now. I never want to see your face again." The menace in his voice was more than a threat. It consumed Belen's father.

Wrenching his body away from the man, Eduardo forced his back against the wall, using it to leverage his balance. He shuddered one last time, and then his whole body stiffened with the anger which propelled it. His eyes bored into the shorter man's for a long moment. All the anxiety and isolation of the last year rushed over him and amplified the rage he had kept beneath the surface for so long.

"Don't. Ever. Touch. Me. Again." He said, his voice so low it barely echoed in the empty hall. "I love Belen. She carries our baby." His gaze never wavered from the older man's face. "You know nothing about love."

He spit out the words. "You don't even know your daughter. All that matters to you is your fear that she will leave you; you didn't even consider her needs. That's why she kept the secret of who I am. She was afraid of what you might do. And she was right. You don't care about her or the baby. You only care about yourself and your pain. That is not love." he said. His face hardened with resolve. "Belen and the baby are my family now. Not yours. She will never be your family again." He turned his back on Belen's father and began the long walk down the empty hall toward the maternity waiting room, abandoning the older man, now a silent, solitary figure in the empty corridor.

10:30 PM

It had been an exhausting few weeks. Ramona dropped into her favorite chair and closed her eyes. Just a few minutes of quiet, she thought, and then I can make it into bed. Annie was at Viola's tonight, the three of them had planned to cap off the concert evening by watching the original version of "Miracle on Thirty-Fourth Street". Apparently, Annie had never seen it, or at least didn't remember that she had. Ramona had made sandwiches for the event because she knew they wouldn't have time to eat before the concert—Janeen always threatened the choir about digestive juices rising to the throat and restricting the sound. Ramona thought the whole idea was ridiculous, but Annie was so anxious, she hadn't been able to sit still long enough to eat anyway. The sandwiches were now in Viola's fridge, but Ramona simply couldn't manage another two hours. She felt as though her entire body had given up the ghost and all that was left was sagging flesh and heavy eyelids. It was time for bed.

****

Next door Annie, on the other hand, was still wired after their performance. She paced Viola's living room too excited to perch anywhere for long. "They loved it, didn't they Viola?" she said for the umpteenth time.

Viola laughed. "Annie, sit down. You should be worn out after all that to-do. Come over and sit by me," she patted the spot next to her on the loveseat.

Annie twirled around the room. "I've never felt like this before. It was so exciting." Abruptly she plodded down next to Viola. "Is it always like that?"

"Like what, child?"

"Does it always feel like angels are singing with us?"

"Angels?"

"I'm sure I could hear them whispering all around us. It was like we were really singing for heaven."

The things that come out of that girl's mouth. Viola could think of nothing to say. But she did admit it had been an exceptional night. In her memory, the soloists had never performed with such precision and clarity. The choir blended as one voice. And when Annie stepped forward to sing, the entire audience held its collective breath. Even the youngest children stopped their fidgeting and listened with rapt attention.

Viola put her arm around Annie; the girl leaned her head on Viola's breast. "Annie, I don't know about the rest of the choir, but there is no question that angels were with you when you sang. Ramona and I were so proud of you."

Annie brushed aside her own performance. "My favorite part," she said, "was when people in the audience stood and sang the "Hallelujah Chorus" with us. Did you see that gray-haired lady with the bun? She didn't even have to use music. She knew every word."

Viola thought for a minute. "Oh, you must mean Ada. She used to sing with us every year; in fact, lots of those folks did at one time or another." She smiled down at the girl. "I was in college the first time I ever sang selections from the *Messiah*," a clear vision of the past rose in her head. "I belonged to the Women's Chorus. All the University choirs were combined for a 'brown paper bag' lunch concert in the central hall of the Fine Arts Center just before semester break. The audience stood all around us on three levels of balconies. During the 'Hallelujah Chorus', I remember a tiny woman so old her face was lined with wrinkles stepped out of a hallway and moved next to me. She took hold of one side of my music, smiled at me, then began to sing. Her voice was gravelly and frail, but it was one of the most beautiful moments of my life." She put her cheek against Annie's soft hair. "I never even heard her name, but I felt as if I'd known her forever. It was the music."

Annie nodded understanding. "Sometimes, when something really matters, we are all the same," she said.

Viola tightened her grip around the girl. Like now, she thought.

11 PM

At the Stagecoach Steak House, Carrie Jane and Mark Gifford were laughing over the look on Mayor Simpson's face as Janeen Baldwin asked all those who had worked to transform Christensen's into a concert hall be recognized. Fully one-third of the audience, mostly young people, rose to its feet. The crowd whistled and cheered, rising to its feet to spontaneously to join the students and teachers whose hard work had performed such miraculous wizardry to the old hall. Mayor Simpson obviously wasn't used to being a minority, but she grudgingly stood with the rest of the group and clapped half-heartedly. Carrie Jane, whose position in the choir was directly in front of the Mayor, described with some delight the look of apprehension that flitted momentarily across the Mayor's face when she realized that her tide of support may have begun to erode.

"There's no question that what you all accomplished was nothing short of phenomenal," Gifford agreed. "When I was a kid, my mom used to drag me to Christensen's on the rare occasions when she found enough money to buy herself something new. I was fascinated by those columns upfront. Seems the early settlers didn't have a way to transport marble from the pit up near Salt Lake, so they cut the columns out of huge trees up the canyon and then hired someone to paint them to look like marble. I kept trying to figure out how they did it."

"Did you?"

"What?"

"Figure out how they did it?"

"Nope," he said decisively. "Still don't know. But I'm guessing some farmer had gone to art school and then was sucked in by the pull of 'rich, new land' in the West." He paused, looking directly into her eyes. "That's one thing you learn as a cop—people have lots of sides to them. What you see doesn't necessarily mean that's what you get. Like you, for instance."

"Me?" she looked genuinely puzzled. "I'm about as predictable as you can be."

"Really? A teacher who can talk a bunch of kids into volunteering hundreds of hours of hard labor without lifting an eyebrow and has a beautiful voice on top of that? What else don't I know about you that I should?" He reached over and brushed a tendril of hair out of her eyes.

Startled, Carrie Jane ducked her head in confusion. "You'd be surprised how many teachers sing." She avoided his steady gaze. "Last year we had a faculty choir perform for a patriotic assembly, and the auto body teacher did the baritone solo. The kids loved it." She relaxed and made a conscious effort to recover her equilibrium. "As for me, I have expensive tastes in food," she teased looking around at the linen tablecloths and candlelit atmosphere, "and I'm deathly afraid of spiders."

"Good news," he said. "I carry a gun. Spiders are afraid of me!"

Sunday, December 22

6 AM

THE BABY WAS BEAUTIFUL. SHE had dark, dark hair which was so long there were even tiny curls along the back of her neck. Because she had been delivered C-section, her skin was an even, silky caramel color, and there was none of the bruising or reddened welts that appeared on some babies after the stress of birth. She was sleeping peacefully, wrapped in a pink blanket, one fist almost hidden under her little chin, her compact little body curled in Belen's left arm. Her mother was dozing, but when Eduardo tried to slip the baby out of her arms, Belen had stirred, smiled sleepily, and pulled the child closer.

Eduardo checked his phone. It had run out of battery. He glanced at the clock hanging over Belen's bed. He hadn't slept since yesterday and exhaustion threatened to overtake him. He could have stretched out on the fold-out chair in Belen's room which was provided for dads, but she wouldn't let go of his hand.

It had been after midnight when she had been rolled into recovery, and now hours later, the doctor was just making her rounds. "You need some sleep," the doctor ordered the boy. "Mom is going to sleep most of today. The surgery went well. Baby is fine too, but this kind of birth is pretty traumatic, so they both are going to need some tender care the next few days. Belen is on some heavy pain meds, and the surgery will leave her sore and uncomfortable for several weeks. Maybe a couple of more days here, and then you can take them home." She searched Eduardo's face. "Where is home?"

"We have a little place by my parents," Eduardo lied, surprised at how easily the lie came to his lips. "I have a few days off. I will take very good care of her and the Little One." His eyes wandered to the sleeping infant of their own accord. "She is so beautiful."

"Six pounds two ounces. A big baby for being almost a month early." The doctor paused, seemingly to consider what to say next. "Mom is going to need some time to recover," she said to Eduardo. "She is young and healthy, but her body won't just bounce back immediately. Do you understand what I'm saying?"

Eduardo nodded, confused. The doctor's piercing stare caused him to squirm uncomfortably. His eyes widened in comprehension. This was something he had never even considered when he imagined what it would be like to be an adult. Not one of the books he had read spoke about what happened after the baby came. He loved Belen. A man would give her time to heal. His heart caught in his throat. What if she is angry with me for causing her this pain? Momentary panic crossed his face.

The doctor put a hand on his shoulder, sympathy and concern in the gesture. "Belen is strong," she reassured him. "She will recover. Sometimes the body doesn't do exactly what it's programmed to. Neither of you could have anticipated that the placenta had a weak spot. It is not your fault." She looked at Belen's hand clutching his even in her sleep. "It's not uncommon for us to have to help nature fix the problems it creates, but fortunately, in most cases, we can. Don't worry. You have a lovely child." She paused, thinking about how young this boy looked. It occurred to her that the girl's father who had been here last night had seemed to have abandoned them. She reconsidered whatever she might have intended to say and changed the subject. "Have you decided on a name?'

"Elinor," said Eduardo. "If the baby was a girl, we were going to name her Elinor, after my mother."

Eduardo wasn't sure how much time had passed when Belen's gentle voice started him. "You must sleep," she ordered Eduardo. His eyes popped open, but his groggy head struggled to focus on what she was saying.

"I am fine. I was just resting my eyes."

"No. Your head was bobbing, and you were snoring—just a tiny bit," she smiled to soften her words. "You haven't eaten since you came to the hospital. Go to the cafeteria—perhaps bacon and eggs?' Belen tempted him playfully. She knew that breakfast was his favorite meal.

He leaned toward her, kissing first her cheek and then the baby's in turn. "I am afraid she will wake, and I will miss something," he said.

She smiled, a new appreciation of her responsibility as the mother of the family already resting on her shoulders. "Then bring a tray and hurry back. I will feed Elinor," the name played on her tongue pleasingly, "when you return. Our family can have its first meal together." She let go of his hand and watched as he shook it to encourage the blood to seep back into his fingers.

He knew she was right, as always. "I'll be back," he conceded. "It will just be a few minutes." Though it took only a moment for him to smooth down his hair and rinse out his mouth, Belen was asleep again before he left the room. He kissed her tenderly on the forehead and slipped the sleeping child from her arms, placing the baby in her bassinet next to Belen's bed.

He checked the hall in both directions as he closed the door behind him. No sign of Mr. Hidalgo, and not a word during the night. Eduardo was both relieved and concerned. He didn't imagine Mr. Hidalgo had given up. The boy shrugged his shoulders. He was still basking in the glow of being a new father. Other problems would have to wait.

The cafeteria was almost deserted--only a couple of tables with lone employees in brightly colored scrubs nursing cups of coffee, one reading the early edition of USA Today. For a moment Eduardo was shocked. Headlines that had nothing to do with Belen and the baby? How could there be any other news going on in the world?

"What can I get for you?" asked a plump, middle-aged woman whose hair was straying outside the confines of her hairnet. He picked up a tray from the stack at the entrance of the food service line.

Eduardo fished a couple of dollar bills and some change out of his pocket. "How much for . . .." He stopped to count how much cash he still had after paying for the few presents he'd managed to purchase.

"I'm buying," said a voice behind him. He turned to discover the white-haired guy who'd helped him find Marisa's Christmas shoes standing next to him. The man smiled, his eyes crinkling in amusement at the expression on Eduardo's face. "Came to see a new baby," he explained. "Quite a coincidence running into you again."

"Yeah," Eduardo said. The was man was dressed exactly as the day before, a white shirt and pants and a fancy camel-colored coat over one arm. "You a doctor?"

The man laughed. "Not hardly. Just a visitor. How 'bout you?"

"Baby. I had a baby girl last night. Her name's Elinor."

"Nice," approved the man. He smiled, "both the baby and the name. How's Mom doing?"

Eduardo hesitated. Maybe this man knew his father, or worse, Belen's? The man seemed sincere, and Eduardo was so tired. He just couldn't see how telling him the truth could cause trouble.

"She's tired. But she'll be OK. She's very special." Eduardo felt self-conscious trying to explain, so he stopped.

"New moms are all special—in the best way possible." The older man nodded in agreement. "I remember years ago I asked an OB-GYN doc why he chose maternity when the hours were horrendous, and the pay was nothing compared to what a surgeon, for instance, makes. I'll never forget what the guy said. 'I've been practicing for 30 years and in all that time, I've never—not once—had a mom ask if she was going to be OK. After delivery, they all say, 'How's my baby?' When you think about it," the old man looked straight into Eduardo's eyes, "that's about as selfless as human beings ever get."

He changed the subject briskly. "Now what are you having? I've always been a bacon and eggs man myself, although you're welcome to order anything you want." He waved off the server's question about his own order. "Too early for me. Just came in when I saw the kid here in line. We're old friends."

"Thank you," said Eduardo. "You do not know me, and yet you have gone out of your way for me twice in the last two days." You must be a very good man, or you want something from me, Eduardo thought but didn't voice the words aloud. He had learned to pay careful attention to people. More than once when he was younger, he'd had kids at school appear to befriend him then simply dismiss him when he refused to do their homework. On the other hand, he was starving. It had been a very long night.

He leaned across the counter and spoke to the server. "Bacon and eggs would be perfect, and maybe some orange juice?" He remembered Belen's plan. "To go, please."

"Coming up," replied the server. "Juice is in the machine right before the cash register. Take a minute to cook the bacon. Why don't you sit down, and I'll bring it over?" The white-haired man pulled out his wallet and handed her a twenty-dollar bill; one of many, Eduardo noticed. Then the man led the way to a nearby table. He and Eduardo grabbed a couple of chairs, and Eduardo carefully sealed a plastic lid on the top of his juice as he sat down.

"So. When does Belen get out of the hospital?"

"It will be at least a couple more days. She had to have a C-section. But soon, I hope." Eduardo pushed the looming medical bills out of his mind. Yet another problem he had no idea how to solve. Best to ignore it and think only of Belen and the baby. Speaking of which, how did the old man know Belen's name?

"How'd you know her name?" Eduardo asked suspiciously. "I don't think I mentioned it."

The man laughed again. It was a warm voice, relaxed and engaging. "You think I'm psychic or something?" He appeared genuinely amused by the idea. "Nah, only three or four moms' names on the ward list upstairs. I've got a good memory, and I just guessed." He shifted the conversation to a more serious note. "Gotta be difficult. Having a baby at your age. What are your plans?"

Eduardo tried to imagine some elaborate bluff he could tell the man to avoid painful reality, but nothing came to mind. He was just too tired to think clearly. Besides, he wasn't likely to ever see this guy again. What did it matter now?

"I . . .." he began, but how could he explain? "I love her," he said. He shrugged his shoulders helplessly. "I don't know what to do, but I love her. We will manage somehow." He hated that he sounded like a stupid kid, but he feared that's what he was.

The man searched Eduardo's face. "I can see that, Son. Things will work out," he reassured the boy. "They always do. Sometimes in the most unexpected ways." He added, "What about your family? Do they know the baby's come? Have you called them? I'm sure they can help."

Eduardo tried to mask the misery he felt at the mention of his father. "I will call them soon," he promised. "I just have not had time."

The man looked into Eduardo's eyes. There was no judgment in his voice when he said, "Give them a chance, son. That's why we have families, at least partly anyway--to smooth the way from one generation to the next. You may be surprised at the results."

Eduardo heaved a long sigh. It's not that he didn't want his family to know Belen and the baby. But he'd put it off for so long, it seemed impossible now to remedy his mistake.

"Here ya go," the server interrupted, handing Eduardo a Styrofoam container. "Bacon and eggs. I added some hash browns. Hope you don't mind. New dads need plenty of energy." She winked and headed back to the kitchen, her soft-soled shoes making a squishy sound with each step on the linoleum floor.

Eduardo felt a wave of gratitude wash over him all out of proportion to the small kindness of the woman. He had been so long alone. Now two people had stepped in to help in only a few minutes. He could scarcely contain the relief their simple actions had produced. "Thank you," he said again to the white-haired man. Then a new thought occurred to him. "Would you like to meet my daughter?"

"I would, indeed," said the stranger. "It would be an honor."

Eduardo led him back upstairs to the maternity ward. He opened the door and held it for the white-haired man, balancing his meal in the opposite hand. "We are going to have breakfast together," he explained unnecessarily.

Belen was asleep, her long dark lashes contrasted with the pallor of her skin. "She lost a lot of blood," Eduardo explained in a whisper. "The doctor said she is worn out, but she is very strong."

The old man studied her face, calm and unlined in sleep. "Lovely," he said. "You are fortunate."

Eduardo nodded. He gestured to the small bassinet next to Belen's bed. Swaddled in pink blankets with the Christmas cap now perched on her head, the baby looked more like a tiny doll than a child--except for the fact that she was wide awake and studying the florescent lights on the ceiling above her. As he lifted the bundle carefully from her bed, she turned her head and looked directly at him. He knew the books said that she wouldn't be able to see clearly for some time, but he had the uncanny feeling that she knew him; he tightened his arms around her and hugged her to his chest. Pride surged through him. He hoped she knew that he would keep her safe, always. "This is Elinor," he said to his visitor, and he turned her little body so that the white-haired man could see her face.

Setting his coat on the chair next to Belen's bed, the older man touched the baby's cheek. Her head moved instinctively toward his finger, her lips seeking an object to suckle.

"Oh-h-h." Eduardo chuckled. "She likes you."

The old man stroked her cheek and touched the soft hair under her cap. "This one will be a blessing to you," he predicted. "Take good care of her."

The child's lips stopped moving. Her eyes roved past Eduardo and focused on the old man. She stared at him without blinking.

"She acts as if she knows you," Eduardo said in surprise.

"Perhaps she does, Son." the man agreed. "Perhaps she does."

8 AM

Morning was flooding the room when Ramona woke suddenly. She opened her eyes and blinked at the glare from the windows. It looked to be snowing lightly, but the sun was shining through the mist of white onto the already snow-covered ground. Its reflection nearly blinded her. Must be six or eight inches out there, she calculated as she shook her head back and forth, blinking at the light. Somewhere she could hear a barely audible rhythmic beat, and then a tiny voice yelling something.

She sighed as she threw back the covers and turned over. She slid her legs off the edge of the bed and groaned slightly as she tried to stand. "Never knew I'd end up an old person," she muttered as she grabbed her robe and pulled it over her shoulders, buttoning it as she went. The noise sounded like it was coming from the front door. "If this keeps up, I'm going to have to hire a butler just to handle the traffic."

She pulled back the deadbolt and opened the door. Marisa stood shivering on her front porch. "Where's the Annie-girl?" she blurted out. "I need her. *Mi hijo* is lost."

Ramona pulled the little girl inside. At least today she had on a warm coat and hat, though her boots had Power Rangers insignia and looked to be about two sizes too big. She helped the child slip out of the boots and set them by the door. They were covered with slush, so Ramona concluded Marisa must have trudged through sidewalks not yet cleared by the neighbors' snow blowers. "Does your mother know you came to see Annie?" she asked.

"*No, señora. Mi papa* is calling *la policía*. I heard him say to Mama that something bad has happened. Eduardo did not sleep in his bed. He does not answer his phone. I am very scared. The Annie-girl. I need her," she insisted.

"Annie is sleeping next door," Ramona said. "I am sorry about your brother, but why do you think Annie can help you?" She asked as she helped the little girl climb onto the couch and then sat down next to her.

"She is lost. She knows what to do. She can help us find him."

There was a certain irrefutable logic there somewhere, Ramona thought. "I am sure Annie would want to help you, but there are many policemen. Perhaps they can be of more help than Annie?"

"No," the little girl said firmly. "I need the Annie-girl."

Ramona nodded in the face of the girl's implacable faith. "Then we will talk to her. First, let me call your mother to tell her where you are and ask permission for you to stay with me awhile. Second, I need to get dressed; then we will go next door and see Annie. Is that OK?"

"Yes, please," the little girl agreed and folded her hands in her lap, prepared to wait as long as necessary.

In less than half an hour, Ramona and the child were sipping cocoa at Viola's table, the little girl sitting on Annie's lap. Large unshed tears hovered at the corners of Marisa's eyes as she explained that Eduardo had rushed out of the house just after dark the evening before and had never come home. "He has a secret," she said looking up into Annie's face. "Papa said it was . . ." she paused, thinking carefully so that she could persuade these women to help her. "Papa said Eduardo could have a secret. It is OK. But now he is not home, and I don't know the secret." Her lower lip quivered. "He needs me to take care of him. He should have told me."

Annie hugged her. "I sure he would have told you if he could have," Annie assured her. Looking at Ramona and Viola for support, she told the child, "When I was lost, I told a policeman, and he helped me. Maybe he could help you?"

Viola nodded. "Marisa, let's take you home and see what the police told your mama and papa. Maybe Eduardo is home already, and there is no need to worry?"

"No," said the child positively. "He is not home. He is lost, and we must find him," but she dutifully climbed down from Annie's lap and went to find her hat and coat.

"What do you think," Ramona asked Viola, who had had years of experience with teens evading their parents for one reason or another.

Viola spoke quietly without turning her gaze from the little girl who was now shouldering her coat with Annie's help. "Probably just hanging out somewhere with a friend. He'll turn up in the next couple of hours and wonder why everyone is so upset." Her words were light, but her face betrayed her worry. Both women chose not to voice the more frightening possibilities that were now commonplace in a society where kids could be victims as well as perpetrators.

Ramona bobbed her head in agreement, but a shiver slipped unbidden up her spine. She'd had a morning like this before, and it had not ended well.

The streets in the area had not been plowed yet, so the trip to Marisa's house was slow. Even at less than 15 miles an hour, Ramona's car skidded into a curb as they went around a corner. The tires slipped and spun as Ramona twisted the steering wheel one way then another, trying to force the tires to find purchase in the slick and icy street. Finally, the little Prius shuddered and inched away from the curb. Viola and Annie exhaled simultaneously, exchanging a glance. Ramona inched back into her lane, barely creeping along. Marisa watched the entire process with fascination, unaware of anything amiss.

Oblivious of their proximity to the street and its possible perils, children on both sides of the block rollicked in the snow as if they'd never seen it before. School was out for the holiday, Christmas only a few days away, and the children were in high spirits. A couple of older children dressed like fluffy snowmen pulled smaller children on worn sleighs. A group of boys had built a snow wall and were pelting each other with icy balls, yelling taunts at each other from either side of the snow barrier.

Their exuberance was lost on the occupants of the car, their minds on Marisa's family, and Eduardo's disappearance. The little girl called out to one of her brothers as they neared the house, but the boy was engrossed in building a snowman and didn't notice her. Ramona parked in the driveway at Luz's house which had already been cleared, banks of snow spilling into the yard on both sides.

When they knocked, Luz opened the door and scooped up her daughter, burying her face in the little girl's hair. She looked over Marisa's shoulder at the women on the porch and held the door open to them, her lovely face stiff with worry.

"No sign of him?" Ramona asked as she settled down on one end of the couch next to the two younger boys who sat quietly by one another, their eyes following every move their mother made.

"Nada," Luz answered shortly. "No," she corrected herself for her visitors' benefits. She described what had happened the night before pretty much as Marisa had related. "There has been no message. Marisa's papa has gone with a policeman to the garage to see if Eduardo has been there."

"Did you see him leave?" Viola asked. "Was he upset? Did he have mention plans with friends? Sometimes kids just forget to check in with their parents. Maybe he spent the night with buddies?"

Luz considered this, shaking her head. "He never speaks of friends. When he is not home, he is at work." Her face belied the steadiness of her voice. "He is good boy. Never," she searched for a word, then gave up-- "*irrespectuoso*," she finished, gesturing with the hand which wasn't curled around Marisa, who was still clinging to her.

"Disrespectful," Annie translated.

Luz nodded. She lowered Marisa to the floor and pulled three mismatched chairs from the dining room table for Viola, Annie, and herself. "He is a good boy," she repeated. She placed the chairs in a semi-circle across from the couch. Once Viola and Annie had chosen chairs, Luz carefully lowered herself onto the couch, automatically lifting Marisa, who had not left her mother's side, back onto her lap and resting her chin on the little girl's soft, dark hair. "There are bad personas," she said. "I worry." She sent a silent message to the older women, who nodded in understanding.

Ramona spoke. "Our children," she began, but she was struck with an unfamiliar loss for words, "they are everything." For a mother, there was nothing else to say.

Luz did not respond, but she hugged Marisa tighter, and she inclined her head.

"We should call Detective Gifford," Annie said. "He likes children. Maybe he can help?

"This detective has helped you?" Marisa asked.

"Yes," Annie replied. "He has come when I needed him."

"This is good," Marisa pronounced. She craned her neck upward to face her mother. "*Mama, vamos a hablar con él.*"

Ramona was already pressing buttons on her phone.

"Gifford, here," Mark answered on the first ring. There were garbled voices in the background so loud that even the women seated across from Ramona could hear the noise. "Sorry? Who is this again? There's a lot of noise here."

"It's Ramona Zollinger." Ramona could hear the clattered of metal and voices laughing. It sounded like a lot of people, maybe a restaurant? "Looks like we've got another lost kid, but at least we know who this one is." She went on to explain the situation. "His name is Eduardo Caballero, and he hasn't been home since last evening. That's out of the ordinary; his parents are worried that something is wrong."

"Hey, Carrie Jane." Ramona could hear his muffled inquiry from her end. "Do any of your kids know an Eduardo Caballero?"

"Where are you, Mark? And what's Carrie Jane doing there?" Ramona asked.

"We're at Christensen's loading up chairs and equipment to return to the high school." He paused to listen. "Carrie Jane says Eduardo is one of her students." He stopped. Ramona heard a jumble of conversation in the background. When Gifford came back to the phone, all he said was. "We're on our way," and the phone went dead.

10 AM

The small living room was not designed to contain so many people, so Ramona and Viola gave their seats to Carrie Jane and Gifford. They picked up the last two chairs from the kitchen table and set them in the doorway to the living room, allowing them to be part of the discussion.

There was an uncomfortable silence until Annie took charge. She introduced Marisa and her family to the newcomers, including a brief summary of how the women had met the family when Marisa had taken it upon herself to collect Christmas money for family gifts. Carrie Jane filled in details about Eduardo's behavior at school and her impressions of him as a student.

"I know he's the brightest kid in that class, but he never does an assignment, never contributes to our discussions. Mostly he just sits in the back and looks angry. To be honest, I was floored when Mr. Caballero told me Eduardo had talked to him about some of the articles we'd read as a class." She turned directly to Mark. "He's very closed. Doesn't reveal anything about himself. I've worried about him since the first day of class. He radiates hostility or worry or something." She stole a glance at Luz, hoping she wasn't making the situation worse. "I can't quite pin it down. It's not that he's openly rebellious—in fact, he's always polite to me. It's as if he's never really present—he's off somewhere else in his head."

Luz nodded. "He is alone, even when he eats *la cena con la familia*. `El no habla de su vida,*" she said thoughtfully, then realized she had spoken in Spanish. "He does not talk about school or friends. He tells nothing." Her fingers crumpled the skirt of her apron into little bunches and then released them again.

Carrie Jane turned to Gifford. "What do we do now?"

"I'll check and see who caught the case and update him with what you've told me. Most likely he just crashed at a friend's house and is still asleep." He turned to the little girl. "We'll find him," he told her. "Don't worry. He'll be home in plenty of time to wrap your Christmas presents."

Marisa's eyes grew large. "He has told you about my present?'

Annie leaned over to hug the little girl on her mother's lap. "I'm sure that is a secret, too. But when a boy has a sister like you, he never forgets her Christmas present."

Luz smiled for the first time that day. "Yes, Little One. You would not let him forget."

12:30 PM

Gifford dropped Carrie Jane back at Christensen's to help Leon finish the clean-up and headed for the office. It was quiet on the Sunday before Christmas. The County Sheriff had won the last election campaigning on the need for the police system to pay more attention to the families who supported its officers. As a result, most of his colleagues were at church with their kids or out finishing last-minute shopping. It was one reason Gifford respected his boss. Being a cop was tough on wives and children as the divorce rates testified.

The lone dispatcher in the small room next to Gifford's office waved at him as he went by, her eyes on the screen in front her and her right hand holding her headphone tighter against her ear for increased clarity. Sounded like a routine call from the couple of words of instruction he heard her give, but he didn't stop to check it out. He shoved aside the mail which was piled on the desk in front of him and switched on his computer. When he found what he needed, he scrolled through his phone list and gave Patrolman Shaloe a call. Shaloe. It figured, he thought as he waited for the call to connect. Vince had probably volunteered to fill somebody else's shift. He'd only been hired six months before, and the tarnish which colored the never-ending routine of interviews, fact-finding, and reports for career guys hadn't affected the patrolman--yet. But it would, Gifford knew. Especially the reports.

"Hey, Vince. It's Gifford. I heard you were working on a missing kid—Eduardo Caballero?" He paused, paying attention to the response. "Yeah. He's the student of one of the teachers you met at Christensen's on Thursday. I told her I'd check on what you've found out. Heard you and the kid's dad were out late knocking on doors last night?"

Gifford listened for two or three minutes. He hadn't expected any progress, but both he and Shaloe knew that the longer a kid was gone, the more serious the possible outcome. "Well, let me know if you need any help talking to his friends or co-workers. I know a lot of the kids around here. Get back to me if you find him, OK?" and hung up.

So far Shaloe had come up dry. No kid. No clue. Gifford leaned back in his chair and closed his eyes. He imaged the picture of Eduardo that Luz had shown him, and the description Carrie Jane had given of an angry or isolated kid. When he'd asked Carrie Jane if it was possible the kid had been bullied at school and was frightened, she'd laughed. "No," she said. "His tongue is a weapon sharp enough that most kids are afraid to tangle with him." Maybe he ruffled the feathers of too many kids? Gifford considered that possibility.

He let his mind wander through a half-dozen scenarios. Personally, it sounded to Gifford like the kid was just hiding out somewhere. He knew from his own experience that adolescent boys tended to spend a lot of time avoiding home. Games, parties, bull sessions. That kind of thing. On the other hand, Eduardo's family clearly cared about him. No sign of serious conflict. Still, the kid hadn't been gone long. Gifford suspected he'd turn up when he was ready.

The day after tomorrow was Christmas Eve. Gifford still had a little shopping to do. At the concert last night, he'd asked Kyra to set aside a couple of her favorite children's books, one for each of his siblings' families to read together. Frequently when one sister or the other invited him to dinner, he'd be roped into joining the family for an evening ritual of enjoying a chapter or two from "Black Beauty" or "Hunger Games", or whatever novel the family was reading. He had fond memories of his parents reading to them almost every night, and the habit had trickled down into the next generation. He figured he'd better go pick up the books first thing in the morning before Kyra got a chance to sell them to someone else. Maybe he could talk Carrie Jane into coming with him and having a little lunch on the way back? Or was that too much too soon? He sighed. Crime, he understood. Most always a direct line between motive and action. He chuckled under his breath. Sometimes the line was really dumb, but still, it was a pretty clear line. Relationships, in his experience, however, were infinitely more complex.

2 PM

Ramona and Annie were wrapping gifts, brightly colored paper spread out on the floor in the living room. Ramona was sitting in her chair attaching tags to last-minute packages, and Annie, scissors in hand, was crawling from one package to the next folding and taping as she went.

"Do you think Marisa's brother is OK?' Annie asked for the third time in the last half an hour.

"He's eighteen. He can take care of himself, I'll bet. I wouldn't worry too much," Ramona assured her. Annie had seemed obsessed with the disappearance of the boy from the moment Marisa told her he was missing. Maybe it was just her own situation, Ramona concluded. Even with Viola and me watching out for her, the girl must feel like she's in limbo. She took a deep breath. It was time to talk about what happens next. Ramona set the roll of wrapping paper with the open end down, so it didn't unravel. "Annie? Are you worried about your own future? Is that why you are so concerned with the boy?"

Annie stopped cutting. She looked at Ramona. "I guess," she admitted, then ducked her head, hoping to conceal the anxiety she felt. Viola and Ramona had been so good to her. She didn't want them to worry about her even more. "It's just that I . . .. I don't want to be lost forever."

Ramona's heart tore at the words. "Oh, Annie," she said. "No matter what happens, you have a home here. Viola and I—we love you. We want you to stay with us."

Annie smoothed a corner of the package she was working on and carefully taped the ends tightly. The only sound in the room was the soft background music of Christmas carols. "Ramona, why doesn't Viola have a family?" Annie asked, changing the subject. "Didn't she want to get married?"

Ramona considered her answer. "I didn't know Viola when she was a young woman," she said. "She didn't buy the house next door until we were in our thirties, and she has never relished talking about her past. I think maybe she would have liked to have a husband and children. It just didn't happen. That's one reason she loves you. You have become like the child she didn't have."

Annie nodded in understanding. "I like being her child, and yours," she added thoughtfully. "But you're both kind of old to be moms," she pointed out.

Ramona laughed out loud. "Very old," she agreed. "However, remember there are all kinds of mothers. Lots of grandmothers are raising their grandchildren. Ask Viola. She knows all the statistics for that sort of thing. When she was a social worker, many of her cases involved helping grandparents cope with the problems of raising the young children of their children when their health was poor, or they were on small fixed incomes."

"What's a fixed income? Who fixes it?"

"Well, that means you get a monthly retirement income, but you are never going to get a raise—you will always get exactly the same amount of money every month. For retired people like Viola and me, that amount is usually smaller than the salary we earned while we were still working."

Annie thought about that for a moment as she carefully folded the edges of the long rectangular package she was working on. "If Viola knew all those children, why didn't she adopt one before?"

"It's complicated," Ramona said. She put down her pen and set the package she had just labeled aside. She debated momentarily about whether it was wise to tell Annie such an ugly story, but she had learned through long practice that giving kids the truth was the best way to help arm them so that they could develop the skills they'd need to manage the inevitably messy situations they would encounter in adulthood. Kids had a sixth sense when it came to a story that didn't add up, even when one parent, or both, were just trying to sugarcoat the severity of a problem to protect their children. It was best to just tell children the truth and tell it as clearly and simply as possible.

"Years ago," Ramona began, "Viola had a very bad experience. Perhaps the worst kind possible in her profession. A child who she was assigned in a custody supervision case died. The little girl's father had beat her. . . very badly," Ramona said carefully. "Viola signed the order to send that child back to her family after the little girl had been in foster care for a while. Viola didn't want to sign it, but Utah law requires that the parents have a second chance. The girl was only two years old. One night several months later, the father was high on drugs; the child woke up in the night, crying. When the father couldn't get her to stop, he beat her again. After the child died, Viola began to believe that she should never have children—that she wouldn't be able to keep them safe."

"But she's so good!" Annie protested unable to think of another word to describe Viola. "She's ...?" Annie struggled with the unfairness of the idea. "What about the mother? Why didn't she stop it?" She demanded.

"As I understand it, the mother was frightened of her husband. He beat her, too. After it happened, the mother took her older daughter and ran away. I don't believe Viola ever heard from her again."

"That's not fair," Annie declared with the adolescent outrage of injustice in the world.

"No," Ramona agreed. "It's not fair. Sometimes we don't get to decide whether something is fair or not. We just have to live with what we've got." She leaned forward in her chair and touched Annie's cheek with affection. "But now we've been blessed with you," she said softly. "For Viola, and me, you are making all the difference."

4 PM

Gifford was on the way out the door when the call from Shaloe came.

"Detective Gifford? You asked me to notify you if I discovered any useful information about the whereabouts of that missing Caballero kid?"

"Shaloe. It's Sunday, remember? Why aren't you home with your family getting ready for Santa Claus?"

"But, Sir. A clerk at the Mini Mart happened to mention he'd seen

Caballero and some girl at the library a couple of times last fall."

"Happened to mention?" Gifford couldn't resist poking a little fun at Shaloe's undisguised zeal. "Did the kid 'happen to mention' the girl's name?"

"Yes, Sir. That's why I called. Belen. Belen Hidalgo. I have an address. Do you want to meet me there?"

The Hidalgo house was on the north end of town, only a few blocks from the high school. It was a pleasant but unremarkable neighborhood, established long enough ago that yards were dotted with large trees whose branches glistened with ice from the storm the day before. The house was an older brick model like most of the ones built in Utah after WWII. Though the trim appeared to be recently painted, it was hard to tell anything about the maintenance of the surrounding yard seeing as how the ground was covered in half a foot of snow. Gifford did note that the sidewalk had been shoveled at some point, but the additional snow from the last day or so which now covered the walks seemed to have been ignored.

Gifford tipped his head, and Shaloe obediently took the lead. Knocking first, then ringing the bell several times didn't rouse anyone. "Looks like nobody home," Shaloe said. Gifford nodded. The two men split up and walked the perimeter of the house. No lights. Not even a Christmas tree visible between the slats of the blinds in the living room.

"Probably out doing last-minute shopping." Gifford felt a momentary twinge of anxiety for his own list, still incomplete. "Girl's probably happy to get out of the house. I checked with the high school principal before I left the station. Principal wasn't happy to be pulled out of a family dinner, and she was careful to point out that she had a few more things to worry about now—like the fact that her school burned down! But she did remember the girl. Hidalgo had withdrawn the daughter last fall. Said he was going to home school her. Doesn't sound to me like the kind of thing a 16-year-old would enjoy."

He leaned back from the door and looked at the houses on both sides. Faint Christmas carols seemed to be coming from the house on the west side. "Want to try a couple of neighbors?"

Shaloe grinned in anticipation. "Yep."

They didn't have to knock or even ring the bell at the little house that sat next door. An elderly stoop-backed woman opened it before they even tried.

She peered up at them from under a cheap pair of reading glasses. "I take it you fellows are the law?" She gestured at Patrolman Shaloe's uniform, not bothering to ask for ID.

"Yes, Ma'am," he said. "Could we come in a few minutes and ask you a couple of questions about your neighbor?"

"Hidalgo? Sure. Don't talk to him much except when he comes over to complain about my Russian olive tree. Says it grows over the fence into his yard and spreads a bunch of dry leaves every fall. Wants me to go over and clean 'em up. They're in his yard; why should I have to clean 'em up?" She turned her back on them and headed into the living room. "Come on in."

Once she settled the two men onto a burnt orange couch that Gifford was certain had been sitting in that very spot since the '70s, the old woman was clearly happy to have someone to talk to. "Name's Ruby. Ruby Stone. Don't bother to say what you're thinking. Heard it already a hundred times. Folks think they're so clever, like they're the first people to notice. I married someone named Stone. What's it to 'ya?"

Gifford steered her back to the subject. "Any idea where we might find Mr. Hidalgo? We need to speak with him."

"Well, I'm no gossip," she said, "but I do keep an eye on my neighbors. Never know when someone will have a heart attack and not be able to get to the phone."

"I'm sure they appreciate your concern, Ma'am. But perhaps you can tell us when you last saw Mr. Hidalgo?" Patrolman Shaloe suggested tactfully.

"Here now, let me see. . . .." Mrs. Forest muttered under her breath as she considered the answer. "Probably day before yesterday. Yep, Friday night. Hidalgo was out there shoveling snow late. I remember the noise from his shovel was interfering with my program. Never occurs to him that he could shovel earlier in the day."

When no one appeared to shovel the additional snow the neighborhood had gotten, she'd taken it upon herself to question a couple of homeowners on the block. "Just checking to see if Hidalgo and his daughter were OK," she told the officers. "That's what neighbors should do," she said. "Hidalgo never pays any attention to the rest of us, but we still try to watch out for him—mostly because of his daughter. Real nice girl. Quiet, but always kind." Gifford got the idea that Hidalgo was not the most popular person in the neighborhood. Mrs. Stone reported that none of the neighbors had seen the girl since Saturday night when she and her father had rushed out of the house in a big hurry.

Gifford jotted the date in his notebook. Same timeframe as Eduardo's disappearance. He'd discuss that point when Shaloe when they got back outside.

"She was all bundled up like she couldn't get warm," the elderly woman told them. "She musta had a couple of layers of coat on because she looked like a snowman waddling out to the car." But the woman had had no idea where they were headed, and as far as she knew, the girl had not been with her father when he came back the next day.

Shaloe was gung-ho to continue knocking on doors all evening, but darkness came early in December, and Gifford finally ordered him to go home to his family instead. Gifford tried to remember when he had been that dedicated to the job. Nothing came to mind. Now when he had vacation time available, he took it. In the long run, a little respite from the tensions of the job had proven to be more valuable than working until his brain refused to operate any longer.

Monday, December 23

7:30 AM

ANNIE WAS ALREADY UP AND, in the kitchen, pulling cereal out of the cupboard when Ramona came in from the bedroom. Outside, the wind howled, and large, heavy flakes of snow had plastered the front window. At least the weather was acting like it was supposed to. Ramona shivered. "It looks like it's going to be a nasty day."

Annie didn't reply. She sat down, hunched over her bowl, and poured milk onto the little squares of shredded wheat which were her favorite. She didn't look up when Ramona entered the room.

"You OK, Girl?" Ramona asked. "Annie?" She touched the girl lightly on the shoulder to get her attention. "You sleep all right?"

Annie lifted her head. Worry clouded her eyes. "I need the paper," she said.

"It's out on the front porch. I haven't brought it in yet."

"Not that paper. The paper Detective Gifford has. The one from my pocket." Annie's voice rose slightly. "Can we call him?"

Ramona felt like she'd missed something and couldn't catch up. "What on earth are you talking about, child?"

"The paper. The paper from my pocket," Annie insisted. "That's what it's for. To help find Marisa's brother."

"Marisa's brother? Why do you think the paper would help? There's nothing on it. You know that." Ramona sat down across from the girl. Maybe the strain of the last couple of weeks was finally overwhelming Annie? She'd half-expected signs of the stress sooner than this.

"Annie," Ramona explained gently. "The police will find him. He's going to be just fine." Now that another day had passed with no word, she hoped to heaven that was true.

Annie sat silent, methodically scooping spoonfuls of cereal into her mouth. A frown creased her forehead. Finally, she spoke. "I kept waking up last night. Over and over again. Is that normal?" the girl pleaded. "I feel like I didn't sleep at all. Every time I closed my eyes, I dreamed about Marisa's brother. He was in a big building somewhere, and I couldn't find him. Then I'd wake up again."

"Oh, Honey," Ramona consoled. "Lots of people have bad dreams when they are worried. My dad used to tell me that our heads are directly connected to our hearts. When the heart cares about something, it won't let the head forget."

Annie shook her head empathically. "No. There's something else. Something important, Ramona. Just before I wake up each time, I remember I am holding the paper. I keep staring at it, trying to read it. And there is something there--something I just can't see. I need it!" Annie was adamant. "It's supposed to help us."

"Well, let's give it another day or so. He'll surely come home for Christmas. And remember, the police are looking for the boy." Ramona patted Annie's shoulder. "They'll find him. Maybe he's home already. I'll check with the Caballeros as soon as we've finished breakfast. You'll see. It will be all right," she assured the girl.

For the first time since Ramona had found the Annie behind the Seaweed Bar, she looked rebellious. "No. Now." she insisted. "I need the paper now! It's important." When she saw the expression of surprise on Ramona's face, Annie apologized anxiously. "I'm sorry. I didn't mean to be demanding." But she was resolute. "But we have to call Detective Gifford. Now. This morning. Please." She was on the verge of tears.

Ramona studied the girl for a moment. "If it's so important to you, Child, we'll call him," Ramona soothed. "But you've got to remember--tomorrow's Christmas Eve. Mark is probably with his family. And I suspect once evidence is recorded and filed, it can't be returned until we find your family and the case is closed. There may be no way at all to get your paper."

Ramona poured herself some Mini-Wheats and sat down next to the girl. She studied her out of the corner of her eye, but Annie avoided looking at her. Ramona noticed that twice the girl dripped milk on the table without even being aware of it as she spooned cereal into her mouth. Ramona had never seen the child so agitated. "Annie." The girl looked up at her expectantly, her spoon suspended between the bowl and her mouth. "Finish your cereal. I'll get my phone."

Ramona was surprised to catch Mark at the office. "You people have to work even a couple of days before Christmas?" she asked him.

"Doctors and cops," he said. "Doctors and cops."

When she described Annie's problem, Gifford was sympathetic but dubious. "We both know there's nothing on that paper; but if it eases her mind for her see it, I don't know why I shouldn't let her. I was on my way to Newman this afternoon to pick up a couple of last-minute gifts. Why don't you meet me at the Courthouse before I go?"

He was pathetic, Mark thought as he ushered the two women into his cubicle. Here it was the supposedly first day of the workweek, and he'd already put in a half-dozen hours yesterday helping Shaloe.

Gifford sighed in resignation. Just isn't a 9 to 5 job, he told himself. Or even 40 hours a week. At least nobody could say he didn't earn his salary. He unfolded a couple of chairs from behind the coat rack and set them up for Ramona and the girl. Annie perched on the edge of the chair and folded her hands in her lap, but the fingers on her right hand drummed unconsciously on the palm of her left. She neither smiled nor looked at him. "So," he leaned down to draw her attention to him, "I understand you need to see the paper that was in your pocket when we found you?"

Annie nodded. "I had a dream." Once she started, she rushed through the rest of her words without stopping. "Marisa's brother is in a big building with lots of halls--there's a message on the paper--it will tell us where he is." Her voice rose as she spoke, but there was an element of certainty in it.

Long practice had made Gifford aware that people conjured up all sorts of ideas to replace their worry with hope. He knew better than to try dissuading Annie. If she wanted to believe there was an easy answer to the boy's disappearance, then it was best to show her that her dream was just that—a dream.

"Hang on here. I'll dig out the evidence box. Won't take a minute." Heading down the long hall to the back-storage area where he'd filed Annie's personal effects just a few days ago, Gifford wove his way between several isles of shelves toward the missing persons' section. The room was filled with floor to ceiling shelves; fluorescent lights glaring down on rows and rows of boxes—all labeled carefully with names of officers, identification of crimes, and dates of collection. He knew Annie's box was near the back wall on the shelf with the most recent acquisitions. When he turned the corner to the last row, as he expected, he found the small box sitting on the third shelf from the floor just where he'd left it. What he didn't expect was that something inside the box was glowing, light seeping out from between the cracks in the cardboard walls that contained it and spilling onto the other boxes nearby and to the floor beneath them.

8:30 AM

As Belen dozed after feeding the baby, the nurse instructed Eduardo on the finer points of diaper changing—something he really didn't need much practice with since Alejandro had joined the family. But if the nurse wanted to give him some tips, he wasn't averse to the lesson. Elinor, however, was not thrilled with the idea of lying uncovered on the elevated crib mattress and was not above voicing her disapproval—loudly. Belen opened her eyes at the sound and then closed them again when she saw that the baby was complaining and not demanding. Deftly, Eduardo cleaned her tiny bottom with antiseptic wipes and applied a little cream to prevent diaper rash, then pulled the tabs on the diaper firmly across the baby's tummy, ensuring that the diaper wouldn't slip.

"Wow. Nice job," whispered the nurse so as not to disturb Belen—a vain hope in Eduardo's opinion. Elinor had had no such concerns. The nurse was fishing a fresh pink nightgown out of the stack of linens she'd brought from the nursery just as the door to the room opened and slammed against the opposite wall. Mr. Hidalgo and a companion filled the doorway. At the back of his mind, Eduardo had known his father-in-law's absence--Eduardo shrank from the unfamiliar words in his mind—was too good to be true. Hidalgo would never give up so easily.

Belen's father bristled with satisfaction as he strode into the room. "I am the father of this patient," he announced to the nurse, "and this is my attorney, Alfonso Sanchez. We are here to make arrangements for my daughter's release."

"Sir," the nurse acknowledged him and put a finger to her lips. "Your daughter's sleeping now. It would be best if we stepped outside and let her rest." Hidalgo nodded without even glancing at Eduardo--or the baby. He turned and headed back into the hall.

Eduardo finished dressing the tiny girl and bundled her up in a soft flannel blanket, lifting her to his shoulder and murmuring quietly in her ear, "There now. Isn't that better? All clean and dry and ready for a nap." He settled into the rocking chair next to Belen's bed and leaned his cheek against the silky fuzz of the baby's hair.

Outside the room, he could hear Hidalgo's strident voice and the nurse's quieter murmur. Eduardo closed his eyes and tried to focus on the slow rhythmic motion of the rocking chair, but he felt the old anger rising inside his head—and something else. Something invading the corner of his mind overtaking even the anger he had nursed for so long. Panic. Its inexorable pressure took hold of him, threatening to pin his arms and legs against a blank wall somewhere in his mind and leave him hanging with no avenue for escape. What could he, a kid, possibly do to stop Belen's father from taking her away from him! And now a lawyer? How could he defend Belen and the baby against the power of the law? Was it even possible that the law would let Belen's father take her away from him? He had no money. No resources to protect himself or his family. His arms around the baby tightened, and she stirred in her sleep, her head flopping against his neck.

Eduardo tried to slow his breathing. Maybe he and Belen could take the baby and just leave the hospital? Get a room in a motel for a few days. One of those places that rented rooms by the week? As soon as the thought crossed his mind, he rejected it. Even a kid could see that Belen needed to be here a few more days. Her father was a big man when he could push people around, but surely, he wouldn't have the courage to defy the doctor. Would he? The baby whimpered, and she twisted her head searching for something to eat.

"Eduardo?" Belen's voice was slurred with sleep. "Is the baby hungry?"

"She thinks she is," Eduardo whispered, grateful that Belen hadn't noticed the disturbance her father had caused. He smiled with affection despite the tension that lapped at the edges of his conscious mind. "Already she believes she is the most important person in the room." He lifted the child into Belen's arms and slid his chair closed to her bed. A surge of strength poured into him when he touched her. Her lips twitched through her half-closed eyes, and his panic subsided momentarily. They were a family now. He turned his head away from Belen and the baby as his eyes filled with tears. He must find a way to keep them together.

9:00 AM

Gifford's phone rang, just as he lifted the lid of the evidence box. He ignored it, glancing at the caller ID before switching it off. Carrie Jane. Call her back in a minute, he thought absently, his attention riveted on the contents of the box, now casting rays of light to the shelf above it. Reason told him that someone must have been using a flashlight to search for a piece of evidence and left it on the shelf behind the box—which caused it to glow. Although, on second thought, he couldn't imagine there wasn't enough light in the room for anyone to need a flashlight. Maybe the evidence clerk dropped something, and it rolled on the floor behind the shelves? It was unlikely, but who knew? Still, the box was lit up somehow. Warily, he reached in and shuffled through its contents--a couple of files of notes on Annie's discovery, a doctor's report guessing at her age and ethnicity, the fingerprint checks he'd had the state do, and at the bottom-- the two evidence bags. One held the red plastic tag which Gifford now knew must have come from Kyra's bookstore, the other--the parchment-like paper Annie said the white-haired man had given her. Gifford lifted it from the box. The gold leaf on the paper flashed as he twisted the plastic bag which held it, and Gifford blinked at its reflected brilliance. But it was not the gold leaf that was emitting rays of light. It was the words now shining from the page.

He squinted, trying to read the lettering through the plastic covering, but he didn't recognize any of the symbols. It wasn't English or anything like the limited Spanish which he knew. Dumbfounded, he studied the page. Someone must have tampered with the paper. He double-checked the chain of evidence posted on the front of the box. He was certain that page had been blank the last time he had looked at it. Now there was clearly some kind of script visible on it, but nothing recognizable to him. He didn't even bother to grabble with the problem of why it was glowing. That was completely outside his experience; his brain rejected every explanation which came to mind. This paper shouldn't be shining. Period.

He turned it over and back again. No change. Annie. Maybe Annie could explain it. Maybe there was something in her dream? Relieved to have some course of reasonable action, he jammed the lid back on the box which, now devoid of the evidence bag, was acting like a box was supposed to—no supernatural evidence in sight. He held the bag containing the gleaming parchment in front of him like a lantern as he headed back to his office and the girl.

Annie had turned her chair toward the evidence room door, watching for his arrival. Anticipation etched her face as if she knew that something extraordinary was about to take place.

Gifford registered Ramona's gasp when she saw the glow emanating from the small plastic bag, but his attention was directed solely at the girl in front of him. "What is it, Annie? What's happening? Did you know about this?" He demanded. Ignoring evidence protocol, he ripped open the bag and yanked the parchment from it. "What does it say? Can you read it?"

Annie's face took on the glow of the paper in front of her. Her eyes widened, and her lips parted in surprise. "There are words. I knew there must be words! He said there was a message!" As Annie reached out and took the paper, the text blazed brightly, seeming to leap off the page.

"What the ???" Ramona swore and gaped at the girl. "Annie …?"

Gifford made no sound; his eyes never leaving Annie's face. "Can you read it, Annie?" he repeated softly.

For a long moment, she stared at the words. As the luminance slowly faded, she raised her eyes to Gifford, nodded, and a brilliant smile widened on her face. "Yes," she said. "Yes, I can."

9:30 AM

Carrie Jane and Flor had made one last check of Christensen's before they headed to the real estate office to return the keys. Overnight the temperature had dropped, the wind had picked up, and the snow pounded against the newly installed windows seeking a way inside. But the sound was dampened in the empty hall. Chairs had been loaded up, instruments and risers returned to the high school, Christmas trees returned to living rooms all over the valley, floors swept, discarded programs and random trash collected. Flor had even found a partially melted candle in one of the dressing rooms, wax congealed onto the floor in a half-dozen little globs.

"Carrie Jane," she called. "Look at this."

Carrie Jane shuddered. "Oh, Lord. Haven't we had enough combustibles for one month?"

"Some stupid kid wasn't thinking," Flor responded. "If I'd have caught him with this, I'd have seen to it that his grade was dropped." She dumped the candle in the bag of trash and carted the whole thing out to the dumpster.

Both women were exhausted. It had been more than two long weeks of 12 to 15-hour days. Teaching full time would have been easier. Carrie Jane looked forward to tomorrow's Christmas Eve service, sitting peacefully in a pew at the little Catholic Church just a couple of blocks off Main Street, the priest reading the Christmas story, sweet children posed in the age-old tableau. She sighed. The work was almost over. And more to the point, a bunch of teachers and a couple of hundred kids with a very big idea had pulled it off. Take that, Mayor Jesse! Flor turned to stare at her when she laughed out loud.

Ollie and Trevor had gone with Leon to unload the last group of chairs at the high school and return the truck that Home Depot had loaned them. All that was left was to lock up the building and head home. It took both Carrie Jane and Flor pulling on the heavy double doors to close them against the snow, which on Saturday night had seemed magical, but now with several more inches in the last two days, it was considerably more threatening.

Flor leaned against the doors listening for the crash bar to fall in place, while Carrie Jane keyed the deadbolt and tested the ornate doorknobs to be certain they were securely locked; then she and Flor headed for her car. Pulling open the trunk, she handed Flor an extra-long-handled brush and grabbed one from behind the front seat for herself. Both were too tired to do anything but haphazardly attack the snow which had piled at least a couple of inches deeper just since they'd been inside. Flor groaned every time she had to lift her brush to shoulder height, her sore muscles crying out in protest. "Good thing you have a compact car, not a minivan," she yelled over the howling of the wind. Carrie Jane didn't respond; she was using her limited energy to clear off the other side of the car.

When all the windows were cleared, the women darted inside and slammed the doors behind them. They sat immobile for a few seconds, breathing heavily and letting their weary bodies sink into the padded cushions. Carrie Jane started the engine and turned on the wipers. Flor closed her eyes. "Let's just sit here a couple of hours."

The wipers whipped snow away from the paths of the two blades, the clicking at the end of each swipe reminding Carrie Jane that she hadn't replaced the blades since last winter. One more thing to worry about, she thought. At the top of the 'worry' list, Eduardo's name appeared, unbidden.

She turned to Flor apologetically. "Would you mind if we go by the Caballero's on the way home? I just want to be sure they're OK. I tried to call Mark to see if he'd heard anything from the cop who was looking for Eduardo, but he didn't answer."

"This whole thing makes you really uneasy doesn't it?" Flor was so tired she didn't bother to open her eyes or lift her head from the headrest supporting it. While she had worked that morning, she'd tied a scarf around her head to keep her dark hair from falling in her eyes. Now it had slipped backward until it bunched her hair into an unruly ponytail caught in the collar of her coat. Dripping snow clung to the hair, the scarf, and the shoulders of her coat. Impatiently, she dragged the hair loose from its confines and twisted it out of her way. Sitting up straighter, she sighed in defeat—it was obvious that a nap was a long way down the road. "Why?" she asked. "Eduardo's a bright kid. Maybe he just got fed up. From what you've told me, he sounds like he's sick to death of school and work and . . . maybe he's just hiding out, trying to punish his parents?" Her eyes narrowed as she mulled over the possibilities from her years of experience with teenagers' points of view. She looked directly at Carrie Jane. "Do you think there's a chance he's suicidal?"

Carrie Jane considered the question. She stared at the snow piling up on the windshield again, icy flakes covered the car and created an island of white which shut out the view of the street and the buildings, the low purr of the engine muffling the sound of the occasional passing vehicle. With every swipe of the wipers, two openings cleared allowing her to see the world outside, but the view disappeared between wiper rotations. "Maybe," she answered. "But he doesn't strike me as depressed. He's just so," she searched for the right word . . . "distracted," she finally concluded.

"It's like his head's always somewhere else. And nothing I've been able to do seems to change that."

Though it should have been only a 15-minute drive to the Caballero home and the main roads were plowed, they were frozen and crusted with ice. Carrie Jane slowed the little car to avoid sliding into a curb or another vehicle. When they turned into the Caballero's neighborhood, it was clear that snow removal in this part of town was at the bottom of the mayor's priority list—not many voters in that community.

Driving carefully along the ruts created by the tire tracks of residents who had already chanced the nasty weather, Carrie Jane finally eased the car alongside Caballero's driveway. Drifts of snow had piled up against Caballero's house, but the porch and sidewalk had been shoveled, though a determined layer of snow was intent on covering it again. Marisa was out the door before they could even exit the car. Snow pelted the little girl's face and covered her eyelashes, but she didn't seem to notice. "You have come to tell me about Eduardo," she demanded as she struggled to pull the driver's side door open a crack. "When is he coming home?"

Carrie Jane climbed out of her seat and lifted the little girl into her arms, pulling her coat around them both. "I don't know, honey; I'm so sorry."

Marisa ducked her head into the lapel of Carrie Jane's coat, retreating into the safety of adult protection. Instinctively, Carrie Jane pulled the little girl closer.

"Marisa, I want you to meet my friend." She pointed to Flor as she came around the back of the car. "This is another teacher—her name is Flor; she knows Eduardo, too. We were worried, so we came by to see if your family has heard anything new?"

Marisa's face fell. The icy wind bit into her bangs and scattered them helter-skelter around her face, snow clinging to her t-shirt and jeans. She wrapped her thin arms around Carrie Jane. "Oh," she said, and her face collapsed into misery.

"Marisa?" Luz called from the doorway. "Please invite our friends into la casa where it is warm."

The child burrowed her head deeper into Carrie Jane's shoulder—the energy in the little body ebbing away and her tears leaving a dark spot the coat collar where her head was tucked under Carrie Jane's chin. "We will find him. I promise," she whispered in the little girl's ear.

Luz motioned them into the kitchen and yanked the front door against the wind behind them. In the minute or two since the door had been open, snow had already blown through the doorway and formed a small drift just inside the entrance. Luz had to kick it away with her foot before the door would shut completely. The boys were nowhere in sight, but Luz didn't bother to check on them—she could hear their laughter floating from somewhere near the back of the duplex.

Light poured from the kitchen, and Carrie Jane could see a small, older woman stirring a pot on the stove. The woman turned to greet the newcomers. "Viola," she said in surprise. "Didn't expect to see you here."

"Thought maybe I could watch the kids in case Luz and her husband were called away." Her face betrayed no emotion, but she chose her words carefully. "Might need to pick up Eduardo--when the police find him. Somebody ought to be here." She tasted whatever was in the pot and added a bit more salt. "You two finished at Christensen's?"

Carrie Jane nodded. "No word at all?" She asked, directing her question to Luz.

"*No, Señorita. Nada. Mi esposo,*" she began, and then recognizing her lapse, switched back to English. "My husband has been gone since early this morning with the policeman. They are knocking on many doors—the policeman does not speak Spanish and some families have reason to fear the *policía* . . .." She shrugged her shoulders in explanation. "Sit, please." She pulled two chairs out from the table, brushing several Legos off one. "*Señorita* Viola makes the excuses, but I know she has come to be with me." Luz walked across the room to put her arm around the older woman. A look of appreciation washed across her face, then was buried again in anxiety. It was clear her composure was at its ragged edge.

Carrie Jane and Flor exchanged glances, but recognizing there was nothing they could say, they remained silent.

Flor took one of the proffered chairs, and awkwardly, Carrie Jane lowered herself onto the other, shifting the burden of Marisa's weight onto her lap. The child settled against the teacher and closed her eyes. In a few moments, her shoulders relaxed, and her breathing deepened.

As she pulled out another chair for herself next to Carrie Jane, Luz brushed aside a patch of Marisa's damp hair which was dripping tiny drops of melted snow across the child's cheek and down onto her t-shirt. "She was up very early this morning watching out the window for Eduardo's return. She has always followed him around like a little. . .." Her English failed her.

"Shadow?" Viola inserted.

"Si. A small shadow." Luz's voice broke. Viola reached across the table and took her hand.

"I am sorry," Luz apologized. "She does not understand what is happening." She stopped, unable to finish. Viola slipped into a chair next to Luz and put an arm around her. Luz leaned her head briefly against the older woman's shoulder. Viola covered Luz's hand with her own. "They'll find him," she said softly. "Try not to worry."

Viola lifted her eyes from Luz and spoke to Carrie Jane. "Anything from Gifford?"

"No. I tried him earlier, but he didn't answer."

The four women and the sleeping child sat silently in the little kitchen, each struggling to voice words of comfort, each aware that as more time passed without word of Eduardo, comfort was less and less likely to be found.

Anger stirred in Carrie Jane. She took a deep, slow breath to quell the rising irritation. What was Eduardo thinking—worrying his family like this? Kids just didn't get it. Most of them were so self-absorbed, all they could think about was their own problems. It never occurred to them their behavior might be affecting someone else. She bit her lip. Lashing out would not be helpful. Besides, what if Eduardo was hurt? Or? A stab of guilt shot through her. She smoothed the little girl's hair off her face, tucked her chin into the sweet smell of freshly shampooed hair, and wrapped her arms more securely around Marisa.

A knock at the door startled the women, and all eyes turned toward it. Luz motioned to the others to stay seated. Answering it, she found Gifford, Annie, and Ramona on the porch, wind whipping snow onto their coats and into their faces. A layer of white had already covered their shoulders just in the brief walk from the car to the door.

"Something's come up." Gifford addressed Luz as he strode into the room and shook the snow off his coat onto the small rug in front of the door. "The problem is, I'm not sure exactly what." He saw the lack of comprehension cross her face, so he started again. "Sorry. I mean I don't know . . .." He knew he was making no sense. But how exactly did one explain the unexplainable? "Annie came to the station to look at the paper.

And it had words . . . And light. But even with the light, I have no idea what it says. Annie can read it, but that doesn't really help. So, we came here, hoping you could help—figure it out, I mean."

"Mark, if that is your idea of clarity, it needs a little editing," Carrie Jane interjected.

Gifford did a double-take. He'd been so intent on his mission that he hadn't even noticed Carrie Jane in the kitchen. Alarmed he looked at her. "What are you doing here? Has something happened?" The others in the room faded into the background. Two steps and Gifford was through the archway. "Have you found Eduardo?"

"No," Carrie Jane responded, her expression warning him not to wake the child in her arms. "Nothing yet."

Luz took Ramona and Annie's coats and seated them on the couch, their breaths shooting little puffs of steam into the warmer air. "*Señor Gifford?*" Luz turned to Gifford. "There is news?" Hope surged in her voice.

"Not exactly." He turned to the girl, "Annie and Ramona came to see me this morning. Annie's had a dream. She says Eduardo is in a large building." He checked with Annie to be sure of his accuracy. She nodded in response. "She says the paper is a clue about how to find him."

Luz was clearly bewildered. "*Señor, no lo entiendo.*"

"Me either, *Señora* Caballero." Gifford spread his arms and shrugged his shoulders. "Nothing seems to make sense." He looked over his shoulder at the girl on the couch. "Perhaps you could explain, Annie?"

Every head rotated toward the young girl. She shrank back at the attention riveted on her.

"It's OK, Annie. Tell them," Ramona urged her.

Straightening her shoulders, Annie leaned forward, reached into her pocket, and pulled something from it. She opened her palm to reveal the little evidence bag containing the parchment. It flashed rays of light across the room at every twist of the paper, dancing in the faces of the seated audience. Luz gasped. "What is it?

"Exactly," said Gifford. "What is it?" Gifford had their attention now. Assuming the mantle of authority, he ordered, "Why don't you all come in here, and Annie can explain." After helping Luz drag the kitchen chairs into the living room, Gifford was careful to maneuver the women so that he could have the seat immediately next to Carrie Jane on the couch.

Sandwiched into between her and Ramona with Annie on his left, it made a tight fit. But his shoulder brushed against that of Carrie Jane and, despite the drama of the moment, he didn't intend to let gallantry force him to vacate his position.

"Annie?"

She began when the white-haired man had given her the paper. Since Carrie Jane, Flor, and Luz had never heard the story, there were questions of confusion, outrage, and then confusion again.

"The white-haired man told me I would need the paper. When he gave it to me, I couldn't see anything written here, but now there is a message." She raised the bag, so the paper was visible to all of them. The symbols now embedded in the paper flashed tiny reflections of gold against the illumination of the parchment itself.

Varying degrees of disbelief crossed the faces of the all but Ramona.

"That's a pretty nifty trick," Flor said. "How'd you do it, Annie?"

Ramona sent her a withering glare. "It's no trick, believe me."

"Willing suspension." Gifford murmured to himself, referring to something he'd remembered from Mrs. Z's literature class.

"What the heck are you talking about?" Flor began.

"Somebody once said that 'fiction is the willing suspension of disbelief.'" His glance at Carrie Jane carried a grudging apology for his inability to explain the paper. "Maybe this is a case where reality requires some willing suspension, too." He shrugged his shoulders in defeat. "Since this whole thing defies any and all of the logic I've been taught," he said, "we were hoping," he included Ramona and Annie in his supposition, "it might make sense to at least one of you."

The women in the room all stared at him blankly.

"I was afraid of that," he admitted. "OK, then. Let's do what we came for," he instructed. "Annie, will you pass *Señora* Caballero the paper? Maybe it means something to her." Obediently, the young girl handed the package across the room to the Luz, who fingered it with some trepidation. She twisted it from side to side, wincing momentarily as the light flashed directly into her eyes. When she seemed satisfied, she pulled the paper closer for a detailed inspection.

"Does this mean anything to you, *Señora*? Anything at all?" Gifford gestured toward the bag. "I know it makes no sense, but there it is." He paused as if to admit the absurdity of what he was asking. "I guess we have to just go with it." Stealing a glance at Carrie Jane, he was relieved that she did not appear to be on the verge of dismissing him as a lunatic.

"Annie believes it's a message about Eduardo," Ramona explained. "I don't know how? English is the only language I know, and those symbols—Annie says they're letters--make no sense at all to me."

Across from her Luz nodded in agreement. *"No es Espanol,"* she murmured to no one in particular. *"Pero hermosa, muy hermosa."*

"Tell them what it says, Annie," Ramona urged, as Luz handed it back to the girl. Annie raised the paper closer to her face, light reflecting in her eyes and shining against her hair, making her head seem to be covered in a glowing crown.

"It says, 'Seek the baby'." Annie read. "There is the beginning of happiness."

"And exactly what does that mean?" interjected Flor. "Eduardo's no baby. Why do you think it refers to Eduardo?"

"That's why we're here," Gifford explained. He looked at Luz. "We were hoping you could tell us."

"Sounds like some sort of enigmatic Christmas mumbo jumbo," Flor grumbled.

"Well," Gifford said. "This whole thing is way beyond my pay grade." He looked exasperated and intrigued simultaneously. "First off, I don't believe in anything I can't see or touch or smell so that rules out paper that can shine without a light source. Second, if that message was written in some sort of invisible ink, I have no idea what triggered its appearance, and third, I leave secret codes to the intelligence guys. That pretty much puts me out in the cold."

"Annie," Viola pointed out, "why do you think this is about Eduardo? It sounds like Flor's right. It's some sort of Christmas message."

Annie looked very certain. "My dream," she said. "In my dream, I was looking for Eduardo, and I was holding this paper."

"Could be just coincidence," Flor suggested. "Sub-conscious connection, maybe?" Even Luz stared in derision at her this time. Flor held up her hands in surrender. "Okay, okay. I give up. Today only," she said mimicking the voice of a TV advertisement, "Today dreams trump reality!"

No one in the room even cracked a smile.

Carrie Jane reached across Marisa's reclined body, taking the bag from Luz and studying the symbols. "Annie, can you tell if the word 'baby' has a small first letter or a capital? Maybe it's pointing out some sort of Nativity display—someplace Eduardo might go? A church? Or that one in front of the library?" Carrie Jane speculated.

"Not the library," Flor interrupted. "It's too cold for him to have been outside this long. He'd freeze out there. And where would he hide? The building's locked up on Sunday. If he were there, you'd think someone would have discovered him when they opened the doors this morning. It's got to be somewhere warmer." Belatedly, Flor realized she might have upset Luz even more than she already was, but Luz gave no visible that indication Flor's words made her any more anxious.

"It is a small letter 'b'," Annie answered Carrie Jane's original question, "not like the 'Baby' Jesus."

No one bothered to ask how she knew that.

"That doesn't mean it isn't some kind of Christmas message." Carrie Jane said. "And it sounds kind of Biblical. 'There is the beginning of happiness.' Odd word choice for a modern writer. Maybe the parchment is a lot older than we think."

"I had the physics teacher at the high school run a few tests for me," Gifford informed them. "There weren't any letters evident visible, but he says the border is genuine gold leaf. And that the parchment is imperious to all kinds of acids and decay. On the other hand, he admitted that he didn't know a lot about paper making techniques before the 20th century. It could be just very old, not some super-paper."

Marisa stirred on Carrie Jane's lap. When she recognized Annie in the living room, her eyes popped open. "He is here? You have found him?" she sat up straight and searched for an answer on Annie's face.

"No, Little One. We have not found him yet," Luz soothed her from across the room. "But your Annie-girl has an idea."

Marisa leaned toward Annie. "What is it? Can I help? Do you know where Eduardo is hidden?" She rushed through the sentences. When she saw the glow coming from the paper Annie held, she leaped off Carrie Jane's lap and clamored into Annie's.

"What is this?" she said fingering the plastic around the parchment, accepting the light without a second thought. "Is it magic? What does it say?" Holding the paper close to her eyes, she poured over the symbols on the parchment. Then her face fell. "I am too little to read," she admitted to the adults in the room with what looked like embarrassment.

"We are trying to figure that out now," Annie answered, smiling down at the little face turned up toward her. "It talks about a baby."

"Like Alejandro?" Marisa asked.

"Yes, like that," Annie agreed.

Ramona snorted. "Eduardo's almost a man. Unless he's had an accident," she glanced belatedly at Luz to be sure her suggestion wasn't devastating to the woman, "he's probably just fine. Doesn't need a bunch of older people hovering over him. Might be disinclined to come home if he guesses the hubbub his disappearance will have caused. Any smart kid would avoid having to face the music." Her voice softened as she directed her words to Annie. "Maybe this paper has no connection to Eduardo at all." She glanced at Flor. "Maybe it is just a convenient coincidence."

Automatically Gifford switched back into cop mode. "In my business, there are no coincidences." Then half apologetically, he admitted sheepishly, "But then in my business, paper that glows by itself doesn't exist. So …?"

"No. I'm sure. It's about Eduardo." Annie was resolute. The stubborn look crossed her face again, and her voice rose. "The paper is about Eduardo; he needs help. We must find him. Now." Her audience unconsciously leaned toward her.

"This white-haired man knew Eduardo?" Luz puzzled. "*No entiendo. Quien es?*"

Gifford answered. "Nobody knows who he is. Or anything about him. I can't find a record of him staying at any hotel or motel within 20 miles of here. But he keeps popping up—then disappearing. Literally." Gifford grimaced. "Nothing about this whole thing makes sense."

Carrie Jane looked thoughtful. "I guess the real question is how Annie is involved in all this." She directed her next words to the girl. "Annie, have you ever met Eduardo?" The girl shook her head in response. "Then why should he matter to you? Why do you have to find him? It's like a jigsaw puzzle, only without all the pieces."

Annie shifted uncomfortably in her chair. "I can't explain. I don't understand." There was certainly in her voice. "I just know that Eduardo is somewhere in a big building, and this paper is a clue. I'm sure," she added. She stared back at the others. "That's the truth. I know it."

Gifford sighed, shaking his head. "Annie, if it were anyone else telling me this, I'd get up and leave right now." He leaned toward her. "But you? Over the years I've known a lot of people who've lied to me and tried to get away with it, so I'm pretty good at spotting a story from a mile off." He wrinkled his eyebrows in concentration. "You? Honestly? I don't think you know how to lie." He looked around the room. There was an unspoken agreement around the room. "Anybody else have any ideas?"

Viola shifted in her seat, mulling over the situation. "OK, say Annie is right. Say Eduardo is in some kind of 'big building'. What on earth would he be doing there? And why not get in touch with his folks if he needed help?" She questioned. "The longer he's gone, it seems to me, the more likely he's not just at some friend's house playing video games. What are we suggesting here? That something's happened to him. That he's being held against his will?" She looked directly at Gifford. "What is the likelihood he's in real trouble, Mark? Maybe even in danger?"

Gifford hesitated. He glanced at Luz and made a decision. "*Señora* Caballero, I don't mean to upset you, but Viola is right. The longer he's gone, the more reason to believe he's involved in some kind of serious problem. Can you think of anything unusual that he's said or done in the last couple of weeks? Something that might give us a clue where he might be or with whom?"

Luz faced him without flinching. "*No, Señor.* He does not make friends easily. There is only the girl." She paused, searching for a memory, and then shook her head. "I have never met her, but Eduardo once told me that her father would not let him see her. I do not know why. He was very upset. He has not spoken of her for many months. If there are other friends, I do not know them. He goes to school. He works. There is no time for other things." Her eyes focused on something beyond the four walls. Twisting the edge of her apron between her fingers, she admitted, "There is something. . .. I do not know what. He will not say. He worries. I can see it. But he does not speak." Without conscious thought, her fingers twisted the corner of the apron even tighter, and her eyes dropped. She said sadly, "I am sorry. It is all I know."

Gifford nodded, his memory of his own high school years rising to the surface. "It's a vulnerable time in a young man's life—almost an adult, but not quite. Everyone telling you what to do, but no one really understanding. It is also a time of immense pride. When I was his age, I knew everything. I was invincible." At Luz's obvious confusion, he backtracked. "Strong. Equal to any problem."

"Men!" Ramona mumbled under her breath.

None of the conversation made any sense to Marisa, her little body unable to sit still any longer. "Where does the paper say Eduardo is, my Annie?" she begged. "Read it again." Catching her mother's warning look from across the room, she added "please" as an afterthought.

Annie held the paper up so that Marisa could see it. The light from the golden letters shone in the little girl's face, the ends of her long eyelashes a burnished flame. Annie kissed her lightly on the forehead. "It says 'Seek the baby. There is the beginning of happiness," she articulated the words clearly so that the little girl could understand.

Marisa furrowed her brow in concentration. "What is this 'seek?'" Her face screwed up in concentration. "I do not know this 'seek.'"

"It means to 'search or look for'," Annie explained. "Like the day you first came to my house, and your Papa went looking for you."

"Ah," she said, including the adults in the room with her new knowledge. "We must 'look' for the baby," she instructed. "Eduardo is with Alejandro," she concluded with triumph. "But where is Alejandro?"

"He is with your abuela, Little One. But Eduardo is not there," her mother answered gently.

Marisa's face fell. "I do not know other babies. How will we find him, if we do not know which baby?" She fell silent, her disappointment too heavy for words.

Gifford's voice was grim. "Any other ideas?"

For a long moment, the room was silent. Suddenly Marisa's high voice exploded in excitement. "Annie. Annie-girl!" the little girl said, reaching up and pulling Annie's face toward her. "I know. I know where there are lots of babies," the little girl insisted. "Mama got Alejandro at the hospital. Maybe the baby is there." She turned to the others in the room. "There are many babies in a big room," she felt it necessary to elaborate. "I have seen them. They are wrapped in blue and pink blankets. I like the pink ones best," she concluded with satisfaction.

Gifford looked at Annie. "Could it mean a hospital? —Didn't you say you saw Eduardo in a large building with long halls? A hospital fits that description."

Ramona considered the possibility. She looked at Gifford. "At least it's an idea. And it's the only one we've had so far," she pointed out. "I can't see any harm in checking it out. Why don't you, Annie, and I head down there and look around?" Ramona saw the look that crossed Gifford's face. "Carrie Jane, too,' she amended without comment.

Protests broke out from the others.

Gifford spoke over the ensuing noise and raised a hand for silence. "May I remind you; this is a police investigation? A bunch of civilians clamoring all over is not going to be helpful. In fact, just the opposite. The rest of you stay put. We'll let you know as soon as we find anything."

"No." Flor had been a silent bystander; listening to the discussion with considerable interest. "No. As in 'NO. I'M NOT STAYING HERE!'" The startled expressions which flashed across the faces of her friends at her outbreak rebuffed her. Flustered, she tried to retrench. "I'm tired. I'm hungry. I want this problem solved so I can go home, close my eyes, and not worry about Eduardo. Till then, I'm going with you. Sitting around here will drive me crazy. Besides," she glanced at her friend from the corner of her eyes, "I love babies. Always have." She closed her mouth and stared defiantly at Carrie Jane.

"Uh-huh." This time Carrie Jane snorted before Ramona had a chance to. "Must be a sudden interest brought on by vending machines."

"Whatever," Flor replied, attempting to make it seem like no big deal.

Lost in thought, Viola appeared oblivious of the exchange. Apparently unaware she was voicing her thoughts, she considered the pros and cons of Marisa's idea. "Nothing to do here but worry." She glanced at Luz, whose face was blank of expression, but whose hands had dropped the apron and were now braiding and unbraiding tiny sections of the long hair that fell below her shoulders. Viola watched her, concern lining her face. "Inaction is making things worse, not better." She caught Gifford's eye and tilted her head in Luz's direction. "Hospital's a pretty public place. Not likely to be any real threat there. Probably no Eduardo there, either. Let's all go. It's better than sitting around here. Change of scene might be good for everybody. Luz told me her mother can take the other children, so there's no reason not to come." As if the whole thing were decided, she added, "Should we call Mr. Caballero and tell him what we're doing?"

Luz's hands fell to her lap. Reaching to untie her apron, she stood-- inaction cast aside, relief easing the tension of her posture. "No. Let us wait. When there is something to tell, we will call him."

Gifford sat stunned as all the women rose in silent unison. They loaded the chairs back to the kitchen, turned off the lights, selected their various coats from the piled at the edge of the couch, and headed for the cars, all without a word of discussion.

Carrie Jane squeezed Gifford's hand, pulling him to his feet. "It'll be OK. Just go with the flow," she whispered, her eyes twinkling for a moment at his discomfort.

"Marisa, you will stay here with your *abuela*," Luz instructed as she buttoned up the little girl's coat and tied her hat securely over her ears.

Stiffening with anger, the child declared, "I will go with my Annie-girl. She does not know Eduardo. He will need me to find him." She stomped her foot. "I am too big to stay at home with the boys." She dismissed her older brothers without a second thought.

"Let her come," pleaded Annie. "I will watch out for her." Marisa glared at her mother expectantly.

When Luz nodded her head, Gifford held up his hands to stop them. "Wait a minute. Just a minute. I don't need a bunch of interfering citizens messing up and on-going investigation. No one is going with me. And that's final!" he ordered. "I will check out the hospital and let you know what I find. Now just relax and wait here until you hear something from me."

The women totally ignored him. Without exchanging a word, Luz fitted Marisa with her oversized boots, and all seven females filed past Gifford on their way outside as if he weren't there. Even Marisa marched past him without a glance.

When she reached her car, Carrie Jane turned and glared at him. "You coming?"

Gifford threw up his hands. "You people are CRAZY!" he yelled. But he jammed the parchment--which had fallen off Annie's lap when she got up--back into the evidence bag, buttoned up his overcoat, closed and locked the door, muttering under his breath to himself as he went down the steps. "They are worse than my sisters! And nobody is worse than that!"

"Oh, what the ???," he consoled himself. "How much trouble can they get in at a hospital?" He shrugged his shoulders in resignation, and he held his hand out to the little girl. "I lost all control the minute I opened that drawer,' he reasoned. "Come on, Marisa. We're going to need your booster chair."

11:00 AM

Belen was groaning in her sleep. Eduardo pushed the call button. A voice answered. "What can I do for you?"

"It is . . .." Eduardo wasn't sure what to call his relationship with Belen. Not wife, surely? Girlfriend? Mother of his child? Finally, he settled on "It is time for Miss Hidalgo to have more pain medicine, please." He was angry with himself. Miss Hidalgo? Belen was as dear to him as life itself, and he was reduced to calling her Miss Hidalgo? "Stupid, stupid, stupid," he swore under his breath. A flash of inspiration shot through him. In an instant realization dawned--they must marry. Soon. Why had he not thought of this before? If they were married, her father would have nothing to say about their lives. They would be free of him. Eduardo allowed himself to imagine a life where Belen and the baby waited for him when he returned from work. Having dinner together. Sneaking the baby tidbits off his plate when her mother wasn't paying attention. Laughing when Belen caught him spoiling the child. He smiled to himself. It was a beguiling picture. Fleetingly, he wondered if they could be married in the hospital. He knew there was a chapel somewhere. Maybe the priest would even come to Belen's room? They could ask the doctor and a couple of the nurses to be witnesses. When Elinor was older, they would show her the pictures and tell her the story of her presence at their fairytale wedding.

Then he remembered. Belen was only 17. She could not marry without her father's permission. Eduardo didn't doubt that Mr. Hidalgo would find a way to stop it. His heart dropped. He could see no way. Slumping in his chair, he felt the weight of his problems descend upon him once again. It was hopeless.

A nurse knocked once and opened the door, carrying a small cup. "Here's the medication. Is mom awake?"

From the bed, Belen's voice whispered, "Yes. Thank you. The pain is worse."

The nurse sat the medication on the tray at the foot of the bed and spoke to Belen, who had opened her eyes at the sound of the woman's words. "On a scale of 1 to 10, how bad is the pain right now?"

"Seven. Perhaps eight. It hurts." Belen bit her lip.

The nurse recorded the information on a sheet of paper folded into quarters which she pulled from her pocket. Pushing the button on the bed, she helped Belen straighten her body enough to swallow the pills. "Usually the second and third days are the worst. By tomorrow, you will be able to tell that the pain is receding. And by the end of the week, you should be much improved. Until then, don't hesitate to ask for something to help the pain. We don't like our moms to suffer if we can help it." She handed Belen the pills and tipped the cup for her to take a drink.

The baby stirred in the crib next to the bed, her little arms pushing against the swaddling blanket she was wrapped in. "She is a beautiful baby," the nurse said. "You are very lucky." Her words took in both parents. Belen smiled agreement, and Eduardo felt some of his tension ease. He was so tired. It was something of a relief to recognize that he must not be thinking clearly.

"Thank you," he said to the nurse, dazed by the tide of emotion the slightest sign of compassion triggered. What was happening to him? Had he lost all perspective? He wondered if this was what they were talking about when he'd overheard girls in the halls whispering and giggling over 'hormones'. If so, men were clearly superior, he had decided. Now if he only he could get some sleep, he might begin acting like a man again. Belatedly, in the nurse's direction, he added, "Thank you for helping us."

The nurse touched his shoulder. "A baby is the greatest gift," she said. "Take good care of her."

Eduardo knew he'd heard that before, but he was too exhausted to remember where. "I will," he promised, his eyes now so heavy, he could hardly keep them open. By the time the door closed after the nurse, he, the baby, and Belen were all asleep.

Eduardo had lost all track of time when the doctor nudged him gently. "How is she doing?" She gestured toward Belen. "How's the pain?

Shaking his head a couple of times, he willed himself to alertness. "She had some medicine a while ago. She's been sleeping since then."

The doctor nodded. "I'll be back when she's awake to check her stitches," she said as she unwrapped the baby and stroked the little feet to test her reflexes. She nodded, pleased when the little girl wrapped her tiny fingers around the doctor's thumb. "She's a strong one," the doctor said over her shoulder. She lifted an eyelid and shined a small flashlight into the baby's eye. Recording something on the baby's chart, she said to herself. "Bilirubin's good. No sign of breathing difficulties." She nodded in satisfaction.

Turning back to Eduardo, she paused a moment as if she was uncertain how to frame her next words. She straightened and looked at him directly. "Your father-in-law came to see me, his lawyer in tow," she said quietly. "He wanted Belen and the baby released in his care tonight. Has he spoken to you about this?"

Eduardo's features tightened as anger flitted across his face. "No," he said shortly. "He does not talk to me. He issues orders."

Understanding, the doctor nodded. "I suspected as much. I was afraid I was going to have to call security to get him out of my office. I would like to help you, but Belen is underage, and he is her legal guardian. I managed to convince him that she needed at least another couple of days in the hospital. However, his lawyer assured me they would be seeking a second medical opinion. I may have no choice but to release her to him." She tucked the blanket back around the now dozing baby and pulled the small stool she had sat on to deliver the baby next to his chair. "What are you going to do?"

"I have no idea." Eduardo hated himself as soon as he had said the words. He couldn't afford to trust anyone, but the doctor seemed sympathetic, and he was so very weary. He didn't know if he had the strength to resist Mr. Hidalgo anymore. Maybe it was best to just let Belen go home with her father? At least she and the baby would be safe. And warm. He had nothing. He could give them nothing. He felt himself collapsing into an empty void which no man should ever know. "I cannot lose her. Or the baby," He whispered, ashamed of his weakness. "Perhaps it is better for them to go with her father." He pushed the momentary vision of his life without them to the back corner of his mind.

The doctor shifted the clipboard, on which she had been making notes, to her other hand as she reached out and touched Eduardo's shoulder. "You need to do something soon. I have asked the hospital social worker to come and speak to you. And our chaplain is usually in his office after lunch. Perhaps he can help you also." The concern in her face was genuine. "Do not wait." Her eyes took in the sleeping baby and her mother. There was the slightest tilt of her head, and a sigh escaped her lips. "I am afraid the odds are stacked against you." Without another word, she rose from the stool, rolled it back against the wall, placed the chart back in its slot at the end of the crib, and walked from the room.

Eduardo sat silent for several minutes, his head in his hands. Eventually, the creeping sense of despair overwhelmed him; he fought the tears, but they came without his permission.

12:30 PM

By the time they had decided who was going in which car and where to put Marisa's booster chair, it was well after lunch, but no one except Flor mentioned being hungry--they were too intent on their errand, even the child. Marisa chattered aimlessly to Annie in the back seat of Ramona's car. "Hush," her mother told her, "or I shall drop you off at *la casa de su abuela*." Marisa went instantly silent.

Flor and Viola climbed into the back of Carrie Jane's car without discussion, allowing Gifford to sit up front.

The day before Christmas Eve meant the parking lot at the hospital was almost empty. Everyone who could take time off was at home. There were a few cars parked in the Emergency Room lot, but the spaces next to the main entrance were almost empty. Though the asphalt had obviously been plowed recently, snow had again covered the markings between the spaces in front of the main doors, so cars were parked in a couple of ragged rows. It was cold, and the blowing snow made it difficult to see. Gifford led the way into the hospital, grabbing Marisa just in time to keep her from slipping face-first onto the ice. She flashed him a radiant smile. Gifford laughed. It was obvious the little girl was very pleased with herself for having maneuvered her mother into letting her come.

The volunteer at the information desk looked up in apprehension when she saw Gifford hold the door for five women, a teenager, and a small child. They all lined up at the desk expectantly. Unconsciously, the volunteer slid her chair back a step. "Can I help you?" She addressed Gifford, but her eyes shifted uneasily from one adult to another.

"I'm with the Douglas Valley PD." Gifford flashed his badge. "I'm looking for a missing kid---18 years old, tall, dark curly hair, blue-green eyes," he checked with Luz for the accuracy of his description. She nodded. "His name's Caballero, Eduardo Caballero. Have you got a patient with that name?"

Checking her computer, the volunteer shook her head. "Nope. Looks like we have a baby Caballero in the nursery, but nothing here about a young man."

"A baby Caballero?" Ramona cast a glance in Annie's direction. "That doesn't make any sense. Are the parents listed on that thing?" She demanded.

"I'm not allowed to give out that information," the volunteer aimed her response at Ramona. She eyed her with irritation. "Hospital rules."

"Common enough name," Gifford interjected. The stubborn look on Annie's face hadn't receded. It was obvious she wasn't going to give up. He sighed and added, "How do we get to the nursery?"

"Up the stairs. Follow the green strip to maternity. They'll direct you from there," her voice trailed off. The whole group had already headed down the hall behind her toward the stairs. "Only two visitors allowed at a time," she called over her shoulder to them, but there was no one left to hear the warning. Annie and Marisa, the last of the group, already had disappeared from sight.

It was a straggly line that ascended the stairs, walked down one long hall, made a right turn, and piled up outside the maternity ward door. Marisa shoved her way past the women to stand next to Gifford. "You push that button," she informed him pointing to a large red disc with instructions in both English and Spanish. "Then the people let you in."

"Thank you," Gifford said dryly.

Reaching past Gifford, Carrie Jane grinned at the little girl, raised an eyebrow in Gifford's direction, and pushed the button. "We're here to see the Caballero baby," she announced. A buzzer rang, and the locks were released electronically.

The nurse at the desk was visibly startled to see five women, one man, and two girls line up at the counter. "Are you all family?"

The group looked uncomfortably at each other. "Sort of." Gifford took the lead, relieved when none of the women superseded him. Reverting back to the theory that authority talks, he pulled out his badge and said, "I'm with the Douglas Valley PD. I'm looking for a boy." He went through the description again. "We understand there's a baby by that name in the nursery."

The nurse looked curiously at the assembled group. "Then are all of you associated with the police?"

"Not exactly," Gifford replied. He shifted his posture uncomfortably. "We have reason to believe," he started and then realized how ridiculous his story might sound. "We're just checking out every possibility. These folks ... er ... women are here to see the Caballero baby." He didn't like the feeling of things spinning out of his control.

"Sorry. Only family allowed in the nursery."

"Well, that's the point. This woman here," he pointed at Luz, "is *Señora* Caballero." He chose his words carefully, avoiding a direct lie. "She may be related to the baby. I'd like to take her in to see him/her?"

"Her," supplied the nurse. "I guess that's OK since you're a cop. But the baby may be in her mother's room. Nursery's down the hall and to your left though." She pointed. "The rest of you can sit down in the maternity waiting room across from the desk." She looked back at Gifford. "Five minutes."

Obediently most of the group walked across the hall to a long, narrow room with assorted chairs and couches, all upholstered in fake leather, which lined the walls. A couple of dog-eared issues of People and Better Homes and Gardens magazines were stacked in one corner. Near the ceiling at the end of the room, a wall-mounted television was flashing pictures of happy patients being served their medications in cheerful rooms with lots of natural lighting. The women settled into a group of chairs and a couch in the colors which every hospital decorator imagined were sure to sooth anxious families. None of the women paid the slightest attention to the colors; their focus was elsewhere.

Down the hall the nursery curtains were drawn, so Gifford tapped lightly on the door. A tall, blond nurse poked her head out the door and smiled. "Here to see a baby?"

Gifford pointed to Luz. "This is *Señora* Caballero. We'd like to see that baby."

"Sure. Hang on a second while I roll her bassinet over to the window."

They heard some shuffling behind the door, and then the drapes were pulled aside. The nursery was a large well-lit room with half a dozen small beds on rollers lined up across the center, a couple of rocking chairs on one end, and one or two isolates pushed against the back wall. As they watched, the nurse pushed a crib with the word 'Caballero' stenciled on one end toward them. Inside was a sleeping baby girl with a red and green knitted hat in honor of the coming holiday. The combination of a pink swaddling blanket and her incredibly long, dark eyelashes made her cheeks look as if they had a light dusting of blush on them.

Luz sucked in her breath. "Oh," she said, staring at the child. "So beautiful."

Gifford wasn't as impressed by the baby. She looked healthy, he thought—that was good. He leaned toward the window, trying to read the first name which was hand-written below the stenciled one. Elinor. Maybe she was named after a family member? "Know anyone named Elinor?" he asked Luz.

Her eyes widened in surprise. "Eduardo's mother," she said quietly. "It is the same."

1:30 PM

In the waiting room, Marisa was too excited to sit still. She pestered Annie and the adults with questions. "Can I see the baby? I will go and look in the rooms for Eduardo. You do not know him, so I will 'seek' him," she said enormously proud of the unfamiliar word she had learned. "Annie, you will come with me?" She trotted from the older women to the younger one, not actually listening for permission or any response at all, for that matter.

Distracted for a moment by the child's enthusiasm, Annie laughed. "Come here. Sit down by me, Little One. Your mother will be back soon. We can't just walk into every room. We must be careful not to share our germs with the new babies. We will wait for Detective Gifford." Even before she finished the sentence, Annie was dismayed to see Marisa ignore her and shoot out of the room, heading down the hall.

"Marisa," Annie called, then dropped her voice in sudden recognition of sleeping mothers and babies. "I'll find her," she assured the other women as she jumped from her chair to follow the little girl, "before she gets lost."

"Kids aren't allowed to wander around by themselves on this floor. She went that way," pointed an exasperated clerk at the desk without looking up from her computer.

Annie glanced down the hall in the direction the clerk indicated, but the hall was empty. "Oh, Marisa. Your mother is NOT going to be happy," Annie sighed. There were several rooms on each side of the long passageway, a couple with doors slightly open. Maybe Marisa had ducked into one of those?

Moving rapidly past the doors which were closed, Annie stopped at the first open doorway and peered in. A grey-haired woman was leaning over the bed of a young mother holding a baby. Both women were smiling, but there were no other occupants of the room. The next open doorway had a curtain pulled across the bed, so Annie couldn't see what was going on inside. She whispered, "Marisa, are you in there?" But no one answered.

By now Annie was at the end of the hall. A bank of large windows overlooked an outdoor atrium below. Two small trees, several bushes, and three or four benches were all weighted down with snow. Annie could just barely make out the twinkle of the tiny, white Christmas lights which must be covering the tree branches beneath the blanket of white. She stopped and stared at the scene, trying to remember another Christmas, in fact, any other Christmas, but her mind was blank. She wondered in passing if she would ever remember the past. Brushing off an instant of unexpected anxiety, she looked both directions and randomly chose the left corridor.

"It's been almost 10 minutes. Do you think I should go after her?" Ramona asked Viola.

Viola shook her head. "Annie will find her. Marisa can't have gone far, and since stealth is not her nature, she's probably just talking to some mom about her baby or arranging to take over all patient care on this wing."

Ramona chuckled. "Good point."

Carrie Jane checked her watch. "Maybe we should call *Señor* Caballero and let him know where we are. I'd hate for him to come home and find the house empty, not when his son has already disappeared."

Flor looked up from the text conversation she had been having since she sat down. "Give it a few more minutes, Amiga. Let's find out what Gifford and Luz say about the baby before we decide what to do next."

Carrie Jane nodded and settled back in her seat.

1:45 PM

Outside the nursery, Gifford and Luz were conferring in quiet voices. "It can't be a coincidence," Gifford said. "It's got to be Eduardo's baby."

"But how? How could he keep such a thing from us? We are his family. We love him."

"I have no idea," Gifford replied. He was relieved to hear no anger in her voice, only sadness. Most stepmothers had a tough time loving the child of another woman. This one appeared to be the exception. Eduardo probably didn't have a clue how unusual his situation was. "What we need to do now is find him and ask him. The baby's nameplate says her mother is in room 204."

Around the corner, pushing with all her might, Marisa managed to open the door wide enough for her little body to slip through. She had ignored the doors which were closed tightly because she couldn't reach the latches to open them. But she'd manage to enter three whose doors had slits wide enough for her to slither inside. The ladies in the beds were nice to her, but none of them knew someone named Eduardo. It was hard for the little girl to figure out.

"Who's there?" asked a man's voice from behind the curtain of this room questioned her.

"It is me, Marisa," she answered.

"Marisa?" Eduardo's voice came through the curtain. He flung the barrier out of the way and gaped at her. "Marisa? What on earth are you doing here? How did you find me?"

"The paper with the gold letters," Marisa announced. "It told us."

"Eduardo? What's going on?" called a drowsy voice from the bed. "Who's here?"

"It's my sister," his voice caught as he took two steps across the room and scooped her up into his arms. "My little sister."

"Marisa?" said a voice in the hall. "Marisa, where are you?"

The little girl flung her arms around Eduardo's neck, her face alight with discovery. "Annie-girl?" she called. "I am here, here in this room. I have found Eduardo." She pulled her head out from under his chin, her two hands holding his face so that he was forced to look directly into her eyes. "You are lost," she scolded him. "You must come home now. Papa is worried. Mama has cried. Now she is looking at a baby, but she will be back soon. You have been very bad," she scolded.

"Marisa?" Annie rounded the edge of the drawn curtain and spied the little girl in the arms of a tall, handsome boy with blue-green eyes. She stopped short.

"Eduardo," she said uncertainly. "Are you Eduardo Caballero?"

He had not noticed Annie's voice at all. Alarm registered in his face; the total center of his attention concentrated on the child in his arms. "Marisa," he said urgently. "Mama is looking at a baby? Here? In the hospital? Now? Where is she?" His arms around her tightened.

"Ouch! Let go! You are squishing me." She demanded, trying to wriggle out of his grasp. "Put me down!"

"Marisa, where is Mama now?" Anxiety colored his question.

"Where they keep the babies. The paper said to 'seek' where they keep the babies."

"*¡Dios mío!*"

He exchanged glances with Belen. "Go," she said.

He dropped Marisa to her feet and pulled her along after him, sweeping past Annie without a second thought.

"Annie," Marisa called as Eduardo dragged her through the open door. "My Annie." But Eduardo paid no attention.

2:30 PM

The four women in the waiting room looked up expectantly when Gifford and Luz joined them.

"Well?" said Viola. "Any news?"

Luz sat down heavily in the chair across from her and Ramona. "We do not know. The baby is sleeping in a small crib. The last name of Caballero is on the bed, but we did not see Eduardo. It is hard to be sure."

Gifford chose a seat next to Carrie Jane. "There is something," he said, addressing her but including the other three women. "The baby's name is Elinor. Luz says it's the name of Eduardo's mother."

Ramona stiffened in her chair and grabbed unconsciously for Viola's arm. "Elinor? How do you spell it?"

"Ramona," Viola commanded sharply. "It's just a coincidence," Viola whispered, patting her hand. She searched her friend's eyes, forcing her not to listen. "Don't jump to conclusions. It's a lovely name, you know that. You used it yourself. Not common perhaps, but many families must like it as much as you and Amos did."

Gifford looked up sharply. "You know someone named Elinor?" At Ramona's moan of recognition, his eyes narrowed. "What's going on?" he asked Viola.

Viola stroked Ramona's arm soothingly for several moments until she could see signs that her friend's tension had eased slightly. "Ramona's daughter, Elinor, disappeared 20 years ago." At the mention of the name, she felt Ramona shudder and her face crumpled into a portrait of pain. "Ramona," she said sharply. "Stop. It's just a baby with the same name. You can't let yourself do this again. Not now. Not after all these years."

But it was too late. Ramona's breathing had become labored, and her body began to tremble with deep, jagged gasps as she tried to get control of herself.

"You had a daughter named Elinor?" Luz asked, puzzled by Ramona's reaction to the news. "What has happened to her?"

Viola slipped an arm around her friend, supporting Ramona as she lost control of the ramrod strength with which she always carried herself. "Sh-shush," she murmured. "It will be all right. We'll figure it out. Don't give in. It's going to be OK."

There was no indication whether or not Ramona understood or even heard Viola's words. She was lost in her own private sorrow.

When Annie rounded the corner into the waiting room, she stopped abruptly at the tableaux before her. Gifford, Luz, Carrie Jane, and Flor were staring intently at a weeping Ramona, who was wrapped in Viola's arms.

"What happened?" Annie asked urgently as she rushed to kneel at Ramona's feet. "Ramona?" The girl touched one of the older woman's hands clutched in a vise-like grip on the arm of the chair in which she sat. At the contact, Ramona reached blindly for the hand Annie offered as if discovering a life raft at the moment of drowning. Annie turned Viola, who seemed to be bearing the weight of Ramona's grief. "Is she all right?"

Gifford gazed unseeing at Annie for a moment, then shook himself out of the trance produced by the reaction of the two old women across from him. He spoke slowly, trying to fit the pieces of information he had gained into some sort of logical framework. "Looks like the baby's Eduardo's. I talked to the clerk at the desk—an Eduardo Caballero is listed as the father. The baby's a girl. Her name . . .."

"Elinor. Her name is Elinor," Luz slipped the words into Gifford's sentence, the sympathy for her two friends in her face mixed with confusion at the chain of events.

"Elinor?" Annie nodded in comprehension. "Like her daughter?" Understanding dawned on her face. "Oh, Ramona." Her voice broke as she joined her arms with Viola's, reinforcing the invisible stronghold around Ramona's trembling shoulders.

Suddenly aware of the girl's presence, Ramona made a gallant effort to get control of herself. "Annie," she said. "Annie," she whispered, finding some small comfort in the presence of the child.

"Maybe she has found the baby?" Marisa's cheerful voice floated ahead of her as she skipped into the room tugging at Eduardo. Then his face appeared in the doorway after her.

He surveyed the room but saw only Luz, the mother who loved him. "Mama." Relief washed through him. "Oh, Mama." He leaned against the doorframe, his face pale with exhaustion, and his shoulders hunched with the effort it took to remain upright. Without a sound, Luz arose from her chair, crossed the room, and swept her tall son into her arms. "My son. *Mi hijo, mi hijo. ¿Dónde has estado? He estado tan preocupado?*" she murmured gentle, musical words of consolation, the sound from her lips so low as to be inaudible to the others in room.

Eduardo buried his head in her shoulder, her strength supporting them both. For a long moment, there was only the sound of the boy's uneven breathing, and the clock ticking the seconds away. Then he lifted his head to search her face. "Marisa said you were here. You went to the nursery...? What are you doing here? How did you find me?"

Looking around, and for the first time taking in the other occupants of the room, he asked incredulously, "Miss Plunkett and Miss Gallegos? What are you doing here? Has something happened?" His body tensed with apprehension. "Is someone hurt? Papa? The boys?"

"Oh no, Eduardo. Nothing like that." Carrie Jane attempted to reassure him. "We came looking for you."

Marisa pried herself away from his grasp, hurled herself into the vacant chair next to Annie and declared, "See my Annie-girl. I told you I would find him." Her face beamed with her success.

Carrie Jane leaned forward toward the boy—man, she corrected herself. "Your parents have been so worried. You have been gone for two days. What are you doing here?"

Eduardo led Luz to the nearest worn couch and collapsed into it. He closed his eyes, exhaustion darkening the hollows of his cheeks. He wasn't sure how to begin. He'd kept his secret for so long, and now it seemed that his months of enforced silence could be swallowed up in only one word—Elinor. So simple. But when he tried to form the words, no sound came out. His eyes felt too heavy to open. He wasn't sure if they would ever open again. What was happening? He couldn't seem to clear his head.

"Who are these people," he asked his mother wearily. "What is going on?"

Gifford took charge, unspoken consent mirrored in the faces of the women in the room. "Perhaps it would be best to start at the beginning. My name is Mark Gifford. I'm a detective with the Douglas Valley police department. I've been working with the patrolman assigned to your case since your parents reported you missing two days ago." Indicating the women on the couch, he said, "Viola Pridgeon and Ramona Zollinger. You know Carrie Jane and Flor." He nodded in their direction. "And this Annie, a friend of your sister. I have been helping your stepmother locate you. Perhaps you could tell us what you have been doing for the last two days?"

Across the room, Ramona opened her mouth to interrupt with a question, but she couldn't find enough air to make a sound.

"Eduardo?" Viola asked on behalf of her friend, her professional voice intentionally low and non-threatening. "Can you tell us why you are here?"

The boy looked from face to face. Confusion rattled around in his brain. The baby. They must know. Couldn't they see the entire world had changed? Surely that was obvious? He lifted his eyes to look directly at the woman speaking to him, but nothing made sense.

"Is that your baby in the nursery?" Viola asked gently.

Eduardo nodded. "Her name is Elinor, after my mother."

Ramona gasped, a glimmer of something washed across her face. "Your mother?" she blurted out. She felt her chest constrict. "How—how do you spell it?"

"What?" Eduardo repeated. "What?" His mouth twisted in anger. "What kind of stupid question …?"

"Easy, easy," Viola spoke to him as if he were a skittish creature in the wild. "It's OK. Your baby. A sweet little girl?" She dragged his attention away from the impossible woman next to her.

Gifford waited. He could see something important was happening here, and Viola seemed to know where she was going. Perhaps, at last, this whole episode was going to settle into some kind of sense.

Eduardo nodded his head. "Yes," he said, nodding his head and intertwining his fingers to stop the shaking they seemed to have started on their own.

"A lovely name, Elinor. Unusual. Where did it come from?" Without moving her gaze from Eduardo's face, she kept up her gentle rubbing of Ramona's handclasp in hers.

"My mother," Eduardo answered, instinctively lowering his voice. "It was my mother's name." A wave of grief so heavy it was palpable swept over him. "She died. She left me when I was a baby." He swiped at his eyes, angry at the emotion over which he seemed to have no control.

Ramona groaned. "Oh, God," she whispered. Horror washed across her face as comprehension dawned. "She died? She's dead?" Her fingers clenched Viola's with such force that Viola gave a startled gasp of pain.

Ramona's intensity enraged Eduardo. Who was this woman and what did she think she knew about his mother? He bent forward in his seat, his eyes taking on the slate blue-gray ocean waves in a stormy sea. He tried to lunge from his chair toward the older woman, but Luz's hands on his shoulder held him back.

"No, no, my son. Listen, por favor. Please, listen." Luz drew him back to her, her arm massaging his back as if he were a child. "Shhh. Shh. It will be all right. Shh," she comforted him.

Agitation had seized Ramona so completely that she clutched her arms to her chest attempting to calm their involuntary shaking, Viola's hand still entwined in hers, "Oh, God, Viola. It's her. It's my Ellie."

"Ramona?" Annie's tremulous voice interrupted. Her eyes flitted from Ramona to Viola and back.

"You have to ask," Viola prompted her friend tenderly. "You have to be sure."

There was silence, Ramona's face transfixed with hope and sorrow simultaneously. She strained to calm the rise and fall of her chest; her breathing slowed. A lifetime of facing loss head-on gradually gave her the strength to straighten her shoulders and release her death grip on Viola's hand. Squaring her jaw, she forced the tone of her voice to mimic normalcy. "What is your father's first name?" she asked Edward.

"Guillermo. Why? What is this about?"

At the mention of the name, Ramona's tenuous self-control imploded. Overcome, her shoulders trembled, and her face was again tight with unshed tears. She looked at Viola in panic. "It's him, it's him," she repeated in a kind of litany to herself, her eyes traveling wildly around the room without recognizing a single object in their path.

Eduardo stared at Ramona, anger rising in his throat. He caught Carrie Jane's eyes, blaming her somehow for this one last straw piled on top of his other impossible burdens. His face hardened, and his eyes narrowed. He didn't give a crap about this stupid woman and her stupid questions. "Who does she think she is?" He asked, his voice rising. "What gives her the right …?"

"Eduardo," Luz warned, her arm massaging his shoulder as she spoke. "Wait. You do not understand. Listen to the *señora. Por favor.*" She drew his attention to her face. "Wait," she hushed him

All eyes focused on Eduardo. Except Gifford's. His were fixed on Annie's face. There was something wrong. The tendrils of her hair around her face seemed to smolder as if lit by some illumination from within. And it appeared that the radiance was increasing in brightness. Denial whipped through him. He blinked. The light faded. He exhaled as relief poured through him. She must be holding the parchment, and light was reflecting from it, he reasoned. Thank heaven. His brain couldn't handle any more of this weird supernatural stuff. Cops knew there was an explanation for everything, he assured himself. He just had to take the time to figure it out.

"Eduardo," Carrie Jane asked softly. "The baby? Who is her mother?"

"Belen. Belen Hidalgo." He didn't dare meet her eyes.

There was a sudden intake of breath from Flor. "That name was on one of my junior class rolls last fall, but she never showed up?" Understanding came. "She was pregnant? That's why she didn't show?"

Ramona's tears slowed. She sat still listening intently, her mind racing at Flor's explanation. She felt Viola loosen the on grip on her shoulders. If this boy was Elinor's son, then the baby must be her great-granddaughter. . ... How could that be? Yesterday she was alone, the only member of her family left, and now she had a grandchild and a great-grandchild. How was that even possible?

Next to her Viola looked up at the boy. She knew that prenatal care could be a rarity among mothers so young. "Is the baby all right?" She relaxed when he nodded.

"She is perfect, like her mother."

Carrie Jane exchanged a glance with Flor. "Eduardo," she began almost tenderly, "why didn't you tell your father?"

Hostility leaked from the boy all at once as if someone had poked him with a pin, releasing the hot air that had inflated his body. "I couldn't." He clenched his eyes shut, shoving aside an almost overwhelming desire to retreat into the safety of childhood. "My father works so hard," he admitted in defeat. "And after work, he helps take care of all of us. He will be so disappointed." Even as he said the words aloud, he felt an enormous reprieve. Now, at last, the secret was revealed; he had to protect it no longer.

"But he loves the babies," Marisa's high voice protested, totally unaware of the emotional deluge engulfing the adults in the room.

Eduardo's expression softened, and his eyes misted at the words of his little sister. "He does love the babies, Little One," he agreed.

"Can I hold the baby? I will be very careful?" she promised. She peeked through her eyelashes at her older brother. "You know I change Alejandro's diapers. I have the practice with babies?"

Eduardo smiled despite himself. "Si, Little One. I am sure the baby will love you."

Luz looked from one of her children to the other. "The baby is a beautiful little girl," she assured him. "She looks as you did as a small boy. She has the little curls over her ears, just as you did."

Eduardo's face clouded at the description of the baby. The enormity of his situation threatened to swallow him up again.

"Do not worry, my son. I am here. Your Papa and I will help you. It will be all right," she soothed him, patting his hand which was entwined with hers.

"No, it will not," said a harsh voice challenged from the desk across the hall. "For you, it will definitely not be all right." Mr. Hidalgo burst into the room, his chest still heaving from the climb up the stairs. He surveyed the crowded waiting room, arrogance plastered across his face. His gaze rested on Eduardo as he announced, "I have come to take home MY Child. I forbid you to see her ever again."

Apologetically, Belen's doctor stood slightly behind Hidalgo at the entrance to the room. "I'm so sorry," she said. In her hand was a document with a formal looking seal. "It's a court order reinforcing Mr. Hidalgo's jurisdiction over Belen and the baby."

Ramona lifted her head. Viola whispered something in her ear.

Gifford approached the doctor. "May I see it please?"

The doctor handed him the document, grateful to hand the problem to someone else. This kind of thing was always ugly. She sympathized with her patient and the boy; they were young, but they obviously cared about one another. She was certain the baby was in safe hands with them. As far as she could tell, Mr. Hidalgo had no interest in the baby at all. She'd delivered literally thousands of infants. They were fragile creatures, totally dependent on their caretakers for years. For a baby, life without love could scar the child forever. In her opinion, Belen wasn't yet strong enough to stand up to her father by herself. The baby deserved better.

Scanning the document, Gifford nodded in agreement. Wordlessly, he handed it to Eduardo. "I'm afraid she's right, son. Belen's only 17—her father has custody."

Luz interrupted. "I could take the baby," she offered anxiously. "Another *niña* would be welcome." Gently her voice pulled Eduardo away from his fixation on Hidalgo and compelled him to look at her. "You are the father. We will love your baby as we do you."

"Mama," he said quietly and caressed her hand, lifting it to his cheek. A faint smile crossed her face at his words.

"Would the judge allow this?" she asked Gifford hopefully.

"I'm afraid not," Gifford answered.

Ramona came to life. "I need to call John." She searched her pocket for her phone. To no one in particular, she explained, "He'll know how to help."

Hidalgo ignored them. "Get my daughter," he ordered the doctor as if she were a hospital aide. "I will meet her at the Emergency door."

"I'll check to see if she's ready," the doctor replied evenly. She glanced at Eduardo as she turned. The hostility now radiating from him was as palpable as a spark of electricity. She slipped across the hall and whispered to the clerk at the desk, "I think we're going to need security."

"So. You have lost." Mr. Hidalgo snarled at Eduardo. "In only a few minutes, Belen and the baby will be coming home with me. I am finished with you!" he pointed at Eduardo. "And you will never see my daughter again."

Eduardo flinched at the older man's words. He struggled to regain his composure; his face tightened with anger. He released his grasp on Luz, rising to his feet to face Hidalgo.

Effortlessly, Gifford slid between him and Belen's father, putting a light restraining hand on the boy's arm. "Wait, son." The boy tried to twist away from him. "Eduardo?" he repeated, but this time his voice held a definite warning. He shouldered the boy a step further away from Hidalgo. "It won't help the baby for you to be in jail. Think!" he ordered.

"Eduardo." Carrie Jane's soft voice reached out to the boy. "Let us help you. All this time you have carried this weight by yourself." Listening, the boy half-turned toward her, his attention still on Hidalgo.

"There is nothing you can do," he said bitterly. "Belen loves me and I her. I want to marry her, but he—he doesn't care about her or the baby. No one does." His shoulders sagged, and despair filled his face. His eyes dropped to the floor, his balled fists hanging loose at the sides of his body.

"Actually, that's not true, son," said a penetrating voice from somewhere outside the waiting room. "Some of us care a great deal."

Gifford's head swiveled from Eduardo to locate the source of the sound. A man with shoulder-length white hair and a spotless white suit walked into the room. An expletive exploded from Gifford-- "What the hell?"

Annie gasped. She rose from her chair, lifting Marisa from her lap and settling the little girl carefully her eyes riveted on the stranger. "It's you," she whispered. "It's you."

A jolt of recognition stunned Eduardo. Only this morning the man had bought his breakfast, even held his baby. The white-haired man smiled at Eduardo and nodded his head in acknowledgment.

Paying no attention to the stranger, Hidalgo moved a step closer to Eduardo, his finger jabbing into the boy's chest. With a cry of fury, he yelled, "You are nothing. I promise you will never see my daughter or that brat again."

The stranger reached out, and at his touch on Hidalgo's shoulder, the man froze, motionless—his head twisted over his shoulder, shock registering on his face. His mouth made no sound. Belen's father was totally immobilized.

Gifford shuddered. He felt for a chair with the back of his hand and sat down unexpectedly.

"Annie," the man motioned her toward him. "Of course, that's not the name we use on the Other Side," he explained to the others, "but it will do." At her tentative approach, he lifted his right arm and embraced her. "Your work here is finished. Well done. It is time to come home." He looked at her with undisguised affection. "We have missed you."

Annie nestled into his shoulder as if she belonged there.

Only Viola had the presence of mind to speak. "What work? Who are you, and what is all this?"

"My name is unimportant," he answered her. "There are myriad numbers of us sent to minister to our Father's children." His voice was quiet, but it pierced every soul in the room. "None of you in this room, or anywhere on earth, is without our protection and concern. When the need is great, we are sent to ease your burdens. Rarely do we have permission to show ourselves to you, but rest assured, we are never far away."

Marisa seemed unimpressed by the white-haired man's words. "Are you a ghost?" she asked.

He smiled at her. "No, Little One. Ghosts are creatures of imagination. We are very real."

"And you know my Annie-girl?" Guilelessly, Marisa climbed out of her chair and walked to Annie's side, stealing her small hand into Annie's.

"Very well," he said. "She has not been with us long, but as you know, she is special. For many years we have heard the prayers of your friend Ramona. Annie was assigned to help her find her daughter."

Annie nodded. Her posture straightened, and she seemed taller, older. "I didn't remember," she apologized to Ramona. "But you and Viola," she included both women in her words, "you loved me. You took me in—you had no reason to protect me, but with you, I felt safe." She stopped, not sure how to explain. The white-haired man at her side smiled down at her, encouraging her. She turned to Ramona. "We have felt the sorrow of your loss. We were called to ease that burden."

"Exactly, Annie," he said. "No life is easy, but despite your own pain, Ramona, for many years you have cared about and loved thousands of children. Now there is a new child who will need you. And you, Viola." He included her in his message. "These parents are very young," he explained. "There will be difficulties which only the two of you have the knowledge and experience to resolve." The tenderness in his voice caressed the two women. "Goodness does not go unrewarded in this life or the next."

"Your love sheltered me when I was alone," Annie said simply. "You were my guardian angels. Now you will watch over little Elinor."

Marisa patted Annie's arm. "I love you, too," the child reminded her.

"And I, you." Annie pulled her close and hugged her.

The white-haired man knelt until he was eye level to the little girl. "Only you, Marisa, understood the message on the parchment which I gave Annie. Because of you, Ramona's prayers have been answered." He closed his eyes, reached down to the child, placed his hands upon her head, and blessed her. Though the occupants of the room could not understand the words he spoke, they saw her small face begin to glow with the illumination which now enveloped himself and Annie.

"Remember," he told the occupants of the room when he had finished blessing the little girl, "you are never alone, no matter how difficult your days may seem."

Speaking to Ramona, he said quietly, "Eduardo is the family you have been seeking all these years. He will be a blessing to you, and you to him."

"Eduardo is her family? But he is my family. How can he be her family, too?" Marisa questioned Annie, puzzled. "He does not look like her. He looks like me." The little girl looked at the honey color of her skin and examined a piece of her jet-black hair.

"Families are found in the heart, beneath the skin," Annie explained to the little girl. "Eduardo is Ramona's family, and because you are Eduardo's family, you are her family, too." Marisa thought about this. It was very confusing, but the white-haired man had said she had helped Ramona find Eduardo. Her face cleared. "It is good," she approved.

"Then it is true?" Ramona asked. "The baby is my great-grandchild." A lifetime of loving the language of words betrayed her now; there was nothing which could express the joy of this moment. "Oh Viola. I have not lost her after all." Overcome, she sank back into her chair.

Once again Viola wrapped her arms around her friend and held her tightly. Together they wept, and as the tears fell, a gentle brilliance began to emanate from their faces. The almost visible curtain of despair was which had haunted Ramona since the day her daughter Elinor had disappeared was washed away in the radiance now emanating from the two figures in the center of the room.

The white-haired man spoke directly to Eduardo. "You and Belen have made choices that led you here. Every choice has ripples." He gestured to Mr. Hidalgo standing motionless in the center of the room. "Do not mistake his behavior as selfishness—it is fear which drives him. Fear has the power to dissolve love and wash it away. You have the power to propel him out of your lives or to ease his road back to you. Remember. He is the grandfather of your child."

"Soon you will celebrate the Child born long ago in Bethlehem," he addressed the others in the room. "Blessed are you who have chosen to shelter and protect His children."

He leaned over and kissed Marisa on the cheek. "It is time, Little One, to let go of your Annie-girl. It is time for her to come Home." Gently he lifted Marisa and settled her on her mother's lap.

He paused in the center of the room and looked into the eyes of each person present. "Do not forget this day," he instructed. "Remember. You have only to ask, and you will find comfort."

He reached for Annie's hand and led her from the room. As they passed through the door, blinding light flooded the room, and without warning, the two figures vanished.

For several seconds no one moved. There was a lingering sense of rightness with the world, and no one dared say a word lest they dispel its magic. Finally, a long sigh escaped from Ramona. "She's gone, isn't she?"

Only Marisa understood. "My Annie is in heaven?" she asked.

"Yes, Little One. I think she has gone home," her mother comforted her. "She is needed there."

The little girl ducked her head into her mother's breast. "When will she come back? What if I need her again?"

"I do not know the answers to those questions." She lifted the child's head so that she could look directly into her eyes. "But she is your friend. Always remember that."

Abruptly, the peace was interrupted by a growl of rage. In the middle of the room, Hidalgo sputtered, shook the tension from his muscles, and looked around frantically to be sure the threat was gone. "What has happened to me? I could not move." His face reddened with fury. "You did this to me!" He pointed at Eduardo. "I warn you. Do not touch me again! Policía! I need the police!"

"It was not Eduardo," Marisa scoffed at his stupidity. "It was an angel. An angel touched you."

Enraged beyond control, Hidalgo shrieked, "Shut up, you little witch. It was no angel. It was that Devil!" He lunged at Eduardo. "I'll kill him! I WILL KILL HIM!" His eyes bulged. His arms flailed in Eduardo's direction.

"I don't think so," Gifford said rising and in one smooth motion snapped Hidalgo's limbs behind his back, confining the man's threats. "But I suspect the judge will appreciate knowing you threatened to murder this boy." Gifford turned to Carrie Jane. "Will you see if those security guys have shown up? And dial 911. We're going to need transport to the jail here."

But Carrie Jane did not respond. She was frozen in place, shock still evident in her expression.

Hidalgo jerked away from Gifford, cursing in what Gifford assumed was Spanish as the man struggled. Gifford tightened his grip and forced Hidalgo's shoulders closer together. Hidalgo howled in pain.

Gifford grunted with the exertion. Hidalgo was several inches shorter, but considerably heavier, and he used his weight as a lever to try force Gifford to release him. "Carrie Jane? Need a little help here. Now!" Gifford raised his voice to attract her attention. "Please." He added as an afterthought.

Flor nudged Carrie Jane out of her trance. "You call 911. I'll find the security guys." Flor ordered.

Shaking herself free of her stupor, Carrie Jane pulled her phone from her pocket and dialed. She looked at Gifford in apology. "Sorry, it's all just so . . .." her voice trailed off as she punched the numbers on the phone. "Did what I thought just happened ...?"

A voice on the other end of the line asked, "What is your emergency?"

A shaky smile crossed Carrie Jane's mouth and ignited her dimples, "We need backup for Detective Mark Gifford at the Douglas Valley Regional Hospital. Maternity Ward. He has a suspect in custody."

Viola's sharp eyes watched the proceedings. "Well," she said. "I think it's time this family got to know each other.

"Eduardo," she told the tall boy standing in front of her, "maybe it would be a good idea if you introduced Belen to your mother and told her what is going on. I suspect she'll be happy to spend another day or so in the hospital." Then she pulled her friend to her feet, "Ramona, come on. You and I are going to see that new great-grandchild."

Tuesday, December 31

9 PM

JOHN SMILED ACROSS THE TABLE at Ramona. "Congratulations. We've made it halfway through our agreement," he said. "Two dinners without complaining. Impressive." A wicked grin crossed his face. "And I can tell you are--at this minute--grinding your teeth to avoid breaching that last part of the agreement." It amused him to see her irritated almost beyond her ability to keep the vow she had given him.

"I'm busy," she said. "I don't have time to be going to dinner with you!"

"Careful, you're about to cross the line between information and whining," he warned her with amusement.

"John. You have always been the most infuriating person I know."

"And you for me," he countered. "We have so much in common," he spread his hands expansively. "It's a bond, as it were."

Exasperated, Ramona shook her head. "OK, OK. Just remember that when we get to the end of this deal." Her tone turned more serious. "And I admit," she glanced at him from under her eyelashes, "that your company has always been diverting—if not always relaxing," she amended. "But tomorrow is beyond anything. . .." she tried to find words to describe what she was feeling and couldn't. That irritated her even more. "I hate it when I run out of words."

"It happens so seldom; I find it quite entertaining. It's astonishingly peaceful."

She glared at him. "John, sometimes you drive me crazy," she said louder than she intended. Diners at nearby tables looked up from their conversations and stared at her.

He grinned. "Good! Helps with your anger management issues. So.

251

Any resolutions for the New Year? Besides taking in a young couple and their new baby, I mean? How's the renovation going?"

"Viola and I have cleared out the office and the guest bedroom. Carrie Jane and Gifford came over day before yesterday and painted the two rooms. I dug the old crib out of the basement and scrubbed it down. Eduardo said he and his dad will refinish it over spring break, but for now, the baby is sleeping in their room anyway." As had been the case all week, at the mention of the baby, her eyes started to mist over. "And to think I almost missed this," she said softly. Her gratitude got the best of her. She reached across the table to squeeze his hand. "Oh, John. Thank you so much."

"For the truck? If that's what you're thanking me for, I'm getting a lot of bang for my buck here!" That did it. Her eyes filled, and she swiped at them angrily. "I'm getting tired of crying," she said. "It's exhausting. You'd think I'd run out of tears after a couple of days, but NO!"

Gently he lifted his linen napkin and leaned toward her so that he could dab at the tears which had fallen on her cheek. "You've waited a long time," he said quietly. "You've earned a family."

"Have I, John? After all the terrible things I said to Elinor that morning? I didn't even know Guillermo, and I condemned him because he was poor and Latino. I was sure he was lazy and up to no good, so I drove my only child so far away that she died without me. What kind of mother does that?" Her face crumpled, and she grabbed at her own napkin to cover the depth of her shame. In the past week, she had lain awake long hours grappling with the guilt she had never been strong enough to face. Each succeeding morning, she had feared she might not have the strength to rise from her bed.

John waited until she had control of herself again. "We can't change the past," he told her, "but it is wrong to use today's knowledge as a bludgeon to punish ourselves for the mistakes of yesterday. It took courage for you to invite Eduardo and Belen to live with you. No one doubts you love that baby, and you will grow to love your grandson and Belen, too."

When her voice steadied, Ramona said, "That's what I was saying 'thank you' for. The wedding. Only you could have managed it." She knew it was the truth, and she had been loath to discover that her take-care-of-yourself-at-any-cost attitude was self-defeating. She had needed him, and he hadn't disappointed her. "Eduardo and Belen didn't want to wait," she said slowly. "It was generous of you to offer to do the ceremony tomorrow--on a holiday." She looked directly into his eyes which were startlingly blue even after all these years. "We could never have managed it so quickly without you."

"You'd have figured out a way. Probably with a bulldozer and a megaphone."

Still clutching the napkin against her cheek, she chuckled at the image. "I actually like that idea. Maybe I'll look online and see how much a bullhorn costs."

Recoiling in dismay, he pointed out, "Well, I admit that it might come in handy at Town Council meetings. Speaking of which, what's your next move with Mayor Jesse and the gang? Isn't the first meeting of the New Year next week?"

"That concert at Christensen's put a bit of a wrench in her plans, I think. Even the newspaper has hinted that the idea of renovation over demolition has merit. But we'll see. I suspect Jesse won't give up easily. On the other hand, neither will I."

"Hmph!" he laughed out loud. "We may be older, but I swear this is the gist of the same conversation we had when we were 18. Then it was something about the dress code and cheerleader uniforms. But the same fire in your eyes. You haven't changed a bit." He shifted in his chair and leaned toward her, then stopped when he saw her smile at the memory. Deftly, he changed the subject. "So, what's on the menu that looks good?"

Wednesday, New Year's Day

8 AM

RAMONA OPENED HER EYES TO a New Year's Day sun flooding her room. The brightness of the light caused her a moment of panic. What time was it? Most of the night anxiety had kept her awake--worry about how she could face the man who had loved her daughter, and in her pride, she had driven away. Ramona had been shocked to discover that Elinor had spent the last two years of her life only a few miles away in a tiny apartment owned by a widow whose family had lived in the valley since pioneer days.

She realized that at some point during the night, she must have fallen into an exhausted sleep. Now anticipation coursed through her. Had she overslept? She groaned as she rolled so that she could see the clock. Only 8 AM. Thank heavens. She lay still for a moment, waiting for her body to catch up with her brain. When her feet touched the floor, she didn't even notice the familiar pain. Today her family would be waiting for her at the Courthouse.

These last few days since Christmas had been a roller coaster of exhilaration and trepidation. Already she loved the baby—the dark fuzzy hair, the bright eyes so like her own, the sweet smell of the child as she suckled gently in her sleep. And she had already grown fond of Belen, who was so anxious to prove herself a good mother that she sometimes wakened the baby from a nap to feed her.

Ramona remembered her own first weeks with Elinor. Perhaps every new mother was the same. Wonder laced with worry. Belen will figure it out, she reassured herself. We all do, one way or another. But school? School was going to be a problem. A new baby made attending classes more complicated, and Belen had already missed the whole first semester.

No great-grandchild of mine is going to grow up with an uneducated mother, Ramona vowed. Belen would be lucky to have a teacher right across the hall.

Grabbing her robe, Ramona headed for the bathroom. She needed to get a move on, or she'd be late for the wedding. Flipping on the light, she stared at herself in the mirror, her graying hair reminding her of her stupid pride. Twenty years not knowing about Elinor. Or Eduardo.

Ramona had never been positive that there was a heaven before she met Annie. Now she knew. And she prayed that Elinor could forgive her, so that when they met again--she shook off her fears. All those years of anger and sorrow—and the answer was less than two miles down the road.

10 AM

John's office doors were wide open, the sun's reflection on the snow so bright that he hadn't bothered to flip on the lamps. He was seated at his desk speaking in quiet tones to Eduardo, who had pulled a chair up next to the front of the judge's desk and was nodding occasionally as if the entire world depended on it. Belen was to his right, the baby wrapped in a white afghan with a tiny pink ribbon woven through the edges which Viola had somehow found the time to crochet over the last week. The two big leather chairs which usually sat opposite the desk had been pushed back against the walls, and two dozen folding chairs borrowed from the Town Hall meeting room set in semi-circles facing the desk.

Eduardo's family sat on the front row, the boys wearing their Sunday best, their hair neatly brushed. Ramona smiled at Alejandro, who was sitting on his mother's lap staring over her shoulder, wide-eyed at the participants as they came through the double doors. He was chewing on three of his fingers, his head tucked shyly into his mother's neck. Marisa had on what must be her Christmas dress—red with ribbons on the sleeves and a ribbon in her hair to match. On her feet was a pair of Cinderella shoes, complete with a sparkling bow and tiny, delicate heels. They fit as if made especially for her.

Mr. Caballero rose gravely when he saw Ramona arrive. He walked to her side. Guillermo reached out and shook her hand. "*Señora*," he said. "Welcome."

She hadn't seen him since the day she'd watched Elinor slip past her and climb into his truck, despite being forbidden to do so. But Ramona knew him immediately. He was handsome then, as he was now. She recognized the young man he had been beneath the steel gray of his hair and the slight wrinkles at the corner of his eyes.

"*Señor* Caballero," she faltered. All of this was her fault. She didn't know how to begin. "Please forgive me," she started and was horrified to discover that once again she might not be able to control her emotions.

"I, too, ask forgiveness." His voice was gentle, his face a mask of sorrow. "I was young and very angry. My family encouraged me." He stopped, lost in a memory. "My beautiful Elinor—I kept her from those she loved—from you and her father--when she became sick." He paused and looked at each of his children seated around him, the younger ones learning forward in their chairs so as not to miss a single moment of this break in the routine of their lives. "I do not know how I could have done such a thing," he finished. Reaching out, he took Ramona's hand. "*Señora.* We both loved your daughter. Let us remember that. There is nothing we can do about the days which are past. Let us rejoice in the days to come."

Overwhelmed by his kindness, Ramona nodded mutely and allowed herself to be led to the chair next to Luz, who smiled at her. Alejandro pulled his fingers from his mouth and reached for her earrings. Instinctively, she leaned away from those small, damp appendages. Then thinking better of her reaction, she reached up and clasped his little hand in hers—wet fingers and all.

Behind her, she felt the warmth of Viola's familiar grasp press her shoulder and heard her whisper, "What a very good way to start a new year, my friend." Viola's voiced stopped, then added, "For all of us."

Ramona twisted around so that she could meet Viola's eyes. They had known one another so long that they could read one another's thoughts. Ramona squeezed the hand on her shoulder. No reply was needed.

The two women turned simultaneously as Gifford, Carrie Jane, and Flor, holding hands with a tall, lanky figure that neither knew, walked into the office, and took chairs in the second row. "I thought you were in Salt Lake," Viola whispered to Flor.

"Just got back. Didn't want to miss this. I thought I'd better show up." There was a second of hesitation while Flor considered her words. "Might outshine my own wedding someday."

"Everybody here?" John interrupted, surveying the audience just as Temp moved quietly through the doors and tipped his head in apology for his tardiness. At the front of the room, Eduardo's face broke into a grin.

"Just wanted to be sure Eduardo here finally managed to complete an assignment," Temp said. The audience chuckled in appreciation.

When the laughter died down, John began, "For those of you who don't know me, I am Judge John Callister, and we are assembled here to join Eduardo Caballero and Belen Hidalgo in holy matrimony. I understand little Elinor thinks it's a requirement for her future happiness." He indicated the baby sleeping peacefully on her mother's lap.

Belen lifted the baby to her lips and kissed the tiny forehead. Obligingly, the infant smiled in her sleep. A moment later a loud thump started the child, her tiny fingers splaying out against her mother's embrace, as the open door banged against the wall. Mr. Hidalgo and his lawyer swept into the room fumbling noisily among the folding chairs until they found seats in the back of the room as far from the rest of the participants as they could get.

"What now?" Ramona hissed under her breath.

Hidalgo stared straight ahead, ignoring the other assembled friends and family—even his daughter.

"Mr. Hidalgo, thank you for coming," John acknowledged. Some sort of message passed between the two men at the judge's glance. Hidalgo's stony expression did not change, but he bobbed his head briefly.

The judge rose from his seat, his black robe adding stature to his position. "Now Eduardo, if you'll bring Belen around with you to stand there in front of the desk?"

Belen handed the sleeping child to Ramona and walked around to take Eduardo's hand. She wore a simple white, knee-length silk sheath with a deep neckline and long sheer sleeves made of the delicate lace that covered the fabric of the dress—a gift from Ramona and Viola. The dark hair Eduardo loved to touch hung down her back in deep curls, a white ribbon clasping the tiny French braids which kept loose ends in check on both sides of her face. Despite the slight bulge of the tummy and swell of the breasts which indicated that Belen was still recovering from her emergency delivery, Ramona was certain she had never seen a more beautiful bride. There was a serenity and certainty of purpose in her face which would have been the envy of any woman, no matter what her age, on her wedding day.

"By the power invested in me by the State of Utah . . .." Callister began.

Clapping erupted when Eduardo kissed the bride three minutes later. Her radiant face was a clear communication of her feelings. Viola pulled a small packet of tissues from her purse and handed one to Luz and one to Ramona. Behind them, Carrie Jane smiled wordlessly as Gifford squeezed her hand

"Is that all!" Marisa demanded, and the guests dissolved into laughter. "Are they married now?"

"Yes, Marisa. They are husband and wife," Mr. Caballero assured her.

Marisa's face clouded. "Papa, I am not your 'Little One' anymore?" she asked.

"I think," answered Mr. Caballero, glancing at the sleeping child in Ramona's arms, "a new Little One will need her aunt Marisa to watch over her."

Marisa considered the idea for a moment. "It is good," she said. Turning to the other guests, she announced, "I am the baby's aunt," with some authority. She straightened in her chair. "When you wish to hold the baby, I will show you how."

Amusement rippled through the guests, and they moved forward to congratulate the newlyweds, hugging them, and oohing and aahing over the beautiful baby in Ramona's arms.

Eduardo could scarcely take it all in. He shook hands and embraced every person in the room—except Hidalgo, who rose as soon as the ceremony was finished, forced the doors open, and strode angrily into the hall. Watching him leave, Eduardo realized in amazement that his year-long anxiety had disappeared. He had never imagined a day like this could be possible. For now, pushing away the worries of tomorrow, he and Belen were husband and wife. They had a home which welcomed them, and a child more beautiful than any he had ever seen. Today was a memorable day indeed.

"What was that about?" Carrie Jane leaned toward Gifford and raised an eyebrow at Hidalgo's hostile exit from the room.

Gifford chuckled. "The good guys won this round," he said, ducking his head slightly to be heard over the happy congratulations surrounding the bride and groom. "Judge Callister told Hidalgo he'd drop the assault charges I filed on Hidalgo's threats to murder Eduardo if he signed the forms for Belen to marry Eduardo. Hidalgo didn't like it, but his lawyer pointed out an assault charge wouldn't be good for his business. Money talks," he said in satisfaction.

"Wedding brunch at my house in one hour," Viola reminded the crowd as the celebratory cheers began to wind down.

Noon

The Christmas tree was still standing in Viola's living room, now covered for the first time since Viola's mother's death with the elderly woman's collection of angels from around the world, each one unique. Ramona had helped her dig them out of a dozen boxes in the attic. "My mother loved angels," Viola had said. "I didn't see much use for them—too much like fairy tales, I guess. But now . . . .." her voice had trailed off.

"For Annie," Ramona had said.

Today two long banquet tables filled the center of the room across from the tree. Tablecloths with intricate silver designs of wedding bells woven through their fabric-covered both tables. Half dozen bouquets of white rosebuds and lilies-of-the-valley graced the coverings, filling the room with a hope of the coming spring. In a portable cradle in the corner of the room, Elinor dozed peacefully. The kitchen counters were heavy with muffins, fruit, biscuits and gravy, scrambled eggs, bacon, sausage, tortillas, and the ingredients for huevos rancheros—including a generous bowl of homemade spicy hot sauce contributed by Luz.

"First introductions, for those of you who don't know each other," Viola called, bringing the wedding guests to order. Obediently, they moved to the chairs surrounding the tables and seated themselves.

Flor jumped up before Viola had a chance to begin. "I'd like to introduce Nash Singleton." She paused for dramatic effect, "My fiancé!" A gasp of delight sounded across the room

"I guess that means my chances have been dashed," Leon complained to Temp seated next to him.

"Yup. Looks like you're on your own, as usual," Temp replied without a smidgen of sympathy.

"What!!!" Carrie Jane squealed. "You got engaged, and you didn't tell me??"

"I'm telling you now," Flor pointed out, flashing a ring with a series of small diamonds set around a larger marquee-cut stone in a platinum band. "My Christmas present." Casting a triumphant glance at Carrie Jane, she added, "I hope you'll all plan on attending our wedding in July."

Carrie Jane jumped from her chair and rushed around the table to hug her friend. "Wow!" was all she managed to sputter. To Nash, whom Flor had pulled to his feet next to her, Carrie Jane said, "Welcome to the ...," she looked around the table seeking an accurate description of the group and settled on "family." Not a soul complained.

"I was hoping you'd be my maid of honor," Flor said, laughing as she attempted to untangle herself from Carrie Jane's embrace.

"I always knew you'd beat me to the altar!" a breathless Carrie Jane declared, oblivious to the fact that Gifford was looking at her thoughtfully from across the room. Once again, the room rang with congratulations.

"Well," said Viola when the high spirits of the group settled into a congenial chatter. "I hope the rest of you don't have any more bombshells because if we don't eat soon, we'll have to throw out the eggs!"

Since most of the two dozen guests had already greeted one another in the judge's chambers, Viola whipped through the rest of the introductions with ease.

"I've asked Marisa to give us a blessing on the food before we began," Viola announced when Carrie Jane had finally finished catching up on the events of Flor's life over the past few days and took her seat again.

Marisa stood up, but she was too short to see the other members of the party, so she climbed up on her chair, the curls her mother had formed so carefully bouncing behind her back. She bowed her head and folded her arms. "Father in Heaven," she began. "Thank you for helping us be happy." She peaked out from one eye to be certain everyone was paying attention to her words, especially her brothers. "Bless my Annie-girl. And my new baby, Elinor. Amen!"

John Callister stifled a hoot of laughter behind his napkin.

Every eye looked at Eduardo to see what he thought of her prayer which had said nothing about the bride and groom or even mentioned the blessing of the food. He regarded the little girl with obvious affection.

"Amen, Little One, I mean, Marisa," he corrected himself, smiling at his father.

In silence, he looked around the table. Gratitude washed over him. So many people who cared about him and his little family. It was overwhelming. "Thank you. Thank you all. We will not forget this day— Belen and me. And we will tell this story to Elinor so that she will not forget it either." He stopped short, his voice breaking. Under the table, Belen caught his hand in hers. Her touch gave him the strength to continue. "A man once told me that there will always be more blessings than problems." No one, not even Marisa, questioned which 'man' he meant. "Now I see that he was right." Embarrassed at the tears which filled his eyes, he swiped at them with his free hand.

Next to him, Belen touched her napkin to the corners of her eyes, careful not to smear the mascara she had applied so carefully early this morning. Taking a deep breath, she said simply, "We are so happy. There are not enough words."

"Oh, for Pete's sake," Ramona interrupted, proud that considering the children present, she had managed to stifle a stronger word. "We've had more than enough blubbering this week. Let's eat." And so, they did.

Thank you for choosing *The Christmas Guardians* as part of your holiday celebration. One of my goals when I wrote the book was to focus on the good people in the thousands of small communities around the world who make a difference in the lives of others without fanfare or expectation of reward. Too often what we hear from the media is that the world is spiraling downhill and there is no stopping its descent. I don't believe that. Hope is stronger than despair; understanding can be the antidote for rage, and love is the universal force that binds us together.

If, as you read *The Christmas Guardians,* you were reminded that laughter and tears are part of what makes us all part of the human family, I would love it if you would post a review on Amazon about your feelings as you read my book. And thanks for spending a little time with Ramona, Viola, Annie, and their friends in Douglas Valley.

Janice Voorhies

Made in the USA
Monee, IL
31 October 2020

46445189R10146